The Whistling Bird

The Whistling Bird

WOMEN WRITERS OF THE CARIBBEAN

edited by
Elaine Campbell
Pierrette Frickey

A THREE CONTINENTS BOOK
LYNNE RIENNER PUBLISHERS
BOULDER & LONDON

IRP

Ian Randle Publishers
Kingston

Published in the United States of America in 1998 by
Lynne Rienner Publishers, Inc.
1800 30th Street, Boulder, Colorado 80301

and in the United Kingdom by
Lynne Rienner Publishers, Inc.
3 Henrietta Street, Covent Garden, London WC2E 8LU

Published in Jamaica in 1998 by
Ian Randle Publishers
206 Old Hope Road, Box 686
Kingston 6

Library of Congress Cataloging-in-Publication Data
The whistling bird : women writers of the Caribbean / edited by Elaine
  Campbell and Pierrette Frickey.
     p. cm.
   ISBN 0-89410-409-8 (hc : alk. paper). — ISBN 0-89410-410-1 (pb :
alk. paper)
    1. Caribbean literature—Women authors. I. Campbell, Elaine,
1932– . II. Frickey, Pierrette M.
PN849.C32W45   1998
808.8'9287'09729—dc21   97-46089
                                                        CIP

British Cataloguing in Publication Data
A Cataloguing in Publication record for this book
is available from the British Library.

Jamaican Cataloguing in Publication Data
A catalogue record for this book is available from
the National Library of Jamaica.
ISBN: 976-8123-51-6 paperback

Typesetting by Letra Libre

Printed and bound in the United States of America

5 4 3 2 1

Contents

Introduction

The Whistling Bird is a book of celebration. It celebrates what was until recently the little-heard voice of women writers from the Caribbean. Its namesake, taken from an obscure *New Yorker* story by Jean Rhys, is a rare and wonderful bird found in the mountains of Dominica and in the neighboring island of Martinique. Almost extinct, the "siffleur de montagne," known affectionately as "Le Solitarie," is a thrush-like bird, plain in appearance with an exquisite voice. Heard only in isolated places like abandoned citrus plantations or the high ranges of mornes, the whistling bird is now valued and may escape extinction. Similarly, the writing of Caribbean women is growing in quantity, exposure, and appreciation. In fact, Caribbean writing in general is becoming recognized as an international treasure. With a Nobel Laureate—Derek Walcott—and two National Book Awards finalists—Edwidge Danticat and Rosario Ferré—Caribbean creative writing exhibits a level of quality that we can celebrate with pride.

This collection is not a "teaching text," accompanied by questions and answers for secondary school or college students. Rather, the works speak for themselves. Rich and melodic, the words and themes reveal the joys, the problems, the hopes, the frustrations of women writers who speak with clarity and conviction. Readers can approach these contributions in the same manner as they have over the years approached creative works in collections like *The Oxford Book of English Verse*. The book is a resource where the reader can find poetry to enjoy, stories to remember, and a truth to ponder.

Nor is *The Whistling Bird* intended to promote a political point or social agenda. It exists as an act of sharing. It does not particularly focus on the works of the fore-mothers of Caribbean literature, although it includes the lively first act of an unpublished play by Una Marson, *Pocomania*, as well as poems by Louise Bennett. While our collection does not ignore the verities of the past—slavery, colonialism, racial and social injustice—it is primarily future-looking. For example, it includes the poetry of a young, little-known writer—Christabel LaRonde of Dominica—it features Zee Edgell's first short story, written especially for *The Whistling Bird,* and it showcases a very recently published writer from Puerto Rico, Esmeralda Santiago.

The organization of the collection is admittedly simple—alphabetical by island. Not all islands are represented. We have been limited by both space restrictions and financial constraints. Unfortunately, a few literary agents who quoted exorbitant permission fees forced us to omit some writers we would have very much liked to include.

As editors, we have been strict about quality and about a definition of eligibility. We have selected only authors born in the Caribbean. Although many second-generation Caribbean writers—those born outside and living outside the Caribbean—are now writing about Caribbean topics, we chose to consider them as U.S. or British or Canadian writers. Neither does *The Whistling Bird* include creative writing by those who have adopted the Caribbean as home. Along these lines, we have identified each writer according to the country where she was born. It is not unusual in the Caribbean to be born on one island and migrate to another. A future edition of *The Whistling Bird* may demonstrate greater flexibility on this issue, especially when exploring writing from the Virgin Islands, a corpus that is still developing.

The Whistling Bird does not pretend to be comprehensive. It includes a selection of poetry, prose—both short stories and excerpts from novels—and drama. Basically, the editors selected material of literary quality. Choices were not based on the popular appeal of such superficial features as tropical images or exotic characters. We believe that elements of universality apply, and that the songs of Caribbean women writers, be they sad or happy, will touch the hearts of the readers.

Some common themes emerge in this anthology. Interests such as mother-daughter relationships, relationships between men and women, love for or rejection of an island home, village life contrasted to city life, education, and issues of race all provide themes that stretch across many of these works. If *The Whistling Bird* is used as a teaching text, we encourage students and teachers to identify other themes that suggest a common bond among women of the Caribbean in the face of diversity.

A word of caution applies, however. If the selections included in this text reveal cultural patterns unique to the Caribbean and issues specific to women of that region, they should not be the object of broad generalizations. There are similarities as well as differences among the islands' geographical, historical, social, and racial features that account for common trends but also significant variances. For instance, one should take into account social class when considering women's issues. Inez's tragic existence and her concerns for basic survival in Merle Hodge's story by the same title are certainly different from Emma's psychological trauma in Suzanne Dracius's "Sweat, Sugar and Blood," in which the heroine finds herself prisoner of a class (the upper Martinican Creole bourgeoisie) and of her husband. Equally tragic, each calls, however, for a different focus. In the first instance, the issue is the plight of the single mother attempting to raise her children without having the money to do so; in the second, it is the complex interaction of class, cast, and marriage.

Non-Caribbean readers need also to be warned against the tendency on one hand to glamorize the exotic setting of Caribbean literature at the expense of the men and women who live in it, as Maryse Condé points out in *La parole des femmes,* and on the other hand to dramatize the role of women as victims. More often than not, essays on Caribbean literature focus on the existence of "broken families" in the Caribbean while ignoring the strength of women and the value of the extended family. In a recent address at the Fourth International Caribbean Women Writers Conference, Merle Hodge warned precisely against such false assumptions, too often made when one evaluates the Caribbean family by western standards. Laetitia in Hodge's *For the Life of Laetitia*—not included in this anthology—feels that it is not worth her time to try to explain to her teacher that a family without a man can be a loving and caring one, and sometimes more so than the traditional nuclear family.

The strength of the Caribbean woman is apparent in many of the selections included in this anthology, a strength that often arises from necessity. She is often a woman of undaunted will and a fierce determination to fight for the welfare of her children and to defend what she has worked hard to build. She is sometimes disconcerting to men for these reasons. In Brodber's *Myal,* Mary Riley, a single mother, takes plenty of time to answer Taylor's repeated advances, and when she does accept his marriage proposal, it is on her own terms. "They would have to draw on a room for the two of them. It would have to be her house." She wonders if he expects her to be "mother to all his children" [the ones he had with different women]. That would call for a bigger house and more beds.

In Craig's "Burnt Hill," Mavis Harris is alone after her husband has left her for a younger woman, but in spite of her loneliness, she refuses to marry Leonard Davis, her new suitor: "At last, I grew angry . . . But I stayed and made a place for myself and I can't give that up." In Dracius's "Sweat, Sugar and Blood," Emma's act of self-affirmation at the cost of physical mutilation is a triumph over and a liberation from the dicta of a religion, of a class, and of a man.

Apparent, too, is the role played by the family as guardian of its own tradition, a unit in which the life of an individual is orchestrated as in a puppet show, to use Maryse Condé's analogy. Cultural patterns of behavior are expected to survive in the face of a changing world, as Condé's "Wayang Kulit" and Madeline Coopsammy's "The Tick-Tick Bicycle" illustrate. In these stories, the child is caught in the dilemma of subscribing to personal impulses and affirming selfhood while violating parental rules. In "Wayang Kulit" the young girl, Oumou, ends up scorning the schoolfriend who had so courageously defended her against the abuses of prejudiced schoolmates in order to conform to the prejudices of her own family. "I was waiting for her protests. But rooted to the spot, Oumou did not say a word. . . . She even made a move towards her mother as if to seek refuge and disso-ciate herself from me." Yet from Queen Without a Name, Télumée Miracle in Schwarz-Bart's *The Bridge of Beyond* learns an important les-son: how to survive adversities by standing proudly for what she be-lieves. "Behind one pain there is another. Sorrow is a wave without end. But the horse mustn't ride you, you must ride it."

Entire books and countless essays have been written about the role of race in Caribbean literature. Early examples are G. R. Coulthard's classic book *Race and Colour in Caribbean Literature* (Lon-don: Oxford University Press, 1962) and Frantz Fanon's *Peau noire, masques blancs* (Paris: Editions du Seuil, 1952). To ignore concerns about race in contemporary Caribbean writing would be remiss. But to name it the central theme of Caribbean or West Indian writing would be to sacrifice truth. More to the point, Caribbean writers of-ten show us that all struggle is ultimately between the powerful and the powerless. By powerlessness, we mean the inability to overcome, not the inability to fight and to struggle, as Velma Pollard's poems "Marine Turtle" and "Mule" teach us. There is also infinite strength and hope in the solidarity and love of the Caribbean family whose members overcome what might be the worst consequence of living in an oppressive system: the division between brothers. Only through love can the bond between them be restored, a lesson Zee Edgell teaches in "Longtime Story."

When race falls into these terms, then it is possible to see beyond conventional positions. Jean Rhys, whose wish to have been born black is well-known, demonstrates in *Wide Sargasso Sea* that to be a member of a powerless minority is painful for any person. The narra-tor, the white child Antoinette, is tricked and insulted by her black playmate Tia, and as "a white cockroach" Antoinette has no means of recourse.

This does not mean we can ignore the fact that the struggle be-tween the powerful and the powerless is linked to race; it was so during colonialism, and it permeates the psyche of people who still struggle against post-colonialism. A minority racial position did not necessarily equate powerlessness during the era of slavery. However, it brought its own terrors: fear of uprisings, destruction of property, and loss of life. These terrors, associated with minority status, provoked horrors enacted on the powerless majority: beatings, mutilations, death, and the general devaluation of life central to slavery. Such issues have not been forgotten or forsaken by contemporary Caribbean writers, and they surface over and over again. Poets such as Grace Nichols commemorate those who perished in the middle passage ("Eulogy"), those who died in torment ("Ala"), those who toiled blindly and despairingly in the cane fields ("Among the Cane"). As Nichols reminds us in "These Islands," our beautiful islands were made fertile by brutality.

Racism tears at the very fabric of Caribbean society, dividing Creoles and blacks, Indians and blacks, whites and blacks. As the excerpt from Michelle Cliff's *Abeng* points out, it has tragic consequences in the development of a young girl's personality and self-awareness. *Abeng* is the story of a buchra girl, more white than black, who is increasingly aware of the difference between herself and her childhood black friend. This realization corresponds to the end of childhood, the end of a time when dreams are still possible. "They did not question who each was in this place.... This was friendship ... kept only on school vacations, and ... their games and make-believe might have seemed entirely removed from what was in the girls' lives.... At the bottom—as it usually was—was race and shade." Color, or rather shade, is what separates Claire from Zoe, but it is also what divides the students in the Catholic school in Kingston. According to Cliff, black is synonymous to invisibility in the white community. After the expulsion of the black student Doreen for having suffered an epileptic seizure, "it soon seemed to the girls that she never actually existed at all."

In a culture in which tradition is essential for the preservation of identity, the disappearance of tradition would have tragic consequences. Tradition links Zoe and Claire and is passed down from generation to generation through customs and stories told by mothers and grandmothers. These customs and stories are a necessary part of child rearing and education, as seen in the works of Simone Schwarz-Bart, Michelle Cliff, and Maryse Condé, to name a few. Tradition is threatened when the language, customs, and values imposed on a society by those in power are different from those that children learn at home. The children learn the most important values from their grandmother, not from teachers, in *The Bridge of Beyond, Abeng, For the Life of Laetitia,* and *Crick-Crack Monkey.* Nor do they learn values from the sterile environment of a school such as the one Télumée attends.

The ambivalent feeling a person born in the Caribbean may feel toward his or her island, then, is not surprising. On one hand, it is home and the place where one has roots; on the other hand, it is a troubled and complex world unified by common concerns, yet racially divided. It is caught between the demands of modernization and a need to preserve its independence and cultural heritage. Greater objectivity can be achieved when one leaves home and looks back from the vantage of exile, but such objectivity leads to a disquieting realization—commitment to one's people calls for a return home.

Away from home, the writer can ponder on this dilemma and can reflect on himself or herself as well. Perhaps the most remarkable piece of Caribbean writing demonstrating ambivalence about an island home is Jamaica Kincaid's *A Small Place.* Although that work is not excerpted here, in it Kincaid expresses her ambivalent feelings for her native Antigua. Sophisticated and richly textured like all Kincaid's writing, *A Small Place* demonstrates the complexity of emotions aroused by literary recreations of home. The dilemma is rendered metaphorically by Kincaid in *The Autobiography of My Mother,* wherein the tale is told by a "mother" who aborts her first child and loses the ability to conceive others. Hence, an autobiography of the author's mother is an impossibility.

Has the displacement of so many Caribbean writers been expressed thematically as exile or expatriation? Are Caribbean novels and poems redolent with a sense of paradise lost?

We think not. We believe that Caribbean roots are so deeply sunk and so richly nurtured that they yield strong growth and creative fruit. Themes of exile and expatriation do not dominate Caribbean literature. We have instead an *Annie John,* a *Beka Lamb, The Bridge of Beyond,* and other powerful works. Rather than lamenting a paradise lost, our writers proclaim the strength of their aunts, mothers, and grandmothers, whose power we have already acknowledged. The energetic outpouring of poetry from Jamaica, the publication of works such as Grace Nichols' *i is a long-memoried woman,* Nydia Ecury's robust English/Papiamentu poetry from Curaçao, the melodious and forceful call of Lorna Goodison's "Mulatta Song"—to name a few—argue for Caribbean literature as song rather than lament.

This introduction has so far focused on serious social issues, since the selections included in the anthology deal with issues of serious concern. More often than not, literary analysts focus solely on such matters, overlooking the antic dimension of Caribbean writing, which we, as editors, value. Much Caribbean humor is captured in the folktales of the area, and calypso lyrics continue to tease and amuse while edifying. In fact, studies have linked calypso lyrics to Rabelaisian prose and Molière's moralist verses: "plaire [rire] et instruire."

The poetry of Louise Bennett offers many instances of sly or sarcastic humor. Bennett was popular in Jamaica in the 1960s. Her poetry was a form of public performance. She delivered it dressed in traditional Creole costume, and her voice helped convey the nuances of street humor. Included in *The Whistling Bird* are two typical poems: "Candy Seller" and "Bans O'Ooman!" "Candy Seller" displays both the charm of the saleswoman narrator and her humorous, sometimes abusive, response to reluctant customers. "Bans O'Ooman!" expresses the narrator's joyous amazement over the turnout for the first meeting of the Jamaican Federation of Women. This poem skillfully conveys social commentary while employing a humorous tone.

Another practitioner of humorous writing—amusingly sarcastic writing—is Puerto Rico's Ana Lydia Vega. Part of Vega's enormous popularity stems from the sense of relief from ponderous commentary that her tone gives the audience. As an example, in a recent speech she described the incessant travel of Puerto Ricans between San Juan and New York City, claiming that a third of the Puerto Rican population is always in the air. While addressing a serious social phenomenon—transience and migration—Vega made her point memorable through her wry sense of humor. She called her address "The Flying Bus." Vega's story "Eye-Opener" starts with a sleepy driver, who in order to keep his eyes open and on the road asks his passengers to "talk, ask riddles, tell jokes." They oblige and proceed to outdo one another with stories as bawdy as any Chaucerian tale. The driver's final joke on his riders and on us, the readers, is that he wasn't sleepy at all; he just wanted to hear their stories.

The lively first act of Una Marson's *Pocomania* and Carmen Tipling's one-act play *Lunchtime Revolution* also offer first-rate examples of writing that conveys information about social realities in the Caribbean without assuming a tone of undue solemnity. Tipling, who has returned to Jamaica from England, continues writing plays, a creative genre not sufficiently practiced by Caribbean women writers.

In sum, this collection of works by well-known, lesser-known, and unknown Caribbean women writers varies in genres and in tones. The works represent the suffering, the joy, the aspirations of women from different racial and social backgrounds and of different locations within the Caribbean. Different and yet alike in their shared concern for self-authenticity and recognition, the authors point to social problems and historical imperatives shared by all Caribbean peoples. They also dispel myths about them and their islands.

As they continue making significant contributions to the corpus of world literature, some of these women writers will convey traditional wisdom through regional humor derived from Calypso, nancy tales, and proverbs, as Erna Brodber has done. Increasingly challenged to write in a voice of their own, like Louise Bennett and Michelle Cliff, these women have discovered that the accurate rendition of truth requires authenticity of language. As they have done in this anthology, they will continue to illuminate concerns shared by their sisters around the Caribbean and around the world. It will be exciting to see what the twenty-first century of Caribbean writing brings!

Elaine Campbell
Pierrette Frickey

Jamaica Kincaid

excerpt from
THE AUTOBIOGRAPHY
OF MY MOTHER

ON THE ROAD BETWEEN Roseau and Potter's Ville I was followed by a large agouti whose movements were not threatening. It stopped when I stopped, looked behind itself when I looked behind myself to see what it was up to—I did not know what it saw behind itself—walked when I walked. At Goodwill I stopped to drink water and the agouti stopped but did not drink water then. At Massacre the entire Church of St. Paul and St. Anne was wrapped in purple and black as if it were Good Friday. It was at Massacre that Indian Warner, the illegitimate son of a Carib woman and a European man, was murdered by his half brother, an Englishman named Philip Warner, because Philip Warner did not like having such a close relative whose mother was a Carib woman. I passed through Mahaut crawling on my stomach, for I was afraid I would be recognized. I did not need to swim across the mouth of the Belfast River, the water was low. Just before I reached St. Joseph, at Layou, I spun around three times and called out my name and so made the agouti fall asleep behind me. I never saw it again. It was raining in Merot, it was raining in Coulibistri, it was raining in Colihaut.

I could not see the top of Morne Diablotin; I had never seen it in any case, even when I was awake. At Portsmouth I found bread at the foot of a tree whose fruit was inedible nuts and whose wood is used to make exquisite furniture. I passed by the black waters of the Guadeloupe Channel; I was not tempted to be swallowed up whole in it. Passing through La Haute, passing through Thibaud, passing through Marigot—somewhere between Marigot and Castle Bruce lived my mother's people, on a reserve, as if in commemoration of something no one could bring herself to mention. At Petite Soufrière the road ceased to exist. I passed by the black waters of the Martinique Channel; I was not tempted to be swallowed up whole in it. It rained between Soufrière and Roseau. I believe I heard small rumblings coming from deep within Morne Trois Pitons, I believe I smelled sulfur fumes rising up from the Boiling Lake. And that is how I claimed my birthright, East and West, Above and Below, Water and Land: In a dream. I walked through my inheritance, an island of villages and rivers and mountains and people who began and ended with murder and theft and not very much love. I claimed it in a dream. Exhausted from the agony of expelling from my body a child I could not love and so did not want, I dreamed of all the things that were mine.

It was the smell coming from my father that awoke me. He had been asked to arrest some men suspected of smuggling rum and they threw stones at him, and when he fell to the ground he was stabbed with a knife. Now he stood over me, and the wound was still fresh; it was on his upper arm, his shirt hid it from sight, but he smelled of iodine and gentian violet and carbolic acid. This smell seemed orderly and reasonable; I associated it with a small room and shelves on which were small brown bottles and bandages and white enamel utensils. This smell reminded me of a doctor. I had once been to a doctor's home; my father had asked me to deliver an envelope inside of which was a piece of paper on which he had written a message. On the envelope he had written the doctor's name: Bailey. This smell he had about him now reminded me of that doctor's room. My father stood over me and looked down. His eyes were gray. He could not be trusted, but you would have to know him for a while to realize that. He did not seem repelled by me. I did not know if he knew what had happened to me. He had been told that I was missing, he looked for me, he found me, he wanted to take me to his home in Mahaut, and when I was well again I could go back to Roseau to live. (He did not say with whom.) In his mind he believed he loved me, he was sure that he loved me; all his actions were an expression of this. On his face, though, was that mask; it was the same mask he wore when stealing all that was left from an unfortunate someone who had lost so much already. It was the same mask he wore when he guided an event, regardless of its truth, to an end that would benefit him. And even now, as he stood over me, he did not wear the clothes of a father; he wore his jailer's uniform, he was in his policeman's clothes. And these clothes, these policeman's clothes, came to define him; it was as if eventually they grew onto his body, another skin, because long after he ceased to wear them, when it was no longer necessary for him to wear them, he always looked as if he were still in his policeman's clothes. His other clothes were real clothes; his policeman's clothes had become his skin.

I was lying down on a bed made of rags in a house that had only the bare earth for a floor. There was no real evidence of my ordeal to see. I did not smell of the dead, because for something to be dead, life would have had to come first. I had only made the life that was just beginning in me, not dead, just not to be at all. There was a pain between my legs; it started inside my lower abdomen and my lower back and came out through my legs, this pain. I was wet between my legs; I could smell the wetness; it was blood, fresh and old. The fresh blood smelled like a newly dug-up material that had not yet been refined and turned into something worldly, something to which a value could be assigned. The old blood gave off a sweet rotten stink, and this I loved and would breathe in deeply when it came to dominate the other smells in the room; perhaps I only loved it because it was mine. My father was not repelled by me, but I could not see anything else that was written in his face. He stood over me, looking down on me. His face grew round and big, filling up the whole room from one end to the other; his face was like a map of the world, as if a globe had been removed from a dark corner in a sitting room (he owned such things: a globe, a sitting room) after which its main seam had been ripped apart and the globe had been laid open, flat. His cheeks were two continents separated by two seas which joined an ocean (his nose); his gray eyes were bottomless and sleeping volcanoes; between his nose and his mouth lay the equator; his ears were the horizons, to go beyond which was to fall into the thick blackness of nothing; his forehead was a range of mountains known to be treacherous; his chin the area of steppes and deserts. Each area took on its appropriate coloring: the land mass a collection of soft yellows and blues and mauves and pinks, with small lines of red running in every direction as if to deliberately confound; the waters blue, the mountains green, the deserts and steppes brown. I did not know this world, I had only met some of its people. Most of them were not everything you could ask for.

To die then was not something I desired, and I was young enough to believe that this was a choice, and I was young enough for this to be so. I did not die, I did not wish to. I told my father that as soon as I was able to, I would return to the household of Madame and Monsieur LaBatte. My father had a broad back. It was stiff, it was strong; it looked like a large land mass arising unexpectedly out of what had been flat; around it, underneath it, above it I could not go. I had seen this back of his so many times, so many times it had been turned to me, that I was no longer capable of being surprised at the sight of it, but it never ceased to stir up in me a feeling of curiosity: would I see his face again or had I seen him for the last time?

Esther Phillips

I Do Not Know My Father

I keep wanting to meet my father,
I do not know who he is.
I know of the smooth
smart-talking impossible dreamer
my mother speaks about.

I remember a man
planing pieces of wood
in the back-yard—
where I longed to play
in the shavings that fell—
who hopped on his bicycle
and left,
those days when anger
spewed out from my mother
and ran like lava
through the house
and all around it.

I know the man
I saw years after,
who tried to fit words
into pictures of the past,
and did not know the
pictures, memories, words
were warped
out of all meaning,
frames twisted out of joint.

I heard him speak
of the glory of God
and the power of angels
and the saving grace
that kept him
through the long years
of cold rooms
and alien faces

But I do not know my father,
I do not know
what is behind the skilled words
and sometimes loud
and reckless laughter,
[Time telescoped into a scene
to fit the stage
until the holiday is over!]

I had no clues
when good-bye came,
to help me gauge the truth
of his embrace,
but I look back
and dare to think
that it was grief I saw
etched on his face.

Zee Edgell

LONGTIME STORY

AT LUNCHTIME, ONE FRIDAY in September, I sat at our dining table contemplating a business matter which I wanted to discuss with my wife.

The vexed expression on her face, however, persuaded me to postpone talking about my idea until another time. Rozalia has an excellent head for facts and figures, which is one thing that attracted me to her in the first place, and not her "pale, freckled skin, grey eyes and curly hair," like Terence said. Terence is my older brother. I don't count on him for anything, and he doesn't, of late, expect much from me either.

I last saw Terence at the bank, in Market Square, about two weeks ago. He was probably withdrawing money from his pension, which is all he has these days between him and the poor house. Giving him a quick salute, I walked into the Manager's office. That's the way things are in Belize sometimes. Even in close proximity, relatives become almost strangers, and there's not much anybody can do.

"What's on your mind, Eddie Campbell?" Rozalia's voice had a slight edge to it.

"Just admiring the view, Roza," I said, which was true enough. Through our windows I see everything I love: the broad Haulover Creek flowing into the Caribbean, the coming and going of the boats near the market, and the public buildings where, as a customs broker, I spent a lot of my time.

"I'd think you'd want a change of scenery," my wife said. Rozalia doesn't want to live in the middle of town anymore. The flat is falling apart, she claims, and the traffic disturbs her rest. At breakfast, I told Rozalia that I would miss my evenings on the verandah. I was only joking, but her look was unfriendly as she said,

"You've become sentimental, Eddie, sudden, sudden."

Reprinted by permission of the author.

I ate a piece of boiled red snapper, always a treat for me. It is a reminder, though, of all the fish heads and fowl feet I had to eat when I lived with Ma, her gentleman, and Terence. I sometimes wish I could discuss those days more freely with Rozalia, but she gets impatient with what she calls, "all those longtime ago stories."

When Rozalia started complaining about the distance from Grand Bogue Boulevard, where we live, to Frigate Bird Lane, her parents' home, I'd bought her a second hand car. We are both in our mid-fifties, and she is close to her family, unlike myself.

"Car working all right, Rozalia?"

"Mmm," she said, patting her mouth with a napkin.

"Mama gave me a few flowers to take to Lord's Ridge, since I had the car."

"Why didn't you remind me?" I said, slapping my forehead. I had forgotten the first anniversary of my mother's death.

"I didn't think of it until I was at Mama's. You can go later, if you have a mind."

"I doubt very much I'll be able to make it," I said, noticing that a slight drizzle was falling, obscuring the distant waves breaking over the barrier reef. "Another ship arrived this morning."

"That's why I went," Rozalia said.

September is one of the busiest months of the year for me. The country goes on a spending spree to celebrate a 1798 battle on St. George's Caye, and to honor our independence from Britain in 1981, two years before.

"Ma would have appreciated your visit," I said, feeling grateful. Rozalia had been closer to my mother than I had been. I feel out of place at most formal occasions, but I was about to suggest that we go out one evening, when she said,

"I met Terence at the cemetery. He took flowers."

Easing myself out of my chair, I walked to the window overlooking the creek. Once when we were in our teens, Terence and I agreed to repair the rotting back stairs in time for Ma's birthday. On the appointed Saturday, he told me he had an errand in town, but would be back shortly. I finished the repairs by evening when Terence returned.

"Good job, Eddie," he said, glancing at the steps. In his arms he held a bunch of red roses. "I spent the morning looking for these." His black eyes were gleeful. "Then I had to listen all afternoon to Mrs. Grenier's life story. She wouldn't cut them before sundown."

I had been so astonished that I couldn't upbraid him as I had planned to do. He and I had been raised differently. Ma was glad to have the steps repaired, but she spent that week, it seemed to me, telling passersby about Terence's search for the roses. Few people in town grew roses when we were young.

"Eddie," Rozalia was saying now, wiping laugh-water from her eyes. "Guess what Terence did? He went by your Ma's house and picked whatever flowers were hanging over the fence. He said Mother Dear had planted them, so he felt entitled to take some."

"He's lucky the new owners didn't call the police. That really would have been a joke." My voice must have held more rancor than I had intended because immediately, and with exaggerated care, Rozalia began putting the dishes onto a tray. "Imagine," I continued, "a retired policeman setting such an example."

"He was complaining to me that your mother's middle name isn't spelt right on the headstone."

"What's wrong about it?" I asked, beginning to feel annoyed. It was a wonder that lunch had been ready at noon since it seemed that Rozalia had spent practically the whole morning listening to Terence. As I pushed the chairs underneath the table, I once again found myself envying Terence his full head of hair, his height, his good looks.

From photographs I've seen, Terence looks a lot like our father who died before I was born, and when Terence was three years old. I also envied his ability to actually enjoy the freedom his retirement brought. I doubted that I would ever feel secure enough to retire, which reminded me of the business proposal I wanted to discuss with Rozalia. But she was saying,

"Terence said that your mother spelt Phebe with an 'o.' I tried to argue with him, but he'd been to the Registry to get out her birth certificate."

I sucked my teeth, a dismissive habit that grates on Rozalia's nerves. I was a bit taken aback. I had lived with my mother from the time I was twelve until I was eighteen, and it was only now that I was learning the spelling of her middle name.

"Was it your mistake, Eddie, or Smithy Johnson's?"

I thought of Smithy, and the loose, hearty, skillful way with which he wielded his chisel and mallet. We had been friends since primary school, and every year he sat with me on our verandah to watch the regatta.

Carrying the tray to the kitchen, I said to Rozalia,

"It was my mistake, but Phebe is Phoebe, however it's spelt. Ma would have been glad for the marble headstone, even if a letter, like bad luck, is missing from her name." My mother had spent many evenings at Lord's Ridge, trying to locate her own mother's grave. There had been little money for bricking graves in her days, let alone for erecting fancy headstones.

"You know very well, Eddie, that if your mother was alive, she'd think that you are still holding malice with her over that longtime story."

"Did Terence tell you that? Well, it may be a longtime story to him, but it isn't to me," I said, glancing at my watch.

"He didn't say that. I think he was surprised and sorry about the mistake. Tears were in his eyes, and I feel bad, too, when I think of all your mother did to help us."

"What exactly does Terence have to be sorry about? He didn't offer to help pay for Ma's stone."

"Be that as it may, we'll have to fix it, Eddie. It's not like you not to check."

"Everybody makes mistakes. Ma would consider fixing that stone a waste of money and time, especially if we have to buy a new one. If Terence feels sorry, let him fix it."

"I hate it when you take that attitude, Eddie."

"What attitude?"

"That hardheaded way, like you have no feelings for anybody, at all, at all. Everything to the letter of the law, Eddie, but no spirit to it. It makes me wonder what you would do if it was my headstone."

"I know how to spell your name."

"Or my mother's."

"How did we get from my mother's headstone to your mother's, Rozalia?"

"Easy, easy. It's the same way you don't want us to move from this stinking creekside. I've put up with the fishy smell from that market for thirty years and I'm tired of it."

My hands were shaking as I collected my car keys from the desk in the living room.

"I'd best be going to work, Roza."

"So go, Eddie, that's what you do seven days a week." She marched back to the dining room, a broom in her hand.

"But I always return," I called, going down the steps. I listened for one of her usual angry retorts like, "more's the pity." There was no sound, so I crept up the stairs again and peered in. She was staring at the doorway, waiting for me.

"If things continue like this, Eddie, one of these days I may not be here when you return, believe me."

Sucking my teeth, I slammed the door. Rozalia was in a huff, but I was in no mood to coax her out of it. If there was a single thing I resented about my wife, it was her habit of turning bad luck into tragedy. Nevertheless, I was disturbed by her last remark, one she had never made before, and which seemed to me a bit extreme.

As I drove from home towards Fort George, I glanced at the sky. If it rained, the workers at Bond Shed would be unable to load the trucks. If the goods, most of them perishable, did not reach the shops on time, my boss would hold me responsible, rain or no rain. In many ways, he has been like a father to me, and I try to spare him unnecessary economic pain.

Inside the Customs House, I moved from office to office, from desk to dusty desk, proffering bills of lading and invoices. The rain had vanished, and the two o'clock sun was blazing down on the zinc roof. Thinking about the error I had made in my mother's name gave me a cold feeling in the pit of my stomach. I seldom made mistakes in my business affairs, but it seemed to me that in my personal life, the harder I tried the worse things got.

Standing in line at the cashier's cage, waiting to pay the duties owed, I thought of the help my mother had given Rozalia and me when our children were small and money had been short.

I saw her moving from bed to bed, when they'd had measles, making them drink unsalted pumpkin water, "to cool their insides." On Saturdays she walked to our house with freshly baked Creole bread and powder buns. Each year, Ma and her gentleman had taken the children upriver during the long school holidays. I had been too proud to acknowledge that Ma's help mattered, or to show her much affection, doling it out, as Rozalia once said, "grain by grain."

But I had been in a terrible state sitting by my mother's hospital bed during the final days of her illness. One morning she touched my hand, which stayed splayed, as if glued, against my knee.

"Feeling all right?" she'd asked. Her eyes, like my own, were large and dark. Stout, and strong, for most of her eighty years, she had lost half her weight in very few months.

"Yes, Ma, and you?" I felt ignorant and powerless in the face of an illness without a known cure.

"Your pride will get the best of you yet, Eddie, if you're not careful," she said, sighing as she looked at me.

Ma knew, I believe, that in spite of everything she had done to make amends, I had not forgiven her for lending me, as a baby, to my father's family and then reclaiming me when I was nearly twelve. I remember feeling angry and resentful living with a mother and brother I hardly knew.

Often, at night, I lay in bed, exhausted from pedalling my messenger bike around town all day. I could hear the three of them telling stories and making jokes outside, on the front steps. Would my mother, I wondered, have brought me to live with them, if she had not needed the weekly paycheck I faithfully put into her hands? The night of my eighteenth birthday I left my mother's house to live on my own. As I packed my trunk, I said to her,

"You have Terence. You prefer him to me anyway."

"Sometimes I wish you were more like us," she replied, "but then I didn't raise you so I can't complain. Money isn't everything, you know."

"That's what you say now," I replied, thinking about Terence, whom Ma had sent to the high school I'd dreamed of attending, while I forced myself to attend night school in order not to be left behind. As I lugged my trunks towards the mule and cart waiting at the gate, I thought of my father's people.

I wondered how, in spite of everything, they could have let me go. Had they asked my mother to take me away? Perhaps with so many other children in the yard to provide for, I became a burden they were glad to relinquish.

I've worked hard all my life because I never want, ever again, to be an economic burden to anyone. But at the same time I couldn't afford to further erode the affection of Rozalia and our children, the only real family I have ever had, because of a flaw in my mother's headstone.

After paying the cashier, I called the boss to explain that he should send my assistant over to the Customs House, as I needed to take the rest of the afternoon off. Surprised, he asked me if I was sick. I told him that I was having a recurrence of a "bad feeling in my stomach," which, I suppose, was true enough. Outside the Customs House, I gave instructions to the head driver waiting near the fleet of trucks and then drove home. At the bottom of our stairs, I began shouting, "Roz! Roz!"

"Where's the fire?" she asked, unbolting the door. Her eyes were puffy, and a handkerchief was balled up in her fist. I tried to put my arms around her, but she pulled away.

"Were you crying, Roz? Don't upset yourself over a little mistake like that. Why don't we go to Smithy's to see what he can do?" At first I thought she would refuse. Instead she gave me a sidelong glance and said,

"We're both crying, Eddie."

"There's something important we should discuss anyway, Roza," I said, wiping my cheeks, and feeling lightheaded.

Smithy's workshop is below his house on Cemetery Road. As we entered the yard, his wife, her hair dripping wet, pushed open the green jalousies of an upstairs window and called,

"Afternoon, Rozalia, Eddie. Smithy is over at the cemetery with Terence, something about estimates for a new headstone?" My heart sank at the mention of my brother.

"I wonder if you've misjudged Terence?" Rozalia asked softly, smiling up at Mrs. Smithy.

"Anything is possible," I said, examining the tiny bird's feather in my brown hat band.

The first, and last, time I had seen my mother's grave, it had been heaped with wreaths and bouquets. But I couldn't remember ever giving her a single flower while she was living. I looked at the red bells trembling in the breeze on Smithy's overgrown hedges. Mrs. Smithy returned to the window, a hairbrush in one hand.

"Mind if I dig up one of your red bell plants, Mrs. Smithy?"

"Take as many as you like, Eddie. A shovel is under the front step." Mrs. Smithy, who seldom left the house, drew a chair to the window, and settled herself into it.

"We have plants at home, Eddie," Rozalia was saying. "I don't know why sudden, you feel you have to dig up Smithy's red bells."

She stood to one side, watching skeptically as I dug up one of the plants, wrapping it carefully in a newspaper I retrieved from the car. "You might need water," she said, picking up an empty paint can from a mound of rubble in one corner of the yard. With Mrs. Smithy's permission, Rozalia filled the can at the vat near the house.

"We could walk," I said to Rozalia, "If you're up to it." Nodding, she lifted up the newspaper with the red bells. I carried a can of water in one hand and the shovel in the other. Mrs. Smithy closed the blinds as we started towards the cemetery about five minutes away.

A year ago, after my mother had been buried, I waited until Rozalia was seated in the car with the family before telling them that I felt like walking back to town.

"Now?" Rozalia asked, removing her hat.

"What's wrong with now?" Nobody else in the car spoke, but I could sense their disapproval.

"We promised Terence we'd go to his house."

"Is it a disgrace to walk there now that everybody has a car?"

"Who is everybody, Eddie?"

"Why do you always pick up on everything I say?"

"Be like that then. We feel bad leaving you to walk there alone. That's all."

"I'll be fine."

After they drove away, I did not look back at the place where my mother was buried. I felt overwhelmingly sad that she was gone. But in an odd way, of which I was ashamed, I also felt free. And the last thing I wanted to do was to sit all evening listening to Terence hold forth.

I hadn't been to his house for years. About five years ago, when his wife Marie died, I went to the church, and, of course to the cemetery. Marie, a distant cousin, had been my childhood friend. I had started out trying to include them in our family life. However, after they lost their only child, Marie only came by at Easter time.

Marie continued grieving for years, and Terence took refuge in our house. He played games with our children, and bragged about the favors he planned to bestow on us once he became a "big man" in the Force. At teatime, whenever he interrupted himself to say things like, "Please pass the condiments," the boys doubled up laughing, and my daughters giggled until they cried. Later they would marvel to me about Uncle Terence's "exciting life, high manners and joking ways."

"Every year," he was promising Rozalia one Sunday, when I arrived home from the club, "you and Eddie will receive an invitation to the September celebrations at Government House. I will see to it personally."

Of course, the moment after I entered the room, silence fell. I felt like an intruder on the intimacies of a happy family, who were fearful of what I would do to them. I retired to the bedroom until Terence left, which he took his time about doing. Listening to the hilarity in the dining room took me back, unpleasantly, to our youth, when I lived with Ma, her gentleman, and Terence.

Marie had been as bad that way about Terence as the rest of my family. She believed every false compliment, every grandiose vision of the future. She forgave Terence his lies ("Well meaning, Eddie," she often told me) and his broken promises. She died not knowing for years I had, on occasion, supplemented their household income. I did not tell Rozalia about this, and she feels that I should do more to help Terence. But in certain ways, I've tried to be loyal to my brother.

On the evening of my mother's funeral, before I'd had a chance to say anything, Terence said to my family, his eyes swollen from weeping, "Why don't you folks come over and have a little bite to eat with me, for a change? We'll have a drink or two, and talk about Mother Dear, and about poor Marie."

"Mother Dear, Mother Dear," I repeated mockingly to myself as he proceeded to include a few of his friends in the invitation. Plain old "Ma" had never been good enough for Terence. But who had taken care of our mother, organized the funeral, and paid for the bricking of the grave?

That evening I had not gone to Terence's house. I was afraid of what I might say after a drink or two. I went home to sit on the verandah. The constant activity of the creek diverted my thoughts to the town's commercial life, in which I played a part.

Rozalia and the children had been outraged by my "unfeeling behavior." They have never really forgotten the incident, and I have been unable to put things right since that night—if things had ever been right specially where Terence was concerned.

Now as we neared the cemetery, a year later, I glanced at Rozalia who had been quiet most of the way. "I am thinking of retiring, Roza, in a year or two, God willing."

The afternoon was still humid, and the air as filled with the exhaust fumes from the trucks, buses and cars making their way to, and from, the Western Highway.

"Retire, Eddie?" She kept her eyes down to avoid stepping into one if the frequent potholes in the road. "So soon? You'll miss your work, believe me." She lifted the newspaper bundle to shield her eyes as we walked towards the sun.

"We might start a business of our own, doing the same thing I've been doing for most of my life."

"This is a surprise, Eddie, a big surprise. What will we do for capital?"

"The bank agreed to a proposal I put to them, and my boss has said he'll co-sign the loan. He has more business than he can handle. What do you think?"

Rozalia was silent, taking deep breaths. I said, "We could buy the building and use downstairs as an office. But if you are dead set against the idea, let's arrange to build a house and go on as we are."

"Why are you rushing to the conclusion that I am against the idea, Eddie? It's a surprise that's all; anybody would be surprised. I wouldn't mind helping you with the books but . . ."

"We'll still build our own home in a year or so, but I'll let you look at the facts and figures."

"If that's a bargain, Eddie, then I agree."

"It is," I said, as we entered the cemetery, more at ease with each other than we had been for a while.

"A family partnership, Eddie! At least one of the children will want to join us."

"For years now they've been after me to start my own business. At lunch on Sunday we can discuss it with them."

"Even Terence might want to work with us, Eddie."

I fell silent as we approached my mother's grave. The bouquets, placed there that morning by Rozalia and Terence, were wilting.

"Don't you sometimes feel sorry for Terence, Eddie?" Rozalia asked. "Think of all the times he was passed over for promotion. He told me that he believed it was all due to party politics."

Terence and Smithy were talking together near Marie's grave, a few yards away. Rozalia stared at me, her face animated, waiting for an answer. I thought of Ma who had died not knowing how much I had grown to love her. I said,

"If you think Terence should be a part of our business, Rozalia, let's give it a try." I bent down and began pulling up the sour grass from around the base of Ma's grave.

"What are Terence and Smithy doing over there anyway?" Rozalia asked.

"Terence is paying his respects, I suppose, probably brought more flowers." The thought of Terence working with me day after day gave me a bilious feeling in my stomach.

I dug a big hole for the red bells. They should bloom all year, un-like Terence's pilfered bouquet. I reached for the can of water as Rozalia said,

"I do believe something is up. Terence is holding his head in his hand, and Smithy is patting his back."

"Crying to Smithy, no doubt, about how I hated Ma and care-lessly gave him the wrong spelling to carve on the stone."

"Why do you always think the worse of Terence, Eddie? He doesn't talk about you like that. Let's find out what has happened." I walked with Rozalia towards Marie's grave, the mosquitoes swarming around our heads.

Smithy dropped his hand from Terence's shoulder, as we ap-proached. "Listen, Eddie," he said, "I was explaining to your brother that I carved that stone as a favour to you. I don't do name carving anymore."

"I know, Smithy, and I am grateful. I am hoping you'll help me out again. I gave the wrong spelling of my mother's middle name."

Smithy scratched his bearded cheek, looking puzzled for a mo-ment, and I wondered why. Nowadays he spent his time carving an-gels and other elaborate memorials to the dead.

"Your brother showed me the birth certificate. What a pity. I may have to buy a new stone, though, if I mess up the old one."

"Do whatever you need to do, Smithy," I said, turning to look at Terence, whose chin was resting in his hands.

"Terence. It's a good thing you spotted that mistake. Spelling was never my best subject."

His eyes were red, and I felt a stirring of pity. But when Rozalia went to sit beside him and began patting his shoulder, I dropped my eyes, feeling my insides contract.

I sat on a grave opposite. Every now and then Terence looked at us as if his heart was about to fail him. If Rozalia hadn't been there, I would have said what I had to say to Smithy and left.

I tried again. "You think that I didn't care about Ma, eh Terence? I've said it was my mistake and Smithy has agreed to fix it."

"I know you loved Mother Dear," Terence said. "And spelling, it turns out, isn't everything after all, dear boy. She used to remind me regularly that you've never let us down in a crisis."

Rozalia was making signals to me with her eyes inclining her head towards Marie's grave. Startled, I said,

"Terence, where's Marie's headstone?"

He looked down at his hands, before folding them in his lap. "I was just discussing that very thing with Smithy. But I haven't got the full amount just yet."

I walked closer to Marie's grave, scarcely crediting my eyes. On the evening Ma came to collect me from my father's people, I hid under my aunt's bed so that no one could see me crying. Marie hunted for me all over the yard, calling my name, running in and out of the small family houses.

Lifting my aunt's bedspread, she saw me huddled against the wall. She swore she would never tell anyone, and she never did. I had loved Marie like a sister.

"Poor old Marie," Terence said.

An unhappy thought surfaced in my mind, growing stronger as darkness fell. I wondered if Terence had seen in the mistake I made in Ma's name, a chance, however remote, of turning the responsibility for marking Marie's grave over to me? I turned to Smithy, and said,

"How about adding a stone for Marie to my bill?" Smithy glanced questioningly at Terence who looked as though he had been relieved from a long stretch of night duty.

"Eddie is our captain, you know Smithy," my brother said. "He's carried the bigger load since we were boys."

Terence came stumbling towards me, arms outstretched. I didn't flinch from his embrace, and I found myself patting his shoulders for the first time in my life. I like to think he saw sympathy in my eyes, not anger or envy, because before turning away, he raised a hand to his forehead in a fleeting salute.

As we walked towards Ma's grave to collect Smithy's shovel and paint can, Rozalia whispered, "Poor old Terence just lost his chance to work with us, didn't he, Eddie?"

"I think he did," I said. I wanted to tell her what I had always known—that the chances to which my brother aspired, and to which he probably felt entitled, had been lost a long time ago.

Nydia Ecury

SONG FOR MOTHER EARTH

In dwelling on your face,
Old Mother Earth,
my soul must cross
a desert vast
and desolate
alone.

I do not even dare
to soothe my pain
with the comfort
of a dream
or a promise
in the wind.

And yet,
I bow my tired head
to kiss
your weary womb
because
I am a Mother, too.

Nydia Ecury's poems previously published in *Kantika Pa Mama Tera*.
Reprinted by permission of the author.

If in this act
of reverence
should you detect
upon my face
a wandering tear,
it is for you,
Dear Mother Earth,
my gift

of gratitude
because today
my son has sung
a song
to me.

KANTIKA PA MAMA TERA

Mama Tera, k'a parimi,
Hesú bo yu su alma
tin di krusa
un desierto largu
anto desolá,
su so.

Ya mi no ta riska
ni di buska
un alivio pa mi pena;
ku bálsamo kisas
di un soño tur bruhá
òf den promesanan
ku ta bai i bin'
ku bientu . . .

Ma at'awé
mi yu chikí
a karisiá mi kurason
ku un kantika dushi
k'el a kanta
pa mi so.

Ta pesei, Mama Tera,
mi ta baha
mi kabes kansá
pa mi sunchi
bo matris gastá.

Si den tal akto.
di reverensia
na mi kara
bo por topa
un lágrima ta dual,
Mama Tera,
pa bo e ta,
mi regalo di gratitut,
pasobra:
Mama mi tambe ta!

THE PROMISE

In my Grandmother's yard
a cotton plant grew
that we picked.
Into wigs, into beards
we shaped the white balls
and in simple disguise
our fancies, most daring,
came true.

In my Grandmother's yard in Aruba,
hundreds of mud-pies were made;
we jumped and we skipped,
we laughed as we played
at all of the games
that we knew.

In my Grandmother's yard
my porcelain doll
fell into shards
and so did my innocent heart.

In my Grandmother's yard
now a child roams about
in a daze . . .
She stretches both arms
to pluck from the heavens
a promise
way out of her reach.

I know her, I know her too well;
by my humming-bird shoes
and my ribbons so red
I can tell.

But all is in vain,
for now it's too late
to protect her
from sorrow and pain.

PROMESA

Den kurá di mi wela
banda dje bliki
ta'tin un mat'i katuna
ku nos tabata piki,
traha bigoti ku barba,
hari kontentu,
bira ken ku nos ke.

Den kurá di mi wela n'Aruba
nos a traha bolo di lodo,
nos a salta kontentu,
hunga kaku korí
i kaku skondí.

Den kurá di mi wela
mi pòpchi di glas
a kai kibra,
mi kurason inosente
huntu kuné.

Den kurá di mi wela difuntu
awó tin un mucha ta dual,
ku sapatu di blenchi bistí.
E ta rèk tur dos man
pa piki fo'i shelu
un promesa,
sin por alkans'é.

Mi konos'é, mi konos'é!
Na mi sapatu di blenchi
i mi streki kòrá
m'a konos'é;
ai, ta lat,
ya ta lat
pa mi por proteh'é.

OLD LADY

Lil' old lady,
are you saying prayers
or do you keep repeating
some sound advice,
that your shapeless mouth
chews constantly
in a rhythm
all your own?

Silly old lady,
are you ironing
your family's laundry once again
or do you wish
to bring to life
a caress of years gone by,
that your gnarled hands
are so busily-occupied?

Daft old lady,
do you feel cold
in summer heat
or does your sinewy neck
upon a call from eternity
shake to indicate
your need
to stay with us,
yet another little while?

Sweet old lady,
with your clogged up veins,
your widow's hump,
your eyes opaque,
I'll have you for my baby,
for a single night, at least,
to hug you—kiss you—love you
before you cease the movements,
before you turn into an object,
cold and still . . .

HABAI

Machi bieu,
ta resa bo ta resa
òf t'un bon konseho
bo ta sigui ripití,
ku bo boka slap
kontinuamente
ta kou sin djente
den un ritmo di bo so?

Machi leu, hei!
Ta strika bo ta strika
dril ku kaki ku kashimir
òf ta un karisia
di den pasado
bo ke rebibá
ku bo mannan korkobá
den konstante moveshon?

Machi kèns,
ta friu bo tin
den tempu di kalor
òf ta miedu di etèrnidat
ta pone bo garganta
tur na lòpchi
tambaliá
pa indiká ku
nò,
ainda nò?

Machi prenda,
ku bo benanan di kalki,
bo lomba di baul,
bo wowonan nublá,
mi ke bo pa mi bebi:
zoyabo—yayabo—stimabo
maske ta ún anochi
promé bo bira inmóbil,
promé bo bira kos,
ketu . . .
friu . . .

Phyllis Allfrey

THE CHILD'S RETURN

I remember a far tall island
floating in cobalt paint
The thought of it is a childhood dream
torn by a midnight plaint

There are painted ships and rusty ships
that pass the island by,
and one dark day I'll board a boat
when I am ready to die

The timbers will creak and my heart will break
and the sailors will lay my bones
on the stiff rich grass, as sharp as spikes,
by the volcanic stones.

Phyllis Allfrey's works reprinted by permission of Lennox Honeychurch.

LOVE FOR AN ISLAND

Love for an island is the sternest passion:
pulsing beyond the blood through roots and loam
it overflows the boundary of bedrooms
and courses past the fragile walls of home.

Those nourished on the sap and milk of beauty
(born in its landsight) tremble like a tree
at the first footfall of the dread usurper—
a carpet-bagging mediocrity.

Theirs is no mild attachment, but rapacious
craving for a possession rude and whole;
lovers of islands drive their stake prospecting
to run the flag of ego up the pole.

Sink on the tented ground, hot under azure,
plunge in the heat of earth, and smell the stars
of the incredible vales. At night, triumphant,
they lift their eyes to Venus and to Mars.

Their passion drives them to perpetuation;
they dig, they plant, they build and they aspire
to the eternal landmark; when they die
the forest covers up their set desire.

Salesmen and termites occupy their dwellings,
their legendary politics decay.
Yet they achieve an ultimate memorial:
they blend their flesh with the beloved clay.

MISS GARTHSIDE'S GREENHOUSE

"BUT WHAT A MARVELLOUS collection!" I cried. "I've never seen anything like it! Wherever did you get them all?"

The Chief Librarian smiled. Was it my fancy, or did he smile somewhat moodily? "We owe them to Miss Garthside. That is, we owed them to her. It's an odd story. . . ."

"This gorgeous plate, for instance!" I exclaimed. The volume was enormous, lavishly gilt-edged, and under gossamer tissue a life-size ruby-breasted hummingbird hung over one of the rarer Cattleya orchids. One whole shelf in the special room was taken up by these magnificent books on the flora and fauna of Venezuela. On that wintry evening the very sight of the pages transported me to a brilliant sizzling continent.

"She was one of our borrowers," said the Chief Librarian. "I cannot call her a subscriber, for as you know this is a free library. Well, we try to keep up a reputation for service and all that. I'm bound to say Miss Garthside made full use of it."

He pursed his lips in melancholy reminiscence.

"Of course she paid her fines—and as far as I remember, she never had a book out which was not eventually overdue. She kept things so long, you see. But most of the books she read were large and expensive. You know we try and obtain for readers the books they especially ask for. Miss Garthside was forever requesting some work that was practically unobtainable. Yet the Committee was very accommodating. They seemed to enjoy indulging her. She never asked for trash, anyhow."

"And I take it she was singularly charming?"—I rather enjoyed pulling the Chief Librarian's leg. But at this he hummed and hawed and looked dubious. "No, I can't say she was. She was a plain old thing, lived quite frugally, and always seemed to wear the same grey tweed costume. Had a certain persuasive manner, of course. But wasn't a *femme fatale,* or anything like that—"

"Was she a botanist, then?"

"No, that wasn't why these books fascinated her. It was simply home-sickness. She came from Venezuela, you see. Always said she couldn't stand the winter without her flora and fauna. We used to call this shelf 'Miss Garthside's Greenhouse.' Birds, too. She had orchids and birds in her bonnet, that poor lady."

I opened another volume. There was a beautiful engraving of a stick insect crawling towards a hibiscus flower. The jutting pistil showered miniature blossoms from a stamen like a painted trumpet.

The Chief Librarian said: "*Nostalgie des tropiques.* That's what she used to say, 'Mr. Hartley, I've got a bad attack of *nostalgie des tropiques.*' In her remarkable bad accent. But one day her father died. We were all surprised to hear that Miss Garthside had a father. She seemed so old—ageless, somehow."

"So he left her a fortune—and she repaid you for all the books that the poor ratepayer had provided!"

"Not so fast, my dear boy. No he didn't leave her a fortune. Just a small sum—a few hundred pounds, I believe. It came one February day, and I recall how excited the dear lady was. 'At last!' she kept on exclaiming, right in this very room. 'At last! My winter dream will come true. I can go home. Away from all this greyness—to the bright colours of the warm south!' She'd never been able to get even as far as Cannes, you see. So poor. We were all very happy for her. She insisted on taking the first cargo boat out, after she got her passport. She came here to say goodbye. Dear me, it was most touching. Holding my hand and all that. 'Mr. Hartley, these books have kept me alive, kept me going all these years so that I could go home.' Quite like a young girl—'blissfully happy!' she kept repeating. We felt upset when we saw that her ship had gone through terrific gales. But she arrived all right—I had an airmail letter. I think I replied to it quite promptly, but it was several months before I heard from her again. And before her letter reached me, she had died."

I was silent. What was there to say? To me, Miss Garthside was just another old eccentric; but it was easy to see that the Chief Librarian had thought her positively lovable.

"The letter is tucked away somewhere, I believe. . . . But the long and short of it was that Miss Garthside's greenhouse was more agreeable than the real Venezuelan landscape—for her, anyway. She suffered out there, you see. She had remembered the hummingbirds, but forgotten the mosquitoes and scorpions. She had remembered the kind servants—all of whom had departed—and forgotten the native birds of prey. She had gone from a borough where she got free medical attention to a place where it cost a fortune to be transported to hospital and have an operation. Worst of all, the change of climate and the blinding sunshine affected her eyes. Poor Miss Garthside died in darkness."

"What a sad story!" I said, a little clumsily.

The Chief Librarian looked shocked. "A sad story? Nothing of the kind my boy—a heroic story. You might as well say that Miss Garthside died to leave these books to the Library. She died for her greenhouse, in fact. We discovered afterward through a lawyer that she had sufficient funds to fly to Caracas and have that major operation. She even had a relative there who might have taken her in for the rest of her life. But she was afraid that if she did that, she wouldn't be able to pay for the books, and as she had written to me, 'those books gave me the happiest evenings of my existence.' You see," said the Chief Librarian loyally, "for all the dreaming and fancying she did among the leaves and orchids and birds in our old books, Miss Garthside was practical and consistent—in fact, a perfect lady."

Christabel LaRonde

SMILE PLEASE

White lilies remain crushed
Their fragrance n'er withers
Out in the ancient philosophy
Where lilies look to sunshine
I. . . . as one in the shade

The midnight caller to your phone
Smile please. . . . Jean Rhys
You live here still
The crushed lily
Your fragrance n'er withered

An unfinished song is in my heart
Your picture on my wall should be
B'neath trees
Not on the walls of cold England
Or Vienna
As they remember you by

Flowers curtain my ring of memories
The dove cries for her young still
In the graven night
All goes well
What is done is done

Mona Lisa smiles
Vaguely though it may be
In the yard
Vines are grown

In the yard
My Jean Rhys
Ella Gwendolen Rees Williams
Smiled not

Smile please .... Jean Rhys

Gilda Nassief

CARIBMAN

caribman
you think of your race
and despair engraves its name
all over your face
and sorrow leaves a trace
across the light in your eyes
down the corner of your lips. . . .
caribman
you look at your people
and count the few
who still bear untouched
the ancestral stamp
of yellowskin straighthair
hawkednose almondeyes
and you know for sure
your race is dying. . . .

    caribman
    your people leave a print
    on the shores of time
    memory of your courage and grandeur
    will linger in the mind of man
    caribman
    the death of your race
    will leave an indelible scar
    in the heart of man. . . .

Gilda Nassief's poems reprinted by permission of the author.

BLACKSISTER

who should be called
blacksister
blackbrother
where does black start
where does white start
among all the infinite shades
which definite shade
is the beginning
of being black
which is the end of being black
gale anne benson
was a whitesis with a blacksoul
and blackbrothers killed her . . .
where does a blacksoul start
where does it end
to begin a whitesoul
oh where where and how and when
and why why why?

C'EST JUSTE UNE GUÊPE

don't be scared
c'est juste une guêpe
it's just a wasp
exploring your forehead
scrutinizing the forest of
your lovely hair
don't be scared
c'est juste une guêpe
it's just a wasp
puzzled and baffled
busy looking
wondering if there's space enough
for shade
in this new type
of frizzly grass
don't be scared
c'est juste une guêpe

MAROUSSIA

maroussia
you're in the making
and i'm helping
trying not to make you
me
trying not to make you
someone else
you're in the making
and i'm helping you
little woman-to-be
i'm helping you
become
you

Jean Rhys

✧

THE WHISTLING BIRD

I FIRST SAW LILIANE, my cousin, at one of the few old estate houses left in Dominica—a baby a few weeks old. She was dark, small, and silent, except that every now and again she would wail, a thin, strange cry, as if she were protesting being born. I was told that she was very delicate and not expected to live, and I remember my grandmother saying something about the sins of the fathers being visited on the children. My grandmother was full of these threatening Biblical quotations, though I don't think that she was at all a religious woman. Soon after this I left the island for England and school.

I met Liliane again in a St. Lucia hotel during my first visit to the West Indies for many years. She was then in her twenties—a tall, energetic girl in spite of my grandmother's prophecies. I had lost touch with many of my West Indian relatives, and I heard for the first time of her family's changed circumstances. Her father had died suddenly, leaving very little money, and his widow and three children were obliged to give up the estate. The son, who was called Don, joined very composedly in talk about their future plans. Then one day he got up from the table at the end of the meal, went into the bedroom, and shot himself. There were various explanations of this. When in England, he'd been anxious to join the Navy. Perhaps he had failed an exam and was unable to forget it. Perhaps he suddenly saw what his future life would be and couldn't face it. Anyway, that was the end of Don. He was eighteen. His mother, whom I remembered so well as pretty Evelina, went back to St. Lucia, the island where she was born, with her two daughters. There she met an English woman who, planning to start a hotel outside Castries, befriended, or perhaps made use of, the entire family. Intelligent Liliane was the cashier, pretty

Monica the receptionist, Evelina the manageress, who dealt with the staff and the food, for she knew a lot about real French Creole cooking, which can be delicious.

We stayed several weeks at this hotel, and I found it every attractive. I was happy there. One afternoon when I asked for tea, the tray was brought up to my room by a woman dressed in the old fashion, in what used to be called the *grande robe*—a long, gaily colored high-waisted dress, a turban, and heavy gold earrings. It was the past majestically walking in.

I did not see very much of Liliane. It was Monica who told me about her long, lonely walks at night—she often didn't come back till dawn, though she was at work early—and that she edited a magazine, writing all the stories, calling herself by different names: "Lady Amelia," "Onlooker," and so on. But there was usually a short poem, which she signed with her initials, L.L. I remember one about English Harbour in Antigua, once Nelson's headquarters but then in ruins, not yet dolled up for tourists, and supposed to be haunted by a Lieutenant Peterson: a long romance about Lieutenant Peterson, wicked Lord Camelford, Captain Best, and a masked ball, belonging more to the old West Indies than to the West Indies as it is now. I was back in London, when I had a letter from Liliane, telling me of Monica's death: the old story—a young Englishman to whom she was engaged had left the island without explanation. When it became obvious that he wasn't going to write or return, she went to bed and was dead in a couple of weeks. For Evelina this was one misfortune too many, and she gave up and died soon afterward. Liliane, the survivor, wrote that she was coming to London, and it was there that I met her and got to know more of her.

She was a strange girl, shying away from any attempt to help her, insisting that what she did was her own business and no one else's. I have never known anyone who kept her contacts with other people so formal. She never said "I'll come tomorrow afternoon" but "I'll be with you tomorrow at a quarter to four and I'll leave at half past five." So it would be. She had found a job, she told me, and something about her voice made me sure it wasn't a well-paid job, or one she liked or wished to talk about.

She lived in a small bed-sitting room beyond Hampstead. In one corner was a silver tea service brought from the West Indies. Also, to my surprise, she had the portrait of Old Lockhart, her great-grandfather and mine, who had arrived in the West Indies at the end of the eighteenth century. He stared as blankly as ever. It was impossible to know whether he was a bad man or a good man lied about, or someone who just did what everyone else did without thinking too much about it. The Spanish great-grandmother, whom

I'd always been so curious about, wasn't there. Liliane didn't talk much about her past or the West Indies but did talk a good deal about her love for England, London, and the Royal Family. Someone once said of her, "I can't keep my face straight when I'm talking to that old Rip Van Winkle."

"Be patient with her—she's an anachronism," I said.

"But such a damn bore."

Underneath all this she could be gay and full of life, and almost crazily generous with the little money she had. After I went to live in the country, she would say that she was the Londoner now, I a visitor and her guest. She as hostess must pay for all our outings. It needed a lot of arguing to convince her that that wasn't how I saw it at all. One day she told me that she had sold one of her poems. "Dorinda isn't mine anymore" is how she put it. "I've sold Dorinda." So she still writes poetry, I thought. She gave me a copy of the poem.

> My name is Dorinda and I live so gay
> In a little hut with flowers on a shilling a day.
> The white man made me but he cannot tell
> The secret of my laughter like a golden bell.
> My name is Dorinda and I live so gay
> In a little hut with flowers on a shilling a day.
> The black man made me but he'll never know
> The secret of my dark heart which he made so.

As we got to know each other better, she showed me other poems. I often wondered when she wrote them. After she came back tired from the office to her little bed-sitting room? Or on Sundays—did she walk about Hampstead Heath to the tune of "Trinidad Selina"?

> Watch her walkin' and stop your talkin'
> See her dancin'—she dances on air.

I was certain that some of her songs were salable, and I knew how badly she needed the money, but I didn't know how to set about selling them. Even if by some miracle someone liked the words, wouldn't they be set to the wrong music and spoiled? Also, Liliane wasn't encouraging. She seemed not to have the slightest wish to make money out of poems—even to be somewhat hostile to the idea. It was as if she meant to keep them to herself, to protect them, and I understood this far too well to argue with her.

I didn't go to London for some time after that. Then I heard from a friend that she wasn't at all well. I'd noticed it the last time I'd seen her. All the spring and pride had gone out of her walk—she had walked beautifully when she first came to London—and she rarely smiled, which was a pity, because her white, even teeth were her greatest beauty.

The last time I saw her, she showed me a poem. "This is different," she said. Unlike the others, it was a sad song, about a man who kills his sweetheart, hides her body in the Dominica forest, and escapes to England before she is missed. But he cannot forget her.

> Devil made me lash her down, devil made me kill.
> Sorrow made me leave her
> Now she's dark in Dominica
> And I'm lonely in the snow. . . .
>
> I wish I were beside her, where the mountains hide her.
> For the whistling bird is calling me.

She said, "The whistling bird—you remember. The mountain whistler?"

"Of course."

"My mother called it the *siffleur de montagne, le solitaire*. I expect there aren't any left now."

"Perhaps a few."

"What about the parrots? Long ago the forest was full of parrots, green and gray. There isn't one now."

"Parrots," I said, "are different. There's money in parrots. Who'd buy a mountain whistler? It it were caught, it would probably die."

"Not at once," said Liliane.

After thinking a lot about her, I wrote and begged her to take a holiday, enclosing some money to help. She wrote back coldly, returning the money and adding that I must know that she didn't want to leave London and didn't need a holiday. I decided that when I saw her next I would argue her into taking one all the same. Then I heard that one morning she'd got up, had her usual obligatory tepid bath, and was dressing to go to her horrible job, when she fell. The landlady heard the noise and rushed to her bedroom. She was dead.

After all, I saw comparatively little of Liliane. She may have had other friends, another life that I didn't know about. But I never caught a glimpse of it.

"Woe to the vanquished," they say. Need it be so much woe and last such a long time? Anyhow, not Don, not Monica, not Evelina, not Liliane will join in that complicated argument. For it is complicated, whatever the know-alls say.

excerpt from
WIDE SARGASSO SEA

OUR GARDEN WAS LARGE and beautiful as that garden in the Bible—the tree of life grew there. But it had gone wild. The paths were overgrown and a smell of dead flowers mixed with the fresh living smell. Underneath the tree ferns, tall as forest tree ferns, the light was green. Orchids flourished out of reach or for some reason not to be touched. One was snaky looking, another like an octopus with long thin brown tentacles bare of leaves hanging from a twisted root. Twice a year the octopus orchid flowered—then not an inch of tentacle showed. It was a bell-shaped mass of white, mauve, deep purples, wonderful to see. The scent was very sweet and strong. I never went near it.

All Coulibri Estate had gone wild like the garden, gone to bush. No more slavery—why should *anybody* work? This never saddened me. I did not remember the place when it was prosperous.

My mother usually walked up and down the *glacis,* a paved roofed-in terrace which ran the length of the house and sloped upwards to a clump of bamboos. Standing by the bamboos she had a clear view to the sea, but anyone passing could stare at her. They stared, sometimes they laughed. Long after the sound was far away and faint she kept her eyes shut and her hands clenched. A frown came between her black eyebrows, deep—it might have been cut with a knife. I hated this frown and once I touched her forehead trying to smooth it. But she pushed me away, not roughly but calmly, coldly, without a word, as if she had decided once and for all that I was useless to her. She wanted to sit with Pierre or walk where she pleased without being pestered, she wanted peace and quiet. I was old enough to look after myself. "Oh, let me alone," she would say, "let me alone," and after I knew that she talked aloud to herself I was a little afraid of her.

So I spent most of my time in the kitchen which was in an outbuilding some way off. Christophine slept in the little room next to it.

When evening came she sang to me if she was in the mood. I couldn't always understand her patois songs—she also came from Martinique—but she taught me the one that meant "The little ones grow old, and children leave us, will they come back?" and the one about the cedar tree flowers which only last for a day.

The music was gay but the words were sad and her voice often quavered and broke on the high note, "Adieu." Not adieu as we said it, but *à dieu,* which made more sense after all. The loving man was lonely, the girl was deserted, the children never came back. Adieu.

Her songs were not like Jamaican songs, and she was not like the other women.

She was much blacker—blue-black with a thin face and straight features. She wore a black dress, heavy gold earrings and a yellow handkerchief—carefully tied with the two high points in front. No other negro woman wore black, or tied her handkerchief Martinique fashion. She had a quiet voice and a quiet laugh (when she did laugh), and though she could speak good English if she wanted to, and French as well as patois, she took care to talk as they talked. But they would have nothing to do with her and she never saw her son who worked in Spanish Town. She had only one friend—a woman called Maillotte, and Maillotte was not a Jamaican.

The girls from the bayside who sometimes helped with the washing and cleaning were terrified of her. That, I soon discovered was why they came at all—for she never paid them. Yet they brought presents of fruit and vegetables and after dark I often heard low voices from the kitchen.

So I asked about Christophine. Was she very old? Had she always been with us?

"She was your father's wedding present to me—one of his presents. He thought I would be pleased with a Martinique girl. I don't know how old she was when they brought her to Jamaica, quite young. I don't know how old she is now. Does it matter? Why do you pester and bother me about all these things that happened long ago? Christophine stayed with me because she wanted to stay. She had her own very good reasons you may be sure. I dare say we would have died if she'd turned against us and that would have been a better fate. To die and be forgotten and at peace. Not to know that one is abandoned, lied about, helpless. All the ones who died—who says a good word for them now?"

"Godfrey stayed too," I said. "And Sass."

"They stayed," she said angrily, "because they wanted somewhere to sleep and something to eat. That boy Sass! When his mother pranced off and left him here—a great deal *she* cared—why he was a little skeleton. Now he's growing into a big strong boy and away he goes. We shan't see him again. Godfrey is a rascal. These new ones aren't too kind to old people and he knows it. That's why he stays. Doesn't do a thing but eat enough for a couple of horses. Pretends he's deaf. He isn't deaf—he doesn't want to hear. What a devil he is!"

"Why don't you tell him to find somewhere else to live?" I asked and she laughed.

"He wouldn't go. He'd probably try to force us out. I've learned to let sleeping curs lie," she said.

"Would Christophine go if you told her to?" I thought. But I didn't say it. I was afraid to say it.

It was too hot that afternoon. I could see the beads of perspiration on her upper lip and the dark circles under her eyes. I started to fan her, but she turned her head away. She might rest if I left her alone, she said.

Once I would have gone back quietly to watch her asleep on the blue sofa—once I made excuses to be near her when she brushed her hair, a soft black cloak to cover me, hide me, keep me safe.

But not any longer. Not any more.

These were all the people in my life—my mother and Pierre, Christophine, Godfrey, and Sass who had left us.

I never looked at any strange negro. They hated us. They called us white cockroaches. Let sleeping dogs lie. One day a little girl followed me singing, "Go away white cockroach, go away, go away." I walked fast, but she walked faster. "White cockroach, go away, go away. Nobody want you. Go away."

When I was safely home I sat close to the old wall at the end of the garden. It was covered with green moss soft as velvet and I never wanted to move again. Everything would be worse if I moved. Christophine found me there when it was nearly dark, and I was so stiff she had to help me to get up. She said nothing, but next morning Tia was in the kitchen with her mother Maillotte, Christophine's friend. Soon Tia was my friend and I met her nearly every morning at the turn of the road to the river.

Sometimes we left the bathing pool at midday, sometimes we stayed till late afternoon. Then Tia would light a fire (fires always lit for her, sharp stones did not hurt her bare feet, I never saw her cry). We boiled green bananas in an old iron pot and ate them with our fingers out of a calabash and after we had eaten she slept at once. I could not sleep, but I wasn't quite awake as I lay in the shade looking at the pool—deep and dark green under the trees, brown-green if it had rained, but a bright sparkling green in the sun. The water was so clear that you could see the pebbles at the bottom of the shallow part. Blue and white and striped red. Very pretty. Late or early we parted at the turn of the road. My mother never asked me where I had been or what I had done.

Christophine had given me some new pennies which I kept in the pocket of my dress. They dropped out one morning so I put them on a stone. They shone like gold in the sun and Tia stared. She had small eyes, very black, set deep in her head.

She bet me three of the pennies that I couldn't turn a somersault under water "like you say you can."

"Of course I can."

"I never see you do it," she said. "Only talk."

"Bet you all the money I can," I said.

But after one somersault I still turned and came up choking. Tia laughed and told me that it certainly look like I drown dead that time. Then she picked up the money.

"I did do it," I said when I could speak, but she shook her head. I hadn't done it good and besides pennies didn't buy much. Why did I look at her like that?

"Keep them then, you cheating nigger," I said, for I was tired, and the water I had swallowed made me feel sick. "I can get more if I want to."

That's not what she hear, she said. She hear all we poor like beggar. We ate salt fish—no money for fresh fish. That old house so leaky, you run with calabash to catch water when it rain. Plenty white people in Jamaica. Real white people, they got gold money. They didn't look at us, nobody see them come near us. Old time white people nothing but white nigger now, and black nigger better than white nigger.

I wrapped myself in my torn towel and sat on a stone with my back to her, shivering cold. But the sun couldn't warm me. I wanted to go home. I looked round and Tia had gone. I searched for a long time before I could believe that she had taken my dress—not my underclothes, she never wore any—but my dress, starched, ironed, clean that morning. She had left me hers and I put it on at last and walked home in the blazing sun feeling sick, hating her. I planned to get round the back of the house to the kitchen, but passing the stables I stopped to stare at three strange horses and my mother saw me and called. She was on the *glacis* with two young ladies and a gentleman. Visitors! I dragged up the steps unwillingly—I had longed for visitors once, but that was years ago.

They were very beautiful I thought and they wore such beautiful clothes that I looked away down at the flagstones and when they laughed—the gentleman laughed the loudest—I ran into the house, into my bedroom. There I stood with my back against the door and I could feel my heart all through me. I heard them talking and I heard them leave. I came out of my room and my mother was sitting on the blue sofa. She looked at me for some time before she said that I had behaved very oddly. My dress was even dirtier than usual.

"It's Tia's dress."

"Why are you wearing Tia's dress? Tia? Which one of them is Tia?"

Christophine, who had been in the pantry listening, came at once and was told to find a clean dress for me. "Throw away that thing. Burn it."

Then they quarrelled.

Christophine said I had no clean dress. "She got two dresses, wash and wear. You want clean dress to drop from heaven? Some people crazy in truth."

"She must have another dress," said my mother. "Somewhere." But Christophine told her loudly that it shameful. She run wild, she grow up worthless. And nobody care.

My mother walked over to the window. ("Marooned," said her straight narrow back, her carefully coiled hair. "Marooned.")

"She has an old muslin dress. Find that."

While Christophine scrubbed my face and tied my plaits with a fresh piece of string, she told me that those were the new people at Nelson's Rest. They called themselves Luttrell, but English or not English they were not like old Mr. Luttrell. "Old Mr. Luttrell spit in their face if he see how they look at you. Trouble walk into this house this day. Trouble walk in."

The old muslin dress was found and it tore as I forced it on. She didn't notice.

No more slavery! She had to laugh! "These new ones have Letter of the Law. Same thing. They got magistrate. They got fine. They got jail house and chain gang. They got tread machine to mash up people's feet. New ones worse than old ones—more cunning, that's all."

All that evening my mother didn't speak to me or look at me and I thought, "She is ashamed of me, what Tia said is true."

I went to bed early and slept at once. I dreamed that I was walking in the forest. Not alone. Someone who hated me was with me, out of sight. I could hear heavy footsteps coming closer and though I struggled and screamed I could not move. I woke crying. The covering sheet was on the floor and my mother was looking down at me.

"Did you have a nightmare?"

"Yes, a bad dream."

She sighed and covered me up. "You were making such a noise. I must go to Pierre, you've frightened him."

I lay thinking, "I am safe. There is the corner of the bedroom door and the friendly furniture. There is the tree of life in the garden and the wall green with moss. The barrier of the cliffs and the high mountains. And the barrier of the sea. I am safe. I am safe from strangers."

Merle Collins

MADELENE

"I DON'T WANT TO be ungrateful," said Madelene, lowering herself on to the sofa. Corinne looked up from filing her nails. She opened her mouth to say something. Thought better of it. Her aunt, she decided, wasn't really talking to her. Madelene moved her hand across the cushion. This was her favourite seat. Her favourite bed, too. Sometimes, at night, she would just relax there and go to sleep instead of bothering to go into the room. These days I don't even like to go to sleep! she thought. I don't like nights. It's not like resting. It's like waiting. Madelene sighed. Corinne glanced up and quickly moved her eyes back to her nails, because her aunt was looking at the photograph above her head.

When I sleep in this room, Madelene was thinking, I'm closer to her. I can't say it's why I spent the money to buy this sofa, because I really needed something decent in here anyway. Friends and relatives and everybody always passing through New York on their way to somewhere and want a night's rest. Anyway, I needed a sofa. But when I sleep out here, it just so happen that I'm closer to her.

Belle, her daughter, the one child God had seen fit to give her on this earth, had had her great grandmother Belle's eyes. But she had looked more like her grandmother, Ma Janie, with those big, thick, long plaits. The one child God had seen fit to give her on this earth.

"You calling you daughter *Belle?*" her sister, Corinne's mother, had asked her. "All the trouble Grannie Belle make you see, you will take your good, good child and call after her?" And Madge had looked at her with something like admiration. "Sister," she said. "If you don't find a place in heaven, it have no justice in this world." And Madge, as usual, had challenged fate by adding, "because if it was what *I* had to

Reprinted from *Rain Darling* by Merle Collins, first published by The Women's Press Ltd., 34 Great Sutton Street, London EC1V ODX. Used by permission of The Women's Press Ltd.

do to secure my place in heaven, I would have lose out. Not me, sese! I couldn't call me good, good child after Grandma Belle."

"Madge," Madelene had told her gently, "don't say things like that. You mustn't speak like that of the dead. Grannie Belle wasn't bad, really; she was just disagreeable because she was sick. That was all."

"Is all right, Madelene. You are the one who mustn't speak badly of the dead. And nobody have to tell you that. Is a known fact that you wouldn't do it. You don't speak bad bout people when they alive, much less when they dead. Me? If Grandma Belle listening now, God rest the soul of the dead and all that, she know well is something I would say right to she face. So is all right. I treat her same way alive and dead. Just as she treat me all the days of me life that I could remember whether she was sick or she was well. No problem."

Madge had been like that. Blunt, straightforward. And people liked her. They knew where they were with her. They would go to cry on Madelene's shoulder, but they didn't go to Madge if they wanted to have a good cry. They went if they were crying and wanted somebody to tell them to stop playing the fool, and why. Madge was like that, except when her tears started, and then because she had always been so strong with everybody, the only person she could lean on was Ancil. And Ancil didn't want anybody leaning on him. That was one reason he had liked Madge in the first place. Because she was so tough. Nobody could hurt her.

Madelene ran her hands along the cushions again and looked around the room. She had no picture of Madge on the wall. She couldn't bear that. All Madge's photos were of a woman who held her head high and had determination and fire in her eyes. A strong face. Thin, almost cruel lips. Only in some of them the eyes took over. And you could see the softness, the love. But in none of them was there the broken, silent woman that Madge had become before she died. Having a photo of Madge on the wall would somehow be a frightening thing.

It was after Madge died that Madelene had developed her fear of heights. Any heights. Even looking out from the window onto the steps below when someone rang the doorbell made her giddy now. And when she was in a car going along a bridge, she had to close her eyes. She couldn't look down at the traffic below without feeling ill and panicky and wanting to scream. Madelene closed her eyes now and thought about it. It's as if it is dangerous just to hold your head high. That couldn't be true. No. She couldn't keep a photo of Madge in the house. That is why it had been so painful and frightening bringing up Corinne and watching her grow into her mother.

Madelene looked at her niece, at the high cheekbones, at the two plaits circling her head, at the determination in the chin, at the scornful tilt of the lips. She closed her eyes. Please God! Please!

The ticking of the clock on top of the television pushed against her eyelids, making them jump nervously. Some days you could watch that clock and not hear a sound. And some days it talked so loudly that you could hear every syllable. Like today.

Madelene opened her eyes and looked around the room. At the refrigerator, the dining table, her shelves full of knickknacks, the 1987 almanac on the wall. The television. Her photograph of Belle. And, opposite her, Corinne's face intent now on the page of the book she was reading. Thirty-seven years of life in New York crammed into four rooms in this apartment. This place was home, more home to her now than that hill in Grenada just over the sea. Now that she had stopped working, she actually missed the early morning trek to the corner of Church and Utica to get the bus. Walking with sleep still in her eyes, sometimes, but then by the time she was walking down the steps into Utica Avenue station, she was always awake. Awake and looking over her shoulder to see who was behind her. You didn't walk sleeping into the train station. No. Perhaps she didn't really miss that daily trek to work in the people's kitchen in Queens! You couldn't miss a thing like that. But it felt empty, still, getting up at five in the morning, and then realising you didn't have to start getting ready for work.

"I don't want to be ungrateful in truth, non, Lord! I don't want to be ungrateful. I have a good life. I don't want to be greedy either."

Corinne looked up again. And this time Madelene's eyes met hers. Madelene chuckled. "What?" she asked. "What you looking at me like that for?"

"I don't know why I bother to come and sit with you, you know. When I'm here, you talk to the Lord, you talk to everyone you have secreted away in your memory, and you ignore me completely!"

"Oh come on, Corinne! You know that's not true."

"Oh no? What's this you're saying about being ungrateful and being greedy?"

Madelene chuckled again. Leaned forward, stretching her arms along her legs, and when she looked up again, Corinne knew from the smile on her lips that she was going to say something her niece would have to unravel. Corinne sighed.

"It's all right, Auntie Madelene. I think I'd better read."

"You see? Now I want to talk to you, you don't want to keep me company at all."

Corinne closed her book. "Shoot!"

"Don't tell me any shoot! I don't carry a gun."

"All right, madam," Corinne stretched, laughing. "Tell me."

"It's a story."

"I guessed as much."

"About a greedy, greedy man."

"Oh! At least it have something to do with the way your thoughts have been going."

"Is nothing to do with me. It's about Konpe Macucu."

Corinne yawned.

"You see the same thing. You young people born in this country . . . "

"I'm just teasing you, Auntie Madelene. Tell me."

"Once upon a time, Konpe Zae, Konpe Macucu, and Konpe Tigre decide to make a big cook one day. They do all the work together, they fish, they hunt, and they go and dig a whole heap of potato and yam, they cut bananas, they knead their flour and make dumplin, and they cook a whole heap of food.

"When food ready, Zae and Tigre watch one another and say, 'The food plenty yes. It should have enough for all of us to eat, but just in case, we better get some more.' Konpe Zae say, 'For how I know I hungry there, I really think we need some more food.'"

Corinne chuckled. Madelene smiled at her niece. "It have people so in truth, you know. Never satisfy. Anyway, Macucu say, 'Me, I well tired. I not going any place now. Is just eat I waiting to eat.' So Tigre decide he will go with Zae to look for more crayfish under the river stone."

"Well I think they were really stupid and greedy. I could see where that story is going already, Auntie Madelene."

"That is the problem. But perhaps you only believe you see. Suppose you think you seeing and you not really seeing!"

Corinne clasped her hands lightly in front of her and looked with more attention at her aunt. Her stories were always like a test. Leaving you unravelling and unravelling. "I'm listening."

"Zae and Tigre set out to get more crayfish. They sit down by the river stone, bend down, push in they hand, grabbing wind and water, wind and water. Whole time their belly grumbling and they thinking of the food they cook already. But they thinking how a few more crayfish would really liven up the taste. So they persevering. Wind and water. Wind and water.

"Macucu, meanwhile, back home, he watching the food and he waiting. He watching the food and he waiting."

"But he was really stupid. They left on such a foolish mission; he shouldn't even think about them!"

"Well, he watching and waiting. He know that their work inside the pot too, so he scratching his head, he watching and he waiting. He scratching his chin, he watching and he waiting."

"Down by the river, no luck. Wind and water. Wind and water. Macucu find, well, he waiting too long."

Corinne's eyes narrowed. She watched her aunt's face.

"At last Macucu decide, 'I will eat a little, little piece on the edge here. Right here. Just a little piece.'"

Corinne relaxed. Chuckled again. "Of course. The others too greedy!"

"Macucu say, 'Oh God, hungry killing me. Let me take another little piece.' So he bite piece of dumplin, drink a little bit of soup, eat piece of fish, dig into a little chunk of yam . . . and whole time he watching the road. No Zae. No Tigre."

Corinne laughed out loud. "Wind and water," she said, "wind and water. That is all they will get!"

"Before Macucu well realise it, he finish the *whole* pot of food!"

"The man was hungry, Auntie Madelene! With reason!"

"When Tigre and Zae reach back, tired, they ain't hold no crayfish, pot empty. Tigre look in; food say, 'If you see me, take me.' Zae look in, he look around; he look up, he look down. He say, 'Non. Well something funny. I could swear we leave a pot here, that was full of food. Somebody if I wrong, tell me I wrong.'"

"He wasn't wrong at all. He was just too damn greedy!"

"So Zae look at Macucu belly how it nearly touching the other partition in the corner over by you there, Corinne . . . "

"No, Auntie Madelene, that is too much!" Corinne looked back at the partition, thumped it, made a show of trying to pull her chair closer to Aunt Madelene's. "Not over here."

"And Zae say, 'Tigre, oh! You know, boy? I think I see the food.' And before Macucu could move, because he so heavy he can't run at all, Zae grab hold of him, and he tell Tigre to hold him on the other side. All how Macucu plead that he didn't do anything, they hold on to him. And Zae look up into the sky quite over where the moon was shining she face nice, nice, and Zae call, 'Konpe Gigi! Konpe Gigi!'"

"Gigi is a bird?"

"Yes, Chicken-hawk! 'Konpe Gigi!' So Gigi flap up he wings and he coming down to hear what happen. And Konpe Zae say, 'Konpe Gigi, do something for us. *Vini. Vini pwan Konpe Maturu epi ale, ale, ale jis soley ba epi lage-y la sou plat woch sa-a!*' Okay! Okay! I will explain! I know you wouldn't understand that where you born in this Brooklyn here. He say, 'Come, come, come and take Konpe Macucu; go with him, go far, far away, like where you see the sun going down far over there. When you reach right up there, just let him go, let him go, let him fall on this flat stone right here!'"

"Oh gosh! Auntie Madelene, where do you get these stories from?"

"But is who really greedy? So anyway Gigi take up Macucu in his claws and he going up. And when he reach far, far up, he look back and he ask, 'Here?' and Zae and Tigre say, 'No. *Ale, ale, ale.* Go, go, go!' He travel, he travel, he travel, he stop again and he ask, 'Here?' And they say, 'No. *Ale. Ale.*'"

Corinne grinned, repeated a patwa word she had heard her aunt say in similar circumstances, *"Tonne!"*

"Tonne is right! At last Gigi reach quite where they can't even see him, and he up there close to the sun in the sky. They hearing the voice from far, far away asking 'He-e-e-re?' And Zae and Tigre shout back 'Oui! Ye-e-e-s!' And Gigi shout out 'Now!'

"And they wait! And they wait! And they wait! Zae watching the sky. Tigre watching the stone! Zae watching the sky! Tigre watching the stone! They wait! But was a long way up Gigi went. So they wait for about almost two hours!"

"Auntie Madelene!"

"How I buy it, so I sell it. I make no profit. But then all of a sudden Zae see this big barrel figure come flying through the sky and before he could look down good Tigre say, 'Woy!'"

Madelene looked down at the carpet, at the lone bedroom slipper which had suddenly become a stone waiting for Macucu's body. Corinne looked, pulled her lips apart in a grimace, drew her feet closer to her, and said, "Yuk!"

"Child, you should see that stone! You should have seen that stone! I tell you! Konpe Macucu belly open up from up here, right under his chest, go right down."

Corinne turned her head away, towards the blank face of the television. Closed her eyes. Opened them and turned back towards Auntie Madelene.

"Split! Burst wide open on the flat stone. Crayfish come out. Chicken come out. Callaloo come out. Dumplin come out. Yam come out. All the waters come out! Everything just mix up, mix up."

"Auntie Madelene! How disgusting!"

"Chile, I tell you! Zae watch and he shake his head. Tigre watch and he hold on to his belly as if he fraid it fall open too. What the two of them do with what come out is another story. But child you ever see? A nice, strong young man like Macucu, look where he end up through greedy! Look where he end up! His close, close friends give up on him!"

"But they were the greedy ones in the first place!"

"You telling me it have *degrees* of greedy? Who to judge? But me? Thirty-seven years in New York! Thirty-seven years! Child, I don't want to be greedy, I don't want to be ungrateful to the Lord for the little he let me put by. Who is to say? Who is to know?"

Corinne wasn't sure what to feel. She was torn between wondering what in fact the two had done with all that came out of Macucu's belly and trying to figure out the whole story. Madelene put her head back against the cushion and closed her eyes. Corinne ran her hands along the mahogany arms of the chair on which she sat. Thirty-seven years in New York, ending up not so far from where you start, and talking about not wanting to be greedy! Corinne sighed.

What was it that made some people feel rich when they had so little and some people want so much?

Corinne wished she knew more about her relatives. Aunt Madelene was the only one, really. "Heaven will be a place full of surprises," Aunt Madelene always told her. And Corinne had once said to her, "The biggest surprise will be the existence of heaven itself!" Aunt Madelene had looked at her strangely. "That is modern talk," she had said, "but for you it not so modern. It sound like you mother anyway. She would say things like that from time. From time."

Once, Corinne couldn't understand the stories about her mother. She couldn't understand how a woman whom people said had been so strong and so full of life could have lost interest in life and literally drunk herself to death because her husband had walked out on her. Then, two years ago, at thirty-two, just when she thought that she would always be in control and she would decide what relationship she wanted and didn't want, she had found herself in the middle of a relationship which she just hadn't known how to handle. Corinne had begun then to understand. Had begun to understand and become so angry with the pain of understanding and drinking and smoking that she talked herself out of madness.

There were times that she had been tempted to talk to Auntie Madelene. But she would rush home from work and begin to cry the moment the door of the apartment closed behind her. Once, after she moved to her own place and had to tackle not just a few narrow stairs but the lift, the tears had actually started in the lift. She had just kept staring at the number 6, right in front of her eyes, until the door of the lift opened, releasing her. Thank heavens the two pairs of eyes which had shared the lift with her had been focused inside themselves, on their own affairs. Those weeks of making sure that she had rum, whisky, beer, anything, so that she could drink herself to sleep! She never smoked in the apartment. She couldn't stand the smell. But she did, on the platform, waiting for trains, when the sight of people sleeping in the corners had made her weepy in a way that it hadn't really before. Well, it had, but she had been able to control it. Would talk about all of that with . . . with . . . him and felt different then. And then, perhaps it had been a television programme, or her friends talking, or her own distaste for smoking, or all of those, that had made her ask herself first of all whether it was worth it smoking herself to death because of some man. It was more the answer than the question that had frightened her. Because she had told herself that she wasn't interested really in whether she lived or died. And then had said, loudly, on the train platform, "Bullshit!"

No-one had turned to look at her, of course. Two youths standing near her were swaying and dipping to the sounds from their earphones. A woman was looking worriedly at her watch. "Rubbish!" Corinne had said, then puffed thoughtfully again at the cigarette and eventually crushed it. It hadn't been the last, but it had been a beginning. What would Auntie Madelene say if she knew it all? Corinne knew for sure that she wouldn't let it happen again. She was learning, now, to value herself more. Although the damn stupid thing was that she had thought she knew that ages ago! But she knew now how it could have happened to her mother. Sometimes she thought that Auntie Madelene had guessed about her. But Corinne never told her. She couldn't tell her.

So when things were really going bad, she had speeded up her plans for going independent and found her own apartment. Needed her own space, she said. She would visit often. Auntie Madelene, of course, hadn't minded. Corinne had only continued sharing the apartment all of these years anyway because she knew that Madelene wanted the company. "I will miss you, child," Madelene had said, "but you have to find your own way." And so she had never seen the packets of cigarettes, the bottles of rum, and whisky, and gin. So stupid! So damned stupid! Poor mother! So impossible!

Corinne looked at her aunt's face, at the lines curving around the sides and over her mouth, at the small, slim hands, loosely linked now below her stomach. Aunt Madelene, she knew, was afraid of death. And she thought that she was dying. There was something wrong, Corinne knew, but she wasn't sure what. Something wrong inside under her stomach just where the hands were clasped. Madelene knew, she felt, but didn't say. And this scared Corinne. She thought perhaps her aunt had some terminal illness; that she was keeping it a secret so that she would not worry anyone; she would carry all of the worry herself.

Madelene was muttering something as she dozed. Corinne stood up and bent over her. Moved away and sat down again. Looked up at the photograph of Belle. In the photo, Belle was about four years old. Four and a half, really. Auntie Madelene could say how many months, how many days after four. She had been buried in the cemetery here in Brooklyn thirty years ago. Auntie Madelene was always amazed because here in the cold, dark pain of Brooklyn all those years ago she had actually managed to find a cemetery called "Evergreen." Auntie

Madelene always said that she wanted to be buried there too. Here in New York, which had become home, bad as it was, she said. Who to say where is home? Over there was home once, but . . . And Auntie Madelene usually shrugged at this point and said, "Bad is bad wherever it is! Wherever it is! Trouble is always trouble! It might feel little better here because everybody little better off, but watch who at the bottom of the barrel! Just watch!"

Sometimes Corinne wondered whether Auntie Madelene really meant that. Or if she was just telling herself that because New York had, like it or not in a way, become her home. Corinne remembered the day when someone had actually tried to snatch her purse one early morning. As luck would have it, she was then walking with her cousin, who had come from Grenada hoping to stay. Corinne smiled. That was just plain bad luck! It was the first time Auntie Madelene had been attacked in the street. Cousin . . . Cousin . . . What was her name again? I don't even remember. Her karma was just bad, I suppose! Corinne chuckled. It wasn't a joke, really, but that had confirmed Cousin . . . oh, Madonna! . . . that had confirmed cousin Madonna's worst fears about New York and, even though they hadn't really lost anything, because Auntie Madelene had shouted and cursed the guy! Imagine! The poor guy, not expecting to hear such words and get such a vigorous defence from a woman that age, perhaps, had run off. Corinne smiled and looked at her aunt's face, as gentle in repose as it was when alive and questioning. "We lucky he was just a novice," Madelene had said when recounting the story. "He didn't ready yet. He only think he want to thief!" Even though he hadn't taken the bag that he was after, Cousin Madonna had booked her return ticket the following week.

Madelene opened her eyes. Moved her fingers along the base of her stomach. "Sixty-seven is a good old age, yes, a good old age," she said without preamble. She looked at Corinne, chuckled.

"What now?"

"I was remembering my husband," she giggled. "Your mother used to say to me, 'That one wasn't husband. Was waste-band.'"

Corinne bit her lip, smiled.

"The man disappear from my house and my bed for seven days and seven nights."

"A biblical man."

"Biblical? I don't know. Was forty days and forty nights Christ went for."

"After this seven-day absence . . . " Corinne smiled in anticipation. She had heard this story often.

"After this absence, I hear me door knock kow, kow, kow one night. And, wait, stop laughing and listen, non. Wait. This disappear you see he disappear there, we didn't have any confusion, you know. He just decide to leave. I didn't even bother to look for him; because I done hear already is so he is, is things like that he would do. So I say, 'Oh yes? Well, let's see!' So this day when the door knock, I look outside. Friend, is Mister, yes, standing on the step. I say to him," and Madelene lifted her chin, held up her right hand with an admonishing forefinger, "'You go right back where you coming from. You know someone here? Go right back where you coming from!'"

Corinne giggled. "What *really* happened after that, Auntie Madelene?"

"How you mean what *really* happened? Is like I always tell you. I say my piece and I leave him there."

"So he just went away?"

"As far as I was concerned he could have stayed there if he wanted to. Wasn't my problem. Anyway, the last I heard of him he was in St Kitts by his people, I think."

"Auntie Madelene, you never looked back? You never found out about him or anything?"

"Why? Is husband I want so? When people show they care nothing about you, what you looking back for?"

Madelene and Madge. Her aunt. Her mother. The weak and the gentle? The strong and the boisterous? Could I have done it? Corinne wondered. Just left him standing there? Perhaps if she hadn't really cared! Nonsense! As Auntie Madelene said, if a person show they don't care about you.

Madelene stood, stretched, switched on the gas fire. "It's getting cold," she said. "You're staying over? Stay, non!"

Corinne thought for a moment. Why rush back to the apartment? In her mind, she surveyed the apartment. Had she put off the iron? Turned down the heat for when it came on? No lights on? She looked towards the window, where she could see nothing, really, but the curtains drawn against the cold. It would be cold outside. One of these days, she would get a car. Could get one fairly cheaply, and a good one, if she could find someone who knew his way around the garages.

"Okay. I'm on nights tomorrow. I can stay, yes. I'll leave in the morning. I'll stay."

"Good. I'm glad for the company." Madelene walked over to the window. Pulled aside the thick, red curtain, lifted the net and stood looking at the tall, grey buildings outside, up towards the distance where you couldn't even see a sky through the mist. She shivered.

A man walked by, light brown jacket, head uncovered, hands in pockets, head down. He was young. There was no way of telling what the weather was like from watching him. These young people wear the most ridiculous things in the cold. Two young women, thick, long coats, collar turned up, scarves, arms folded, heads down. It cold! Behind them, a middle-aged man, thick jacket, hood up, scarf, hands in pockets, shoulders hunched. It well cold!

"Look at me, eh!" Madelene said, turning back into the room. "Look at me!" running her hand over the plastic tablecloth. *"Dimi millionaire na l'Amerk."*

"Come again?"

Madelene chuckled, ran her hand along the waist of the thick trousers she usually wore during the cold evenings.

"When I used to take care of my grandmother, Grannie Belle, up on the hill in Hope, she was well disgusting. Your mother always say so, and was true, but poor thing. Nothing I do for her she ever used to be satisfied. That time my mother, your grandmother, was dead already. Grannie Belle used to say, *'Ich-nwen se dimi millionaire na l'Amerik zu ca ba nwen "inject" shak jour!'* That time my father was up here, so what she saying to me was, 'My son is a little millionaire in America; you here giving me "inject" every day!' So now I say is me that is the little millionaire. Me self, yes, here in l'Amerik."

"But what is 'inject'?"

"The green banana they used to sell after they export what they consider good. They used to call the rest, what they selling to us, 'reject,' so she just didn't get the word good, and she called it 'inject.' Inject, reject, same thing."

"My mother used to be with you at that time, Auntie Madelene?"

"At first. But she really didn't like it in that house. Your grandmother wasn't easy. She used to call us the worse names possible. And after she had the stroke and couldn't walk, she get even more miserable. She used to go down on the floor, sit down, and drag herself right across the floor. And sometimes if something annoy her, she would drag the centre table or anything she could pull or push, right across the floor. And if that back door open, she would push it right over. Right outside. It sounding funny now, but you know how often we run outside behind things and run down the hill over the sea there before things disappear?"

"Yes."

Madelene sat down, her eyes staring at the wall opposite, but clearly not seeing it. "I remember the tourists always used to stop and come up on the hill by us to take pictures. 'Lovely spot,' they used to say. 'It must be a joy to you to live here; it's the most *divine* spot.'"

Corinne said nothing. The old house was no longer there, she knew. But she had gone to Grenada with friends on two occasions, had taken them to that very spot over the sea. They had stayed at a guest house in St George's, the capital, although Corinne had stayed

some nights by friends and distant relatives of her aunt. Had met people who kept saying things like, "So this is Madge own, eh! Look at
that, eh! These children and them doesn't take time to grow, non!
And she look like the mother, eh! God ave is mercy! Child, you don't
lose road at all!" Corinne smiled, remembering the voices, the faces,
the unquestioning acceptance. On the occasions when they had gone
to Hope, Corinne and her friends had walked down to the sea, back
up again to sit in the sun and just gaze at the view. Corinne and her
friends, too, had thought the view divine. If they had that, they said,
they wouldn't live anywhere else.

It was when she thought about that sometimes that Corinne wondered if her aunt was serious about New York being her home. You
couldn't come from a place like that and call New York home and really mean it! Could you? Even now, sometimes, Auntie Madelene
would sit down looking dreamy and say, "All those white people and
them going out to the West Indies buying land and settling down in
the sunshine! It nice in truth, yes." And sometimes she would suck
her teeth and say, "Perhaps I better retire there in truth!" And laugh-
ingly she would ask Corinne, "You will come too? Or visit me sometimes?" Sometimes Corinne didn't answer; sometimes she said, "Of
course I will come too!" And then her aunt just smiled and said, "Of
course? Of course?" And at times she added. "I just joking, child! You
have your own life!"

"After a while," said Madelene now, "your mother got a job working for a Mistress Anderson not so far away. Estate people, you know.
So they used to live in the Great House. Grenada white. And that Mistress Anderson was a special lady."

"Special how?" Corinne pulled Auntie Madelene's other pair of
slippers from the corner by the television, slipped off her high-
heeled shoes with a sigh.

"Specially mean," explained Auntie Madelene, and Corinne
laughed. "She had two disgusting little boys that Madge was supposed
to take care of. She was so mean that she didn't even want your
mother and the other servants to use her pots to do their cooking.
And she said she not boarding anyone; she paying them, so they not
to eat her food. Find their own."

"But she was sure taking a lot of chances! And she let them *cook*
for her? Wasn't she afraid that they'd *do* something? Put something in
the food or something? Come *on!*

"Same thing Madge used to say. Come on is right! But some of
these people were so important they didn't think they were dealing
with people at all as long as you poor. And black wasn't nothing. So
the servants would share the food for the family, and 110 chance to
take something because she measuring everything she put out. She

say she pay a few pence extra, so that they could find their own pots to do their own cooking. But *ki extra sa?* What extra is that?

"So your mother used to stay around and cook sometimes in one of the other servant's pot. But then I said to her, 'Don't take her on; come down here and eat. Is an hour for lunch, so you will have time; don't stay up there. Come down!' Because what the lady used to do, you see, is that as she know Madge around, before the hour up, she going to sleep and she know the children will go to Madge and she will be looking after them. But that can't work. You can't let people take you and tie wood like that.

"So Madge started to come down to the village in Hope for lunch, and take her full lunch hour. And you don't know? The lady then offer her a little pot of her own, saying that she could stay up there and cook."

"She didn't take it, of course?"

"Not at first. She tell me the lady could take the pot and put it back right under her bed or wherever she had it; but then the lady come and press her, press her, and I believe Madge self was afraid she lose the job, because job wasn't so easy to find that time, so eventually she come and take it."

Corinne didn't say anything. She had never heard this story about her mother before. It didn't sound, somehow, like the big, tough mother she had come to believe existed in those early days. Fancy going back eventually and accepting the offer of that pot! Madelene looked at her niece's pensive face.

"You children don't know anything, you know," she said, almost gently. "You don't know trouble at all. Talking about things is one thing. Living it is another. When you have time to read about hardship and talk about it, always remember is because you don't have to live it." Corinne looked at her aunt's face, at the lines running across her forehead, down at her hands. Madelene rubbed her hands together, pushed the fingers through each other. "Because you don't have to live it," she repeated softly.

She leaned back, cupped her hands at the base of her stomach again, and this time Corinne was very afraid. Her aunt looked so tired.

"Auntie Madelene," Corinne said quickly, wanting to say something, anything. "Tell me about my mother!"

Madelene kept her eyes closed. "Your mother," she said, "sometimes I think I tell you as much as I could about her. She live a short life, she didn't even make it to forty. She barely pass thirty, in fact; she live a short time, but she live a lot. And she live strong, mostly, except when she close her eyes to life and forget." Aunt Madelene opened her eyes and studied Corinne's face. "You have her looks," she said, "you have her looks, and you have a lot of her manner. She was strong, very strong like all of us. Like all of us, Corinne." Aunt Madelene closed her eyes again. "Except when she close her eyes and let somebody make her forget how much she go through already, and how much she could go through again. Except when she close her eyes and forget."

"And Aunt Madelene," said Corinne desperately, thinking that there were so many things she didn't know about her aunt and about that whole life back in Grenada, and feeling frightened because of the way Aunt Madelene was talking, "tell me about you, now. Tell me some more about your life."

"Tomorrow, child. We will always have a lot of time to talk. Tomorrow, if God spare life. And you young people don't have patience for all those old time stories, anyway. Tomorrow."

"What do you mean we don't have patience?" Corinne was kneeling in front of her aunt's sofa, holding her hands in hers. "I'm asking you Auntie Madelene."

Madelene opened her eyes briefly. Smiled gently at Corinne. "Madge," she said. Closed her eyes, and just when Corinne thought she was asleep, Aunt Madelene said, "I know, honey. I know you care. I'm not as young and as strong as before. I'm a little bit tired, now. So tomorrow; okay? Everything have a pattern. We never miss nothing, really. Tomorrow, if God spare life." Madelene placed her hand lightly on the younger woman's head, her thumb just touching Corinne's forehead.

Maryse Condé

WAYANG KULIT

MY FATHER IS THE palace puppet master.

So was his father before him. And his father's father. And his grandfather's father. It's been like that for eternity. I too was destined to become the puppet master after him if the world had not altered its course. I know the faces of every puppet, their domed foreheads, their elongated noses and the brightly colored greasepaint around their eyes and mouth. I know the coarse fiber of their hair, the soft silk of their costumes and their shaky movements against the transparent screen that is used as a backdrop in the theater. I know the high and low-pitched sound of their voices and their cries of anger or ecstasy. But above all I know every note of the gongs and cymbals of the orchestra that accompanies their every movement. Because my mother is one of the musicians. She sings. Like her mother before her and her mother's mother and her grandmother's mother. It's been like that for eternity. When I was just a baby at her breast, newly emerged from the warmth of her womb, she would carry me in her arms and lay me on the ground among the musical instruments that shone like pieces of gold. When the music stopped she gave me the sweet milk from her breast to drink. When I was full, I fell into the sleep of the blessed with little fists tightly clasped. Neither the clash of the metal around me nor the roars of my father, as he changed from man to beast to spirit, nor the shrieks of laughter from the audience could wake me. On the contrary. All this mingled in my dreams and, in a certain way, arranged them into colored images that were both forbidding and pleasurable. When I ventured my first steps, it was against the hard edges of certain instruments that I stumbled while I held on to others to stop myself from falling. My childhood, I could say, was confined to the universe of the theater pit where my father sat with the other artists.

Reprinted by permission of the author.

All their life my parents have lived behind the walls of the palace. A palace where you can lose yourself, almost as big as a city with its inner courtyards, its ornamental pools of stagnant water covered with splashes of green, its centuries-old trees, its statues that glare or stare benignly and its rows of pavilions squeezed under their tiled roofs. That's where they were born and that's where they would die. They have never traveled and never visited the capital. They have never seen with their own eyes the green of the sea or the green of the rice fields. All they know is what they glean from the words of our court poets. My father sometimes goes out—seldom I must say—to attend some ceremony at the Central Mosque or to convey his sympathies to one of his friends who has been rushed to hospital en route for the journey of no return. As for my mother, she never goes farther than the second courtyard. She was born, she grew up, she became a woman and married my father, all within these narrow confines.

Recently my father has been going out more often to attend the meetings organized by the members of his profession; for the puppet masters from north to south, from east to west of this land are worried—their art is in its death throes. Movies, television, videos, all these things that come from countries on the other side of the world, are changing the hearts of men. During the days they are fostering other desires and at night dreaming of other dreams. Everything that entertained their elders now bores them. When I was two or three years old I would attend the puppet shows every afternoon in the midst of a crowd. The room was packed. People clapped, whistled and made a commotion. Sometimes the grown-ups, more boisterous than the children, would roar with laughter so loudly that my father had to thunder out his words to make himself heard. Nowadays the puppet theater is deserted, except for a few loyal supporters. All that's left are a few tourists sent by the travel agencies. Some are blond, others brown-haired, most of them gray or quite simply white as if for them life goes on while ours ended a long time ago. Some are dirty and scruffy, others dressed impeccably in white, but all with the same deeply convinced look they are attending a religious ceremony. Every time my father comes back from one of his meetings, he has aged several years. His face is ravaged. He sits me on his knees and looks as though he is about to cry while he caresses me.

"My son, my only son, the apple of my eye, what's to become of you? Tell me what is this I'm leaving you in? A world where there's no place for your art, a world where you won't be able to earn your living."

My mother gently chides him while she pours out for him the strong, sweet tea he is fond of.

"Why do you worry so? The boy's learning hard at school. There will surely be another profession for him when he's old enough."

But I have the feeling she says these words of comfort as a dutiful wife and that she does not believe a word of them. She too is worried. My father and mother have never set foot inside a school and know nothing of books or newspapers. But then came the Revolution and education was declared compulsory for everyone. So the sultan ordered a school to be set under the fig trees in the fourth courtyard next to the ancient water tanks. Of course he didn't send his own children—those of his wives and his concubines—those continued to study in the serenity of the palace with their own private tutors. The school in the fourth courtyard was intended for us, the children of the servants, the gardeners, the butchers, the cooks and batik painters right down to the stable boys. Alas, as time went by, it became increasingly difficult to find teachers who were not merely interested in idling their time away and flirting with the many servant girls in the palace. So the sultan closed the school and all the children went to school in town. His own children left for the United States of America.

I love school.

Almost as much as the puppets.

Books make me dream as do the names of all those countries colored dark brown, green and yellow on the blue of the seas and oceans in our atlases. Canada. Chile. Russia. Ethiopia. Benin.

But my school friends can't abide me. First of all because I come from the palace. They say I act superior to them when I'm nothing but a slave and the son of a slave. Secondly because I'm small and puny and I don't know how to fight. Lastly because I didn't wear jeans or Nikes and have never seen Batman. The school mistresses, however, like me and always refer to me as an example of politeness and obedience. This only encourages my class mates to make fun of me even more.

Last September, shortly after we had gone back to school, I went down with bronchitis. However many cups of tea boiling with mushrooms my mother gave me, however many thick poultices of efenil she laid on my chest, I went from bad to worse. I coughed, I had a fever. All in all I was away from school for two long weeks. The day I went back, still shaky on my legs, I had no sooner set foot inside the yard than the mistress bore down on me like a typhoon.

"Well there you are, at last. Allah is great. You're well again. I want you to meet someone."

She briskly took me by the hand and dragged me to the Administration. Seated in the air-conditioned office we were never allowed to enter was a little girl. I had never seen a little girl like this one before. Her skin was black. Not brown like ours. Nor even very dark like one of the musicians the others make fun of. But really black. Like the water in an ornamental pond whose bottom is never scrubbed. Her hair too was something I'd never seen before. As black as her skin it was cropped so close it clung to her head like a rough woolen bonnet. In the middle of all this blackness her fleshy lips were as pink as litchis. And yet despite her strangeness she seemed to me to be the loveliest little girl I had ever set eyes on. She looked at me in a frightened, brazen way, as if she were about to put up a fight, but knew she was beaten in advance. The mistress put our hands together in the way you celebrate a marriage and said:

"I'm entrusting you with Oumou. She's from Nigeria."

Nigeria? I had seen that name somewhere in my geography book. A large green square of forests crossed by the meandering line of a river that ended in a delta.

Oumou was the daughter of an agronomist sent to improve the production of our rice fields. He worked for an international organization. Her mother was an African-American who drove a car and dropped her off at school every morning. She had a baby brother a few months old. Since her arrival, two weeks earlier, the schoolchildren had been horrible cruel to her. During class they had to keep quiet for fear of punishment. But once the bell for recess rang, all hell broke loose. Gangs of boys, some already as tall and sturdy as a grown-up, would hide behind the mango trees in the yard and swoop down on her. They would roll her in the dust and swipe her with their metal rulers while the girls clapped their hands and spun round shouting the song they had composed specially for Oumou.

> You're as black as a cauldron's behind.
> You're as ugly as the spit of a toad.
> You're black, you're ugly,
> You must disappear from the face of the earth!
> You're not fit to be called a human being!

Once, one of the girls threw a stone that hit her right in the middle of the forehead, and it left a scar, a rosette of hatred encrusted on her ebony skin. I was certainly ill suited to play the role of defender, for more often than not I returned home to the palace in a state that made my mother weep—my face all bloodied and my clothes all torn. Yet the mistresses thought that I was the only child capable of accepting differences. This was a huge compliment they were giving me. Unfortunately, I was not in a position to understand it, even less to be proud of it. I was terrified by a responsibility that at the same time I could not refuse.

Every morning I would wait for Oumou in front of the school gate. As soon as she got out of the car and kissed her mother goodbye I grabbed her hand and together we made our entrance into hell. Yet when I recall those days I forget the suffering and the blows and remember it as a time of happiness. When school was over at four, Oumou and myself would take a flight from our aggressors. Running as fast as our legs would carry us we took refuge inside the palace walls. At first, everyone, including my parents, were surprised and even a little frightened by Oumou. Infants in arms would cry and yell when they saw her. Then everyone got used to her color. They realized she was gentle and shy. Inside the palace the centuries-old trees would hug us tightly in their long arms. The statues would tell us their story. We would take off our clothes and bathe in the pools of stagnant water. We would enter the theater pavilion and watch the puppet show, surrounded by foreigners, Dutch, English and Americans, who, after having delivered their death blow, have now become the most ardent admirers of our ancient culture. The musicians sat down in their respective places. Then the women raised their voices in song. Queen Kausalya, her hair untidy and dishevelled and dressed like a hermit, meets Sita in the forest of Chitra-kuta and wails at his feet. Ravan, the cruel king of Ceylon, turns Marisha into a deer in the hope of tempting Rama. Episodes followed one after the other and sent us into raptures. After the show we went back home where my mother gave us tea and ginger-flavored cookies. Just before nightfall I would accompany Oumou to her doorstep. She lived in the residential district where only the foreigners live. She never invited me in and usually I said goodbye in front of the hedge of Bougainvilleas.

One evening, to my great astonishment, she made an exception. It was the day before school broke up for the end of year holiday and we were not going to see each other for many weeks.

"Are you coming in?" she murmured.

I did not heed an intuition that whispered to me to say no. I was tempted. I had never been inside another house except for the humble dwelling of the palace servants. Once a year, at Tabaski, dressed in new clothes, I went with my parents to present our greetings to the sultan. But he received us in a hall reserved for us, far from the splendors of his living quarters.

Holding my breath, tiptoeing on my dusty gray feet in their worn-out sandals, I remember crossing a series of rooms, each more sumptuously furnished that the next, it seemed to me. The floors were thick with carpets. Chandeliers hung from the ceiling. We entered the kitchen and there she opened a huge white cupboard that I guessed was the freezer.

"Would you like some coke?"

Would I! She put some cubes as clear as crystal into a little bucket and then she filled two blue glasses on long stems. All this beauty took my breath away. She gave me some chips and peanuts. I was in seventh heaven. Then she asked:

"Would you like to watch television?"

Would I! We went back to the living room. I sat down in an arm-chair. I carefully set down my glass and my chips on a small table and the magic eye began to radiate its fairyland of colors. It was a Walt Disney film: "The Lion King." My eyes were brimming with tears when suddenly a voice behind us thundered out:

"Oumou!"

Startled, we turned round. It was her parents who had come home, probably earlier than expected. Her father had a beard and a mustache with a skin even blacker than Oumou's and a forbidding face. Her mother was lighter-skinned, made up like my father's puppets but with less on, and her arms and legs were bare. There was fear in her eyes as if the ten years old that I was could scare her. In the father's, however, I could read contempt and saw myself poor, puny, ridiculously rigged out with dusty feet.

"Who's this little urchin?" she asked in a threatening voice.

I was waiting for a protest. But rooted to the spot, Oumou did not say a word. She made no attempt to explain who I was, me, her friend, her loyal defender for weeks. She even made a move towards her mother as if to seek refuge and dissociate herself from me.

He father then made a threatening gesture in my direction.

"Get out! Get out immediately!"

I didn't wait a second longer. I rushed out into the garden and ran like a madman to the palace. Everything was spinning around me. I threw myself onto my bed.

After the holidays Oumou did not show up at school. What had happened? Had she finally told her parents the way she was being treated at school day after day? Horrified, had they decided to send her back to Nigeria or to America? Or had there been something else?

Simone Schwarz-Bart

excerpt from
THE BRIDGE OF BEYOND

OUR TALKS UNDER THE tree were known to all Fond-Zombi, from
the tiniest little green fruit to those already crumbling to dust. There
were a thousand different versions of the business, everyone standing
up for his own. In Fond-Zombi the night had eyes and the wind ears.
Some had no need to see in order to speak, nor did others have to
hear in order to know what was said. But Grandmother understood,
and said I had inherited her luck, and how rare it was for a star to
come out so early in a little Negress's sky. She looked at Elie through
the same eyes as I did, heard him with my ears, loved him with my
heart. When I went into his shop, Old Abel's usual glum indifference
would disappear. His eyes would come to life again, he seemed suddenly a man, and he would ask me a thousand little questions, just,
he said, to sound out the future a little.

"Are you patient, little one?" he would ask, mischievously. "If
you're not, don't go aboard Elie's barge, or on any other for that matter, for above all a woman should be patient."

"And what should a man be above all?"

"Above all," he would answer, "a bit of a swaggerer. A man should
have no fear either of living or dying." Then he would take a mint drop
out of the jar, quickly, and hold it out with a smile. "May this little taste
of mint make you forget my words—empty cartridges in a rusty gun."

By common accord the Queen and Old Abel let us spend all
Thursday, the weekly school holiday, together. If there'd been only
Elie I'd have been a river, if there'd been only the Queen I'd have
been Mount Balata, but Thursdays made me the whole of Guadeloupe. On Thursday we'd be up before the sun, and, in our own cab-

ins, we'd watch through the chinks for daybreak. The crack of dawn saw water fetched, vegetables dug, the yard cleaned out; and at eight o'clock Elie would appear with a collection of big tins slung over his shoulder. Queen Without a Name nodded, and, as we set off, said: "Don't be in a hurry to grow up, little Negroes. Frolic about, take your time—grown-ups don't live in paradise." Then Elie would hunch his shoulders, and I would fall in step, an enormous heap of the town's dirty linen on my head. We took the path to the river, the one where he had appeared for the first time, the one where my star had risen. The river of Beyond had three branches. Instead of going to the ford that served Fond-Zombi in place of a fountain, we leaped from rock to rock until we reached a more isolated stretch of the river, where a waterfall tumbled into a deep basin called the Blue Pool. While Elie hunted crayfish, turning the stones one by one, I chose a good rock for my linen and began to pound and wring and larrup it as a torturer does his victim. Every so often Elie would let out a yell as a crayfish pinched his finger while he was putting it in the tin. The sun climbed slowly over the trees, and when, at about ten, it shone full on the river, I would splash myself with water, go back to my washing, splash myself again, and then, unable to resist any longer, jump fully dressed into the river. This happened every hour, until the whole pile of washing was done. Then Elie joined me and we'd dive together with all our clothes on, leaving our fears and youthful apprehensions deep at the bottom of the Blue Pool. Then we dried ourselves on a long flat rock, always the same one, exactly the right size to hold us, and as the words went back and forth I would be overcome by the thought that there was a small thing on earth, the same size as me, who loved me, and it was as if we had come out of the same womb at the same time. Elie would wonder if he'd get on well with his letters, because, if God willed, he wanted to become a customs clerk. He always drove before him the same dream, and I was a part of it.

"You'll see," he'd say, "you'll see, later on, what a fine convertible we'll have, and we'll be dressed to match, I in a suit with a ruffle, you in a brocade dress with a cross-over collar. No one will recognize us. They'll say as we go by, 'What beautiful young couple is this?' And we'll say, 'One of us belongs to Queen Without a Name and the other to Old Abel—you know, the chap that keeps the shop?' And I'll give a toot on the horn and we'll whizz away laughing."

I wouldn't say a word or utter a sigh, in case I gave voice to some evil influence that might prevent the dream from ever coming true. Elie's words made me proud, but I would have rather he'd kept them to himself, carefully sheltered from bad luck. And as I was silent, guarding hope, one of Queen Without a Name's stories came into my mind, the one about the little huntsman who goes into the forest and meets—"What did he meet, girl?"—he met the bird that could talk, and as he made to shoot it, shut his eyes, aimed, he heard a strange whistling sound:

> Little huntsman, don't kill me
> If you kill me I'll kill you too.

Grandmother said the little huntsman, frightened by the talking bird, lowered his gun and walked through the forest, taking pleasure in it for the first time. I trembled for the bird, which had nothing but its song, and lying there on my rock, feeling at my side Elie's damp and dreaming body, I too set off dreaming, flew away, took myself for the bird that couldn't be hit by any bullet because it invoked life with its song.

Going down again to Fond-Zombi we felt as if we were still floating in the air, high above the wretched cabins and the abused, vague, fallow minds of the Negroes, and at the mercy of the wind, which lifted our bodies like kites. The breeze set us down in front of Queen Without a Name's house, by the smooth pink earthen steps. A wide band of setting sun swept in through the door on to the old woman, sitting scarcely raised above the ground on her tiny stool, in her everlasting gathered dress, rocking slowly back and forth, her eyes elsewhere. Elie would go and fetch wood for Old Abel, I'd spread my washing out for the night, and Queen Without a Name would set about cooking a crayfish sauce fit to make you go on your knees and give thanks. Already, here and there in the distance, a few lamps were already lit, though low, and the hens were starting to go up into the trees for the night. Elie would come running back, and Grandmother turned up the wick of her lamp so that we could see to shell our crayfish. Then she would seat herself carefully in her rocker, we would take our places at her feet on old flour bags on either side of her, and after a De Profundis for her dead—Jeremiah, Xango, Minerva, and her daughter Meranee—she would bring our Thursday to a close by telling us stories. Above our heads the land wind made the rusty corrugated iron roof creak and groan. But the voice of Queen Without a Name was glowing, distant, and her eyes crinkled in a faint smile as she opened before us a world in which trees cry out, fishes fly, birds catch the fowler, and the Negro is the child of God. She was conscious of her words, her phrases, and possessed the art of arranging them in images and sounds, in pure music, in exaltation. She was good at talking, and loved to do so for her two children, Elie and me. "With a word a man can be stopped from destroying himself," she would say. The stories were ranged inside her like the pages of a book. She used to tell us five every Thursday, but the fifth, the last, was always the same: the story of the Man Who Tried to Live on Air.

❧

"Children," she would begin, "do you know something, a tiny little thing? The way a man's heart is set in his chest is the way he looks at life. If your heart is put in well, you see life as one ought to see it, in the same spirit as a man balancing on a ball—he's certain to fall, but he'll stick it out as long as possible. And now hear another thing: the goods of the earth remain the earth's, and man does not own even the skin he's wrapped in. All he owns are the feelings of his heart."

At this point she would stop suddenly and ask:

"Is the court sleeping?"

"No, no, Queen, the court is listening," we'd hasten to reply.

"Well then, children, since you have hearts and ears well set, you must know that in the beginning was the earth, an earth all bedecked, with its trees and its mountains, its sun and its moon, its rivers, its stars. But to God it seemed bare, to God it seemed pointless, without the least ornament, and that is why he clad it in men. Then he withdrew again to heaven, in two minds whether to laugh or cry, and he said to himself, 'What's done is done,' and went to sleep. At that very instant the hearts of men leaped up, they lifted their heads and saw a rosy sky, and were happy. But before very long they were different, and many faces were no longer radiant. They became cowards, evildoers, corruptors. Some embodied their vice so perfectly they lost their human form and became avarice itself, malice itself, profiteering itself. Meanwhile the others continued the human line, wept, slaved, looked at a rosy sky and laughed. At that time, when the devil was still a little boy, there lived in Fond-Zombi a man called Wvabor Longlegs, a fine fellow the colour of burnt sienna, with long sinewy limbs and greenish hair that everyone envied. The more he saw of men the more perverse he found them, and the wickedness he saw in them prevented him from admiring anything whatever. Since men were not good, flowers were not beautiful and the music of the river was nothing but the croaking of toads. He owned land, and a fine stone house that could withstand cyclones, but on all that he looked with disgust. The only company that pleased him was that of his mare, which he'd named My Two Eyes. He loved the mare above all else, and would let her do anything: she sat in his rocking chair, pranced over his carpets, and ate out of a silver manger. One day, up early and full of yearning, he saw the sun appear on the horizon, and without knowing why he mounted My Two Eyes and rode away. Great pain was in him, he was wretched, and let the horse carry him where it willed. He rode from hill to hill, plain to plain, and nothing had power to cheer him. He saw regions never seen by human eye, pools covered with rare flowers, but he thought only of man and his wickedness, and nothing delighted him. He even ceased dismounting from his horse, and slept, ate, and thought on My Two Eyes' back. One day as he was riding about like this, he saw a woman with serene eyes, loved her, and tried to dismount. But it was too late. The mare started to whinny and kick, and bolted off with him far, far away from the woman, at a frantic gallop he couldn't stop. The animal had become his master."

And stopping for the second time, Grandmother would say slowly, so as to make us feel the gravity of the question:—

"Tell me, my little embers—is man an onion?"

"No, no," we'd answer, very knowledgeable in this field. "Man isn't an onion that can be peeled, not at all."

And she, satisfied, would go on briskly:

"Well, the Man who Tried to Live on Air, up on his mare, one day he was weary of wandering, and he longed for his estate, his house, the song of the rivers. But the horse still carried him away, further and further away. His face drawn, gloomier than death, the man groaned on from town to town, country to country, and then he disappeared. Where to? How? No one knows, but he was never seen again. But this evening, as I was taking in your washing, Telumée, I heard the sound of galloping behind the cabin, just under the clump of bamboo. I turned my head to look, but the beast aimed such a kick at me that I found myself back here, sitting in my rocker telling you this story."

The light of the lamp faded, Grandmother merged into the darkness, and Elie said goodnight nervously, looked out at the dark road, and suddenly took to his heels and fled to Old Abel's shop. We hadn't stirred, Grandmother and I, and her voice grew strange in the shadows as she began to braid my hair. "However tall trouble is, man must make himself taller still, even if it means making stilts." I listened without understanding, and got on her knees, and she would rock me like a baby, at the close of those old far-off Thursdays. "My little ember," she'd whisper, "if you ever get on a horse, keep good hold of the reins so that it's not the horse that rides you." And as I clung to her, breathing in her nutmeg smell, Queen Without a Name would sigh, caress me, and go on, distinctly, as if to engrave the words on my mind: "Behind one pain there is another. Sorrow is a wave without end. But the horse mustn't ride you, you must ride it."

Beryl Gilroy

excerpt from
FRANGIPANI HOUSE

A STRIP OF ROAD, brown as burnt sugar, and tender as old calico led to a large low house which had become a home for old folk. Aged old folk—black women. All relics of work-filled bygone days. Forty-three of them paying for the privilege of confinement while waiting, waiting, waiting for the "call from heaven."

Anyone who came upon the house, sitting sleek and comfortable on the town's edge, stopped outside its finely wrought iron gate as if under a spell. It was that kind of house—eloquent, compelling and smug. Sleepy headed windows dressed in frilled bonnets of lace and fine, white cotton, hibiscus shrubs that danced their flower bells to the songs of the wind, and a mammee apple tree that kept the grounds clean by never bearing fruit, marked the house as a place of professional comfort, care and heart's ease.

A circular skirt of closely-cropped grass, with ruched panels of bright low-growing flowers offered familiarity and friendship to passers-by. But it was the ring of frangipani trees, just inside the slender, white painted spears of railings that marked the limits of the grounds, which named the house and caused folk to whisper darkly "Over yonder—Frangipani House! People dies-out dere! They pays plenty to die-out inside dere! Death comes to lodgers in Frangipani House!"

The women were never objects of derision. Most people were curious about them. Their incarceration was sometimes envied, and often pitied. Some of the women, too demented to care, set out each day on wordless wanderings. Others talked alone as they walked alone, or argued with some long-gone foe or friend, or gestured at those ghosts that somehow learnt to survive the light of

Reprinted from *Frangipani House* by Beryl Gilroy. Used by permission of Heinemann Publishers Ltd.

day. A few suddenly turned from frenzied laughter to frenzied song. But there were days when a resinous silence seized the house and bound it fast and held it still. It was both a mysterious and an assertive place.

The occupants of Frangipani House were the lucky—few lucky to escape the constipated, self-seeking care which large, poor families invariably provide. After much heart-searching, children who have prospered abroad bought what was considered superior care for their parents, when distance intervened between anguished concern and the day-to-day expression of that concern. Then admission to Frangipani House became an answer to a prayer.

The sole proprietrix and administrator of the home was Olga Trask, a comely, honey-brown predator of a woman, short and crisp, with blue-grey eyes and a full head of coarse black hair. True to history there had been a rampant European among the women of her tribe and it showed in the shape of her nose, and in the eager, seeking hands that would confiscate the copper pennies on the eyes of a corpse. With practised sincerity she professed undying love of her mother who had died in Olga's care. When the old lady had aged to helplessness, Olga returned home, and rather than abandon her mother to cursory care, she bought and developed Frangipani House. She made a convincing job of running the business and when the old woman finally died, Olga's reputation for good works had spread like grass fire. People pointed her out in the street and called her Matron. Not many noticed that she was insatiable for power in a serious and efficient manner. On admission the women placed everything in her care. Those who still felt the pulse of life, however weakly, found soon enough that not only did the walls of the house recede to leave them exposed and vulnerable, but suddenly it compressed them enough to cause consternation before they adjusted to their new surroundings. The hopes and emotions the women shared grew hazy with the passing of time. Finally they disintegrated, leaving only faint smudges when they were finally blown away.

Mrs. Mabel Alexandrina King, Mama King to all who knew her, had been ailing for a considerable time and her daughters, concerned with the rapid disappearance of their resources as various relatives tried to provide care, telephoned Miss Trask from New York to obtain a place in Frangipani House for their mother.

"There is no single bed at the moment," replied Miss Trask. "Only a single room. Your mother being lady-like would want a room. Old people like doing certain things in private. My own mother, I remember her. She is the same."

Token, the older of the two girls agreed.

"She will be all right here—good food—good care—morning and evening prayer in case the call comes in the day-time," assured Miss Trask. "The doctor come regular. I pay for that."

"How much, we have to pay?" Token asked uneasily.

There was a long silence after Miss Trask said, "Ah well, four- five hundred dollars a month." "Five hundred!" "Yes, you can afford that?" She could hear breathless calculations and even more breathless argument at the end of the telephone, and then just as she was about to ring off, Token cleared her throat and replied "Very well. We will pay. But we want white people care for her. We'll come over as soon as we can. We want her house left as it is—in case she want to go back home. My mother is independent and determined. Treat her well—please treat her well."

Miss Trask pushed the sobs and intercessions away from her. She was used to them.

"They always coming and they always crying. Damn them! Who they think they are?" she said as she dropped the telephone. She walked quietly and deliberately back to her desk and gave the order to prepare "the room by the garden."

"Do anybody know dis Mama King?" she asked her day-duty nurses.

Nurse Douglas, a tall, thin, conscientious village girl who was glad of the work and the status, explained that Mama King had been ill for quite a long time with malaria, then quinsy, then pleurisy.

"I hear the talk. I hear her daughters paying-out all the time. Paying for things the old woman never see nor taste. I feel sorry for all them. It's good she coming here. I hear she did do a lot of good in her young days."

"Hm," said Miss Trask. "In that case, see she settle down. Don' go mad. Jus' keep a close eye. Make her feel welcome."

The very next day Mama King was installed in a tiny room with the minimum of clutter and a fair-sized glass window on one side. The window gave her a close-up of grass and tree and the large iron gate which sometimes locked her in. It also gave a distant view of the world beyond the frangipani trees. Life was pleasantly confined to the house and the well-kept grounds. The strangeness of the routine, the ordered rhythm of life, the cleanliness of everything excited her at first and she slowly regained her health. But after the pleurisy vanished, the urge for freedom reasserted itself as the days passed without variety or change. As a model inmate Mama King was allowed to walk around the grounds reading such notices as "Keep off the grass," "Off limits to residents." She encountered passages from the psalms or the Book of Proverbs that had been scrawled on the paintwork from time to time, and laughed as she used to laugh with her loved ones not so long ago.

She loved the grass. She remembered its feel underfoot as she walked barefoot to school. Her thoughts swung slowly like the pendulum of a weary clock, and touched those memories of the time she lay beside her husband somewhere out there on the grass. They talked and hoped and planned then, but where was that time now? Buried out there? Gone forever? She touched the grass with the tip of a slippered foot, but Matron's voice swept over her like a fly-whisk.

"You walking on grass Marma King? The sign mean you too, you know!"

The old woman looked up. A strained intensity that became sheer eloquence even as Matron watched, took over her face. "Don't worry yourself, Marma King. You must feel strange here but you just come . . . You get used to it!"

"Why you callin' me Marma King? I am Mama King. Mama mean mother. Don't call me dat stupid name! Marma King! I ask you! What kinda name dat is?"

"You not happy here?" Matron asked. "You talkin so bad? For a old lady you talkin really bad about everything."

"Nothin' doin' in here!" The old woman's voice seemed to come from somewhere inside her that had been encrusted with pain.

"I sit down. I rock the chair. I look out. I see the same tree, gasping for breath in the same sun. I see the same cross road where the beggar meet up with them people selling fowl. I see the same scatter of feather and rags like embroidery on the carrion crow bush, where the beggars hang they things. And the time—it nibble away at me life like rat eating cheese. You don't see it going. But you wake up one morning and it all gone. Wha kinda place dis is!"

Mama King suddenly noticed that she was alone—talking to herself. Matron had disappeared. She walked back to her room with discontent biting into her being like a plague of fleas.

Scratching her arm, her leg, her neck, made her conscious of the form of her body. It responded to her in a way that made her aware of being alive in the home, and of the larger awareness of being alive in the world.

Just then Miss Tilley started screaming and as if to ease their own anguish several other old women joined in—their voices blending the guilt, remorse and resentment of old age.

There was nowhere to hide from the screams, they formed an invisible barrier around her. And when at last they stopped she felt compelled to seek out and be grateful for a place of her own. Since her entry into the home, she had begun to see the world through the glass window of her room as was the destiny of many old people. Mr Carey the druggist told her once, "Too often old people get to see the world through window. To make it interesting, they must pretend it's magic."

Grace Nichols

WEB OF KIN

I come from the Season-of-Locusts
from scorch of sun
and days of endless raining

from the sea that washes the Ivory Coast
I come from coral reefs
from distant tum-tum pounding

from muddy rivers
from long and twisting niger-rivers
I come from web of kin
from sacred new yam reapings

I come from a country of strong women
Black Oak women who bleed slowly at
the altars of their children
because mother is supreme
       burden

Still, at nights the women come
bearing gourds of sacrificial blood—
the offering of their silent woman
suffering

Permission to reprint poetry by Grace Nichols from *i is a long memoried woman* granted by the publisher, Karnak House. Copyright © 1983, 1995 by Karnak House.

I will have nothing to do with it
will pour it in the dust will set
us free
the whip will have no fire the sun
no flame
and my eyes everywhere reflecting

even in dreams I will submerge myself
swimming like one possessed
back and forth across that course
strewing it with sweet smelling
flowers
one for everyone who made the journey

and at evenings I will recline
hair full of sun
      hands full of earth
I will recline on my bed of leaves
bid the young ones enter sit them
all around me

feed them sweet tales of Dahomey

WE THE WOMEN

We the women who toil
unadorn
heads tie with cheap
cotton

We the women who cut
clear fetch dig sing

We the women making
something from this
ache-and-pain-a-me
back-o-hardness

Yet we the women
who praises go unsung
who voices go unheard
who deaths they sweep
aside
as easy as dead leaves

THESE ISLANDS

These islands green
    with green blades
these islands green
    with blue waves
these islands green
    with flame shades

these cane dancing
    palm waving wind
blowing islands
these sea grooving
    mangroving
hurricaning islands

these blue mountain islands
these fire flying islands
these Carib . . . bean
Arawak. . . . an
islands
fertile
    with brutality

Edwidge Danticat

NIGHT WOMEN

I CRINGE FROM THE heat of the night on my face. I feel as bare as open flesh. Tonight I am much older than the twenty-five years that I have lived. The night is the time I dread most in my life. Yet if I am to live, I must depend on it.

Shadows shrink and spread over the lace curtain as my son slips into bed. I watch as he stretches from a little boy into the broom-size of a man, his height mounting the innocent fabric that splits our one-room house into two spaces, two mats, two worlds.

For a brief second, I almost mistake him for the ghost of his father, an old lover who disappeared with the night's shadows a long time ago. My son's bed stays nestled against the corner, far from the peeking jalousies. I watch as he digs furrows in the pillow with his head. He shifts his small body carefully so as not to crease his Sunday clothes. He wraps my long blood-red scarf around his neck, the one I wear myself during the day to tempt my suitors. I let him have it at night, so that he always has something of mine when my face is out of sight.

I watch his shadow resting still on the curtain. My eyes are drawn to him, like the stars peeking through the small holes in the roof that none of my suitors will fix for me, because they like to watch a scrap of the sky while lying on their naked backs on my mat.

A firefly buzzes around the room, finding him and not me. Perhaps it is a mosquito that has learned the gift of lighting itself. He always slaps the mosquitoes dead on his face without even waking. In the morning, he will have tiny blood spots on his forehead, as though he had spent the whole night kissing a woman with wide-open flesh wounds on her face.

In his sleep he squirms and groans as though he's already discovered that there is pleasure in touching himself. We have never talked about love. What would he need to know? Love is one of those lessons that you grow to learn, the way one learns that one shoe is made to fit a certain foot, lest it cause discomfort.

There are two kinds of women: day women and night women. I am stuck between the day and night in a golden amber bronze. My eyes are the color of dirt, almost copper if I am standing in the sun. I want to wear my matted tresses in braids as soon as I learn to do my whole head without numbing my arms.

Most nights, I hear a slight whisper. My body freezes as I wonder how long it would take for him to cross the curtain and find me.

He says, "Mommy."

I say, *"Darling."*

Somehow in the night, he always calls me in whispers. I hear the buzz of his transistor radio. It is shaped like a can of cola. One of my suitors gave it to him to plug into his ears so he can stay asleep while Mommy *works*.

There is a place in Ville Rose where ghost women ride the crests of waves while brushing the stars out of their hair. There they woo strollers and leave the stars on the path for them. There are nights that I believe that those ghost women are with me. As much as I know that there are women who sit up through the night and undo patches of cloth that they have spent the whole day weaving. These women, they destroy their toil so that they will always have more to do. And as long as there's work, they will not have to lie next to the lifeless soul of a man whose scent still lingers in another woman's bed.

The way my son reacts to my lips stroking his cheeks decides for me if he's asleep. He is like a butterfly fluttering on a rock that stands out naked in the middle of a stream. Sometimes I see in the folds of his eyes a longing for something that's bigger than myself. We are like faraway lovers, lying to one another, under different moons.

When my smallest finger caresses the narrow cleft beneath his nose, sometimes his tongue slips out of his mouth and he licks my fingernail. He moans and turns away, perhaps thinking that this too is a part of the dream.

I whisper my mountain stories in his ear, stories of the ghost women and the stars in their hair. I tell him of the deadly snakes lying at one end of a rainbow and the hat full of gold lying at the other end. I tell him that if I cross a stream of glass-clear hibiscus, I can make myself a goddess. I blow on his long eyelashes to see if he's truly asleep. My fingers coil themselves into visions of birds on his nose. I want him to forget that we live in a place where nothing lasts.

I know that sometimes he wonders why I take such painstaking care. Why do I draw half-moons on my sweaty forehead and spread crimson powders on the rise of my cheeks. We put on his ruffled

Sunday suit and I tell him that we are expecting a sweet angel and where angels tread the hosts must be as beautiful as floating hibiscus.

In his sleep, his fingers tug his shirt ruffles loose. He licks his lips from the last piece of sugar candy stolen from my purse.

No more, no more, or your teeth will turn black. I have forgotten to make him brush the mint leaves against his teeth. He does not know that one day a woman like his mother may judge him by the whiteness of his teeth.

It doesn't take long before he is snoring softly. I listen for the shy laughter of his most pleasant dreams. Dreams of angels skipping over his head and occasionally resting their pink heels on his nose.

I hear him humming a song. One of the madrigals they still teach children on very hot afternoons in public schools. *Kompè Jako, dome vou?* Brother Jacques, are you asleep?

The hibiscus rustle in the night outside. I sing along to help him sink deeper into his sleep. I apply another layer of the Egyptian rouge to my cheeks. There are some sparkles in the powder, which make it easier for my visitor to find me in the dark.

Emmanuel will come tonight. He is a doctor who likes big buttocks on women, but my small ones will do. He comes on Tuesdays and Saturdays. He arrives bearing flowers as though he's come to court me. Tonight he brings me bougainvillea. It is always a surprise.

"How is your wife?" I ask.

"Not as beautiful as you."

On Mondays and Thursdays, it is an accordion player named Alexandre. He likes to make the sound of the accordion with his mouth in my ear. The rest of the night, he spends with his breadfruit head rocking on my belly button.

Should my son wake up, I have prepared my fabrication. One day, he will grow too old to be told that a wandering man is a mirage and that naked flesh is a dream. I will tell him that his father has come, that an angel brought him back from Heaven for a while.

The stars slowly slip away from the hole in the roof as the doctor sinks deeper and deeper beneath my body. He throbs and pants. I cover his mouth to keep him from screaming. I see his wife's face in the beads of sweat marching down his chin. He leaves with his body soaking from the dew of our flesh. He calls me an avalanche, a waterfall, when he is satisfied.

After he leaves at dawn, I sit outside and smoke a dry tobacco leaf. I watch the piece-worker women march one another to the open market half a day's walk from where they live. I thank the stars that at least I have the days to myself.

When I walk back into the house, I hear the rise and fall of my son's breath. Quickly, I lean my face against his lips to feel the calming heat from his mouth.

"Mommy, have I missed the angels again?" he whispers softly while reaching for my neck.

I slip into the bed next to him and rock him back to sleep.

"Darling, the angels have themselves a lifetime to come to us."

Louise Bennett

CANDY SELLER

Candy lady, candy mam?
Bizniz bad now-a-days,
Lady wid de pretty lickle bwoy
Buy candy, gwan yuh ways!
Yuh right fe draw de pickney han,
Koo pon him nose hole,
Him y'eye dem a-tare out like him want
Hickmatize me candy-bole.

Nice young man come here. Wat yuh want?
Pinda cake? Wangla?
Ef yuh nah buy wey yuh stap fah!
Beg yuh move yuhself yaw sah.
Me noh ha nutten dah-gi way,
Gi de lady pass fe come,
Wey yuh noh go jine de air force?
Dem have plenty use fe bum.

Come lady buy nice candy man?
Dem all is wat I meck.
Which kine yuh want mam, pepper-mint?
Tank yuh mam. Kiss me neck!
One no mo' farden bump she buy!
Wat a red-kin ooman mean!
Koo har foot eena de wedge-heel boot,
Dem favah submarine.

Ah wey she dah-tun back fah? She
Musa like fe hear me mout
Gwan, all yuh should'n walk a day,
Yuh clothes fava black-out.
Me kean pick up a big sinting
Like yuh so draw dat blank.
Afta me noh deh a war, me naw
Colleck no German tank.

Cho goh way—Come here nice white man
Don't pass me by soh sah!
See me beggin by de roadside
Come buy a nice wangla.
Wen w'ite people go fe ugly
Massa dem ugly sah.
Koo 'ow dat deh man face heng dung
Lacka wen jackass feel bad.

Me dah-liff up now yaw Dinah,
Lacka 'ow dem lock up store
An everybody dah-go home
Me naw go sell much more.
Me wi cry out as me go along,
Me mighta get a brake—
Buy peppermint—till later awn
Me gawn—Fresh pindacake.

BANS O'OOMAN!

Bans O'Ooman! Bans O'Ooman!
Pack de place from top to grung
Massa lawd, me never know sey
So much ooman deh a Tung!

Up de step and dung de passage
Up de isle an dung de wall
Not a Sunday-evening Hope tram
Pack like St. George's Hall.

De ooman dem tun out fe hear
How Federation gwan.
Me never se such different grade an
Kine o' ooman from me bawn.

Full dress, half dress, tidy-so-so
From bare y'eye to square-cut glass,
High an low, miggle, suspended,
Every diffrent kine o' class.

Some time dem tan so quiet, yuh
Could hear a eye-lash drop,
An wen sinting oversweet dem,
Lawd, yuh want hear ooman clap—

Me was a-dead fe go inside
But wen me start fe try,
Ooman queeze me, ooman push me,
Ooman frown an cut dem y'eye.

Me tek me time an crawl out back
Me noh meck no alarm,
But me practice bans o' tactics
Till me ketch up a platform.

Is dat time me se de ooman dem
Like varigated ants,
Dem face a-bus wid joy fe sey,
"At las' we get we chance."

Ef yuh ever hear dem program!
Ef yuh ever hear dem plan!
Ef yuh ever hear de sinting
Ooman gwine go do to man!

Federation boun to flourish
For dem got bans o' nice plan,
An now dem got de heart an soul
Of true Jamaica ooman.

Erna Brodber

excerpt from
MYAL

FIVE YEARS AGO WHEN Maydene Brassington first went to visit Amy
Holness, Mary Riley had got their message and had gone to the
teacher's cottage. She had later gone on to Morant Bay to the
methodist manse and had come home to think over what the ladies
had said. No. She didn't mind at all. Didn't mind sharing Ella. For
that was what the lady said. Parson's wife. Parson Brassington that is.
The lady said that a child should have two parents. Two people
should share the load and since the child didn't have a father, she
and Parson would act as father, something like godparents. She said
that she Mary had carried the load by herself for all these years and
could do with a little break. So after a few years when her age was up
in school, she and Parson would take on the burden completely and
see to it that she was fitted out for life. But right now, it was sharing.
Ella would stay with Mary and continue to go to Grove Town School
but on Friday evenings she would come to the mission house in
Morant Bay and stay there until Sunday evening. Not to worry about
clothes. She would see to the clothes that Ella would wear while she
was in her house. That sounded real fine.

No. Mary didn't mind at all. Because what? To tell the truth, she
was becoming a bit worried. The worry began when Ella started to
see her health. Anything could happen to her and with she Mary
down the wharf on weekends and up at property sometimes during
the week there was nobody to protect the child. The district children
still called her all sorts of names. She knew that that meant that they
were curious about Ella. It worried her that some little boy's curiosity
would one day get the better of him and the next thing she would
know is that Ella would come home with her clothes torn off her back

Excerpt from *Myal* by Erna Brodber, first published by New Beacon Books
Ltd. in 1988. Used by permission of the publisher.

and something in her belly. It was worse now that she was springing breasts and soon needing something to hold them up. And slim little Ella was spreading at the hips. Must be the father's blood for her people were slim, slim, slim. Taylor had teased her and said "All them who was laughing, soon want touch, for seeing is believing but touching is the naked truth" and he would sing the last part. Taylor was like that, so jokify. But it was a true word. True word.

Then there was Taylor. Long time now he been around. Running around. Four, five children now and not living with any of the baby mother them. Telling her that it is her fault. That he want to settle down and make a decent man of himself. Well pass him 30 now, a year from 40. Want to set up the blacksmith business on a good footing, want to join a church and go out Sunday mornings like a big man, want to pull all his children together. "You see Mass Levi, that is a big man. Everything under one cover. Nobody calling his name on anything. No need hide from anybody. They want you, they come to you. So man to stay! And is because him have Miss Iris to pull things together with him. One finger can't kill nit." She was the woman to help him pull his life together. He had always told her so. If she had been with him long time, he wouldn't have been having them patchwork children—one here, one all over the place. Thirteen years now.

From the time she had come back from Morant Bay with the belly, and he noticed that no one was coming around to claim it, he had made his way to her door and in a very proper manner offered to take it. That time he must have been about twenty-five. Came in his full drill suit with his shirt buttoned right up to his neck. And shoes. Dressed like Sunday on the Friday evening. Didn't bother with any story about just passing by. Had come right to the point. He had been watching her for a long time. From she was young girl in school. And just when he thought he could put that kind of question to her, she had gone off to Morant Bay. It wasn't too late. He had still been watching and he didn't see anyone coming around, so would she let him act the part. She had cried and he had held her.

Taylor was a couple years older than her well. Must have been in 'bout sixth book about to leave school when she was in third book, or even lower down. Remembered her first and only fight—a nearly fight really. The bigger ones had wanted a display and they were pushing her and another little one—can't even remember who now—on to each other hoping that one would push the other away and a fight would begin. The other one was warming up, ready to go into action when Taylor from his huge height, or so it seemed then, came up with "Leave the little pickney them alone," and she was saved. And whenever storms threatened she would glance around and know that he was there. But she didn't know that he thought of her in that way. He was popular, always in demand, he could play the fiddle and the fife and they had put his name with Delaceita who was dancing own master. He had come. And had put a very sensible argument to her. "You one can't manage. No see Miss Kate can't help herself?" She had cried and cried, but she had shaken her head. No. And she had told him: she wasn't going to let him carry a whiteman's child. He would be a laughing-stock. Let her carry her own disgrace. That way it would pass off quicker. She was adamant.

He had continued to come around. Sometimes he carried a little parcel of liver if it was a Friday evening: "Quick, cook this for me May"—he used to call her May though he knew full well she was Mary. Said he was christening her himself. Sometimes it was a couple fingers of plantain and Mary didn't bother to try to resist because she knew that Taylor knew that things were short with her and he had come to help her and she was not going to insult a kindness which she needed by refusing it. When she decided to build the little house in her mother's yard, Taylor was right there helping her to organize. Seemed he always let anyone who was his woman at the time know that they couldn't come between him and her because no one ever tried to fight her and she knew Taylor had plenty women. Many more times he would suggest that he move in with her and they become man and woman. Her answer was always. "No. Taylor you don't want to tie up yourself with a strange woman and her strange daughter." He had always laughed it off, gone off to some woman and would always come back, sometimes complaining about the woman, sometimes laughing at how he had had to part two of them and that kind of thing.

This last time he had come differently though. Like the first time he had come this time, hat in his hand and standing. He had called her Miss Mary Riley and said this was Newton James addressing you. "As you know my father is a tailor (that's why they call me Taylor). Not living with my mother like your father and mother, but my grandmother bring me up respectable and my father had enough to school me and send me to trade. I am a saddler and a blacksmith by trade and I can more than support myself and you and whoever you carry. I am asking you to let me be the man." That first time, her mother had been in the room next door them and could hear everything; he had been with her in the hall. "Miss Kate knows everything already, so I am not hiding. But is you I have to talk to before I go back and make my request of her." And she had turned him down. He had made a monkey face and they had laughed and left it there. He had come back this time in the same way: "My father was . . . I am . . . I am asking you to let me be the man . . ." He was very very serious this time. He added that he had been seeing Euphemia. Yes, she knew that. She was giddy but she was settling down. He hadn't asked her any proper question but he was ready to settle down and if it wasn't she Mary, he was going to try Euphemia. Marriage before a parson was going to be in it this time and if it wasn't she, there wasn't going to be much visiting between because he didn't want her pulling him this way and Euphemia the other. He was now going to pull in a team. It was for her to decide if she was going to be in the team. He was very serious this time. No laughing. No monkey face. He had left and said that he would come back end of month. It was now mid month.

So it was deliverance when the lady asked about Ella. She couldn't give Ella what she needed. She had faced that. Ask Ella to scald the little milk and you would hear the phew-phew and smell the milk going down the side of the pot and being burnt by the flames. Ella was right there in the kitchen but she had made the milk boil over! Nothing left in the pot. Or simply ask her to roast two cocoes. By the time you call Ella to bring them to the table, you would get nothing but a loud silence because Ella fraid to tell you she can't find the cocoes. Can't find? The cocoes turn bright red fire. Is true what people did tell her. Ella was not bush mout pickney. So the lady was going to fit her for life. That good. And she would have Ella with her for two more years every weekday. In any case whatever path God had chosen for her, it would not be long before all kinds of calls of nature would separate them from each other and she would be left without a soul to call her own. And according to Taylor she would lose him too.

Marriage have teeth and she wasn't too much for those certain things but she could work hard. Perhaps they could make it. They would have to draw on something more upon the house. Was only a room and hall. Ella could get the room for now until she go up to mission house. They would have to draw on a room for the two of them. It would have to be her house. She wasn't leaving go nowhere. Moreover, Taylor's shop was too near the road with everybody stopping by. Too difficult for people to understand that things change. Let him keep the shop out there and then at night-time he come home. Yes. That seemed alright. And as a matter of fact, with Ella going up in the world, it would suit her to have a married mother so everything would turn out alright. It was just that she didn't know Taylor in those ways. There had only been the man O'Grady and she never so much did like it to all that. Guess them things never mek to like. She had to try it though. When Taylor come next time, she would tell him that she would give it a try. Lord. Wedding is expense, and all them people looking at you. Wonder if Taylor would let them go quietly to Town and come back. No. And she laughed to herself. "Mi know Taylor. Him going want to fling him foot and mek speech." That is one more thing to get accustomed to. But it wouldn't be now.

House have to extend and all that. Money have to find for it, so she really had plenty time to get used to the idea and to talk out more things with Taylor. He had said he "wanted everything under one cover." She wondered whether he was expecting her to be mother to all his children. That she must ask. That would call for bigger house and more beds to be built and all kind of things. This thing might really have teeth fi true!

But it would work. Then she worried a little bit about Ella, whether she was doing the right thing by her. "Taylor say the man no too righted. 'Parson read too much book,' him say, 'That's why him can't look straight in people eye. Is just that. But the woman have sense.' Is him Taylor look after them buggy. So that is another thing. Though him live right here, he know 'bout what go on in the mission house. And him and Mr. Smith that drives for them is his bosom friend, so he will keep an eye on Ella. And nothing fi hinder me from go dey go haul wey mi pickney if she nah meet no good treatment." What a lot of change! She could hardly wait the two weeks for Taylor to come. "Guess as him hear that Parson wife was looking for me, he will come to see why." But Mary changed her mind and decided not to wait. She would begin the revolution. After all if she was going to make her life with Taylor, she might as well begin to meet him half-way and so she betook herself down to his shop to tell him how things were. And he said it made sense, so Maydene Brassington began coming down to Grove Town on Fridays to take Ella O'Grady home with her to the house in Morant Bay for the weekends.

Michelle Cliff

excerpt from
ABENG

ZOE AND CLARE MET one August when each was ten, and Clare had no one to play with. Miss Mattie did not want her to disturb Joshua at his work, getting in the way as he carried water from the river and forever bothering him to play catch or tag or dominoes when he was supposed to be feeding the hogs. And she was getting too old to be running around with boys anyway. But there was not much to do in the country alone. Without someone to join with, the days stretched out and the only way to fill them was to read—schoolbooks or newspapers or the Bible—or to walk within the limits set by Miss Mattie.

The loneliness Clare felt before she met Zoe, or later, on days like the day of the hog-killing, when Zoe was not around, was hard to bear. There was an absolute stillness about the country. There were no sounds which were not heard day after day. Roosters crowing—not just in the dawn but at steady intervals until nightfall. Hens complaining to each other and scratching around the dirt yard. Dogs barking now and again—at nothing, at a passerby a mile away. Sound traveled far in St. Elizabeth.

The steady noise of the river was mixed with the voices of women at the river—on Mondays, the washerwomen. As she sat on the porch, Clare could hear their voices and the water split by the slap-slap of cloth against rock. On Saturdays, the voices of the butcher's wife and her daughters traveled up the hill, as they cleaned the tripe the butcher would later carry from yard to yard, along with other meat, peddling Sunday dinner. At about two o'clock on each Saturday afternoon Clare saw him, trudging up the hill—over one shoulder a sack of freshly killed and freshly cleaned meat, over the other, his scales, on which he balanced the flesh on one tray against small brass weights on the other. "How you do, Miss Clare; beg you call Miss Mattie fe me." Each time he said the same words. Each time Clare fetched her grandmother, who appeared and pondered the contents of Mas Wilbur's sack and decided whether they would have goat or beef or pork—or the usual Sunday chicken.

There were only a few tasks which Miss Mattie allowed Clare to take part in. She was too young. She was not a girl who should be spending too much of her time on chores. Her childhood did not need to be filled up with work. All these things her grandmother said. But Miss Mattie let Clare help her with the preparations for her Sunday meeting. And together they prepared coffee.

In the coolness of the early morning or the early evening, Clare set off with her basket down into the coffee piece and returned with the basket filled to the brim with crimson-red berries. Within each berry were two beans, and the process of making coffee had to do with releasing the beans from the hull of the berry. Out back, near to the outhouse, was a long and wide pavement made of cement, called a barbecue. Clare poured the berries from her basket onto the barbecue, taking care to separate them so that each berry would catch the sun equally. Over the next few days the berries blanched in the sunlight, and Clare raked them with a bamboo rake now and then, turning the still red sides to the light—crimson gradually disappearing until the berries were colorless.

Once blanched, Miss Mattie set aside an afternoon to attend to the rest of the process. She and Clare built an open fire near the barbecue and roasted the berries until they were almost black. They took turns, shaking a flat steel pan over the fire, steadily back and forth across the flames, until the heat accomplished its purpose and the coffee was ready for pounding and threshing.

Miss Mattie brought forth a huge wooden pestle and mortar—the mortar deep and worn and scarred, the pestle shiny and smooth. She fixed the mortar firmly between her legs and pounded until the coffee was fine enough to pass through a wire sieve. Her brown and muscled upper arms worked the pestle against the beans, each stroke seeming to release more of the smell of the roasted coffee, bits of hull flying out and sticking to her apron and her hair. She sweated and grunted from the work of pounding but did not stop until every last bean was crushed fine. Clare's job at this stage was to pass the ground coffee through the sieve, discarding the pieces of hull, and to store the coffee in Golden Syrup and Ovaltine tins—for the use of the family and people around who did not grow their own coffee trees. When their task was finished, Miss Mattie took some of the fresh coffee and filled a tightly woven cotton sack with it. She immersed the sack in boiling water for a time, and the two workers drank enamel mugs of hot coffee and condensed milk around the dining-room table as their reward. The smell and taste of the new coffee, mixed with the sweet thickness of the milk, was a pleasure almost impossible to bear.

But grandmother and granddaughter did not do this often—"There is too much to do on this place, and no rest for the weary."—and for the most part, Clare's time in the country, until she met Zoe, was spent waiting to return to Kingston.

Miss Mattie sent to Breezy Hill to ask Miss Ruthie whether Zoe would be her granddaughter's playmate. Zoe was at the porch steps the next morning and came many mornings over the next two months.

The two girls walked the roads barefoot, and used the mud from the roadbed to make dishes and cups for their tea parties. But the creation of vessels from clay was the real aim of their activity, and the tea parties never came to an end, in fact were barely begun, because they were interrupted by a desire to climb a star apple or custard apple tree—and the girls soon abandoned what was really a town pursuit for what the country held for them. They crushed blossoms from bushes and mixed them with water, and with the dye drew patterns on the branches where they sat together and dripped from the juices of the apples. They said they were making secret totems, in a language only they could decipher, a pictographic system like the Mayans had invented. Clare repeated to Zoe all that Boy had told her about the Mayans and Aztecs and Incas, and these ancient peoples became part of their games.

Sometimes they climbed into the high branches of the ackee and picked some of the red-podded fruit. Concealed within the fleshy yellow pouches which were edible was a sprinkling of red powder—"deadly poison." Zoe explained what Mr. Powell had told her; that Jamaicans were the only island people daring enough to eat the ackee. They scraped the poison into old condensed milk tins and hid it in a secret place for use against their enemies. Secrecy was something they held between themselves. Enemies was an abstract term which they usually put no face to.

They found an old piece of red cloth in Miss Mattie's sewing basket and used it to taunt the bull Miss Mattie kept tethered by the river, until poor Old Joe nearly went crazy with frustration and they laughed and jumped in the river and splashed him until he retreated to his guinea grass patch.

In the beginning they were shy with one another. Clare was afraid that Zoe would not like her—would resent Miss Mattie's request, tied as it was to Miss Ruthie and her daughters squatting on her grandmother's land. Although Miss Mattie would never have mentioned such a thing. Zoe didn't really mind, though; Miss Mattie's invitation got her out of keeping house so much and having to play all the time with her younger sister, because Miss Ruthie kept her girls close to their yard. And Miss Ruthie explained that it was little enough they could do in return for their shelter, and land which gave them a livelihood.

But Zoe did not know what to expect—realizing that Clare was a town girl and fair enough to be taken for *buckra*. "One big fat buckra papa she have," Miss Ruthie told her daughter. "But she mama a decent woman." Suppose Clare thought she was really somebody—suppose she looked down on Zoe because she was the pickney of a marketwoman? Zoe would just have to wait and see—something Miss Ruthie was always telling her anyway.

For Clare, Zoe would be the first girl she would know from Kitty's home. Kitty had told her about the friendships she had had with girls in her childhood—how these were the friends she remembered. All the friends she would ever need, she said.

The two girls—who had lived all their lives in Jamaica and had been taught about themselves not only by Miss Ruthie and Kitty, but by Lewis Powell and Boy Savage—were well aware that there were differences between them, of course. Had it not been for the differences, the friendship probably would not have begun in the first place. But in their friendship the differences could become more and more of a background, which only rarely they stumbled across and had to confront. They had childhood—they had make-believe. They had a landscape which was wild and real and filled with places in which their imaginations could move.

Their friendship over these years was expanded and limited in this wild countryside—the place where they kept it. It was bounded by bush and river and mountain. Not by school or town—and felt somewhat free of the rules of those places. They could walk up a hillside together without once speaking. They could take a machete and carve a ball from the root of the bamboo plant by the road and play hard catch—trying to burn the palms of each other's hands, trying to hold out until the other one yelled "Stop!" and ran to squeeze some juice from an aloe plant on her hand-middle. They did not yet question who each was in this place—if the need to question was there, it remained in the back of their minds. For now they spoke to each other through games and codes, secrets and enemies.

But there were times, as they got closer, when they were able to speak more from their hearts, drop some of the games, and make promises neither one would be able to keep. Like having a school together, when they became teachers. Or a free clinic, when they became doctors. Just another form of make-believe.

This was a friendship—a pairing of two girls—kept only on school vacations, and because of their games and make-believe might have seemed to some entirely removed from what was real in the girls' lives. Their lives of light and dark—which was the one overwhelming reality. But this friendship also existed close to the earth, in a place where there were no electric lights, where water was sought from a natural source, where people walked barefoot more often than not. This place was where Zoe's mother worked for her living and where Kitty Freeman came alive. To the girls, for a time, this was their real world—their true plane of existence for two months of the year when all other things fell outside.

The real world—that is, the world outside country—could be just as dreamlike as the world of make-believe—on this island which did not know its own history.

e⁓

On another plane, in Clare's school in Kingston, there were girls as dark as Zoe, like the girls at the bus stop Clare had called "inhuman." These dark girls were at St. Catherine's mostly on scholarship—but then Clare herself was a scholarship student. Boy was unable to keep up the payments; it was the only way she could stay in school. For Clare it was different, though—and that was part of the confusion she felt—part of the split within herself. There had been an incident the previous October which Clare would never forget, and which had given her a clue to the difference between herself and the other scholarship students. Color. Class. But not in those words.

The entire school—mistresses and students—were standing at prayers, at attention, in the gymnasium which was also an auditorium and chapel, and the headmistress, Miss Haverhill, was leading them in the school hymn: "God of Our Fathers, Whose Almighty Hand, Leads Forth in Beauty All the Starry Band." The hymn which began with the organ imitating a trumpet call. As all sweated under the zinc roof—the mistresses in their light cotton dresses, the girls in their heavy gabardine uniforms, waiting for an end to the hymn, a dark girl had an epileptic seizure. She was, or had been, standing not far from Clare, when suddenly she was face-down on the floor of cold stone, cracking her nose and cheekbones on the flagstones with incredible force, as if all the energy in her body was drawn together in this one exertion. As it must have been. The girl's name was Doreen Paxton; her mother was a maid for an American family living in Barbican and Doreen lived with her grandmother on Mountainview Road, not far from the Tabernacle. Doreen was a genius at the western roll, the teachers said, and every games-day leaped and flew over the highjump bar beyond the heights charted by the girls of Immaculate Conception. Her deep-brown body now rolled and jerked on the gymnasium floor and the girls moved back to give her room. The headmistress sang louder, as if to convey to the girls that they must not stop, must work to cover the sound of Doreen's skull and face hitting against rock, and the low groans coming from inside her. But the voices of the other girls, which had thinned considerably in volume, could not mask the noise—and the headmistress's spindly second soprano moved forward almost in a solo, with only small support from the other mistresses.

Finally, Miss Maxwell, the tall and herself-dark physical education teacher, came over and knelt beside Doreen. She drew the cloth belt from her white tennis shorts and slid it between the girl's teeth, clamping it to make sure that Doreen did not swallow her tongue. When the seizure was over, Miss Maxwell, in one smooth and graceful motion, lifted Doreen from the ground and carried her to a tumbling mat in a corner of the gym. She covered the girl with a few towels so she wouldn't take a chill, and sat beside her until she came out of the deep sleep which follows a seizure. A sleep which wipes away the memory of what has happened to you.

When the child awoke, Miss Maxwell had to tell her what had happened, that her grandmother had been called, and there was now, or would be, some trouble about her scholarship. Before she left the gym, after she gave her benediction, Miss Haverhill had conferred with Miss Maxwell and instructed her to tell Doreen "as gently as possible" that she could no longer represent the name of St. Catherine with her western roll, and so her funds would have to be stopped. The headmistress had stressed that Miss Maxwell convey this information as soon as possible—but it was hard for her to bring herself to say all this, and hard for the girl to take it all in. Doreen's body ached from its violent contact with the stone floor. Her head burned and throbbed from the explosion of the seizure. She was exhausted and scared. She was not certain what had happened to her, and did not know why. Her cheekbones were already beginning to swell and to distort the planes of her young brown face. Her nose pained her about the bridge and her eyes were darkening. Miss Maxwell left her there for a minute to take in what she had said, and went to the school gate to meet the old lady who was Doreen's grandmother and tell her what had happened. She took grandmother and granddaughter up to U.C.W.I. hospital so Doreen could be examined, because Miss Haverhill was concerned that the school might be liable for any lasting injury. The old lady—in her best dress of navy cotton with tiny white spots on it—sat in the backseat of Miss Maxwell's small Austin and wept and prayed alternately. "Wha' fe do? Lord Jesus, wha' fe do?" She repeated again and again. Terrified that her granddaughter might be damaged in some irreparable way and well aware of the mystical and strange nature of epilepsy which would shame them, she prayed and cried and cried and prayed, until the words became a chant. Miss Maxwell, whose own grandmother was not unlike this old lady weeping and chanting in her car, tried her best to explain to Mrs. Paxton that Doreen would most likely be all right but that St. Catherine's felt the pressure of the scholarship would be too much for a girl subject to fits.

Clare knew nothing of these details, only that when she asked Miss Maxwell about the incident, she was told by the gym teacher that Doreen would not be returning to school because she was an epileptic and might be a "danger" to herself. And like Claudia Lewis, it soon seemed to many of the girls that she never actually existed at all. Her name was not mentioned in the school after that.

But Clare could not erase from her mind what had happened in the gymnasium that morning. She would not forget the banging of Doreen's head against the floor, the way her mouth had foamed, and her eyeballs had rolled back in her head—the deep brown disappeared and all you could see were the whites. She came back from school that day and asked her parents about fits and they told her about epilepsy. A terrible disease. An incurable disease. Boy recounted the stories of the famous epileptics of history—like Dostoevsky and Julius Caesar. Kitty told her that epilepsy could travel through families—although the Freemans were uncontaminated. It was a curse—Kitty said. A stigma—Boy insisted.

Something else about the morning bothered Clare, and she turned to Kitty.

"But, Mother, how come no one came forward to help except Miss Maxwell? No one came forward at all. They acted like it wasn't happening."

"Well, dear, Miss Maxwell is trained in first aid, and the other teachers were probably afraid that they would do the wrong thing."

"But even when the fit was over, none of them went to see if Doreen was okay."

"Clare, you know how Englishwomen are—they think that they are ladies; they are afraid of the least little sign of sickness or anything like that."

To Clare's mind a lady was someone who dressed and spoke well. A lady was a town creature. A lady often had people in her home where they talked about the theater or books. Above all, a lady was aloof—Clare knew all of these criteria from the Hollywood movies she saw and the lessons of her teachers. They did think they were ladies. They taught her to drop her patois and to speak "properly."

Proper was a word they used very often. Fountain pens were proper, ballpoint pens were not. Laced-up oxfords were proper, sandals were not. Woolen berets were proper, panama hats were not. The ladies at her school disdained corporal punishment, which they thought suitable only for state schools, and preferred wrongdoers to sit beneath the lignum vitae in the quad and ponder their sins. In silence. Ladies, Clare had been taught, did not speak in a familiar manner to people beneath their station. Those with the congenital defect of poverty— or color.

So these women did not come forward because they were ladies. That was simple.

Of course, Clare held an unspoken question about Kitty. What would she have done? Kitty was certainly no "lady"—she had no pretensions to be one. Kitty was more comfortable speaking patois and walking through the bush. She confined her social world to St. Elizabeth and an occasional lunch with the women who worked beside her at the hotel desk. If Boy insisted, she would have a few of his business acquaintances in, and dress herself up, and be polite to them; but for the most part, Boy entertained his business acquaintances in hotel lounges without his wife.

Lady or not, Clare knew that Kitty would not have come forward. Even though Doreen was the color of the people to whom Kitty was tender. Later, when Clare thought about Anne Frank, and Anne's mother, Clare would have similar thoughts to those she had now. What was missing. In her own mother. In Anne Frank's mother. In the mistresses who only stood there, trying to turn their eyes from the sight of Doreen smashing against the stones. And the sight of the dark Miss Maxwell tending her and carrying her across the floor. As Kitty Hart's mother hid her under the mattresses. What made some women able to come forward, and others only to hold back?

Clare's mind got caught in a tangle with her mother and the mistresses and she didn't realize that the creole and white teachers at St. Catherine's were different from Kitty in ways other than lady ways. At the bottom—as it usually was—was race and shade. It was easy to lose sight of color and all that went with it within the imitation-English quadrangle of brick buildings. A school with a tuck shop that sold English sweeties and copies of *School-Friends*, stories of English girls in English boarding-schools. It was so easy to lose sight of color when you were constantly being told that there was no "colour problem" in Jamaica. Or anywhere in the Empire, for that matter—Her Majesty's Government had all that under control. Apartheid, for example, was only a way of keeping the peace—Black people in South Africa, the geography mistress told them, had as equal chances as the whites. Just like in Jamaica.

Light and dark were made much of in that school. It was really nothing new in Jamaica—but, as in the rest of the society, it was concealed behind euphemisms of talent, looks, aptitude. Just as Kitty had called Clare's teachers "ladies" when she knew full well that they were damned narrow-minded racists as she told herself—that was why they let that child nearly kill herself on the rockstone. Color was diffuse and hard to track at St. Catherine's, entering the classrooms as seating arrangements, disciplinary action, entering the auditorium during the casting of a play. The shadows of color permeated the relationships of the students, one to one. When the girls found out that Victoria Carter, whom everyone thought was the most beautiful girl in school, was the daughter of a Black man who worked as a gardener and an Englishwoman who had settled in Jamaica, her position in their eyes was transformed, and girls who had been quite intimidated by her, now spoke about her behind her back.

⟨

In the town, in the school, girls talked and talked about one another. Disagreements were always settled by talk and gossip and raised voices; and punishment between the girls was meted out by sending someone to Coventry—the English name for the silent treatment.

In country, between Zoe and Clare, talk or silence was not their primary means of settling their disagreements. They fought each other.

Their battles usually occurred when the differences-already-there surfaced in such a way that they couldn't be avoided or dismissed or passed over by a suggestion from one girl to the other that they retreat into the bush or dive into the river or pretend their argument was only part of a game. These surfacings were sometimes suggested by seemingly trivial things, othertimes by things which started out trivial and then moved out to become things of importance.

Their second summer together, when they were eleven, Clare was sent to country with a new bathsuit. And Zoe had asked to borrow it. Not to wear it swimming but to try it on. Clare at once refused her friend, falling back without thinking on her grandmother's instructions.

"No, man; dis is fe me suit. Grandma say wunna is to wear the other one."

"Oh, man, let me try on the sint'ing, nuh?"

"No, man, Grandma say no."

"What you mean 'Grandma say no'—is wunna say no."

"A no fe me to decide. Grandma e'en told me."

"Wunna is friend?"

"Lord, have mercy, Zoe, I can't help it."

"What you mean? Wunna is one wuthless cuffy, passing off wunnaself as buckra."

"Me no is cuffy."

"Wunna is fe true. One true sheg-up cuffy."

They wrangled on and on. Then Clare struck first, clapping Zoe at the side of her head, boxing her ears and knocking her down. This dispute began on the porch of Miss Mattie's house and they fought themselves down the dirt road toward the river. Zoe chased after Clare and kicked her in the shins. Clare moved fast, grabbed Zoe's foot and pulled, so Zoe fell over backways. Then Clare ran toward the river and Zoe caught up with her as she was balancing over the rocks. Zoe pushed her down in the water until Clare sputtered and gasped for "peace."

"Okay. Okay. I give wunna peace, but only if wunna say wunna is sorry and that wunna is one true cuffy and stingy as one dog."

Clare recited all these things to her friend, and they got up and turned back up the hill to the house, where Clare gave Zoe the new bathsuit, and told her she could keep it. And Zoe refused.

"A fe wunna bathsuit. Me have me own."

Later, at the river where they had gone to swim, Clare got a flame-red blossom of hibiscus and put it behind Zoe's left ear and told her friend that she should be a princess and that Clare would be the prince and lead an army of red ants, biting ants, which were now on their way, marching toward them, in an attack on their enemies.

She thought—or needed to think—that they had a common enemy. She dressed Zoe in flowers and palm fronds and sat her on a high rock, as if to make up for the bathsuit incident she wanted to forget.

"But, Mama, why she no let me try on she bathsuit?"

"Lord, child, why wunna worry wunnaself. She no buckra child? De buckra people dem is fe dem alone."

"But Clare is fe me friend."

"Clare is de granddaughter of Miss Mattie. Dem is rich people. Dem have property. Dem know say who dem is. She can't be wunna true friend, sweetie. Fe she life is in Kingston. She no mus' have friends in Kingston. In fe she school. Wunna is she playmate. No fool wunnaself."

"No, Mama, we be friends."

"Den why she no let wunna borrow she bathsuit? Sweetie, mus' not get too close to buckra people dem."

Christine Craig

BURNT HILL

HE ARRIVED IN BURNT HILL at the beginning of July, parked his old truck under a guango tree and started building his house. The village had heard that old Sam Davis' land had passed to his grandson but it had lain fallow and dry for eight, ten years and the grandson had never even come to look at it. Now here he was, in the middle of the July heat, just arrived and starting building with hardly a word to a soul. He had brought a quantity of supplies with him and all day long and far into the evening they could hear him sawing and planing, preparing his wood. He turned up at the rum shop one night. Didn't have much to say for himself except that he wanted a youngster to help him for the next few weeks. They discussed it in the shop for a while and suggested he get Miss Robbins' big boy Marcus seeing as he was going to the new Technical school and should know how to handle himself. It was arranged that someone would send a message and Marcus would show himself the next day.

When he left they puzzled about him for some time. Leonard Davis was as unlike his grandfather Sam Davis as mutton is to pork. Sam had been an easy going man, friendly with everyone and content to live his life simply. His wife Miriam, now there was a woman. She had a back as straight and hard as a church pew and a terrible, fierce ambition to go with it. When their three children were high school age, she picked up and took them all off to Mandeville and from that day on she was finished with Sam Davis and Burnt Hill. Said she wanted higher education and something more out of life for her children. Sam used to go to see them every now and again and take a good sized crocus bag full of whatever produce was in season at the time. His friends marvelled at him. As his good friend Simon Harris said . . . "If I did have a hard face woman like dat leave

Excerpt from *Mint Tea* by Christine Craig, first published by Heinemann Publishers Ltd. Used by permission of the publisher.

me, I woulda say 'tank God fe Jesus' and fix up meself wid a nice young gal."

Sam ignored them and continued his visits to Mandeville, but it seems like his family were getting very high tone for they started sending the maid to meet the country bus and relieve Sam of his crocus bag of yams and cassava. So gradually the visits dwindled and he spoke less and less of his family. As the years drew on he used to hear occasionally from a daughter who lived in England, and when he died, his son and other daughter from Kingston came to bury him. They had arrived, very pleasant but very citified and it was clear they, neither of them, would be coming back there to live.

Now here was Leonard Davis, a big, strapping, young dark-skinned fellow, not citified like his father, but not friendly either like old Sam Davis. Heavy and quiet, just arrived and started building. Marcus, having been accepted for the job, was questioned but could say very little. Seems like Leonard was building a simple enough house but he was very fussy with it. Everything had to be just so. He was even renovating the lattice work from Sam's old cottage. Marcus had felt strongly enough to intervene at this point.

"But Mr Leonard why you don' trow way dat ol someting. Better you get some a dat new grille work to finish up de verandah."

But Leonard had persisted and when they had stripped off the old paint and sanded it down, Marcus had had to agree that it was fine workmanship and it looked good on the new verandah.

The end of August came as hot and dry as July, but the house was growing at a great speed. Malcolm Jones, who ran a small shop which sold odds and ends of hardware, seemed to be the only person who had actually spoken more than a few words to Leonard. Not that he was unfriendly mind you, more that he kept himself to himself and got on with his work. Malcolm had taken a walk over there one day and reported to the rum shop later, that it was a nice enough house but very old-fashioned. Wooden floors and sash windows and goodness knows what else that took time and trouble to make.

Malcolm was a bit of a handyman in his way and he took to going over some evenings to help out. He liked furniture work and they would sit in the yard of an evening, sanding down some of the old furniture that had been lying around in Sam's house. One evening they were working on two straight back chairs when Leonard asked: "Who lives over there, in the blue house?"

"Oh, dat's Mrs Harris' house. She keep de basic school but she gone to Kingston since school give holiday. She told de children say she was going back to school herself but she soon come back. Why you ask?"

Leonard shrugged. "Nothing. I just like the house. I wondered why nobody was there." He paused to get at the inside of a chair leg. "So, where is her husband?"

Malcolm laughed. "He gone way long time. Well, you know here is too country for anybody wid a little education and ambition. Sooner or later dem pick up an leave. Mek it worse, dem was married five, maybe six years an all she try she couldn't mek a baby for him. Well it happen dat him get a coolie gal pregnant. De next ting we know, him up and gone to Sav-la-Mar. Set up house an business dere wid de coolie gal."

After he left, Malcolm put away the tools and sat for a long while looking into the cool darkness. He had inherited about three acres of fairly flat land and a derelict house. But there was a good-sized water tank, a big guango tree and several fruit trees. The land adjoining his was smaller and slightly hilly but it was thickly planted out and also had its own tank. It was a shame that everything there would die from lack of water. The next evening he walked over to the blue house, found a bucket by the tank and started watering. It was slow work with only the bucket but he moved methodically through the front garden and started on the back. What must have been a vegetable garden was only limp, brown stalks but she had a row of young citrus plants struggling to stay alive. Leonard emptied bucket after bucket of water on them and listened to the slight hiss of the water going into the dry earth and smelled the strong, warm smell that rose from the wet earth. There were two large pots of ferns on the verandah and he hesitated a moment before pushing open the little gate, going up the three steps, and watering the ferns.

August turned into September and not a drop of water fell from the open sky. Burnt Hill seemed determined to earn its name as even the customary night dews seemed to have stopped and the land rolled out red and dry every morning. The farmers, who were famous in the rest of the island for their dry-weather farming techniques, had mulched their plants carefully and accepted the dry spell as part of the order of things. But Leonard was aghast at it, it seemed to him that some great force was withholding something simple, effortless to give. He was amazed at the painstaking way in which the farmers carried water out to the plants, just a little trickle for each as the level of water in the tanks grew lower and lower. He took to going over to the blue house every evening to water the plants. He didn't think about it much, he wanted the plants to survive and he liked the small, blue-washed house. He admired the gingerbread carving over the doors and he liked the simple squareness of it on the hilly plot of land. On the evenings when Malcolm came, he didn't go. One evening Leonard started over and stopped abruptly. There was a light. So she was back. He felt curiously angry, turned and went back to his house.

Burnt Hill took on a new look in September. Children appeared in groups, starched and khakied, going to school. The rains came and the men and women who had seemed half-dead in the still, heat of July, unbent, moved as if released from some ancient frieze. There was digging and hoeing and planting. Voices calling, snatches of song moved in the still air. Leonard felt the movement around him and he too set to work on the land. Almost imperceptibly the evenings came earlier and then there was not enough light to work on anything.

One evening, Malcolm came over. He had heard of a fine mahogany felled over at Topside and he had bought a few pieces. Working on the furniture had renewed his interest in wood and he thought he would make something himself, but there was enough if Leonard wanted a piece. Leonard said yes, he would buy a piece to make a table. They disagreed mildly over possible designs. Malcolm was all for an ornately carved table with curved legs. Leonard preferred a simple oblong with straight legs.

"Mrs Harris have a fine old table. I help her french polish it one time. You know dose ole time table wid a pedestal an de legs dem curve an end wid sort of claws. You know de one I mean Leonard?"

"No," Leonard said.

Malcolm wouldn't let it drop. "How you mean 'no.' You don' meet her yet? Seeing as you is neighbours, I surprise at you man."

Leonard shrugged, "Cho Malcolm, you know I'm not one for visiting. I'll meet her soon enough. I'll come over to the shop tomorrow to pick out that piece of wood."

Leonard spent the next morning designing his table and working out the dimensions. In the afternoon he went over to the shop and waited for Malcolm to finish serving ice pops to a group of school children. Malcolm's shop was a one-roomed affair but he had enclosed the side verandah and there he kept stocks of odd things like nails, shoelaces and paint. The last child was ushered out clutching his tube of bright green ice and the men were just about to go through to the verandah when a woman rushed in.

"Evening Malcolm, hope you have some kerosene, don't know how I've run out already."

She was small, slim and her voice was low, rushing out from her small frame.

"Evening Mrs Harris. You in luck, truck coming tomorrow but I have a little put by you could have. But stop, I don' think you know your new neighbour. Dis is Mr Leonard Davis."

"Evening," they said and there was a silence as they looked at each other.

Mrs Harris broke it.

"I've been admiring your house. I hear you built it yourself."

"Thank you," Leonard said, "Malcolm helped me with the furniture."

"Oh," she sounded interested but Malcolm was handing her the kerosene and she was paying, saying goodnight and hurrying out. Leonard chose his wood and walked home slowly.

That evening he sat on his verandah and looked at the blue house. He wondered how the garden was doing. He could imagine her now, active, quick hands planting a new garden. He had imagined that she was old, an old woman teaching other people's children. But she was not old. Older than he perhaps but not more than mid-thirties he guessed. She was pale skinned with dark hair, colouring that Leonard found strange, unattractive even. Quiet and the night came early and he sat there feeling a flicker of restlessness. He needed his books, a radio perhaps, he wasn't sure why he had been delaying going into Kingston to fetch his things. The pattern he had established of working on the house had completely absorbed him, but, he thought, stretching lazily, it was time to make the trip into town. He would go the next day, get it over with. If he went like that, mid-week, there would be nobody there. He could simply pick up his two boxes and leave the key with the next door neighbour. He would not have to face his parents and their aggrieved comments, the small guilt-making jabs, "after all they had done," giving up his job, "such good prospects," to hide himself away "in the depths of beyond," as they put it. And, of course, he could not explain. He could not say that the prospect of working to buy things did not interest him, of drifting into a marriage, much like theirs, did not interest him. It was all sound, solid, and it frightened him, the years stretching ahead, known even before they had happened. He wanted to make something very simple, very different, for himself. He could not explain because they were so proud of having lived out Grandma Miriam's dream, to be educated, professionals, a far remove from Grandpa Sam, travelling in on the country bus with his country talk and his bag of yams.

By the weekend he had his few possessions unpacked. In the evenings now he had company and as September grew full and wet he would sit and play his guitar. He played all sorts of music, music written years before and some never written but passed along the generations like a great fishing net, drawing in and giving out as it moved through time. Sometimes he played his own music, haltingly, then finding the thread he wanted, repeated, woven together and finally noted down. In the blue house, Mrs Harris heard the notes dropping wetly in the September evening. She wasn't sure if she liked his being there or if she slightly resented him. In the afternoons she would see his dark, heavy body moving slowly between the rows he had dug. He might be a good builder and a good musician but his farming looked rather pathetic. She couldn't see even a smudge of green starting in the red earth.

One Friday evening she came home from school, bathed and changed and for the first time in years, felt the weight of the weekend stretching heavily in front of her. She went out to the garden and saw with pleasure the feathery green tops of her carrots. She stood staring at the soft, small leaves, remembering all the other years she had planted, the excitement when they started growing, the despair when drought or floods or insects threatened to leave her with no crop at all. Slowly she went back to the house, fetched some newspaper, a small shovel and started digging up some of the plants. Wrapping them carefully in the paper she set off towards his house. Dusk was edging into the sky and wisps of pink cloud floated there as if they had snatched their colour from the red land.

In front of his verandah she stopped. There was no light in his house and she turned quickly to go away, but he was coming through the doorway.

"Evening," he said.

"Evening," she said and her voice hurried on. "I was thinning out some carrots and beans. Planted too many this year. You want some seedlings?"

"Yes," he answered. "Thank you." There was silence and she felt she hated him. Could he not say something? She held the parcel out and he reached for it.

"Thank you," he repeated, "though I don't seem to be much good with them. None of mine have even sprouted yet."

She felt silly, standing there in the dark. "Perhaps you didn't get good seed."

"Malcolm said it was good," he said.

"His stuff is always good," she said, sounding defensive. "Maybe you didn't prepare the beds right. This land hasn't been worked for years."

"I think I may have planted them too deep," he said. "Yes, maybe that's what I did."

He seemed to have forgotten about her and she turned to go.

"I'll just put these down," he said quickly, "and light a lamp."

He returned with a lamp, holding one hand cupped around the top of the shade even though there was no breeze to snuff it out.

"Won't you come in?" he asked with an old-fashioned stiffness.

She stepped up on to his verandah and sat on one of two chairs drawn up beside the table. His guitar was leaning against the other and he moved it aside to sit down.

"I hear you playing in the evenings," she said. "I can't make out the tunes from where I am, I just get a sort of outline." She stopped abruptly and looked at him. His eyes were heavy lidded, deepset, and in the lamplight they gleamed oddly. He seemed like a large, slow cat, cautious and self-contained.

"Do you like it?" he asked.

"Yes, I like music but," she shrugged, "I don't know much about it." She sounded more definite as she added, "I like all sorts of music as long as it's not all electrical . . . you know."

He laughed. "Yes, I know. I do these things and send them in and, if I'm very lucky, a group will get hold of it and make it all loud and electrical. Sometimes I can't bear to hear them when they are finished. But sometimes, the group improves on it, somebody picks up on something I hadn't fully developed and it ends up being, well, more exciting somehow."

"So you write music then," she said smiling.

"No," he was almost gruff, "just tunes. But it buys me this," he looked past her. "Independence, no noise, no hassle."

They sat for a long while, talking and silence in little patches until the sky was black, scattered with stars and only a small curl of a moon. She got up to go and he walked with her across to her land. There was something cool and heavy between them out there under the dark sky yet at her gate she said, "Will you come over some time and play your guitar?"

He could hardly see her face, only the smallness of her and her quick voice.

"Yes, I'll do that," he said and watched her go into her house.

The weather changed. The days passed wet and thundery with sudden flashes of lightning. There were days when school was closed early and the children admonished to get home quickly before the rain. But they dawdled and their shrieks could be heard as they ran and splashed and held their faces up to the wet. Mrs Harris was conscious, on those wet afternoons, that she was waiting. She wished that she had never walked over there, for now she was waiting and she felt a sharp irritation with herself. One day, the skies opened just before she got home. She let herself in and tore off her wet clothes. She put on an old bathrobe, made some coffee and stood by the window watching with stiff anger as the rain flattened her plants. "Bloody immoderate country, if the drought doesn't get you the floods will."

There was a knock at the door.

"Yes," she called, "come in."

Leonard stood there very wet, staring at her with his heavy eyes.

"I'm too wet to come in," he said.

"Take your shoes off then," she said. "I'll get you a towel."

He sat in her small room with his shoes off and mopped at himself with the towel, then she saw that he had brought his guitar wrapped in an old jacket.

She gave him some coffee and sat away from him drying her hair. It was thick and curly and as she brushed it it sprung away from her head, alive and dark. She was like that, he thought, alive and tensed up, angry at something.

"You know," he said, "I don't know your name. Other than Mrs Harris, that is."

She laughed, looking at him and he felt slightly frightened of her, all her small brittleness frightened him. "It's Mavis," she said. "Horrible name isn't it?"

"Almost as bad as Leonard," he smiled. He looked around the room. "I like this house, I used to look at it. . . . "

"Why?" she asked abruptly, startled by the idea.

"I don't know, it's a simple, workable design I guess. When you were away I used to come over and water the plants. I liked it here. Only, I imagined that you were an old lady, that you wouldn't mind."

She pulled her bathrobe more closely around her and looked at him with strangely dilated eyes.

"Did you. Thanks for doing that." Then she laughed. "But I am old. Old Mrs Harris who keeps school!"

He laughed then, looking into her eyes and picked up his guitar.

Outside the rain was slowing down but the sky was still grey. A grey and red landscape wrapped around the house as he played, his bare feet moving slightly to the sound. The music and the dense grey evening swirled through her head in thick patterns and she got up and started preparing a simple supper. She seemed to stand off from herself, seeing herself standing in the kitchen, aware of a soft dishcloth in her hand, rubbing and rubbing at a white cup, trying to focus away from the patterns and his slowly moving feet.

He sat, head bent, wrapped up in his sounds, hardly moving when she brought a lamp and set it on the table.

"I'm hungry," she said. "Will you eat?"

They ate, speaking occasionally with a curiously stiff, old-fashioned sort of politeness. He watched her clearing the table and the room felt very still after the soft rushing of her voice. He felt hot in the small room, hot and closed in with this woman. He wanted to touch her hair, touch her throat where her voice lived. When she had cleared the table she sat and said awkwardly,

"I'll put something on and walk part of the way with you. It's stopped raining. Did you notice?"

He reached out and touched her throat. "I love to hear your voice. I wish there were notes like that I could play."

She held herself very still as he touched her throat. His hand was so large, so rough at the tips of the fingers, it seemed separated from his smooth, cat body. It seemed to him that something waited in her. Waited tense and coiled and withheld from him. He kissed her strange face, closed like a small flower.

In the weeks that followed Leonard thought it would never stop raining. His tank overflowed and washed away all his efforts at gardening. He felt helpless against the great weight of the sky and the smaller yet equally persistent weight of the woman in the blue house. He wanted not to think of her. He worked quickly to finish the table he was making, to push her away from him with planing, with careful fitting of joints together. He wanted only to see her and take her, not to fill his days with the sharp edge of her. Sometimes, in the evenings, she would speak of her day at school. Of the children she found exasperating and of those who were responsive to learning. She did not speak of her past so their talk was often filled with other people's children, other people's doings and sayings and in the midst of it their lives stood rooted, unyielding in their separateness. But slowly he was making up his mind about her and as October came he was badgering Malcolm for more wood. He started on the last piece of furniture he planned to make. When it was finished he asked her to come to his house. She had been strange about this, welcoming him to her house but seldom wanting to go to his. She said though, yes she would come. She would come on Saturday at six.

Leonard made supper, amazed at himself for the fuss he made over it.

He watched her crossing his washed out land. The sky was full of that strong gold light that comes in the evening towards the close of the year. She seemed herself all golden and lit up as she walked towards him and took his hand. She was more relaxed and affectionate than he had ever seen her. She had put a sprig of jasmine in her hair and the room was full of its scent and their voices and the food shared on their plates. After dinner he showed her his gift and she laughed and threw herself across it. It was a four poster bed, made in dark mahogany and she was full of admiration of him.

"But really, it's so lovely, and you made it!"

Then she fell silent and looked at him. He looked away and said quickly,

"It's for us. You must come and live here. Yes, marry me and come to live here."

She walked round the room looking at the bed, at its simple lines and dark, glowing wood. She stopped, far from him and spoke abruptly.

"But I can't do that. I was married. You've heard all the stories. When he left I stayed in the house. I made a place for myself there. Can you see that? It was very difficult. There were nights when I cried. There were days when I couldn't get up. The house was dirty and I couldn't clean it. I was cold and barren and I could do nothing. I wasn't a woman at all. At last I grew angry. But it took a long time. I am ashamed of it. There were days when I couldn't bear to see other people's children, couldn't bear their noise and chatter and their beautiful limbs, their beautiful faces. But I stayed and made a place for myself and I can't give that up." She paused and looked at him. "You are young. You will find someone, start a family . . . ."

Leonard heard her and his own voice came darting out into the room.

"I don't care about the children thing," he said, "but you must stay. I don't care about marriage if you don't want that although we are being talked about as it is. I don't want you to be talked about. I want you to stay here."

His will was like a large, live fire behind his darting voice, she couldn't move away from it and yet she couldn't let herself be swallowed up in it either. She stood straight and stiff by the bed and her eyes held a great coldness. But he reached out and took her hand twisting it hard against his chest. They made love in a rage. They filled the bed with a bizarre almost tangible rage of love and despair.

She wept. Large, noiseless tears rolled into her hair where the creamy coloured flowers drooped close to her cheek. He looked at her then, saw the flower of her own will opening as the tears slid into her hair. He understood then, not in any way he could formulate into words but in some silent, instinctive way.

Burnt Hill talked for a while about Leonard Davis and Mrs Harris but as more Julys and Septembers rolled past the red land, as the citrus trees bloomed behind the blue house and cassava plants appeared on his land, the village looked away. They found new and more changeable topics to discuss.

Lorna Goodison

MULATTA SONG

Very well, Mulatta,
this dance must end.
This half-arsed band
blowing its own
self-centered song.
The bass slack stringed
slapped by some wall-eyed
mother's son.
This session must done
soon done.
O how you danced Mulatta
to the music in your head
pretending that their notes
were your notes.
Till the gateman whispered
into the side of your head
"Mulatta, mulatta, that's the
dance of the dead."
So you rubadub and rentatile
and hustle a little
smiling the while
pretending that
this terrible din
is a well-tuned air
on a mandolin.
And mulatta your red dress
you wore here as new
is a wet hibiscus

what will do?
Fold the petals of the skirt
and sit this last long
last song out.
Bind up the blood-wound
from the heart on your sleeve
and now Mulatta it's time to leave.

MISSING THE MOUNTAINS

For years I called the Blue Mountains home.
I spent my days faceting poems from rockstones.
By moonshine I polished them, they flashed like true gems.

I was included then in all the views of the mountains.
The hand that flung me down to the plains
was powered by the wrath of hurricanes.

Now from the flat lands of Liguanea
I view the mountains with strict detachment.
I remark upon their range and harmony of blues.

Respect due to their majesty, I keep my distance.
I must now carry proof of my past existence
in the form of one blue stone mined near mountain heart.

I show too a wildness, and intensity
drawn from the mountains' energy.
This is a request to all left behind me.

Bury me up there in the high blue mountains
and I promise that this time I will return to teach the wind
how to make poetry from tossed about and restless leaves.

Reprinted from *I Am Becoming My Mother* by Lorna Goodison, published by New Beacon Books Ltd. in 1986. Used by permission of the publisher.

Una Marson

excerpt from
POCOMANIA
A THREE-ACT PLAY OF
NATIVE LIFE IN JAMAICA

The Cast

Sister Kate, a revivalist leader and a member of the Elizer Church
Sister Mart, her assistant
Brother Kendal, leader of choir and chief man among revivalists
Rev. Peter Craig, a very conventional young parson
Deacon Manners, a stern Baptist deacon
Dawn Manners, a rather plain girl
Stella Manners, frail and attractive
David Davis, typical young West Indian doctor
Elijah Higgins, Pocomania singer
Singers, entertainers, dancers, drummers, mourners, etc.

Time, 1938

[The play has a Prologue and Three Acts of Two Scenes each. Only
Act I, Scene I is included in *The Whistling Bird*.]

Act I

Scene I. *(Sister Kate's Yard. Sister Kate sitting on a box in front
of her door and Sister Mart beside her. Five Sisters and three Brothers standing to the right. One Brother conducting singing with
wand. Dressed in white, turbans, etc. Sister Mart leans on wall and*

Excerpt from the play *Pocomania* reprinted by permission of The National Library of Jamaica.

seems half asleep. Sister Mart watches the antics of the singers. Be-
fore curtain rises they start singing:)

> Go before us Lord,
> Go before us
> And do Thy work, Thyself;
> Go before us Lord,
> Go before us
> And do Thy work, Thyself;
> Roll, Jordan, roll,
> Roll, Jordan, roll,
> Roll, Jordan, roll,
> And do They work, Thyself.

LEADER KENDAL: Now unno is all to open your mouths and sing. Remember you is the choir, when de oders hear you sing they must feel in de spirit to join wid you.

FIRST SINGER: We can't sing without the drum.

KENDAL: De drummer is coming.

SISTER KATE: *(jumping up)* I tells you I don't want drums here in me yard. Next thing the parson hear de noise and come down. I is done tell him I don't keep meeting in me yard.

KENDAL: Sister Kate, him is coming now, but I will make him play soft. Dese gals and men here won't feel to sing widout some accomplishment.

SISTER KATE: Broder Kendal, you want get me into broil. I done, I done.

(She goes back to doze; enter drummer)

KENDAL: Softly, broder, Sister Kate don't wish no noise in her yard. Bat dat drum as softly as you can.

(Conducts, singing starts, they shout, and Kendal conducts. In the midst of the singing Sister Beale spies Deacon Manners and Parson Craig coming. She jumps up—Sister Kate jumps up)

SISTER KATE: Clear out, quick, quick, all of you, round de back quick, and stay dere.

*(They all rush out. Sister Kate composes herself comfortably and
Sister Mart goes to greet the Parson. Enter Parson Craig and
Deacon Manners)*

Sister Mart, get two chairs from de inside. I know me good Minister
will like sit in de cool. Is it not so?

PARSON: That's right, Mother Kate; how are you?

(Shakes hands with her; Sister Mart brings chairs)

DEACON: How do you do, Mother Kate? *(Shakes hands)*

SISTER KATE: Please sit down. *(Exit Sister Mart)*

DEACON: I thought we heard some drums and singing as we came
along.

PARSON: Yes, it seemed very near, I thought it was in your yard,
Mother Kate.

SISTER KATE: No Minister, not in here. I tell you I don't hold meetings in me yard.

PARSON: Mother Kate, I have been having a talk with the Deacons
about your work.

SISTER KATE: *(smiling)* Yes, Minister.

DEACON: Yes, it was a very serious talk.

SISTER KATE: And you is all very pleased about how I bring de people in de districk to de Lawd?

DEACON: On the contrary, we are very displeased.

PARSON: Allow me, Deacon Manners. You see, Sister Kate, as you
are a member of the Elizer Church it puts me in a very difficult position.

SISTER KATE: How you mean, Minister?

PARSON: Well, you must know that you are taking away a large number of my congregation to your meetings and they have given
up the Church though you still attend.

SISTER KATE: The devils, I is tell dem to go to Church and worship de Lawd dere too. You can't worship de Lawd too much, Minister.

PARSON: I quite agree, but you see, these poor people cannot support you and me; it must be one or the other, and for you to break up my long years of labour here. . . . well. . . .

DEACON: Why don't you make a move?

SISTER KATE: Move? Move from me home, from me yard where me grandmodder lived before me, move Sir, it is not possible, I cannot do dat.

PARSON: Mother Kate, that is not all. You know I am a humble servant of the Lord. I want to see my people do right. I am told that much that is done at your meetings is of the devil. That troubles me most of all.

SISTER KATE: Who told you dat Minister, who tol' you dat?

PARSON: Never you mind, Sister Kate, never you mind. But I don't think it is right, that shouting and jumping all through the night.

SISTER KATE: De people is praising de Lawd, they can't praise de Lawd too much, Minister.

DEACON: You know that some bad things have happened at your meetings.

SISTER KATE: Look here, Deacon, I will tek you to Court to prove that.

PARSON: Now come, come, Mother Kate, there is no need for hard sayings, we came here to have a quiet talk with you.

SISTER KATE: Well Minister, if dees people should hol' deir peace de stones would cry out.

PARSON: May be it would be a good thing if they would give the stones a chance once in a while. But now Mother Kate, to come to the point: we are agreed that we must ask you to leave our Church.

DEACON: We have no alternative.

SISTER KATE: And what have a good Church member like me done to leave the Church; I is not living in sin.

PARSON: We did not say that, but we have one or two cases of your converts come before us and we have come to the conclusion that Christ is not pleased with what is going on at Brown Down Hill.

SISTER KATE: I is proud of me Church even though when de spirit move me and I feel to cry out you don't like it, but I is proud of me Church and I don't wish to lef it.

PARSON: You have your own Church which I would advise you to purify. But because of these cases we cannot let you stay, as it will appear to the world that we are condoning things that are not of the Lord.

DEACON: Surely Mother Kate, you can see this.

SISTER KATE: Is what you coming to say, Deacon Manners. You know I have a min' tell Parson about you.

DEACON: My conscience is clear, you can tell Parson anything.

SISTER KATE: Conscience clear, well, I will talk. You used to send you servant and all you pickney, you two daughters and you two godsons to de meeting. Dem stan' in a bush oneside but de spirit tol' me dem was dere. It was many years ago but I not forget.

PARSON: Is that so Deacon? Surely not children! You would never have allowed. . . .

DEACON: It is a direct untruth. You know I would never dream of doing that.

SISTER KATE: I have witness to prove dem was dere.

PARSON: And to prove Deacon Manners sent them?

SISTER KATE: Well, no Sir, no Minister.

DEACON: I have no knowledge of this, Minister, but I will find out if it ever took place.

SISTER KATE: If you all don't want me in de Church well unno can do what you like. I not moving, I not stopping me meeting. Beside, you can tek me name off de register but you can't stop me from come to Church.

DEACON: But you are ruining the Church.

PARSON: That's enough Deacon Manners. Well, Mother Kate, you must ask God to keep the devil out of your meetings. As long as you entertain him there you will get the crowd and you know that. Do not let your conscience go to sleep.

SISTER KATE: Minister, would you tell me what you mean by dat?

PARSON: Mother Kate, you know quite well, and therefore the greater will be your condemnation.

SISTER KATE: Don't condemn me, Sir.

PARSON: When you can come to me and say that your meetings are purified and pleasing in the sight of God, then we will take you back in the Church.

SISTER KATE: Amen.

PARSON: Good morning, Sister Kate.

SISTER KATE: Good morning, me Minister.

DEACON: God bless you, Sister Kate.

SISTER KATE: God bless you and good morning Deacon Manners.

(Exit Parson and Deacon Manners)

SISTER KATE: Sister Mart, Sister Mart, where is you, where is you? Sister Mart!

(Sister Mart comes running)

SISTER MART: What happen, Sister Kate, What happen? O my Sister Kate, is what it is?

SISTER KATE: Dat spineless and creeping Deacon Manners mek de Parson goin' cross off me name of de Church roll.

SISTER MART: And why mek so? Why mek so, Sister Kate?

SISTER KATE: O, O, Lawd have Massy, dem say evil tings gwine on at we meeting.

SISTER MART: I did tell dat wotless Josiah dat would happen. Dem niggers don't know when to stop and dem know de Church was watching we. But no mine, no mine, Sister Kate.

SISTER KATE: No mine, no mine? But you see me trial. I tink when de people hear bout it dem will doubt me, dem will say, Sister Kate is off de church rool, may be we should not follow Sister Kate.

SISTER MART: Don't think so, Sister Kate, dem love you too much, and de sweet songs and de drums, dem can't keep way, dem must come.

(Enter Leader Kendal)

KENDAL: We can go on sing now, Sister Kate?

SISTER KATE: *(standing)* Yes Broder Kendal, and I charge you dat you mek de singing sweeter dan ever you did before. Charge de sisters to shout and sing and de broders to invoke de Lawd so de spirit can come and we get more and more.

KENDAL: De fame of we dance and song is spread abroad Sister Kate. People is coming even from Seven Miles to join we.

SISTER KATE: Dat is de ting. Now I have fresh courage. De dance and de song. O, Parson Craig can go to de debil wid him Church, my people want de dance and song and de spirit. Dem will give me money, dem will shout and cry out. Dem can't show dem feeling in a Church. Where de Choir? Call dem.

KENDAL: Unno come, and let us shout unto de Lawd; shout sisters!

(Sister Kate gets up and spins round. Takes her switch from its place beside the door and stamps about the singers. She stops before one girl, drags her forward and shouts)

Join de chorus
We feel it flowing o'er us
You is no chile of Satan
So get the spirit
And shout, Sister, shout
Hallelujah, Amen
Shout, Sister, Shout.

(She starts in singing, Kendal conducting and singing too.
Great enthusiasm, Sister Kate uses switch around. All burst into
chorus and swaying rhythm, the particular girl forward gradually
working herself up to frenzy and falling on the ground—drums
join in, very bright and stirring)

Get you ready
Dere's a meeting here tonight
Come along
Dere's a meeting here tonight
I know you by your daily walk
Dere's a meeting here tonight.

O, I'm not ashamed to say
That my sins are washed away
I am waiting now for the kingdom coming
And de last great Judgment Day.

O, run about, you jump about
You skip about, you hop about
To hear Jerusalem roll,
O Lord, O my soul,
To hear Jerusalem roll.
You come to me house
And you drink me tea
To hear Jerusalem roll
Yet you go next door
And you lie pon me
To hear Jerusalem roll.

Curtain

THERE WILL COME A TIME

Each race that breathes the air of God's fair world
Is so bound up within its little self
So jealous for material wealth and power
That it forgets to look outside itself
Save when there is some prospect of rich gain;
Forgetful yet that each and every race
Is brother unto his, and in the heart
Of every human being excepting none,
There lies the selfsame love, the selfsame fear,
The selfsame craving for the best that is.
False pride and petty prejudice prevail
Where love and brotherhood should have full sway.

When shall this cease? 'Tis God alone who knows;
But we who see through this hypocrisy
And feel the blood of black and white alike
Course through our veins as our strong heritage
Must range ourselves to build the younger race.
What matter that we be as cagéd birds
Who beat their breasts against the iron bars
Till blood-drops fall, and in heartbreaking songs
Our souls pass out to God? These very words
In anguish sung, will mightily prevail.
We will not be among the happy heirs
Of this grand heritage—but unto us
Will come their gratitude and praise,
And children yet unborn will reap in joy
What we have sown in tears.

                  For there will come
A time when all the races of the earth
Grown weary of the inner urge for gain,
Grown sick of all the fatness of themselves
And all their boasted prejudice and pride
Will see this vision that now comes to me.
Aye, there will come a time when every man
Will feel that other men are brethren unto him—
When men will look into each other's hearts
And souls, and not upon their skin and brain,
And difference in the customs of the race.
Though I should live a hundred years or more
I should not see this time, but while I live,
'Tis mine to share in this gigantic task
Of oneness for the world's humanity.

Velma Pollard

MARINE TURTLE

for Evelyn

In silver half-light
beamed from wave to shore
a flattened hound . . .

bound from one sandhill
to another sand

frightened
I turn on trembling heel
and flee

The moonlight silvering her coat of husk
the turtle mother
lumbers in the sand
scratching like cat
making his private hole
scratching and stretching out
this clumsy paw then that
until the sand engulfs her in its tub

and now and here
she lays her precious eggs
to bear her light years forward . . .

Velma Pollard's poems reprinted by permission of the author.

Counting off her hope
if one of six
will brave the friendless stretch
will crawl the fearsome sand
and safely back to sea
his birthing done . . .

covering her new birthed loves
with tender sand
she shuffles back to sea
terrible with hope with fear
tuwhoo the night owl sadly warns

the fisher is hungry for your flesh
the fisher is hungry for your turtle eggs

How could I flee from such a game of hope?
What could I fear from such a sacrifice?
this mother mothering against fearful odds
turns my uncertainties to certainty
in danger yes
but not endangered I

MULE

hag ask him muma wa mek im mout lang so im se yu a grow
    yu wi si

I

Mules
dragging heavy carts
when I was young
up unpaved country roads
suddenly
would seem to kneel
no bucky massa

the cartman
whip in hand
angry would shower
blow on blow
and I would watch
the mule face pain
and shudder

"stubborn (like mule)" he'd hiss
"stubborn" he'd puff and blow
his nostrils swell and shrink
and other sweaty, muscled men
come crowding round
to help him lift her
save his cargo
urge him on
"lick im" "lick im"
they'd say
"stubborn like mule"

they'd lift the cargo
not the mule
and slowly slowly
when the cart was light
the lady mule would rise

now my own knees
swollen and tight
would wish to buckle
mule-like in their pain
no bucky massa
only pride . . .

and only now
I understand

II

Half-crippled Legba
rests at the crossroads
considers
starts another journey
needs no whip to urge him on
nor hands to tell him
what his load should be

the finger-post
will tell me
where my journey lies
the gods will tell my knees
the time to halt
on this new journey
when to kneel
and rest
Bucky massa

Olive Senior

DISCERNER OF HEARTS

SHE LET HERSELF OUT by the back door and carefully shut it behind her, and ran through the short cut that led to the main road, hoping that no one would see. At the main road she hesitated, not because she didn't know the way but because she was terrified at what she was doing, her heart was thumping loudly against her chest, and because they were always being told never to walk on the road alone. They could get killed, Mama said, everyone drove so fast. Because of the Blackartman, Cissy said. Cissy never tired of talking about the Blackartman who drove up and down in a car and snatched children. That's why, Cissy said, you must never get into a car with a strange man, no matter how heavily it's raining or anything. Because you can never tell just by looking whether or not he is the Blackartman.

"What does the Blackartman do when he's snatched you, Cissy?" they would ask.

"He take you home and cut out your heart."

"And what does he do with your heart?"

Cissy always looked around carefully when they got to this part before leaning forward and whispering, "He want it to *use*."

"Use for what?"

But after that, Cissy's mouth clamped shut. No matter how hard they tried, they could never get her to say more. If they pressed too much, she would become sullen and serious and say, "Not good thing to talk about," and leave them to go about her business.

Because they liked being around Cissy, liked hearing her talk about her life, all the things she knew which were different from the things Mama knew, they never pressed her about the Blackartman. But they believed her, knew he was there, waiting to snatch whichever one dared to go on the road alone. Yet here she was in the bright sun-

Reprinted from *The Discerner of Hearts* by Olive Senior. Used by permission of the Canadian publisher McClelland & Stewart, Toronto.

light, standing alone by the main road waiting to cross it, clutching a shiny new sixpence in her hand. She looked to both sides and, when there were no cars in sight, ran across the road and headed for Mister Burnham's house.

She knew the house well because it wasn't far from where they lived, and when Cissy took them for walks she often stopped to chat to Mrs. Burnham. She would stand by the gate let into the thick shoe-black hedge growing in front of a tall split bamboo fence which went all the way around the yard. They never went inside, though they were intensely curious.

Mister Burnham's yard was like no other. For one thing, it had any number of poles which towered above the house and from which flew squares of cloth like flags. The ones that were up for a long time got tattered and torn and the colours washed out in the sunlight, but then new flags were always going up. Aside from the flags which signalled the yard from afar, and the zinc roof of the house above the fence, they couldn't see much else. They always tried to peek through the gate as Mrs. Burnham stood behind it talking to Cissy, but Mrs. Burnham always stood close to the gate and leaned over it with her large arms crossed and Cissy stood close as she faced her. Since they were both very broad, there was little room left to peep around or between them. Cissy said it wasn't good manners to peep inside people's yards, how would you like them peeping into yours? But people were always staring openly into their yard. And Mister Burnham's wasn't just any yard: apart from the flags, sometimes behind the hedge they heard the cooing of doves, and occasionally while they watched, entranced, a large flock of white birds would rise from the back yard and circle several times before flying west.

When they asked Cissy about the flags, she said how else would you know it was a balmyard? How else could *they* find the place?

"Who are *they*, Cissy?"

"You don't worry bout *them*. You faas too much. What you don't know can't hurt you. Not everything good to eat good to talk."

"What's a balmyard, Cissy?"

"Where people go for healing."

"What is healing?"

"What people need when they have sickness."

"Why they don't go to Dr. Carter?"

"There is sick, and then again there is sick."

"But Mister Burnham isn't a doctor."

"There is doctor and there is doctor."

When Cissy carried on like that, they knew it was no use pressing her. She would just get mad and flounce off or chase them away so loudly that Mama would call out for them to stop annoying her and let her get on with her work. All they ever got out of her was that Mister Burnham—whom she called Father because that was what he was called—was a special kind of healer and that many people went to him when they had troubles. "Father Burnham a great healer. A famous man. Father have the *key*. People come from all over the world to beg Father *read* them," Cissy would boast.

They knew that wasn't possible because Mister Burnham couldn't read; like everyone else, he always came to their father for help with filling out forms or writing letters to the government or reading letters from the government, which were the only kinds of letters most people received. But they didn't bother to point this out because Cissy couldn't read either and she was extremely sensitive about the subject.

Sometimes she would pick up one of their books and hold it up, pretending to read, and if anyone pointed out that she was holding it upside-down, she got so mad. "Eh. Just because my skin black, people think I am idiot, eh? People think I fool. Just because I couldn't get to go to school like *some* backra people children, because I had was to stay home and help my mother look after the baby them. Never born turn-skin and rich like *some* people, couldn't get to sit round like princess, every one of them, like Missis-queen herself, and can't do one god-thing, spoil hog-rotten, the lot of them. Think because *some* people go school they can faas and facety as they like, eh? Think is only book have learning? Ai. I wouldn't bother to tell *some* people all the things I know that they will never know. And you know why?" she would ask, suddenly eyeing each of them in turn as they cowered, ashamed, before her. "You know why?" Arms akimbo, she would wait for an answer. But of course, none ever came. "Because," she would end triumphantly, "no book make yet that could write down everything. Learn that!" And she would fling the book across the room and stalk out. They would get terrified when Cissy carried on like that because they never really knew why she got so angry. And so nobody bothered to contradict her about Mister Burnham reading.

Whenever they got the opportunity, they would scrutinize Mister Burnham carefully to see what Cissy saw in him to make her so proud. He certainly didn't look or behave like anyone else they knew. He was a short little man with a mischievous round face and reddish eyes. He always wore a cloth cap which he touched whenever he came to their yard and loudly greeted their father and mother even before he saw them. "Morning-Justice-Morning-Mistress-and-how-is-the-morning?" he'd call out as he approached in a voice of surprising depth and richness for one so small, and in a tone that was almost mocking. "Morning-Little-Mistresses-and-how-the-pretty-damsels-today?" he would call in a teasing voice if he caught sight of any of the children.

He came once a month to pay for the milk. His little boy Calvin came every morning with the shutpan for the quart of milk, but he himself came once a month to pay for it. They always peeped round the corner of the verandah and watched, fascinated, as he pulled a thread-bag from inside his shirt, the way a higgler would pull hers from her bosom, and poured from it onto the table in front of their father a stream of bright, shiny sixpences.

"You old reprobate," their father would laugh and, without counting the coins, he would scoop them into a paper bag from the bank.

Mister Burnham would laugh heartily too, hang his empty thread-bag around his neck and tuck it into his shirt, and if he had no other business he would touch his cap, call out, "Good day, Justice," and leave, their father's laugh ringing out after him.

Their father always seemed amused by Mister Burnham, called him "the old reprobate" both behind his back and to his face, sometimes teased him by calling out as he arrived: "Wait! Burnham, you still walking about free? Inspector don't lock you up yet?" or "Black Maria don't come for you yet?"

Mister Burnham's merry smile never wavered. "What for, Justice?"

"You damn well know what for, you scoundrel. You wait! Every day bucket go to well. . . . One day, you're going to send and beg me to run and bring these same sixpence to bail you out. But, Burnham, I couldn't do that. They would use them as evidence against you, man."

Mister Burnham would laugh along with their father till his eyes squeezed shut. "Lawd, Justice, you love make joke, eh? But you know the righteous have nothing to fear." And he would pour out his stream of bright silver sixpences and go laughing from the yard and Calvin would bring the shutpan every morning for more milk.

Sometimes in their play the girls would mimic Mister Burnham, cap on head, walking his staggering walk, pulling out his thread-bag—"And-how-are-the-Little-Mistresses?" Although Cissy would laugh at their imitations of everyone else, she never liked it when they poked fun at Mister Burnham.

"Hm. You can gwan run joke. Think Father is man to run joke bout? Father is serious man. But you is just like yu father. Have no respect for people. Unless their skin turn and they live in big house and they drive up in big car. But one day, one day the world going spin the other way though. And then we will see."

᧍

Of the three of them, Theresa, the middle one, was the only one Cissy would say a lot more to, when they were alone, because she liked Theresa the best. Theresa didn't get uppity and proud and facety sometimes like Jane, the eldest, Cissy often told her friends, and she wasn't spoilt and whining and tattletale like the little one, Maud. Plus, you could say Theresa had been born into Cissy's hands, for Cissy's mother had sent her to work for the Randolphs the month before Theresa was born. Cissy was only fourteen then, and she loved the baby passionately, treated her as if she was her own.

Theresa was the only person Cissy allowed into her quarters. Nearly every afternoon, Theresa would sneak across the back yard to the little one-room cottage beneath the breadfruit tree where she knew Cissy would be resting in the hour or two before she had to head back to the kitchen to cook dinner. Nobody knew Theresa was in Cissy's room, for she was always going off by herself and hiding in inconvenient places. Sometimes it would take the combined efforts of the entire household to search for her and most of the time they would give up, since Theresa had the habit of keeping absolutely still when it suited her. They'd be standing beneath the breadfruit tree and she'd be up in the tree, right above their heads, but so unmoving, nobody would spot her. "Theresa. Theresa!" they would call. And Theresa would sit perfectly still, reading her book up in the small breadfruit tree, or in the crotch of the orange tree at the bottom of the garden, or under the house, or behind the tank, or snugly inside the chocho arbour, for she was not afraid of lizards, as the rest of them were. Or she would be in Cissy's room.

She wouldn't answer until they all gave up, but by then they would have forgotten what they wanted her for. They wouldn't dare call out to ask Cissy if she'd seen her, for Cissy refused to speak to anyone when it was *her* time off. No one would even dare to go near Cissy's cottage, for she'd drawn an invisible territorial line around it which everybody respected. Except Theresa. Theresa would sit on the rickety chair at Cissy's dressing table and play with Cissy's things, her huge comb and her hair pomade, her bright pink face powder, her Khus-Khus essence, with which she doused herself whenever she went out, her string of beads, her shiny plastic handbag, her brightly coloured brooch, her earrings, which had what she said was a real diamond, her hairnets, her hat pins. She would try on Cissy's big church hat with the red cherries and green velvet leaves, admire her new shiny satin blouse. And Cissy would lie on her narrow bed and tell her things. Mainly, Cissy would talk about Fonso.

Fonso drove Mr. Rogers' truck all the way to and from Kingston and was therefore quite a catch; all the girls were after him, Cissy said, and Theresa, glimpsing his bright smile from the cab of the truck as he tootled past, thought him glamorous, too. But Cissy was the one who was going to take him away from Ermine, with whom he lived and had three children. Cissy was positive this would happen, because she had got *something* from Father that would make Fonso fall for her.

Theresa didn't see why Cissy needed to get anything to help her take Fonso away from Ermine, because Cissy was cool-dark and plump and beautiful and had hair she could wear in an upsweep when she was going out and white shoes with platform soles and straps, while Ermine was like a stick with picky-picky hair and a long mouth. "Yes," said Cissy, when Theresa pointed these things out, "but you don't see that Ermine *tie* him, how else she could get a man like Fonso?" So Cissy had to get something even stronger for binding.

Theresa was not surprised to go into Cissy's room one day and find Fonso there. After that, she could tell whenever Fonso was back from town, because even when she scratched at the door and called softly and Cissy knew it was her, Cissy wouldn't let her into her room. Theresa didn't mind though, because she could go back to Cissy's room later and hear all about her love life.

Cissy wouldn't say what Mister Burnham had given her to capture Fonso. She just laughed and said that Father was a powerful man and if you wanted anything at all, and you consulted him, he would help you to get it. Whenever Cissy was even slightly ill, or troubled, she would go to Mister Burnham, "for a *reading*," she said. Or a bath. When Theresa asked what was wrong with her good-good galvanize bathtub in the wash-house, Cissy explained that she was not talking about an ordinary bath.

"Is like a *spiritual* bath, Theresa, to wash over you and console you and draw out all the evil the devil plant in you that cause you to do wickedness, or feel faint, or get fever, or have belly-come-down pain, or lose the diamond from yu best earring somewhere on the road from church, or step on a flint-stone that just lying in wait to give you bruise blood, or make you see a galliwasp."

Each bath had just the right combination of *bush*—herbs, leaves, flowers, bark, and roots—for Father collected them special for each and every one of his clients, from the seven hundred and seventy-seven growing things he had in his yard, plus (if he found it necessary) oil from the doctor-shop, sulphur to fight the devil with, clove, frankincense and myrrh. Theresa knew the names of many of the plants and treatments by heart, for Cissy would sometimes recite them like a litany, her eyes sparkling: "Jack-inna-bush and see-me-contract, oil-of-comeuppance and essence of keep-me-strength-good, oil-of-turn-them-back for yu enemy, powder of rose-of-sharon to strengthen nerves, strong back and chainey-root for gentlemen, leaf-of-life for ladies' complaint . . . ."

Cissy was always buying from Theresa whatever silver sixpences she got as presents or could lay her hands on, for Mister Burnham had to be paid in silver sixpences.

"Why?" Theresa demanded to know.

But Cissy couldn't say. "That is just how it is. Have to pay Father in sixpence. Or the treatment don't work."

"How many sixpences you pay him?"

Cissy said it didn't matter. "As much as you have. Even one sixpence will do, if that is all you have. But you must have even one. Sometimes that is all I have to give Father. But him treat me same way. If you are big man now, say drive big car and come from Kingston, then you would give him plenty sixpence. For that is what you have."

She had been going to Mister Burnham for regular treatments for the longest while now, because she couldn't have a baby for Fonso. The fact that she was twenty-two and hadn't had a child was for Cissy the source of unimaginable discontent. Sometimes in the afternoons she would lie on her bed and cry while Theresa tried her best to comfort her.

"But, Cissy, what you want baby for? Baby isn't everything."

"Theresa, you too young to understand, chile. I am nothing but a mule. Everywhere I go, I know them calling me mule. Even my own mother start up bout it now. What good is a woman if she can't have pickney? Everybody else have baby but me poor soul. The girls my age, some of them have all two, three pickney. And me can't have even one little one. My own little sisters and all having pickney. Everybody except poor-me-gal."

Cissy crying in her room was a very different Cissy from the one who ruled the household. Theresa was the only one to whom she showed this side. Theresa wasn't pretty like the other two, and people were always so busy making a fuss over either the oldest or the youngest that by the time they got around to her she would feel let down, as if it were somehow her fault that she wasn't as engaging as they were.

She felt comfortable only when she was alone with Cissy. Cissy always told the truth. Cissy said things like, "Well, is true you not pretty like them other one there, but when you turn big woman you can fix yuself up. Straighten yu hair and wear lipstick and rouge and high-heel shoes. That time you can pretty up yuself, girl. Look just like them. Even better. For that Jane there kinda winji. She'll never get nice and fat for she hardly eat. Though a tell her all the time, 'Jane, man don't want no mawga gal.' And that Maudie? Cho. She like cry-cry too much. Bound to spoil her countenance. Furthermore," Cissy would say, "you have good-mind, you hear, better than all of them put together. You are a good girl, Theresa, for you know how to treat people like them is people. Me tell everybody seh, you are my girl, the bestest of the lot."

She would glow under Cissy's compliments and bear her truths, especially since no matter how hard Cissy was, she was always encouraging in some way. What she couldn't bear was Mama always trying to make her feel better and making her feel worse, because she knew that what she said wasn't true. "But dear, you are just as pretty and sweet as Jane. All my girls are pretty." And because she wasn't sweet and pretty, she knew, she always seemed to be doing the wrong things. She would break glasses and knock over vases and spill ink and make a mess and tear her hems down and lose her schoolbooks and forget what Mama asked her to do and just generally cause everyone to get annoyed with her about something.

"Theresa!" people were always shouting. And she knew she had done, or failed to do, something again.

Sometimes she made Mama so cross. Mama was always talking about it when Mrs. Miller or any of the other neighbour visited. "Jane is the neatest child in the world and Maud take after her. But Theresa! My goodness, within one minute a entering a room that child has it looking like a hurricane hit." Or, "Maud is the lovingest child imaginable. Every morning she brings me little wildflowers from the garden. She pick them for me and I have to arrange them in this tiny vase. It makes her so proud. She is the kindest, most affectionate child." She didn't say, "But Theresa . . . ," but Theresa knew she didn't appear as loving as the other girls, was too shy to go an bury her head in Mama's lap and throw her arms about her or leap into her father's arms as he arrived home, hung back where they came forward, kept to herself most of the time, hid away or sat in dark corners until somebody forcibly dragged her into the family circle.

ᵉ⁓

Cissy began to fret to Theresa and shouted and yelled at a three of them for the slightest thing, slammed down the pots and pans in the kitchen, kicked at the dog, and Theresa wished that Mister Burnham would hurry up and let her have a baby.

Then one day, Theresa heard Cissy humming as she dusted, something she hadn't done for a long while, and Cissy whispered to her as she passed, "Lizard drop on me," and laughed. Normally, Cissy was as terrified of lizards as all the other women about. Theresa couldn't understand why because she herself thought lizards were shy little creatures, but everyone knew that a croaking lizard losing its grip on the ceiling and dropping onto a woman meant only one thing.

From the minute Cissy knew she was going to have a baby, she was a transformed woman, was back to the old self they knew and loved, laughed a lot and sang and told them Anansi and Duppy stories at night, even played Johnny-coopa-lantan with the coconut brush as she shined the floor. Cissy grew happier and more beautiful as the days passed—and fatter. Eventually Mama noticed something and called her into her bedroom and locked the door and could be heard raising her voice to her, something she didn't normally do.

"Imagine," she could be heard telling their father that night. "Imagine, after all we've done for her, Cissy has turned out just like all the other girls around here. All any of them ever want to do is make baby. Imagine. We take her to church, christen and confirm her. She promised to be such a good girl, and I thought she was good, never wanted to go out at night and run around like the rest of them, and now look at what she's been doing behind my back. God knows what her mother will say. She'll swear we haven't been taking good care of her."

Mama was even more vexed when she finally got Cissy to confess who the baby was for.

"Imagine," she told their father, "that Fonso Tomlinson. That ram goat. Sweet-mouth every one of the young girls around. Fall every one of them. Every girl around here has a baby for him. And now Cissy."

Mama could often be heard lecturing Cissy now. "Well, Miss, see what happens when you're careless? I hope you'll learn your lesson." Yet each day Mama would go digging in trunks and boxes to find all her old baby things for Cissy. And she got Marse Dick, the carpenter, to come and fix and paint up the old crib, and she made Cissy two dresses with lace edging around the collars for when she got really big.

Cissy didn't care about Mama's warnings and lectures. Nor did she pay any attention to Mama's orders that she should go and register with the district nurse. She did nothing of the sort, she just got bigger and more contented.

ᴇ᷄

Just as Cissy's happiness had come so swiftly overnight, one day some months later it as swiftly vanished, though Theresa was the only person who really noticed. She couldn't help noticing, for Cissy had gone back to lying on her bed and crying in the afternoons.

"Cissy, what is the matter?" Theresa asked her.

But for several afternoons, Cissy said nothing, just bawled into her pillow until Theresa, getting nowhere, was forced to leave. No one but Theresa noticed the redness of her eyes as she served dinner, the heaviness of her steps.

Finally it all came out. She was never going to have the baby now, Cissy said, because that Ermine gone and obeah her.

"Lawd, Theresa. Ermine get a obeah so bad that I will never have baby again. Lawd Jesus, Theresa. My inside turning to ashes."

"But why?" Theresa asked. "Plenty other people have baby for Fonso that Ermine know about, and she don't do them anything."

"Yes, but that Ermine mussa find out seh Fonso going take me to town. Once I have the baby, Fonso going carry me and the baby to Kingston, set we up in our own room there. Once he do that, that Ermine know Fonso would never bother with the like of she again."

Theresa felt hurt by the fact that Cissy was planning to leave her, yet hadn't mentioned a single thing, but the word obeah put everything else out of her mind. The thought of obeah caused her to shiver the same way the thought of the Blackartman did, for, said Cissy, they were one and the same, the worst thing in the whole wide world. Not even good to talk about. Now here was Ermine working obeah on Cissy.

Once, Theresa had heard her parents talking about Mister Burnham, heard her mother refer to him as "that obeahman," and was startled and frightened to have the terrifying word associated with the kindly faced, smiling Mister Burnham they knew. Was Mister Burnham also then a Blackartman ? She had rushed to ask Cissy, even though it was night and they were all supposed to be in bed. Cissy was outraged.

"Shame on you, Theresa, to even say such a thing. I should wash out your mouth for you with soap, Miss. Father Burnham a obeahman? So yu mother say? Is yu father she get it from, sure as day. Is what I telling you all along, you know. Just because yu skin turn and you live in big house and drive big car, you don't know everything. Father Burnham is a good man. A bush man. He only deal in growing things, things that natural—bush and root and herb and what come from doctor-shop. He don't deal with dead thing—blood and feather and grave dirt and all them sinting. Father spend his whole time counteracting wickedness that obeahman do. If obeahman put it on, Father will take it off."

So now that Cissy said she was obeahed, Theresa asked her, "What you worrying for, Cissy? Just get Mister Burnham to take it off."

But this caused Cissy to weep anew. "Oh, Theresa," she cried. "You are just an innocent chile. The world don't go easy so, you know." And she turned her head to the wall again for a fresh bout of weeping. Eventually it came out. Some obeah was just too powerful even for Mister Burnham. And this was such an obeah.

"How do you know?" Theresa asked. "That's what Mister Burnham tell you?"

"No. I don't even have to go to Father. I just know. Only one man in the whole world work them kind of thing. French obeah. As you look at it you know. Is Haiti fe him mother did come from. A real Madame. Everybody know that. And fe her father was the seventh son of a seventh son and could fly straight to Africa and back in one living second. As you blink yu eye, me a tell you. Nothing can stand against that."

Cissy absolutely refused to say anything more about the obeah, though Theresa knew it must have been something she found outside her room when she woke one morning, or on the path to the water tank, maybe, or when she went to pick chochos or hang out the washing on the line. Something placed where only Cissy would find it, and know it was meant for her. Theresa was so frightened she was glad that Cissy refused to talk any more about it.

But each day Theresa could see Cissy looking wilder and more scared, her eyes becoming more sunken and shadowed. She began to lose weight, she became nervous and irritable, started forgetting things, smashing dishes, dropping pots of food. They heard Mama saying to their father that Cissy was having a serious case of nerves, but it wasn't until the day Cissy actually fainted, dropped boof as she walked across the yard, that Mama took matters in hand. She bundled Cissy up and got Papa to drive them to Dr. Carter. Dr. Carter spent a long time examining her but he couldn't find a single thing wrong with Cissy or the baby. "First-time nerves" he said, and packed her off with something to calm her down.

Cissy didn't believe him. "But, Cissy," Theresa kept telling her, "he says the baby's all right. Mama says he told her that you and the baby all right. See, nothing wrong with you."

But Cissy knew better. She began to talk wildly to Theresa about going mad, about wandering spirits and her Aunt Millie, about how unbearable it would be not to have a child. She went about her work in a daze, her eyes unseeing, her hands shaking. And she got thinner and thinner.

Theresa kept pleading with Cissy to go and see Mister Burnham.

"How you stay so, Cissy?" she asked whenever they were alone. "Why you just don't make up your mind to go and see Mister Burnham? What you waiting for?"

"Ai, mi chile," Cissy would say, sighing and shaking her head and breaking into a fresh bout of weeping. "Girl, is not everything you understand, ya. Some things not even Father powerful enough to undo."

Theresa became so disturbed that she too began to have sleepless nights, or she slept fitfully and had terrible nightmares and would jump out of bed screaming and drenched with sweat. Her mother kept on asking her what was wrong and she kept on telling her "nothing," until she also was dragged off to Dr. Carter. "Too highly strung," he said, and prescribed something to settle *her* nerves.

℮

One morning, during the summer vacation, Theresa woke up and knew what she had to do. It came to her just like that. If Cissy would not go to Mister Burnham, then she, Theresa, would have to go to him on her behalf. The minute she decided this, her heart felt lighter and she could hardly wait for breakfast to be over and for everyone to go about their business so she could sneak off to Mister Burnham's. She had decided not to tell anyone, not even Cissy. As soon as Theresa saw her mother settled at her sewing machine, she slipped out of the house and ran, taking the short cut to the main road, dashing across it with her heart beating wildly, to stand trembling in front of Mister Burnham's gate. She was so frightened, it took her quite a while to recover her voice and call out, "Hello. Anybody home? Hello. Mrs. Burnham?" To her own ears her voice sounded so thin she knew no one would hear her, and she shifted the silver sixpence she had carried from her right to her left hand and bent down and picked up a small stone and used it to knock on the gate. But though her knock got bolder and bolder there was no response and no sign of life inside that she could see when she peeped through the slats of the gate. Her courage began to fail and she would have turned back but, thinking of Cissy, she lifted the latch, pushed open the gate, and entered Mister Burnham's yard. She had barely shut the gate behind her when two dogs came rushing out from around the back, barking madly as she stood stock-still, too terrified to move as they bounded towards her. But as they neared, they seemed to recognize her from the earlier visits with Cissy and their barks turned to happy sniffs and wagging of tails. They followed her as she went up to the front door of the house and knocked, out of politeness, but she knew that Mrs. Burnham would have shut the door only if she were going out, and the windows were closed.

All at once the sound of doves cooing drew her to the side of the house, where she looked open-mouthed with amazement at all the things in Mister Burnham's yard. There were the flagpoles, which could be seen from the road, and the dovecotes, but there were other strange structures: tree stumps with calabash bowls perched on top of them; in some of the calabashes there were bougainvillea flowers and croton leaves, on another pole there was a strange metal object. Horseshoes were nailed up on the side of the house and on the dovecote. There were plants and bushes growing everywhere, some up against the house, at the far side a whole field of them planted out in rows, looking not at all like the plants in other people's gardens.

But what really drew her was the building right behind the house, separated from it by a clean-swept yard. She never knew it was there, for it could not be seen from the road. It was a rectangular structure, much bigger than the house itself. The narrow side nearest the house was walled in wattle-and-daub to form a room which she couldn't see into, for the windows were shuttered. It had two doors, one on the side facing the house and the other leading to the larger room, but these were also closed.

She could look right into the big room, for there were no walls, only the poles which held up the roof. In the centre of the thatched roof was a small circle, open to the sky, and through it the centre pole projected. The dirt floor was tamped hard as cement, and around the centre pole strange pictures and symbols had been freshly drawn in chalk; she could see fragments of earlier pictures that had been rubbed out in the clay.

At one end, where the smaller room was located, there was a wooden platform. Every inch of the wall behind it, including the door cut into it, was covered with paintings. She recognized scenes from the Bible, Jesus and his disciples, and signs and symbols like those in her church. But these didn't look quite like the religious scenes they got on their Sunday School picture cards. For one thing, they all ran into one another with nothing to define each one, and they were much more colourful and lively. And all the people, Jesus included, were black. On a stand in front, which looked like an altar, for it had a white lace cloth draped over it, there was a large book that looked like a Bible, a large wooden cross, lots of jars with water, some with flowers and croton leaves, and rows and rows of candles.

Although she had never seen a room like this before, more and more it reminded her of a church, for rough benches were arranged in two rows in front of the platform. It seemed natural for her to go in and sit on a bench in the front row to wait for Mister Burnham. As she sat, the dogs which had been following her came in and lay at her feet. She felt very safe and peaceful there.

Now she was inside, she could see a large board nailed to a post to the left side of the platform. Someone had written all over it in white paint, the words spilling over the edges and continuing onto the next line in eccentric fashion, the letters badly formed, the spelling funny, too, as if the writer had never been taught. But, as if the person didn't care, the painted letters were jauntily decorated with swirls and squiggles and dots. She thought she recognized the drawing of a key, and, as far as she could make out, for it took her a long time to read it, the writing below it said, or was trying to say: "Come unto me all ye that are heavy laden and I will give you rest."

Below that was a drawing of a dove with a twig in its beak. Then:

> All Welcome.
> Father Burnham. M.H.C., G.M.M.W., D.D., K.R.G.D.
>   Bringer of Light.
>   Professor of Peace.
>   Restorer of Confidence.
>   Discerner of Hearts.
> Consultation and advice.

Theresa read the phrases, not understanding what all of them meant, but she was sure nevertheless they were saying something about Cissy's problems. Who more than Cissy needed Light, Peace, Confidence? She didn't know what "Discerner of Hearts" was, but she liked how the words sounded.

Just then, though she hadn't heard a sound, the dogs bounded up and Mister Burnham himself appeared through the painted door. He didn't seem at all surprised to see her, as he came and sat on the edge of the platform in front of where she sat, smiling and beaming as he always did, his short legs barely touching the ground.

"And how's the Little Mistress today?" he asked in his big booming voice.

"Well, thank you, Mister Burnham."

"The Little Mistress is troubled?" he asked in a softer voice.

"It says 'Restorer of confidence. Discerner of hearts...'" she started to say. She wanted to ask him what this last thing meant but suddenly she stopped. Suppose Cissy was wrong and Mister Burnham was the Blackartman. Suppose discerner meant stealing, stealing children's hearts. Her own heart was beating so loudly she was sure he could hear it, could know exactly where it was located, could simply grab it and tear it out. She desperately wanted to get up and run, but, as in the nightmares, her body felt like lead.

But Mister Burnham only said in an even softer voice: "Ah. You are the Little Mistress that can read so good. You are the bright one."

She was so surprised to hear him say this, it took some of her fear away. Surely the Blackartman couldn't be someone who knew her? Plus, Mister Burnham didn't have a car. And he drank their milk.

"I'm Theresa," she said.

"I know. Cissy friend. Long time I don't see Cissy."

"Mister Burnham. Cissy . . . ," but she couldn't go on. Embarrassed, she held out the sixpence. He took it without comment and, pulling out his thread-bag, dropped it in.

"You want a consultation?" he asked.

"Well, not for me. For Cissy. Mister Burnham, you know bad obeah on Cissy. Ermine put it there. Mister Burnham, please do something to take the obeah off Cissy. Or else she going mad. And she's my friend. I can't let her go mad." And she burst into tears.

Mister Burnham didn't say anything but produced a newly pressed handkerchief and handed it to her. In between wiping her eyes and blowing her nose, she noticed that he was not looking at her, he was looking out the window and seemed very serious, quite unlike the clownish Mister Burnham who came to pay for the milk.

Finally he said, "I know all about Cissy."

"So you can help?"

"Perhaps. Perhaps not. Cissy own self must ask."

"But she won't come."

"Right."

She waited for him to say more about Cissy. Instead, he said, "You mustn't worry so much about those other ones, you know. You worry that you not pretty, that you don't have tall hair, that you don't hear when yu mother talk to you. You fret that nobody love you. Now, what you need to do is stop fretting. Cast yu eye around you. Look at the flowers, the clouds, the butterflies. You see them worrying? No sah. They just going about their business same way, happy to be alive. Look at you. Such a sweet little gal. You not sick. You not poor. You have a nice Mammy and Daddy to look after you. Much more than all those other children about. You are going to grow up to be a fine lady, for you have a big, big heart. But you must stop feeling bad bout yuself."

She didn't say anything but looked at him. How did he know? But then she thought, this Mister Burnham knows everything. Cissy was right. This Mister Burnham was not the silly little man who came to their yard making jokes with their father. He was not an evil man, as their mother thought. This Mister Burnham was a serious man, someone you could put your trust in.

"Cissy . . . ?" she asked.

"If you want something really bad, you see, you must make sure that it is something that good for you," he said. "Plenty time we want something bad-bad but when we get it, it stick in we craw." She wondered what that had to do with Cissy.

"Well, Little Mistress, they probably wondering what happen to you," he said briskly and stood up, and she found herself standing, too, walking with Mister Burnham out through his yard to the road.

Although she had not got what she came for, she felt happy, as if relieved of a great burden. Mister Burnham held her hand and walked her across the road, and at the short cut to her yard, he wished her good day.

"Come again, Little Mistress, any time you want. You have a friend." She set off smiling, proud to have a friend like Mister Burnham. When she had walked quite a distance, she heard him calling out to her: "Cissy. Maybe you can help Cissy. You have a big enough heart."

She started to ask him what he meant, but he was gone; and when she got back home, without anyone seeing her, she was surprised to find the silver sixpence in her hand.

⌁

Theresa kept her secret to herself all day, though she was almost bursting with excitement. She kept away from Cissy, so afraid was she of spilling the news to her at the wrong moment. She knew that the story of her visit had to be told to Cissy only when they were alone and Cissy was in the right mood to receive it.

When she finally entered Cissy's room that afternoon, she had started to talk before she even closed the door, and was gratified to see that her news made Cissy show some interest for the first time in weeks in something other than her own problem.

"You!" Cissy said. "You go alone to see Father?" She was incredulous because Theresa was the shyest person she knew; she would hide even when her own aunts and uncles came to visit. Now here was Theresa going off alone. "By yu own self. What a thing!" she exclaimed in admiration.

"Mister Burnham send you greetings," Theresa said, wondering how this could have popped into her head. "Say he long to see you till he short. Say you going to have a bouncing baby boy."

Cissy was interested despite herself. "Him really say that?"

"Weighing seven and a half pounds."

"Theresa! You taking me mek poppyshow."

"If you think a lie, spit in mi eye," Theresa boldly offered Cissy's own challenge to her.

"Well . . . a don't know." Theresa could see Cissy filling up with doubts again. "You tell him it real bad?"

"The baddest. But I didn't have to tell him. He know all about it already. Cho. Mister Burnham just laugh. Say why you don't have more faith? Say nothing put on yet that can't take off. Say you need a bath bad-bad. Need to have River Jordan wash right over you. Cleanse you of evil. Bring you light. Restore your confidence."

Theresa wondered where all of this was coming from; she knew she was not half as good a liar as Jane, yet here she was making up all these things to tell Cissy. Cissy wondered too at how Theresa could suddenly talk so well, she really sounded like Father Burnham. Perhaps she wasn't telling lies, perhaps she had been to see Father after all.

But it was an uphill battle with Cissy. For weeks she seesawed between wanting to believe in Father Burnham and falling prey to her fright about what Ermine had put on her. Wanting to believe Theresa and remembering how her heart dropped clear to her footbottom, how she wet herself, felt that her whole insides had fallen away, when she saw it, the thing that she had stepped on. That was the worst part, if only she han't mashed it, had sidestepped it, then she wouldn't have seen, might have gone on unknowing, believing it was just any little thing, something she could get Father to deal with.

But her own mother had told her what to look out for, how to know, told her that time when Cissy was small and Aunt Millie had gone right off her head and the police had come in a Black Maria and taken her away in a straitjacket to Bellevue asylum. They had done something their people had never done before: asked the police to come and take one of their own to Bellevue, for there was mad and there was mad, and they knew that no power on earth could help her, so they let the white people look after her in their hospital since the Millie they knew no longer existed.

When she finally drowned herself in the hospital water tank, ripping apart the protective wire mesh with her bare hands to throw herself in, they said, "Jesus be praised." One year later, they held a memorial for her like nobody had ever seen before, dancing three nights straight to summon her to be reunited with her family. But the power that had been used on Aunt Millie was so great she couldn't find her way back, not even when the drumming went on for nine hours one time, when Isaac dropped with exhaustion and Clayton grabbed the drum without missing a beat and Isaac came back and took over from him again, for the spirits were arriving so fast the room was thick with them, spirits from everywhere, but no Millie. No matter how hard they tried to call her, Aunt Millie couldn't find her way back. To this day, her spirit hasn't rested.

After what happened to Aunt Millie, Cissy's mother had taken her to get all extra powerful new guzu to wear around her waist, but she had also warned her that there were certain things that no guzu could protect her from, and she had to learn to be careful about everything and not offend a soul. She had to learn to live right.

Which is exactly what Cissy used to tell Theresa all the time when Theresa was small.

"Theresa," she would say, faithfully repeating what her own mother had taught her, "never, never fling water outa door like that when you done wash yu face at night." Theresa had a slop pail, part of the pretty china set on her washstand, but she never used it, preferring the big-people feeling it gave her to open the window wide and lift up the basin and dash the water outside.

"I keep telling you, you suppose to be polite at all times to them Ol' People, for if they be good people, only their body leave this earth, their spirit come back after the nine night and they right out there, protecting you," Cissy would patiently explain. "If you treat them good, and show respect, and feed them now and then, they will look out for you, keep you from harm's way. That's why I keep telling you, Theresa, never fling anything outa door without first say, 'Ol' People: mind yuself,' so they can get out of the way. For you wouldn't feel insult and want to do bad things to somebody who fling cold dutty water in yu face that way?"

But Theresa never seemed to pay any attention to Cissy's warnings and, after a while, Cissy stopped worrying about her, for it came to her one day that people like Theresa didn't need that kind of protecting for nothing seemed to threaten them, people with their turn-skin and big house and big car. They were born protected. It was only people like her who needed charms and baths, ceremonies and drums to protect them, who needed to be so careful, to live good in the world, for there was nothing else between them and the night, between them and the whole world full of dangers out there, nothing else to fight off straitjacket and Bellevue. No big house with electric light to drive away duppies at night, no big car to whisk them safely past dark corners and crossroads where Rolling Calf and Three-Foot-Horse waiting for every poor black sinner forced to walk foot.

So Cissy ignored Theresa's breaches of etiquette and carried on as her own mother had taught her: Never spill salt without flinging a pinch behind you. Don't talk loud at night or duppy will catch yu voice. If you want to gaze at full moon, look at it in a basin of water. Always walk with corn grain or rice to throw in case Rolling Calf follow you. Don't comb yu hair at night for it will make you forgetful. Wrap knife and fork in a page of the Bible and sleep with it under yu pillow to keep evil spirit away. Don't walk backwards or you will curse yu parents. Don't throw fingernail cutting and hair from comb away careless; hide and bury them, or people will use them against you.

And Cissy always remembered to tread carefully, day or night, as she went about her business, in order to sidestep certain things, should you happen to make somebody grudgeful enough to put them in your way. For, if you didn't, no power on earth could save you from what befell Aunt Millie.

ᵔᵕᵔ

Theresa thought she could see a change of some sort in Cissy and it made her try harder.

"Mister Burnham, that day I went to see him, say he see you big woman with five sons. And two daughters," she would say casually as she played with Cissy's beads. If that got no response she was amazed to find that she could continue talking. "Say you make to have children. Say you'll have them easy, too. You will have children and grandchildren around you in your old age. To play with my children and grandchildren."

"Father never say that!" Cissy would angrily protest. "You too young to know anything bout having children."

Theresa would laugh and say, "No, I made that part up." And occasionally, now, Cissy would laugh along with her.

Cissy desperately wanted to believe that what Theresa was telling her was true; desperately wanted to be able to go to Father Burnham and have him take this heavy burden off her and give her peace. She didn't want to die or go mad like Aunt Millie, didn't want to become a wandering spirit. Suppose her mother wasn't always right? After all, Father had helped her many times before, been like a true father to her from the time she left her mother's house as a young girl. And her mother was far away: she hadn't seen her for a long time now. What did she have to lose by going to get a bath from Father Burnham?

Maybe she needed more than a bath. Maybe Father would arrange a special ceremony for her. She could request a Table, a feast to placate the spirits and beg their forgiveness with dancing and singing and drumming. If everything went well, the ancestors would answer the drums, their spirits would come and dance through their children. She felt lightheaded as she thought of the drums talking to the spirits, calling them down, of the nights she had crept out when everyone was asleep to go to Father's yard, danced and fallen into the spirit herself, got home as dawn was breaking. Tired, yes, but ready for the night to come again so she could dance and catch the spirit summoned by the drums at Father Burnham's yard.

But her mind was only fully made up the day Theresa casually said, "You know Mister Burnham did even know what Ermine set on you?" What had Theresa said? Cissy was so shocked she couldn't speak. She had never breathed to a soul what she had seen on the path that day, what her own mother told her to watch out for. Yet Father had known. How could he?

"Theresa, Theresa girl, tell me true. Father did really say so, or you joking?"

"Cissy, you think I could joke about a serious thing like that? Mister Burnham told me he know. I didn't ask him. And Cissy"—Theresa was feeling inspired now—"he say he know what he going to have to put in the bath to counteract it."

"What you saying?"

"Well, he did tell me, he call plenty name, but it's too much for me to remember. I only remember it was seven times seven different bushes and roots and herbs, Mister Burnham said, mix with nine different oil from doctor-shop."

Cissy was convinced now that Theresa couldn't have made that up, because she had known Father to use exactly that kind of recipe to drive out a troublesome duppy that was causing rockstone to fall on a house and pots to go flying off the fire and dishes to smash into the wall and the people inside to run for their lives. Father was particularly proud of that case for it was a celebrated one. It had even been written up in the *Gleaner*, and many learned men from the university had gone down to the house where this was happening to see what they could do. But nobody could do anything, the duppy even chased out the university men, flung stones at their car, caused one to drop his briefcase and another to lose a sandal as they rushed to get away. Nobody could do anything until Father Burnham was called in, but there was nothing in the *Gleaner* about that, for this thing had gone on too long and people had lost interest.

Father Burnham had right away traced the cause to a young boy living in the house. He had had to use all his powers to get rid of the duppy which had taken up residence inside him. He had been proud of that case. It was the toughest he had ever had, he said, it was such a troublesome duppy. But he chased that duppy so well, the people were never troubled again and could go back to their home. Although Father was not a boastful man, one Sunday afternoon when Cissy was there, he couldn't help talking about it to her and Mrs. Burnham, he was so pleased. "Seven time seven bush root and herb I had was to use. The highest remedy for the baddest cause. Pick them myself. Oh, that was a tough one. Seven time seven and nine different oil from the doctor-shop."

How could Theresa know about this, Cissy wondered, unless she had got it straight from Father Burnham?

Cissy decided that she didn't want to go mad, or have her womb turn to ashes, or die, or turn into a wandering spirit, if Father could prevent it, and he seemed to think he could. She wanted to get better and she wanted to have her baby. She would go to him.

Once she decided, she felt a lightening of her spirits, a quickening of her body, as if the baby was still alive. But she didn't think about that. She didn't want to hope too much.

Yet she kept putting off going, as if she were bothered by something else. And she finally had to admit that she was ashamed to go to Father, she'd been ashamed from the start, for in a way she knew she had brought the evil on herself. Her mother had taught her to live right and not offend a soul: Don't act better than other people. Don't be grudgeful and don't cause other people to grudgeful you. For grudgefulness will cause spite and cut-eye and bring you more than you can handle.

And hadn't she herself attracted Ermine's wrath? She had to admit now, she never suspected that Ermine had it in her to get such a bad obeah, she had seriously miscalculated that little dryfoot girl. But she had grudged Ermine her man, taken him away, was going off to Kingston with him even, and that had caused Ermine to turn around and grudge her. As for the man himself, for the first time she realized that she hadn't seen Fonso once since Ermine obeah her. Imagine that. He would have known what Ermine had done, for she would be sure to tell him. And that had been enough to keep him away.

Cissy had been ashamed to go to Father Burnham because she had sorely deceived him. When she went to get something to get her man, he didn't ask who it was, but because he was like a real father to her, he said, "I only hope his name don't begin with the letter F. For I could never encourage you with that at all." And she had lied and said, no, his name began with the letter D. And Father had believed her, for he had given her the charm. But now he knew she had lied, and it was Fonso after all.

The whole thing served her right, Cissy told herself, for if she hadn't been thinking about Fonso that day, hadn't been actually smiling to herself when she thought of Fonso and herself cozy-up together in their own room, in Kingston, she would never have mashed the thing Ermine put in her way, her mind would have been clear as it always was, on the lookout for just that kind of trouble, and she would have been able to sidestep it. That Fonso was the cause of all her troubles.

When it came down to it, she didn't care now if she never saw him again. He could go back to long-mouth Ermine and his other baby mothers. She didn't even want a room in Kingston. "What I want room in Kingston for when I have good-good room right here where I can raise baby?" she asked herself. A son, Father had said, seven and a half pounds.

Cissy screwed up her courage and went to Father Burnham and Father could look into her heart and discern that it was pure again, so he gave her the bath with seven times seven bushes, roots, and herbs. And he said, yes, if she wanted, he could arrange a Table for her. Soon, soon, she begged, for the baby was getting bigger and kicking like mad.

Cissy told Theresa about her visit to Father Burnham and what was in the bath he gave her and how she had decided to give up Fonso and have the baby right there and what kind of guzu she would get for the boy and what she was going to name him though she changed her mind every day and how she would take him to church to be christened by the parson because you couldn't have too much protection in this world and how Theresa would be his godmother and would have to teach him his ABC as soon as he was old enough, before he went to school.

But there were some things she didn't tell Theresa. For although Theresa was her friend and had a big heart, she knew that her kind of people wouldn't understand why someone like her could take the last farthing she had to her name, everything hidden under the floorboard, and give it all to Father Burnham to pay the drummers and prepare for the feast: buy goat and white rooster, rice to cook without salt, rum and showbread and condensed milk for the chocolate tea, candles and everything else for the Table.

Theresa wouldn't understand how badly she needed to be there in Father's yard with everything set up just so, the Table laid with the showbread and the fruit, the candles, the water and the rum, the Bible and the flowers, incense, frankincense and myrrh. The right signs on the floor and the fresh new flag flying to attract the right spirits down the pole. Wouldn't know how badly she needed to be with her own people dressed all in blue robes for cutting and clearing, Sister Brooks with her scissors for cutting away evil, Brother Thom with his whip for driving out devils, Shepherd Casey the warrior with his sword to guard the door, Sister Icilda who cooed like a dove, all her own people feasting and praying and singing with her. And the drums finally calling down the spirits, inviting the ancestors to enter, to possess, to shower her and her son with blessings.

❧

Everyone was surprised by the change in Theresa. Overnight, she seemed to have lost her shyness. Didn't hide away so much, chatted more, hugged her mother every now and then, ran with the other girls to greet her father as he came in, didn't seem as clumsy as she used to be, looked at herself in the mirror almost as often as Jane.

"She's growing up," her mother could be heard telling their father.

Much to their astonishment, when next Mister Burnham came to pay for the milk, she ran out from the side verandah, where the girls usually hid to giggle as they watched him pour out silver sixpences, and rushed to greet him at the gate before he even opened his mouth. "Good morning, *Father* Burnham," she called in her strong new voice. Everyone was amazed to see her chatting away with Mister Burnham as if they were the oldest of friends, to see her proudly walk with him on to the verandah where her father sat, as if she were ushering in an honoured guest.

Carmen Tipling

LUNCHTIME REVOLUTION
A ONE-ACT PLAY

The Cast

Bernie Saunders
Big Joe
Miss Lizzie
Matilda
Postman
Fish Woman
Man
Boy
Announcer
Four Sailors
A Crowd

    Scene 1. *A yard in West Kingston. A building with three rooms, a veranda with about six posts and three or four steps leading into the yard. A table with two chairs on the veranda. Right of the steps sits Big Joe, an old shoemaker, at his work bench. He is a fat, balding Sambo-type in his sixties. He is wearing a striped shirt, brown pants and a blue apron. On the other side of the steps, Miss Lizzie, a washer-woman, is scrubbing at her tub. She is a short, slim, black woman. She wears a simple, faded house dress with large flower patterns on it. Her tub is mounted on a fruit crate. There is an empty stool beside her, also a zinc pan into which she tosses her clothes. Further left from her is a stand-pipe. Two clothes lines are extended from a veranda post to another post offstage.*

Bernie Sanders, a lean, tired-looking black man, in his early twenties, is sitting in the middle of the steps. His hair is high on his head. He wears a faded yellow tee shirt, brown slacks, brown socks and sandals. It is about midday. Throughout the play, Miss Lizzie washes her clothes and hangs them on the line, Big Joe hammers leather and patches the soles of shoes, while Bernie has just finished eating some ackee and saltfish and bread.

BERNIE: *(plate in hand)* This ackee and saltfish set well with me. *(belches)* Thank you, Miss Lizzie.

BIG JOE: Had some meself, boy.

MISS LIZZIE: *(takes plate and returns to tub)* Always willing to feed another mouth, Bernie.

BERNIE: *(relaxes)* Well, the way things tough with me these days, is a good thing ah know you and Big Joe.

BIG JOE: Things always look tough when you just come from country and trying to make it in a big town like Kingston.

BERNIE: You know, when ah was coming to town, me mother tell me about how she used to live in the yard with you and Miss Lizzie. But ah really didn't expect to find you.

MISS LIZZIE: Your mother is a good woman, Bernie—See Big Joe there, ask him—is me and him advise her to go back to Clarendon when she couldn't make it here.

BIG JOE: True. She used to work for some people in St. Andrew, but when them went back to England she just couldn't pick up anything. And you, you was just a little dry foot boy running all over the place, mashing you finger with me hammer and picking up me scraps of leather 'bout you making shoes.

BERNIE: *(leans back laughing)* Maybe ah should really learn the trade, eh, Big Joe?

BIG JOE: It wouldn't do you any harm since you can't find any work.

MISS LIZZIE: Nuh the same thing you say when Bernie first came to live with you, nuh Big Joe. True, you know, Bernie, him sit right where him is now and say: "Miss Lizzie, ah should teach the boy the trade."

BIG JOE: *(nodding his head)* That's exactly what ah said.

BERNIE: *(toying with a piece of leather)* Ah thought about it meself, but ah don't think ah was cut out to be a shoemaker. Ah just don't have the rhythm that Big Joe have when him pounding out a piece of leather.

MISS LIZZIE: Is one whole year since you came here, Bernie. About time something turn up for you, man.

BERNIE: These are key-soap times, Miss Lizzie. Ah tried to get in on some farm-working, them cut down the quota; tried pushing a cart in the market, somebody steal me cart; tried cleaning street, them go on strike and ah lose the work. Things just too tough for me.

BIG JOE: *(hammering leather)* Boy, you think things tough now?

BERNIE: *(picks up foot of shoes)* Things tough, yes . . .

MISS LIZZIE: *(wringing shirt)* Bernie, you sit down on them steps everyday talking 'bout things tough. A big man like you should go back to country go cut cane or dig bauxite dirt.

BIG JOE: *(hammering)* So me tell him. Big man like him ought to be able to find work easy.

BERNIE: *(polishes shoe)* Day in, day out, me tried to look for work, man.

MISS LIZZIE: *(throws shirt into zinc pan)* Ah thought you was supposed to join the army?

BERNIE: Ah made an application.

BIG JOE: *(laughs)* All now you should turn corporal, boy. If you can't get into the army, join the police force. Them need man to catch thief all the time.

BERNIE: Is my fault if the army don't answer me letter?

BIG JOE: No, that is not your fault.

MISS LIZZIE: But it seems to me that the army need able-body young men all the time.

BIG JOE: Thing is, them is taking them own sweet time to answer Bernie's letter.

BERNIE: Is true that.

MISS LIZZIE: You better do something before something do you.

BIG JOE: When him least expect, him might just hear from them.

MISS LIZZIE: Bernie too lazy for my use.

(Bernie and Big Joe laugh out loud)

BERNIE: *(still laughing)* What this country needs is a revolution. *(more serious)* We ought to shake it up a bit. Everybody taking everybody else for granted. What we need is a revolution to shake up things so that a small man can have a day.

MISS LIZZIE: Talk, talk . . . Go out on the street and hustle like everyone else.

BERNIE: Is steal you want me to go steal?

MISS LIZZIE: *(squeezing pants)* Bernie, nobody not sending you to go thief . . . just to help youself. If you ask me, you stay bad, boy, you stay bad.

BERNIE: *(smiles, shines shoes)* Now, Miss Lizzie, is your condition any better?

MISS LIZZIE: *(scrubbing)* You hear me complaining?

BERNIE: When the revolution comes is people like you going to mess it up.

MISS LIZZIE: I don't want any part of any revolution.

BIG JOE: So you planning to revolt, eh Bernie?

BERNIE: First thing, Miss Lizzie wouldn't even know what side to be on.

BIG JOE: Tell us about it, Bernie. Talk, boy, talk.

BERNIE: I don't have to wear a beard and carry on like a Rastafarian to believe that it will happen.

BIG JOE: Just warn me, my boy. I'll come and see you in action.

BERNIE: *(rising, strikes pose like a preacher)* It will be a new day for people like you and me. You, Big Joe, you won't have to make new shoes for other people and patch your own. You will have new shoes for yourself. *(turns to Miss Lizzie)* Miss Lizzie, no more washing other people's clothes.

MISS LIZZIE: *(laughs)* Yes, Mister Bernie, sir. You just tell me what I will be doing.

BERNIE: *(sits, disgusted)* If people like us don't believe in the revolution, it will never happen.

BIG JOE: I don't see how any revolution is going to make me better off.

MISS LIZZIE: Better off? You likely to end up dead.

BERNIE: Why should anyone die?

BIG JOE: Boy, shut you mouth. You ever see a revolution where nobody died? *(snicker from Bernie)* If nobody dies, then you can't tell me that it is a revolution.

BERNIE: It's going to be a bloodless coup, man.

BIG JOE: I have to see it first.

BERNIE: And when it's over there will be jobs for everyone. All me might even find a work.

BIG JOE: All that just to find yourself a job, boy?

BERNIE: Cho, Big Joe, man, as 'cording to how I understand it, things always improve after a revolution.

MISS LIZZIE: *(laughs out loud)* Improve, yes . . . not for people like you, though.

BIG JOE: Right. All we would end up with is some new leader.

BERNIE: Cho, new leader no mean nothing. A revolution will turn things around; give us more of the action.

BIG JOE: Us? Miss Lizzie, him talking like you and me involved.

BERNIE: You involved yes. When I listen to the talk ah can't help but believe it meself.

BIG JOE: Whoever filling up you mind with all that revolutionary talk just don't know what them talking 'bout.

MISS LIZZIE: Rumour, Bernie, me boy. Just plain and simple rumour. As the Bible says: there will be wars and rumours of wars. Well is like you now—rumouring 'bout a revolution.

BIG JOE: True word, Miss Lizzie, true word.

BERNIE: Ah telling you both like ah naw tell you: all this revolution needs now is a plan and some real strategy.

BIG JOE: Hear them big words, Miss Liz. The man serious.

BERNIE: Serious, yes. Some people don't see the need for a revolt here, but that's just it. There is no one big reason to point out why there should be one, but all sorts of little things hiding in various corners. Little things that we all take for granted. But when the revolution comes, you will see the light.

(As the door behind Bernie opens, there is the blast of a radio playing a Reggae tune. A young American sailor steps out. He closes the door behind him, cutting off the sound of the radio. The sailor quickly makes his way down the steps and out of the yard)

MISS LIZZIE: *(watching sailor)* God protect us from the sins of that whore. Dear God, *(looks to the sky)* help her to see the light so that she can mend her sinful, wicked ways.

(as Miss Lizzie continues to stare in the sky beseeching God, Bernie and Big Joe are laughing)

MISS LIZZIE: *(back to earth)* You go on laughing, Missa Bernie. Everyday you sit there talk, talk. God only help those who help themselves.

*(Matilda, a young, good-looking black woman, steps out
on the veranda. Blast from the radio again. Matilda
is wearing a tight, slinky black dress. She stands before
her door, hands akimbo)*

MATILDA: For the last time, Miss Lizzie, keep your big mouth out of
my business. *(Matilda turns back into her room, slamming the door
behind her)*

BERNIE: *(in faked confidence to Joe)* Now, there is one person who
don't need no help. *(the two men laugh again)*

BIG JOE: True word, true word.

MISS LIZZIE: You talk about revolution, Bernie. One day, one day,
this place is bound to go up in smoke. With all the sinning going on around here, it won't need any revolution to burn this
place down.

*(the door behind Bernie opens again. Matilda steps
out wearing black dress, red shoes, red clutch bag. She
wears a lot of make-up and has the general appearance
of a small-town whore)*

MATILDA: *(stops beside the two men)* Hi, Bernie, Big Joe . . .

BIG JOE: Good afternoon, Matilda. How's business?

MATILDA: *(moves nearer to Joe)* It's better than repairing shoes.

*(Matilda digs into her purse for a cigarette,
comes up with one and lights it)*

BERNIE: You look sharp today.

MATILDA: *(smokes, purse in right hand)* It pays to look sharp these
days, Bernie. *(Matilda laughs lightly as she turns away from the two
men and swings her hips past Miss Lizzie)*

BIG JOE: Watch out, Bernie, watch out. *(Miss Lizzie begins to hum a
nameless tune)*

MATILDA: *(at the gate)* More time, Bernie . . . Big Joe . . . *(she puffs on
her cigarette as she swings down the street. Bernie rises from the steps
and points after Matilda)*

BERNIE: Now, there goes one person I would like to get some help from.

BIG JOE: *(amused)* You have money, boy?

> *(both men laugh. Miss Lizzie carries her zinc pan to*
> *the clothes line to hang out her clothes. Throughout the*
> *next section she sings: "Running up the shining way,"*
> *as she pins her clothes to the clothes line)*

MISS LIZZIE: *(singing)* Satan on my track, and he tries to turn me back, I am running up the shining way . . .

BIG JOE: Matilda is a business woman, Bernie.

BERNIE: This is business talk, Big Joe.

> *(sound of a postman's bell ringing)*

BIG JOE: Small talk and promises won't get you anywhere with her. You have to talk cash before you can talk big. *(sound of bell ringing as the Postman rides up to the gate and holds out the mail)*

BERNIE: My money is as good as dollar bills.

BIG JOE: Stop talk in vain. Go for the mail before the postman ride off with it.

MISS LIZZIE: *(sings and hangs cloths)* I am running up the shining way, running up the shining way, Satan on my track and he tries to turn me back, I am running up the shining way.

> *(Bernie gets the mail and reads the envelopes*
> *as he walks back slowly)*

BERNIE: *(holds up envelope)* One for you, Miss Lizzie. Look like it's from Son-son in New York. What a way the American stamp pretty . . .

> *(Miss Lizzie comes forward wiping her hand on her apron.*
> *She takes the letter from Bernie and goes to the stool*
> *beside her tub and reads it)*

MISS LIZZIE: Thank you, Bernie. Is about time that boy write me.

BERNIE: *(surprised)* The other one is for me.

BIG JOE: *(laughs)* Bring me letter, boy. Is you know who to send you letter through the mail?

(Bernie opens the envelope dramatically. Sits on the steps)

BERNIE: Serious, man. It's from the Defence Force . . . addressed to me. Remember I told you that I used this address . . . is my letter fe true. *(pause)* Hey, hey, hear how them start out. *(coughs)* Dear Sir, *(pause)* to rawtid, *(stamps his foot)* Dear Sir . . . you see it dey now . . . see it dey . . .

BIG JOE: Well *(pause)* Them want you or dem don't want you?

BERNIE: *(leaps up from steps)* Them want me, yes . . . them want me to come in with the next group of recruits for training. *(pushes letter into Joe's hand)* Read that. *(Big Joe puts down his shoes and takes the letter. Reads it quickly)*

BIG JOE: Now you can get off your arse and do something for a change.

BERNIE: Congratulate me first, huh man . . .

BIG JOE: Boy, you don't have to worry about one thing now.

BERNIE: Cho, Big Joe, me just get the letter, man.

BIG JOE: Not a thing. Them army man get free everything.

BERNIE: *(back on steps)* Give me little time. Ah want it to sink in good.

BIG JOE: Free food, free place to live, free clothes, free protection.

(Miss Lizzie finishes her letter, but remains seated. she stares ahead unaware of Bernie's joy. Then she hangs her head. In the street the ice man goes by pushing his cart and shouting: "Ice water man, ice water man." Suddenly, Bernie jumps up from the steps and snaps to attention)

BERNIE: *(marching)* Left, right, left . . . left, right, left . . . halt . . . up one, up two . . . h-a-l-t. *(prances back to steps)* Just imagine me at

Review. You can see me marching in all kinds of ceremonial parades. . . . and for Independence!

BIG JOE: Cool it, boy. Just wait till them get you up into New Castle. Cold bus' you shirt so hard . . . cold night push parades and ceremonies straight out of you mind. You begin to wonder what kind of fool you is to join up in the first place. Just wait. *(Bernie turns to Miss Lizzie who is wiping her face in her apron, letter in one hand)*

BERNIE: Miss Lizzie, you hear me good *(slowly)* fortune. *(loud)* Miss Lizzie. *(moves closer to her)* What wrong? Something happen to Son-son? Anything wrong in the letter?

(Miss Lizzie shakes her head, unable to speak. Waves letter and wipes tears from her eyes. Big Joe joins them)

BIG JOE: What wrong, Miss Lizzie?

MISS LIZZIE: Son-son gone clear to America and go get himself arrested.

BERNIE: What?

BIG JOE: Say wha'?

MISS LIZZIE: Son-son arrested.

BERNIE: Arrested for what?

BIG JOE: Hold on, Bernie man, take it easy. Miss Lizzie tell us what the letter say.

MISS LIZZIE: The boy gone clear to New York, gone demonstrate and now them arrest him. *(cries)* Him in jail . . . my Son-son . . . who don't even know how the inside of a reform school stay. Here, read it, Big Joe. *(Joe takes the letter)*

BERNIE: Is how Son-son so stupid?

BIG JOE: *(reading)* Hush. The boy should know what him doing. *(pause)* It don't sound so bad, Miss Lizzie, the boy is alright. See where him say that them let him go, *(points to line and shows her)* right here on the other side of the first page.

MISS LIZZIE: Is where him say that. Me never read that part.

BIG JOE: *(reads aloud)* "They allowed me to leave the station two hours after it was clear that I had nothing to do with the demonstrations. I know that . . . "

MISS LIZZIE: Thank God. Thank you, Massa Jesus, thank you.

> *(suddenly the sound of someone singing draws their attention to the gate. Matilda appears at the gate, struggling with a young sailor who is singing: "Rum and Coca-Cola . . . working for the Yankee dollar." He is drunk. Matilda holds him firmly and leads him through the gate)*

SAILOR: Hi, you-all. *(he breaks away from Matilda's hold and does a version of the rumba)* Can you-all do the limbo, man? *(the others look on silently as Matilda struggles with the sailor. She takes him across the yard and up the steps)*

MATILDA: Let's go, Sailor-boy. Up the steps, one, two, three . . .

> *(she opens the door, pushes him inside, steps in, and then slams the door behind her)*

MISS LIZZIE: *(recovers)* Heaven protect us . . . *(Miss Lizzie sticks her letter in her apron, goes up to the clothes line and continues to pin up her clothes. Big Joe goes back to his bench and Bernie back to the steps)*

BIG JOE: Well, Bernie, all I can say is good luck in the army.

BERNIE: Sure, man.

MISS LIZZIE: *(struggling with clothes)* Dear Lord, have mercy on our souls . . .

> *(the lights fade slowly as they hold their positions)*

Scene 2. *Same yard. Early morning about three months later. Same setting. Big Joe at work bench. Miss Lizzie comes through the gate with her fruit basket on her head, a stool under one arm. She unloads near her wash tub, which is in the same position as before.*

MISS LIZZIE: Morning, Big Joe.

BIG JOE: How the fruit sales going today?

MISS LIZZIE: Ah don't know why ah bother with it.

BIG JOE: Good business or bad business?

MISS LIZZIE: Is just a few school children passing by bother to stop and buy something.

BIG JOE: People stop buying oranges in the morning?

MISS LIZZIE: It would seem so, but ah think the supermarket down the road putting me out of me little sideline.

BIG JOE: *(cleaning up bench)* Don't make that stop you. You see me . . . them could build a hundred shoe factories I still carrying on with my trade right here. Plenty people still rely on a fruit woman like you and a shoemaker like me. Don't let any big-time competition force you out of you business. Me and you too old to start to look for new lines.

MISS LIZZIE: *(laughs lightly)* Is true, that. With a little here and a little there both end bound to meet now and then.

(the voice of a fish woman is heard coming up the street)

FISH WOMAN: Who buy fresh *(drawls)* f-i-s-h. Fresh fish again, who *(drawls)* b-u-y. Who buy fresh *(drawls)* f-i-s-h. Fresh, fish again, who *(drawls)* b-u-y.

BIG JOE: *(runs to gate)* Fish woman, fish woman, stop. Ah want some fish.

(the woman comes to the gate and Joe selects his fish. Improvising dialogue, they go through the ritual of type of fish, weight, price, and finally he buys a large parrot fish. As the fish woman leaves, Big Joe glances down the street and sees Bernie in uniform approaching)

BIG JOE: *(shouts)* Hey, hey. Watch the soldier man, nuh. *(calls)* Miss Lizzie, come watch Bernie goose-stepping down the road.

(Miss Lizzie comes to the fence and looks down the street.)

MISS LIZZIE: Is Bernie that?

BIG JOE: Him look good, een. *(Bernie comes to the gate and into the yard. Pleased, they surround him)*

BERNIE: Hi, Miss Lizzie, Big Joe . . .

MISS LIZZIE: *(steps back)* Make me step back and get a good look at you. Boy, you look good fe true.

BIG JOE: The uniform fit you. In three months them make him look like a good, good soldier.

BERNIE: *(snaps to attention)* Private Sanders, sir. *(Big Joe slaps him on the back and all three laugh heartily)*

BERNIE: How's everyone?

MISS LIZZIE: Just as always . . . washing, fixing shoes, selling fruit, and God only knows what Matilda is up to. Haven't laid eyes on her for days.

BERNIE: How Son-son?

(Big Joe leaves with fish)

MISS LIZZIE: Fine, me dear boy; him coming home for Christmas.

(Big Joe returns to his bench and proceeds to cut up strips of leather. Bernie brushes off one of the steps and takes his regular seat. Miss Lizzie begins washing at her tub)

BIG JOE: How New Castle treat you, boy?

BERNIE: Migod, Big Joe, the place cold, you see.

BIG JOE: Ah told you . . .

BERNIE: Hearing about it and feeling it is two different things.

MISS LIZZIE: *(washing)* Is what them teach you besides marching, boy?

BERNIE: *(rises, walks towards her)* All kinds of things: emergency tactics, about guns, mechanics, history. Miss Lizzie, I never realise that there was so much I didn't know or even heard about.

BIG JOE: *(pleased)* Now you on the right track.

MISS LIZZIE: And him just start . . .

    (Bernie takes a stance like the "Thinker," one foot on the steps.
    Big Joe takes a keen look at his boots)

BIG JOE: Them shoes tough . . . look real tough, boy . . .

BERNIE: *(stamps foot)* Built for life, man, built for life.

BIG JOE: *(laughs)* If the soles ever wear out you know where to get them fixed. *(they both laugh)* If, that is . . . if.

BERNIE: *(picks up one of Big Joe's shoes)* May as well help with the polishing while I'm around.

BIG JOE: Thanks, boy. Sure missed your help around here. *(looks up into Bernie's face)* How's the revolution coming?

BERNIE: *(polishing)* You seem to take this thing for a joke.

BIG JOE: Not exactly.

BERNIE: You ever ask yourself why I join the army?

BIG JOE: No.

BERNIE: Guess.

BIG JOE: 'Cause you was looking for work?

BERNIE: *(puts down shoes)* You ask me about the revolution, right?

BIG JOE: *(smiles)* You join the army because of the revolution?

BERNIE: Right . . . to learn about guns . . . to be prepared when the revolution comes.

BIG JOE: That still don't tell me anything, man.

BERNIE: What do you want to hear?

BIG JOE: I want to hear some factual things about this revolution.

BERNIE: Such as . . .

BIG JOE: Such as who is going to be in it.

BERNIE: The people . . .

BIG JOE: Where is it going to happen?

BERNIE: Right here on this island.

BIG JOE: When? And what signs to look for to know that it is the real thing? *(Bernie rises and paces back and forth beside Big Joe)*

BERNIE: I don't know all those things, man, but I'll tell you this much: when it begins, you will say to yourself *(faces Big Joe dramatically)* this is it, man, this is what Bernie was talking about.

BIG JOE: *(laughs)* Beautiful, Bernie, beautiful . . .

MISS LIZZIE: Forget that nonsense about revolution, Bernie, and listen to the sense the army trying to teach you.

BIG JOE: Miss Lizzie, you and I will either have to choose sides or watch it from the sidelines, eh?

MISS LIZZIE: Sidelines for me . . .

BERNIE: *(relaxes)* One day . . . one day . . .

> *(the lights fade as he leans back on the steps and
> stares blankly ahead of him.)*

Scene 3. *About a month later. Same scene as before. The sun is high in the sky. Loud sound of a factory horn announcing the lunch hour is heard in the distance.*

BIG JOE: Hear the conchie, Miss Lizzie?

MISS LIZZIE: Lunch-time already?

BIG JOE: *(putting down shoes, rises)* Those of us who don't have the lunch can always take the time.

MISS LIZZIE: *(wiping her hands in her apron)* True that. *(shouts of "Fire, Fire" are heard in the distance. Sounds of sirens and loud blasts and screams)*

BIG JOE: What kind of thing is that in the middle of the day, een? *(Shouts toward Matilda's door)* Fire! Fire!

   (Big Joe and Miss Lizzie run to the gate. They turn around as a young sailor comes rushing out of Matilda's room, still in the process of dressing. The blast of a radio is heard)

MISS LIZZIE: *(laughs)* Is what going on around here? *(Miss Lizzie and Big Joe step back from the gate to let the sailor through, just as Matilda comes to her door)*

MATILDA: You haven't paid me, you bastard! *(a group of people from neighbouring yards has gathered quickly at the gate at the shout of fire. They laugh at Matilda and the sailor coming down the street)*

BIG JOE: *(shouts after sailor)* Boy, you forgot to pay. *(more laughter from the group at the gate)*

MISS LIZZIE: Divine retribution catching up with some of us.

MATILDA: *(shaking her fist)* Dirty, rotten bastard! *(Matilda turns back into her room and slams the door behind her)*

BIG JOE: *(To Man outside gate)* Is what going on with all the fire and shouting?

MAN: Ah not so sure meself, but a young boy just come off the bus up the road say that a whole heap of ragamuffins swarming all over town and Spanish Town Road burning and looting all the stores, stopping buses and carrying on most disgraceful . . .

BIG JOE: Say what?

MAN: I was heading for town meself when I began to see the smoke and hear the noise.

BIG JOE: Hey, hey, this must be the revolution, man. This has to be it . . .

MISS LIZZIE: I have to go see this.

BIG JOE: *(grabs her arm)* Hold on . . .

MISS LIZZIE: Hold on, for what?

BIG JOE: If this is the revolution, the best place for you is right here.

MAN: I wouldn't advise anyone to set foot in town according to what I hear.

BIG JOE: According to how I understand it, we should all be taking part.

MAN: Me, take part?

BIG JOE: Yes, you and everybody else.

MAN: Not with police and soldiers all over the place.

BIG JOE: Soldiers? *(a Boy comes running up the street with loot in his hands. He carries several pairs of shirts, pants and shoes)*

BIG JOE: Hey, you. *(the Boy stops)* Where you coming from? *(as the Boy comes to the gate, the Crowd gathers around him)*

BOY: *(breathless)* Spanish Town Road. You want to see people a-loot . . .

MISS LIZZIE: Where?

BOY: Everywhere. Everything burst open, everything crash and the small man is having him day.

MAN: Where you got all those things?

BOY: Free things out there like sand . . .

BIG JOE: How you get them, boy?

BOY: When me see man start to grab things, ah just walk into a place and start helping meself. Ah don't even remember the name of the store. Police and soldiers all over the place now. *(the Boy runs down the street holding tightly to the loot)*

BIG JOE: Watch that boy run, nuh. Hey, hey, Bernie must be having the time of him life.

MISS LIZZIE: *(turns into yard)* Ah wonder what side him on?

BIG JOE: Cho, man, that boy will be on the right side.

MISS LIZZIE: You know, Big Joe, I really don't know which side is the right side.

BIG JOE: *(hand on her shoulder)* Miss Lizzie, in times of crisis and change, the right side is the side that win.

MISS LIZZIE: Ah don't care about sides. I would just like to see Massa Bernie in action.

BIG JOE: *(shakes his head in agreement)* Yes, I'd love to see me boy in action, man. Look, Miss Liz, ah change me mind. If them having the revolution during our lunch-time, ah don't see why, on God's earth, we should miss it.

MISS LIZZIE: *(takes his hand)* Come, Big Joe, we have to go see this for ourselves.

(amid the sound of sirens, the lights fade quickly as Big Joe and Miss Lizzie hurry through the gate and down the road.

The lights come up slowly. It's later the same day, about dusk. Miss Lizzie is on the veranda sitting by her door. Big Joe leans against his work bench. Behind him on the bench a radio plays mood-type music. Joe is drinking a beer from a bottle. A pile of looted shoes is stacked up against the edge of the veranda. There is a break in the music and the Announcer's voice comes on)

ANNOUNCER: *(very British accent)* This is your big news station and here is the news brought to you by Linval Williams. All is quiet in downtown Kingston this evening following a lunch-time free-for-all along Spanish Town Road and King Street. The fracas left fifty men wounded. Ten persons were taken into custody. The riot, fondly called "The Revolution" by those arrested, lasted approximately one hour. Area policemen and a task force from the army quickly put things back in order. The rioters burnt several buildings, including Mason's Drug Store, Smelley's Meat Mart and Winston's Furniture Shop. A total of ten buses, property of the bus service, were also destroyed. Damage has not yet been estimated. This reporter . . . *(Big Joe turns off the radio and takes a long sip of beer)*

MISS LIZZIE: Well, a lot of people thought it was the real thing.

BIG JOE: This should be a warning to the powers that be, them better take notice and see what can happen.

MISS LIZZIE: Such a pity though . . .

BIG JOE: Pity about what?

MISS LIZZIE: We never even see Bernie.

BIG JOE: Huh-huh . . .

MISS LIZZIE: *(kneels beside shoes)* All these shoes . . . and not one of them can fit us.

BIG JOE: True.

MISS LIZZIE: *(picks up a shoe)* Size four, size five, size three . . . not if ah was ah Ugly Sister me foot could grease one of these.

BIG JOE: You would have to be Cinderalla herself.

MISS LIZZIE: *(laughs)* Right, I would have to be Cinderally herself.

BIG JOE: *(puts down beer bottle)* That's what them call the law of averages. People like us never win. *(there is a movement at the gate. Matilda enters. She is alone, looks haggard and tired. Big Joe moves toward her)*

BIG JOE: *(softly)* Anything wrong, Mattie?

MATILDA: Is a long time since you call me Mattie, Big Joe.

BIG JOE: Is a long time since ah see you alone . . . *(Miss Lizzie quietly withdraws to her room)*

MATILDA: You saw the riot?

BIG JOE: Just the tail end. But I was expecting more, much more.

MATILDA: Plenty police and soldiers, all over the place tonight so everyone keeping in them shell.

BIG JOE: *(sits beside her)* And business?

MATILDA: Business slow, real slow . . . not even the merchant sailors on shore leave tonight.

BIG JOE: Everything so quiet. You would never believe all that lunch-time ruckus.

MATILDA: It so quiet, you can hear the sea breeze coming in.

BIG JOE: This kind of breeze force a man to stop and think serious about what happened today.

MATILDA: Ah don't understand it.

BIG JOE: Bernie used to talk about change, and ah just realise what him mean.

MATILDA: Bernie is all talk.

BIG JOE: No, him right. What happened today is just a sign. Ah can imagine the real thing.

MATILDA: Big Joe, you should know better than Bernie. A revolution won't make a bit of change in your life.

BIG JOE: Ah used to laugh at Bernie, but I can see it . . . you just look around you.

MATILDA *(rises)* I like what I do. And no revolution is going to change that. *(sound of Bernie's voice outside the gate)*

BERNIE: Okay, young boy, head on home. It's long past the curfew. Head on home before you get yourself into some real, real trouble.

SECOND VOICE: Okay, sah, okay. *(Bernie comes through the gate. He is wearing full army battle gear and has a rifle with a bayonet in his hand. He stops a short distance away from Joe and Matilda)*

BERNIE: You people heard about the curfew?

MATILDA: *(walks toward him)* Bernie, is that you?

BIG JOE: What a sight for sore eyes!

BERNIE: *(laughs nervously)* Matilda, Big Joe . . . Ah didn't even realize that it was me own yard me reach.

BIG JOE: Bernie, what you doing in that get-up, boy?

BERNIE: *(relaxed)* Keeping the peace.

BIG JOE: What a ruckus today, een?

BERNIE: Miss Lizzie okay?

BIG JOE: Everybody okay. *(shouts)* Miss Lizzie, Miss Lizzie, Bernie come. *(to Bernie)* She gone to bed disappointed that she didn't see you in action.

BERNIE: Well, she didn't miss anything. *(Miss Lizzie sticks her head through the door)*

MISS LIZZIE: Bernie, Bernie, you safe?

BERNIE: *(moves to the step)* Safe and sound, Miss Lizzie.

MISS LIZZIE: Thank the Lord. Ah can sleep peacefully now.

> *(she turns back into the room and closes the door behind her. Bernie sits on the work bench and leans his rifle next to him. He takes off his hat and plays with it)*

BERNIE: Bad timing, man. This is not the way it should happen.

BIG JOE: What was supposed to happen?

BERNIE: Tactics, man, well-planned strategy.

BIG JOE: Who say you can train hooligans to fight?

BERNIE: It can be done, but it needs planning and timing. Some stupid ass jumped the gun.

BIG JOE: Ah, Bernie, things don't usually turn out the way you plan them.

BERNIE: Months before I joined the army I sat around and talked about revolution. But I was not talking about what I saw happening in the streets today. People just destroying other people's property . . .

BIG JOE: Ah told you that is so revolutions go . . .

BERNIE: A well-planned uprising . . . planned down to the last man . . . that's what I thought about.

BIG JOE: For a while back there I saw what you were talking about. But every time I listen to you, Bernie, ah could see it . . . ah used to laugh at you; but every time you talk it took me back to what me grandfather used to tell me about the Morant Bay uprising.

(Matilda climbs the step, moving toward her room)

MATILDA: I don't care what the both of you have to say about this riot or revolution. Not that I don't understand what is happening, but riots put me out of business.

BERNIE: *(picks up rifle)* Well, that's the end of that. I have to get back on the beat. Take care, Big Joe . . . Matilda . . .

(Bernie looks up at Matilda for a long time, turns and heads for the gate. He walks into a young sailor at the gate)

SAILOR: Say, man, is this where Matilda lives?

BERNIE: This is it, man. *(shouts)* Matilda, your time . . .

(Matilda wiggles to the gate, takes the Sailor by his hand and leads him to her room as Bernie and Big Joe look on)

BERNIE: *(going through gate)* Nothing seems to change around here, eh Big Joe?

BIG JOE: *(rising)* That's right. Nothing seems to change.

(the lights fade slowly as Big Joe stretches his arms above his head. Bernie slings his rifle over his shoulder and moves slowly down the street)

Slow Curtain

Suzanne Dracius

SWEAT, SUGAR AND BLOOD

I DON'T KNOW IF Emma loves Emile. But that's not the point.

The mulatto girl is sixteen. As milky white as a corrosol, as tender as a heart of palm, in just two days a wedding will officially make her my great-aunt Emma B.

The day after tomorrow Emma is going to marry the eminent Mr. Emile B., Esq., a lawyer from Fort-de France. Everything is ready: from the lilies, the organdy, the damask, the tulle, the vertiginous chiffon down to the royal orchids brought from Balata, still trembling and damp from the tropical forest, everything is immaculately white. All you hear around her is talk of trousseaus, hairdos, veils, fittings, her train, her posture, and then her attire again.

Emma getting married is like being engulfed in a whirlwind of white.

The third day after the wedding Mr. Emile B. gave her a quick peck on the lips and then advised her in leaving that under no circumstances should she venture off in the direction of the distillery. Besides his law office located on the rue Perrinon in Fort-de-France, in the center of town, Mr. Emile B. has inherited an ancient little distillery that has managed to subsist up on the Didier plateau. Because the property is vast, he has restored the old plantation house, made of old stones and wood from Guiana. This is where Emma is now living with a new husband—new to her alone, for there's quite a bunch of chabins in Morne Coco now who can claim that they're B.'s little bastards. But Emma never meets any of these illegitimate kids. She never goes to Morne Coco on the other side of the road. That's not a place for her, according to the plump cook Mama Sonson. Every God-given day, Mr. Emile drives to his office, leaving her alone at Haut-Didier with the women of the house: Mama Sonson and the little Da Sirisia. Emma didn't think she needed any other help.

Every morning it's the same peck, the same "have a good morning," and the same advice: "Don't go walking in the direction of the distillery."

"What does he think?" wonders Emma, protesting to herself. "Is he worried that I'm going to get drunk on rum? Who does he think I am? I'm not a baby anymore! Besides the decanters are all within my reach on the pedestal table in the living room; they're not even locked up. If I felt like getting drunk, I'd just have to reach for them."

Maybe Emile is afraid of the powerful erotic charge that emanates from those big, supple bodies with their long, bulging muscles and their skin pearled with sweat? Emma barely caught a glimpse of the workers from the distillery when they came—their hair all marcelled and slicked down with vaseline, all dressed up wearing ties and smelling of eau de Cologne "Etoile"—to present their congratulations to the newly weds. But they disappeared as fast as they came.

Thus went the first weeks of her marriage.

On the morning of the eighth day, while Emile was busy washing and dressing—a daily activity which always seemed to last as long as a day without bread—Emma made sure, by peering into the bathroom, that her husband was busy passing his straight-edged razor over his greenish mulatto beard, carefully tailoring the contour of a goatee that Emma caught herself at that moment finding a tiny bit ridiculous. Only half awake, the young bride flew as in a dream to the end of the veranda, at the other end of the house from the bathroom, to the spot where she knew she'd be hidden by the foliage of the poinsettias and the crimson curtain of the Barbados hibiscus. From there she knew she could look all she wanted at a couple of the turns in the road leading to the distillery. True she'd never be able to take in the whole road in a single glance: tufts of giant bamboos hid most of it. But there was a spot, a part in the vegetation's woolly crop of hair, where a spot of light shone through revealing a part of the road. That's all Emma needed.

The veils of early morning had lifted in silence. The blackbirds in the filao trees had begun their racket: between chirping and squawking, they had enough to keep them busy until nightfall. Noisy but serene, the early morning dampness gave new, throbbing life to trees alive with the rocking of sissis, to roosters rushing to cockadoodledoo just to beat out the cackling hens and prove their supremacy, to acrobatic anolis spread out on the frond of a dwarf date palm hoping to catch their first prey, and to Emma, who had leaped from her bed, barefoot on the damp tiles, drawing the lace of her nightgown over her breast with her hand.

"How cool it is at dawn!" Emma says to herself shivering—with cold? with fear? with a sense of having no business being there?

Suddenly, clearly, penetrating the air, there arises the masculine voice of some fellow that unfortunately Emma can't see.

She closes her eyes and listens carefully:

'I pé ké ni siklon, man di'w! Pa fè lafèt épi mwen! Asé bétizé, ou ka plen tèt mwen epi tout sé kouyonnad-la!"

(Ain't gonna be no hurricane, ya hear me? Don't want to hear nothin' about it! Stop that nonsense. I've had it up to here with your crap.)

A second voice loses patience, rings out stubbornly.

"Fè sa ou lé! Mwen, man za paré. Zalimet, luil, pétrol, bouji, man za fè tout provizyon mwen. Kité Misyé Siklon vini!"

(Do what you want! I'm ready. I've got me enough matches, oil, kerosene, candles. Come and get us, Mr. Hurricane.)

"Gadé'y! I pa ka menm kouté. Yen ki chonjé i ka chonjé toubonnman."

(Look at him! He's not even listening. All he does is daydream, daydream . . .)

That voice is new; it's trying to cover the other one and will succeed, without any difficulty. It's a third man who's speaking. Emma can't recognize either the tone or the language of the first two. This one speaks a heavy creole that sounds rough and choppy. So, he's from the North! she thinks, without wondering why.

"Sa ou ni an ka-kabèch ou, nèg? Asé dépotjolé ko-ko'w! ou ka sanm an t-toupi mabyal."

(Hey, what's got into your sk-skull, man? stop wo-worrying so much! You look like a crazy spinning t-top, a higher voice snickers.)

Which one of them just spoke? She can't figure it out. She's sure it's not the first man. Now that she's heard it she'd recognize his voice out of a thousand. She becomes flushed. She represses a shudder. This time is it a fever? Oh, she can't wait for them to get to the clearing soon so that she can see them!

But when they get there she can't hear them anymore. Their voices are already fading, the words wafting off in the air. She can't make out what they're saying anymore. All she hears now is a burst of the same, incoherent, hammered-out syllables—té-té-ké-ké-pé-ka-pou-pouki—the steady barking of the one who stammers and articulates louder than the others, probably to compensate, she thinks.

"The air is healthy in Haut-Didier, but at this time of year you still have to be careful about spiders, moths, and cockroaches that are leaving deposits and laying all kinds of eggs in the hems of your clothes," the little Da explains to Emma.

Startled, Emma quickly leaves her secret observation point.

And Mama Sonson adds.

"You keep your clothes in the closet forever and ever, ain't no way you're still going to find them there! . . . Hey Sirisia, girl, stop jumping around, you're not going to be able to do your ironing, girl, my lord! You'll work yourself up into a fever! . . . If you think you're going to use that hot iron wearing sopping wet clothes and you all covered with cold sweat you've got another thing coming."

Mr. Emile must have finished his endless morning routine by now for, tall and straight, with triumphal beard, he comes to perform the daily ritual: have a good morning, here's a good kiss, take my good advice.

There, it's over, he's left at the wheel of his Panhard.

Up there in the big house, Emma is bored.

A hot smell of caramel and sugar cane alcohol rising from the distillery tickles her nostrils. They're making rum, and the young woman enjoys the mystery that comes from inhaling the disturbing emanation, stronger than the odor of punch, more intoxicating than a planter's punch or that tropical cocktail they serve at the Annual Grand Officers' Ball.

As she waits for Madame to get pregnant, the little Da busies herself fancifully tending to the trousseau of the future first-born child. There's no end to what you can do with a trousseau. Sirisia never stops washing, rewashing, ironing, and then washing again the diapers, bibs, little shirts, little sheets with English embroidery, the minuscule mosquito-net. There's no point in keeping in mothballs anything that will touch the newborn in any way! "Poor little thing, his skin would come off and he'd suffocate from the smell," Mama Sonson asserts knowingly. It's a matter of honor for the Da to keep a jealous guard over Mr. B.'s future progeny, even if he hasn't been conceived yet, even if there's more going on in Emma's mind now than in her womb. Whether Madame likes it or not, a child will be born and he'll be male, there's no two ways about it, "no squirming out of it," Mama Sonson would chime in if there were any questions on the matter. Besides, a boy's first name has already been designated; if the misfortune of its being a girl arises, they'll just put an 'e' at the end. If Mr. B. had picked "Arsene" instead of "Henri," it would have been even easier, there'd be nothing to change at all. That's Mama Sonson's opinion; even though "Arsene" means virile, she sees nothing wrong with imposing it on a girl, who'll be feminine enough, you can be sure! Anyway Mama Sonson doesn't know Greek. That's really the least of her concerns. On the other hand, there's a serious problem for the baptism, because the person who's been picked in advance refuses to be a godfather for the first time in his life for a member of the feminine race: "It's bad luck. He's only agreed for a boy. For a girl it's another matter: he hadn't even thought of that possibility when he proudly said yes. It's an honor to be the godfather of a little male, but for some little female pissecrette . . .

Sure Emma enjoys listening to the moralistic lamentations of Mama Sonson, who tells the beads on the rosary of past, present, and future miseries while she scales fish.

But then there's the mystery of those men!

Mr. B. announced in leaving that he won't be back for lunch today. As is often the case, he has a business luncheon that will keep him in Fort-de-France. Sometimes he even lowers himself to buy lunch at the market, eating off of big wooden trestle tables, getting a blaff or a fish stew seasoned with red pepper served by imposing câpresses.

Mr. B. has never mentioned bringing Emma there some day.

She assumes that it's not done.

"Little rummy, so you're sipping your punch without even waiting for me?"

Aunt Herminie just arrived.

Of course, Godmother's having lunch here today, obviously! Every time Mr. B. needs to have lunch downtown, he assigns "Cousin Herminie"—Godmother for Emma, for she's not only her aunt but was her godmother for her baptism. She's a B. from Saint-Pierre, not from Fort-de-France, and that's a big difference. The B. family from Saint-Pierre has a certain paternalistic condescension toward the B. family from Fort-de-France; a square bears their name in the center of Saint-Pierre in honor of one of their family members who was a notable personage of that city—Emma can't remember why—but the B. family of Fort-de-France has more money.

The historically prominent but nevertheless impoverished mulatto lady gargles with pride as she affirms that the B. family is a great family, but Emma responds by bursting out laughing:

"You shouldn't confuse 'great family' with 'large family'!"

Great or not, the B. family has never intrigued Emma.

Lunch drags on. Godmother talks to herself without realizing it: Emma's not with her anymore. Emma's lost in thought. Emma's thoughts wander off from the house.

If there's one thing she can't stand it's not being able to know things, to know only one side of life.

She can't see or know anything, at least not by herself. Because she's "the mulatto's wife," "the boss' wife," a mulatto herself, she doesn't have the right to go see what's going on below, what they're doing over there, inside, within the distillery. All she can do is steal a few bits of conversation when they arrive in the morning or when they leave in the evening, when their workday is over. If she hears them it's because they're still invisible and, finally when she sees them, she can't hear them anymore because they're too far away. Then they go into the distillery. There she can't see anything, she can only imagine what happens afterwards, after the last twist in the road where she has her last view of the group of tall men walking, who despite the distance always seem tall: she's never stepped foot inside that beastly distillery! For her the interior of the distillery is an unknown world. She wants to go inside, see what they do there, know how they go about it, find out about these men that she sees from afar every day, that she observes on the sly and, yes, find out how they manage to perform the metamorphosis of the juice from sugar cane into rum. Emma has drunk rum, with a lot of syrup and lime.

She's tasted sugar cane. But what about the forbidden alchemy . . .

Oh! She learned many things at the Colonial Boarding School on rue Ernest-Renan, attended in Fort-de-France by all the daughters of the "best families," snobbish, straight-laced but nonetheless tolerant and committed to humanist values. But she stopped learning things all of a sudden! Emma yearns to know more. She wasn't a bad student, she digested whole chapters of the history of France and Navarre; she's very familiar with school programs in the natural and physical sciences and even in world geography; she knows quite well who broke the Soissons vase and there's nothing she doesn't know about auricles and other ventricles. Yet she knows nothing about the fabrication of rum that's taking place over there, a few feet away from her.

Nothing seems more mysterious to her today than what's right there, so near to her, in that distillery that holds within its walls the tall men that she only sees passing by, with their handsome blue-black bodies. Here she is now: married, a woman, a wife, the lady of the house, potentially a mother. Yet nothing is more foreign to her than that world that is so close by, than that side of humanity to which she has no access.

A barrier has been built between Emma and that world, between Emma and their creole language.

A barrier has been built between their world and hers, between their language and hers, between their skin and hers, between their sex and hers.

Taking advantage of Godmother's nap, Emma has slipped away like a swift mongoose to the edges of the Other World. She's gotten away secretly, furtively, without Mama Sonson suspecting anything, and even without Sirisia knowing, she who normally knows everything.

It's the hour of the break, for them too, it would seem. That's to be expected: with Godmother you have to eat early out of respect for her age.

At the doorway stands a man, naked to the waist. After the work he's done he puts his shirt back on so as not to catch his death. The stretched-out fabric of his jersey sticks to his sweat-covered skin. Emma recognizes him right away: he's the one with the voice, the first voice, the clearest, the one that cuts through the air the best at sunrise each day. She'd swear to it.

What he needs is a good shower. But a cold or even cool shower on a body all covered with sweat is just what you need to get sick. At least that's what grown-ups always preach, so forget the shower, there's no way around it. If Mama Sonson was there, that's what she'd say, Lord, she would! Just as long as he knows it.

The man with the sweat-drenched jersey stretches his long limbs and then goes off slowly to crouch down in the shade, off a way.

Others join him outside, sit down with him under the biggest mango tree. From their lunchpail they extract a big piece of breadfruit, some fried balao, some acra, a piece of codfish: it's Friday. They concentrate on eating, saying not a word. Wet Jersey pours everyone big glasses filled with a clear liquid, probably rum, or maybe just water?

Emma doesn't dare go over to talk to them. She doesn't even dare come close to them. Is it their silence that intimidates her? She only knows them when they speak, when she spies on them each morning. It's first and foremost through language that their complicity has arisen, it's through the shared secret of all those words that she steals from them, day after day—those creole words. Is it their silence that stops her, or is it the Insurmountable Barrier between her and their universe? It may be Insurmountable but surely one can get around it.

Emma goes around the group of men, at some distance, so as not to be seen.

She almost gets down on all fours to reach the back of the building, which she succeeds in entering by crawling through the opening of a low window.

Her blood spurts on the sugar cane, splattering the cane trash.

The escapade at the distillery has cost Emma three fingers. That's the price. And at that, only because she screamed and because the men ran back, amazed by the sound of the machine inexplicably set in motion. They thought quickly and stopped the crusher in time while one of them, the strongest, Wet Jersey, grabbed onto Emma's body with the full force of his muscles, straining to the breaking point.

The man managed to hold back the voracious movement of the machine.

"If he hadn't it would have crushed her hand, her whole hand, and then her arm, and then her whole body, who knows! . . . Ah, Jesus, Mary and Joseph and all the saints, why did Madame need to go play with those machines!" laments Mama Sonson.

One of their cousins, a good doctor who answered the emergency call, has given the necessary treatment to Emma's mutilated hand, and Mr. Emile B., called away from his office, makes no comment. Hasn't she been punished enough for her disobedience? He has never been so silent. She has never been so pale, but with a glow in her eyes that will never go out. Yes, it is a light of jubilation that illuminates Emma's eyes.

Having lost the use of the fingers that she used the most, Emma B. lived her life as a lady from Fort de France awkwardly, wearing a glove on one hand, the left one: first a white glove, then a navy one, and finally a pearl grey one. Fools would say, "Fortunately it wasn't her right hand!"

For some people the whole thing was mysterious, for others it had a sort of troubling charm; still others interpreted it as a sign of uniqueness or a kind of provocation, although they would have been hard pressed to say what kind. Very few knew what it was all about; very few knew the secret of Emma's rebellion.

When Emma died, at the age of one hundred and two, Oreste, her seventeenth child, approached her deathbed—or should I say her wedding bed?—and slipped on the pearl-white glove, the first one that she had worn until the day of her silver wedding anniversary. Washed, rewashed, and ironed, it wasn't even yellowed with age.

Forget "Crick, crack."
This is not a story.
It really happened to my great aunt, Emma B.
Thanks to that mixed frenzy of sweat, sugar and blood, Emma had at least one strong sensation in her lifetime.

Translated by Doris Y. Kadish
University of Georgia

Glossary

Acra: Fritters made with codfish or vegetables.
Anolis: Little green lizards (author's footnote).

Balao: A type of tropical seafish, also known in English as halfbeak.

Blaff: A plate of fish seasoned by cooking on Indian wood (author's footnote).

Câpre, Capresse: Dark-skinned child of black and mulatto parents.

Chabin, Chabine: Person of mixed-blood who appears to bear the characteristics of only one, the lighter skinned parent; sometimes referred to in English as being "yellow."

Cockadoodledoo (translation of "coquiyoquer," a word invented by the author): to crow.

Corrosol: A tree of medium height resembling a European pear tree bearing a juicy, refreshing fruit considered to have a calming effect.

Crick, crack: Caribbean expression, like "Once upon a time," used to begin the recounting of a story.

Da: Black nursemaid for creole families.

Filao: Casuarinas; graceful trees from Madagascar that resemble weeping willows.

Marcelled (translator's choice for translation of "calamistre"): A style of carefully waved hair attributed originally to the nineteenth-century French hairdresser Marcel.

Pisscrette: Creole word for a little tish which, while evoking smallness, also evokes the image of a "little pisser" (information provided by the author).

Sissis: Little birds comparable to sparrows (author's footnote).

Vaseline: A special hair product used in Martinique made from vaseline and a mixture of other cosmetic products (explanation supplied by the author).

Ana Lydia Vega

EYE-OPENER

And for to make you the more merry,
I myself will gladly ride with you.

Geoffrey Chaucer, Canterbury Tales

AN EXPLOSION OF RED clouds lighted the sky and the shadows of ya-grumo trees lay in long slanting lines across the Guavate Forest when our driver made the disturbing confession that he could barely keep his eyes open. "Talk, ask riddles, tell jokes," he entreated, rubbing the merry eyes that looked at each of us in turn in the rearview mirror. The radio, that last resort of drivers lulled in the arms of Morpheus, was broken. It was life or death: we either gave him his dose of Eye-Opener Tonic or the *público* would take a short-cut to eternity.

There was a brief silence that seemed to drag on forever while one of us could screw up our courage to break the ice. Fortunately, the passenger from Maunabo, loose-tongued even under less de-manding circumstances, moistened his lips and took the plunge:

"In the town where I live, out near the lighthouse, down by Cape Malapascua, there once lived a man that had thirty-seven children, all of them by different mothers. I don't know what that man had be-tween his legs, but whatever it was, apparently the Virgin Mother her-self couldn't have resisted it."

The narrator paused, to await his audience's reaction. You could have cut the silence with a knife, and the faces looked as though they'd been cast in cement. I turned my head toward the window to hide my sinful grin. When the driver gave a good hearty laugh to cel-ebrate the minor sacrilege, the storyteller plucked up his courage and continued on:

English-language translation by Andrew Hurley. Reprinted from *True and False Romances*. Used by permission of the author and the translator.

"Yessir. *BIG* family this guy had himself. And a good husband and father he was, too. So nobody would get their feelings hurt, he took turns sleeping one night in each different house."

The driver snickered again, but this time he had company—a retired schoolteacher type in a dark suit coat.

"But the best part was that this man's wives were all just as happy as could be with this arrangement, and it was them that worked out the calendar for where this man would sleep each night. Why, if one of them had to run some errand or something, one of the other ones would take care of the children for her. You'd've thought they were Mormons!"

The driver's hilarity was irresistible. The other passengers laughed just to hear the driver's asthmatic wheezes. I must confess that I personally didn't think that last part was so funny.

"Things were going just fine for this fellow. He worked hard farming and such, and he'd do part time jobs in town whenever he got a chance to, and with the help of God and that flock of wives of his and his Uncle Sam's food stamp program, he pretty much kept food on the tables and clothes on the backs of everybody in those thirty-seven houses."

A charismatic lady wearing a white habit tied at the waist by a rope with red balls on the end couldn't contain her indignation.

"Very nice! He didn't have to change the dirty diapers or peel the plantains for the *tostones*."

"Now don't get yourself all worked up there, ma'am," the Maunabo man said gently. "You'll see what happened to this gentleman in a minute. Good things don't last, and when they do . . . well, as the old saying goes, It's a mighty good wind that blows nobody ill. As I was saying: Like any good citizen, this man filled out his income tax form every year and paid his taxes. And every year the list of dependents this fellow claimed on his tax form got longer and longer. At first, the income-tax people let it slide, but when things in the government started getting bad economically speaking—or started getting worse, rather—one of the inspectors they've got there, a real little hornet of a fellow that had ambitions to rise in the government as a reward for the way he squeezed the good honest hardworking folks out of their hard-earned money, this little inspector-fellow sent this man a letter. 'You must present,' read the letter, or words to that effect, 'a birth certificate or evidence of baptism and social security number for each dependent claimed.' What a problem, ladies and gentlemen, because neither he nor his wives had ever bothered to register those children—not in town at the Registry Office and not at the church. And can you imagine what that man would've had to go through at this stage of the game to get that flock of thirty-seven

Christian children all registered at once—and with two weeks to go before April 15 at midnight, when that income-tax form has to be postmarked or else? I'll tell you, if it was me, I'd take out a loan even if I had to be in debt up to my ears for the rest of my life before I'd voluntarily get myself into such a mess of red tape as that . . ."

"So what did he do?" the kid with the Walkman asked. When he'd seen everybody laughing he'd taken off his earphones, and now he was hooked on reality.

"A lawyer-friend of his told him to obey the law, that was the best thing he could do, but this fellow had neither the time nor the patience for that route. Several nights he lay in his bed cogitating, and then all of a sudden the light dawned. The next day he went over to this car dealer's place in Maunabo—the dealer it seems owed him a favor—and he reserved himself three vans—those big ones they're using these days to ferry kids to school in, with the doors that slide on the outside? He reserved himself three of those vans and he found himself two out-of-work *público* drivers, and him driving one van and the two guys driving the others, they went from house to house picking up children of all sizes and colors. There were kids in those vans from little tykes two years old to big husky eighteen-year-olds. The kids, imagine, they had themselves a ball. They rode along singing songs and yelling dirty words out the windows at people along the highway. The other two drivers drove through the mountains like a bat out of hell—they couldn't wait to get rid of those holy terrors they had for passengers. But this fellow I'm telling you about just drove along like he was out for a Sunday drive in the country, smiling to himself and humming.

"When they came in sight of that big new Treasury Building, there at the entrance to Old San Juan, this fellow motioned the vans over to the side of the road, got out, and went from van to van with their instructions: 'When we get there, I want you children to get out of the vans with me, and then I want you to get up those stairs you're going to see inside there, and I want you to make all the racket you can . . . I want you to make the biggest fuss these people ever saw, and if anybody says a word to you about hushing or behaving yourselves, you tell them to talk to your daddy—I'll be right there with you. Everybody understand?' Did they understand? Is the pope Catholic? Those poor people in the Treasury Department didn't know what hit 'em. When that flock of kids erupted through the front door of the building, it was a wonder the roof didn't cave in. You'd have thought it was an earthquake. And their daddy behind them, just smiling to himself."

The driver's belly was rising and falling, brushing the steering wheel with every new gale of hilarity. We passengers couldn't wait to hear what . . .

"Yessir, ladies and gentlemen—this man walks up to that little inspector-fellow's desk as calm as you please, and that gang of young heathens right behind him. Those kids were into everything, opening and closing drawers, poking around in the wastebaskets, picking up telephones, sharpening pencils, everything they could think of, and you could hear the noise all the way to the Plaza Colón.

"So anyway, the man says to that inspector, as meek as can be, 'Here are those thirty-seven dependents you were asking me about, mister. If you want to get a piece of paper we can write their names down for you . . .'

"The little inspector-fellow looked at him a minute. He didn't know what to say. And those children still opening and closing drawers and stapling papers together and playing tag around the desks in the office. Finally the inspector stands up, straightens his tie a little, and goes off to find his supervisor, to see if he couldn't get him out of this fix. And those kids running after him, jumping around and doing cartwheels and pinching him on the rear. The supervisor comes out about then, and he goes berserk—within ten minutes he'd lost his voice from yelling at those infidels to keep quiet and settle down, and finally he threatened to call security if this fellow didn't get out of there that minute, himself and his thirty-seven wild animals. No sooner said than done, don't you know. Still yelling and jumping around and screaming like a pack of banshees, they were down those stairs and out of the building.

"As a reward for how well his kids had behaved themselves, this fellow took 'em all to McDonald's in Puerta de Tierra before he trucked 'em back to Maunabo. That was ten years ago. And this fellow is still making out his list of dependents every March, and to this day the Treasury Department hasn't even *thought* about bothering him again. As the saying goes, 'You want to be real careful what you ask for, because you might get it.'"

There was applause from the driver and the retired schoolteacher. The storyteller from Maunabo smiled contentedly, and said now it was somebody else's turn.

Surprisingly, it was the kid with the Walkman that stepped in next.

"In Arroyo, where my grandmother lives, there's been all these fires. There's been businesses, cane fields, houses burned to the ground, and there's even been some women that've poured gasoline all over themselves and set themselves afire. My grandmother says it's the curse of this sailor that got sick on a boat one time, he got sick with something real contagious, I don't remember exactly what she said it was, and the crew put him off in a little boat and set him on fire."

"When he died?" the Maunabo man, a little confused by this last part, asked.

"That's the point, dude, they *torched him*, get it? They. Burned. Him. Alive." The kid pronounced each word separately and very, very carefully, as though he were talking to a lip-reader. He was a little upset that nobody had gotten the point of the story.

The brevity of the story was a disappointment to the driver; again he threatened to fall asleep if we couldn't do better than that. The charismatic lady took up the challenge next.

"I'm from Arroyo too, and it's a fact—you'd think fire had something against my poor home town. This story I'm about to tell happened quite some time ago. I'm not going to mention any names, in case some of you know the people—down in Arroyo, everybody is related to everybody else, or about to be.

"What happened was that sometime around the turn of the century a widow lady from the Canary Islands came to Arroyo to live. This woman had a grown son and a lot of money. Pretty soon what was bound to happen happened, and this son fell in love. He fell in love with a nice girl from there that he'd met in town, and he decided he wanted to get married. Only problem was, the girl's skin was a little darker than his. Well the mother wouldn't hear of it, and not only because of the girl's color—truth was, no girl was going to be good enough for her boy. And in order to keep 'em from having that wedding she even got sick and everything. But the son stood his ground, and since he was of legal age there wasn't much the mother could do about it. Finally one day he gets tired of waiting for his mother to change her mind, and he grabs that dark-skinned girl and they go talk to the priest and the next day she had a wedding ring on her finger. They went off to live in a little house he'd rented right there in town. Now this young man was a good son, and he would visit his mother every week, regular as rain. She'd open the door to him, but she wouldn't let her daughter-in-law so much as set foot on her porch. She wouldn't give that girl the time of day.

"Well, as time went on, the son and his new wife discovered that with the blessing of God they were going to have a baby. It was born as white as the father, but even so, the grandmother refused to even look at it.

"About a year after the baby was born, strange things started happening in the son and daughter-in-law's house—keys would disappear, the water would turn itself on and off, smoke would come up out of the toilet. One night a pack of big black dogs got into the yard and barked all night. Things were getting ugly. So finally the girl sent for the priest. The priest said two or three *dominus vobiscums* in the living room, the bathroom, and each bedroom and sprinkled holy water all through the house. But that same night those black dogs were back again, and the bed shook, and all the shutters in the front room opened and closed all by themselves."

The narrator had lowered her voice, which accentuated the sinister atmosphere of her story. All of us, including the driver, were leaning toward her, not wanting to miss a word of the tale. Night had fallen now, and the air on the highway through the forest was cool. I surreptitiously rolled up the window beside me, in case some venturesome spirit should take a mind to join us.

"The girl then sent for her aunt, who had the understanding. And that black *espiritista* no more than walked through the front door into the living room when the light fixture came crashing down from the ceiling and landed practically on top of her. '*Ay Santa Marta!*' she says, looking around warily, 'the evil work is in this house,' and she starts trying to find it. She looked high and low—she practically turned that house upside down hunting for the thing that was causing all this trouble. But she looked and she looked and she still couldn't find the lock of hair or whatever it was anywhere. So she took up one of those spirits that's loose just about anywhere and she took it up and it began to speak out of her mouth. 'Your mother-in-law has done this,' the spirit says to the girl, 'she's the one that's doing this to you, and until you find the thing that's doing it, the spirits she's set on you will never leave you in peace.'"

"What they ought to have done is send a couple of guys over to that mother-in-law's house to teach her not to meddle in other folks' business," pronounced the driver, though he had his fingers crossed, just in case.

"Or put a spell on her that was bigger than the one she put on *them*," said the retired school teacher type, who not for nothing was from Guayama, which anyone will tell you is the witching capital of Puerto Rico.

"Anyway, that night, when the widow's son found out about all this, naturally he refused to believe it. How could such a thing be? His mother, such an upright, Catholic woman. But his wife was convinced, and she refused to sleep another night in that house until the spell had been found and undone. She stood her ground, too, so finally her husband promised her that the next day he'd find them another place to live. Meanwhile, they went to bed, scared to death, and it took them hours to ever get to sleep. Along about morning, they suddenly woke up to the smell of something burning. The smell was strong, too. He ran to find out where the fire was, and she had her housedress about halfway pulled on, when they heard the baby crying. So the girl, dressed in nothing but her nightgown, ran into the child's room. And there—*ay Virgen del Carmen*, it gives me goosebumps just to think about it—she found her baby on fire, like some human torch lying there under the mosquito net."

Thank goodness we'd gotten onto the expressway by now, so the lights of the cars helped not only light the way but dispel our fears a bit as well.

"What happened to the widow? Did they get her for it?" the driver demanded, unconsciously taking out his vengeance on the accelerator.

"What happened to somebody didn't happen to the widow, it happened to the poor daughter-in-law. The widow accused her of murdering the child, and since the old lady had money and lots of connections, she fixed things so her daughter-in-law was carried off to San Juan and locked up in the lunatic asylum."

The retired schoolteacher then asked the question we had all been silently asking:

"And what about the husband? Didn't he do anything?"

"Yes, of course he did," she said, with a gesture of disgust. "He went back to the Canary Islands with his mother . . . just so you'll see how false and cowardly some men are."

The moral of the story aroused protests from some quarters—the four representatives of the male sex, who were in the majority in the car. The retired schoolteacher was determined to save the honor of his sex, and no better way could he find than to take up the challenge with a further tale:

"In a town on the south coast whose name I do not wish to re-member, there was a businessman with a great big elegant house sit-ting beside his store, which was right near a fire station. His wife was elegant, also—a tall, white-skinned foreign lady with blue eyes. She was very lovely, but she was a little, you know . . ."

The charismatic lady pursed her lips in preparation for the ex-pected offense to her modesty; the driver, as was his wont, noisily greeted the possibility.

" . . . too hot to handle . . . One man was not enough for her, shall we say. Or two. Or three. Or four. Her poor husband had horns growing every which way out of his head—he looked like one of Santa Claus's reindeer. Of course, he didn't even realize he was be-ing . . . *cuckolded,* I believe, is the polite name for it, since he was a little . . . you know . . . slow on the uptake himself."

The driver now was choking with laughter, the Maunabo gentle-man joined in, and the lady from Arroyo opened her eyes and took a deep breath. The kid with the Walkman winked at me enigmatically; I had no idea how to take that.

"The wife's taste leaned to firemen, of all things. And since she had them right there at hand, you see, why every night she'd give her husband a cup of linden tea sugared with two or three sleeping pills, and while he lay there snoring she'd spend the night putting out fires."

"Good god!" the charismatic lady muttered softly, and looking for moral reinforcements she cast her irate eye on me. I didn't know whether to look serious or just get it over with and laugh out loud, so I sat there with a sort of half-smile on my face, looking wholly idiotic.

"The husband's friends found out what was going on, of course, and they alerted the guy so he could take patriotic action. The fellow thought about it a good long time, because it was hard for him to believe that his beloved wife was cheating on him with half a battalion of firefighters. One night he decided to just *pretend* he was drinking the linden tea his wife always fixed him, and so he just lay there awake studying the ceiling for a long time, *pretending* he was asleep. Pretty soon he heard sounds in the room next door, so he got up, sneaked out the back door, went around the house, and crossed the street and found himself a lookout behind a tree. What he saw was a whole parade of firemen in and out of his house, so finally he woke up to what had been going on all this time. But he controlled himself—he waited for the last one to come out before he did anything. Then he crossed the street and went back in the house."

In spite of the narrator's perverse sense of storytelling, the story had us all by the throat. Even the charismatic lady was holding her fire so that we could come more quickly to the ending.

"Those who were there say that husband was like a madman. They say his face was purple with rage. He threw open that door, stalked into the bedroom, grabbed his wife by the hair, dragged her out onto the porch, and threw her out in the street as naked as the day she was born."

Now nobody was laughing. The abruptness of the finale had taken our breath away.

"So you see, missus," said the narrator without missing a beat, "we men may be false, but women can be a whole lot falser yet."

"Those that are, are," intoned the man from Maunabo in a conciliatory tone of voice, "but most women are truer than we men, you know, my friend, as my mother is, and I imagine your own."

The sentimental evocation of our mothers calmed tempers a bit. The latest storyteller, in fact, was rendered so tender-hearted that he did not even realize that his mother's purity had been called, ever so delicately, into question.

"There's more to the story than that," said the charismatic lady suddenly, and we all turned to look at her. "You haven't told but one side of it. You've made that poor woman sound like the villain."

The man from Guayama opened his eyes wide and shrugged his shoulders in a guise of total innocence. But the lady in the habit was adamant. She looked him straight in the eye and crossed her arms censoriously.

"Then *you* tell the story, you tell it," urged the driver, his tired eyes taking on new light. The lady considered the invitation, hesitated a few seconds, and then without further ado launched herself into the tale, her fingers fiddling with the rope-ends at her waist, her eye set on the window.

"What happened was that this businessman we were talking about was no saint himself. His idea of fun was to take the ignorant young girls from the countryside around there and carry them to a house of ill repute there used to be in town and have his way with them."

The phrase made the kid with the Walkman smile. But he contritely lowered his eyes when my gaze met his.

"That place was famous for the parties they used to have there—the most degenerate men along the whole southern coast with their mistresses and whores and scarlet women. Orgies was what they had there, orgies that'd put the Roman emperors to shame."

"Well, now . . ." murmured the schoolteacher, who was beginning to be distressed by the turn the story was taking. The charismatic lady, though, was not so quick to relinquish the floor.

"The wife, of course," she forged on, "knew nothing about any of those shenanigans. The whole world knew what was going on, but since her husband kept her all shut up in that great big house of theirs all the time, with no family and no friends, there was no way for her to hear anything about it. So about that time a pretty young girl comes to work in the house. This husband of hers had sent the girl supposedly to help out. The girl was polite and obedient, a real nice girl, and the wife was delighted.

"One day, as she was cleaning, this young maid stuck her hand back behind a bookcase in the room the husband used for an office. And what did she put her hand on, behind a false wall, but a whole stack of books all wrapped up and tied with a cord. Since the poor girl didn't know how to read, she didn't realize she'd come across a collection of dirty books—every one of them, every single one, on that Index, that list the Church keeps of forbidden books. But she did know how to look at pictures, and since the books had gotten her curiosity up, she started thumbing through one particular big thick album that she found sticking out between two smaller books. Imagine the look on that poor innocent young girl's face when she sees what's in it—all these photographs of the husband and his filthy friends doing terrible things with little girls twelve and thirteen years old, and with negro women and even with animals, oh my God . . ."

"Those orgies must have been something," said the driver, fascinated, and nobody dared to laugh.

"She didn't want to get into trouble, so she kept her mouth shut about what she'd found. *To each his own, I guess,* she thought. But God works in mysterious ways, and what happened was that this business-man we were talking about, he'd had his eye on this girl he'd brought in to help his wife around the house, and around this time he begins to fondle her a little bit every time she'd get within reach. At first she tried to brush his hand away, like this, you know, not too much fuss about it, but the man kept on and kept on, and he'd watch and try to corner the girl whenever he could. The night he tried to get into her room, she drew the line. She packed up her things and the next morning she went in to say goodbye to the wife. But the truth was, she liked the wife, the wife had been real good to her, so when she opened her mouth to tell her she was leaving, she broke out crying like a nine-year-old child. The wife didn't know what to think, of course, so she started asking questions. And she kept asking ques-tions until finally the girl told her the truth. The woman didn't want to believe her, of course, but the girl took her by the hand and led her into the husband's office and showed her the false wall and the album of dirty pictures and everything."

After the requisite pause to let her words take effect, the charis-matic lady couldn't resist hammering in one last nail:

"So you see," she said, smiling, "how the story changes depend-ing on who's telling it."

The man from Guayama, though, was not altogether abashed.

"I hope you'll forgive the question," he said, in a tone entirely too polite for the moment, "but where exactly did you get that ver-sion of the story?"

Surprisingly, it was the driver that came to the lady's aid.

"From the same place you got yours, and did anybody ask *you* how you came by it?" And he broke the tension with one of his inim-itable bursts of laughter.

A comfortable silence fell over us. The driver, as he shepherded us along the Caguas highway, looked bright-eyed and awake now. We'd soon come to the exit for Río Piedras. I knew that by all rights my turn had come, but fortunately the trip was almost over. Then just as I thought I was safe, the voice of the man from Maunabo checked me:

"Well, young lady, aren't you going to tell us a story?"

The driver and the other passengers joined in. But I shook my head and began trotting out my entire arsenal of cheap excuses—I didn't have anything interesting to tell, life in San Juan was so boring, nothing ever happened, and of course we were coming to the plaza now and we'd all be getting out and going our own ways, so I really didn't have time to tell one. But everyone was so insistent that finally

I even had to claim I had a sore throat. Suddenly turning up the volume on his Walkman and blasting us with the latest hip-hop hit, the kid with the Walkman came to my rescue. So with youth arrayed against them, the older folks from the south coast finally stopped insisting and resigned themselves to traveling the last short stretch of the trip in silence.

In the plaza at Río Piedras, the goodbyes took a while. People introduced themselves to each other (by name, I mean, at last) and shook hands warmly. The man from Guayama, who turned out to be a fireman and not a retired schoolteacher, drew us a map on a napkin so we could all get to his house sometime. The driver even gave us his card, and he told us several times not to hesitate to call him the next time we wanted to "go down that way."

"Next time, have a cup of coffee before you leave," suggested the charismatic lady, picking up a box, tied all round with twine, that smelled deliciously of ripe mangoes.

The driver laughed one of his unmistakable laughs again.

"Goodness gracious," he said, "that's just a trick of mine to get to hear people tell stories . . ."

I walked down Georgetti toward my apartment, and I hadn't got far before I had the eerie sense that someone was following me. Given the all-too-real possibility of a mugging to welcome me to the metropolitan area, I turned around, only to discover that it was the kid with the Walkman. I thanked him for coming to my rescue in the *público* and we walked on together toward Ponce de León. He told me he went to the university days and sold ice cream nights in Los Chinitos.

"Come in sometime and have an ice-cream courtesy of the management," he said, this time with a less ambiguous wink. And then, just as we were about to part—

"Hey, listen, what do you do? Do you work here, or what?"

I just smiled, coyly waved goodbye, and kept walking. I didn't want to break the magic of the moment. My head was full of words, and I could hardly wait to sit down at my typewriter and roll in that first piece of paper.

Esmeralda Santiago

excerpt from
WHEN I WAS PUERTO RICAN

Con el agua al cuello y la marea subiendo

With water to the chin and the tide rising

THE SKY FELL TO the tops of the mountains. The air hung heavy, moist. Birds left the *barrio,* and insects disappeared into hidden cracks and crevices, taking their songs. A cowboy rounded up the cattle in Lalao's *finca,* and on her side of the fence, Doña Ana led her cow to the shack behind her house. The radio said Hurricane Santa Clara was the biggest threat to Puerto Rico since San Felipe had destroyed the island in 1918.

"Papi, why do they name hurricanes after saints?" I asked as I helped him carry a sheet of plywood he was going to nail against the windows of our house.

"I don't know," he answered. The hurricane warning must have been serious if Papi couldn't stop to talk about it.

Mami bundled our clothes, pushed her rocking chair, the table and stools, her sewing machine, and the pots and pans into a corner, tied everything to the socles, pressed it all against the strongest wall of the house, and covered it with a sheet, as if that would keep everything from being blown away.

"Negi, take the kids to Doña Ana's. We'll be there in a while."

I rounded up Delsa, Norma, Hector, Alicia, and Edna. For once I didn't have to chase them all over the place, didn't have to threaten, yell, or pull their ears for ignoring me. They lined up solemn as soldiers, Alicia and Hector hanging on to Norma's hand, Edna on Delsa's hip. The baby was asleep in his hanging cradle, but Mami took him out, bundled him in flannel sheets, and handed him to me.

"Take Raymond. Make sure no drafts get to him."

The baby was thirty days old, and we had to be careful about infections, foul breezes, and the evil eye. Mami had strung a nugget of coral and an onyx bead on a safety pin and attached it to Raymond's baby shirt at birth. It was the same charm she had used on all of us, kept in a little box among her thimbles and needles between babies, to be brought out and pinned to the tiny cotton shirts, supposedly for the first forty days and forty nights of our lives. She claimed she didn't believe "any of that stuff," but each time, the charm stayed on long after it was supposed to.

We trudged single file along the path connecting our yard with Doña Ana's. Her sons had nailed plywood sheets to the windows and along the front of her house, so that the only way in was the back door leading to the latrine, barn, and pigsty. These structures had also been reinforced with plywood, and debarked tree limbs buttressed every wall. As we passed from the barn, we heard the muffled and frightened moo of the cow, the frantic squealing of pigs, and the rustle and cackle of hens and roosters.

Inside the house, every crack and chink had been plugged with rags to keep the wind out. Mattresses were stacked, bunches of green bananas hung from the rafters, the gash where the machete had cut dripped white sticky ooze onto the floor. The room was shadowy, lit with *quinqués* and fat candles, steamy with the fragrance of garlic and onions. Several old hens had been sacrificed and everyone contributed something to the communal meal that would be cooked on our kerosene stove, spiced with Doña Lola's fresh oregano, and shared by the four families who would pass the hurricane in Doña Ana's one-room cement house.

Papi and Mami brought in bundles of food, clothes, blankets, and baby diapers. Papi put his battery-operated radio on a shelf and kept it tuned the whole time the hurricane blew, even though all we heard was static. Although Doña Ana's house was no bigger than ours, its sturdy concrete walls and roof made it safe and cozy. The warmth of the thirty or so people inside, the familiar aroma of spices and good cooking, and the hushed play of children was extraordinarily comforting, the way wakes were, or weddings or baptisms.

The men set up a domino table and took turns playing, the losers giving up their chairs to the ones waiting their turn. The women cut up chickens, peeled plantains, cubed potatoes, made *sofrito*, washed dishes, brewed coffee, and tended babies. The *muchachas* huddled in a giggly group between the plantains and the mattresses, while the *muchachos* crouched against the wall opposite, pretending to play cards. We kids played among ourselves or circulated among the various groups, observing the domino game, snatching boiled chicken hearts or livers, carrying mysterious messages from the older boys to the older girls.

Every so often a thump quieted everyone, and arguments erupted about which tree had fallen in which direction. The cows and pigs couldn't be heard above the roar of the wind, the thunder, the crashing zinc sheets from less sturdy roofs, and the flying outhouses lifted in one piece by the wind and swept from one end of the *barrio* to the other.

After we had our *asopao* with plantain dumplings, we curled against one another on the mattresses and slept, lulled by the crackling radio inside and the steady gusts of the hurricane outside.

We heard the ominous quiet of the hurricane's eye as it passed over us. Papi and Dima, Doña Ana's son, pried the door open a crack. It was raining lightly, gray misty drops like steam. The men stepped outside one at a time, looked around, up to the sky, down to the soaked ground that turned into muddy pools wherever their feet had sunk. The women clustered at the door, forming a wall through which we children couldn't pass, although we managed to catch a glimpse by pressing against their hips and thighs, crouching under their skirts, between their legs, against their round calves striated with varicose veins and dark, curly hair.

Mist hung over the yard littered with branches, odd pieces of lumber, a tin washtub that seemed to have been crushed by a giant, and the carcass of a cow, with a rope around her neck still tied to a post. Doña Ana's barn still stood, and the animals inside whimpered softly, as if their normal voices would make the wind start up again. The men walked the edges of the yard in a semicircle, their hands outstretched like the stiff figures I liked to cut from folded newspapers.

A sliver of sun broke through like a spotlight and travelled slowly across the yard, forming a giant rainbow. The women pointed and held up the smaller children to see, while those of us big enough to stand by ourselves crowded the door in awe of that magic spectacle: the figures of our fathers and brothers moving cautiously in a world with no edges, no end, and that bright slice of sun travelling across it, not once touching them.

"We had eleven avocado trees and nine mango trees," Mami was saying. "Now there's only the two avocados and three mangos left."

"My entire coffee patch washed right off the hill." Doña Lola spit into the yard. "And you can see what it did to my medicinal herbs. . . . Even the weeds are gone."

Doña Lola's house, nestled at the side of the mountain, had been spared, but the adjoining kitchen had disappeared, except for the three stones of her *fogón*. Our outside kitchen, too, had flown away, as had our latrine. The whole barrio had been stripped of anything too flimsy, too old, or too weak to withstand the winds and rain that had pelted the island for hours, flooding towns and washing downhill entire communities built along the craggy slopes. No one in Macún died, but many lost their belongings, poultry, pigs, milk cows, vegetable gardens, kiosks for selling fried codfish fritters, and shops where rusty old cars received one more chance at the road.

"Pablo said the government will help rebuild . . ."

"*Sí cuando las gallinas meen!*" Doña Lola laughed, and Mami chuckled, her eyes twinkling at me to see if I understood what Doña Lola meant by "when hens learn to pee." I'd been around enough hens to know they never would.

Papi and Uncle Candido repaired our house, replaced parts of the roof, extended the house to incorporate a kitchen and a site for a bathroom, anticipating the day when water would be piped down the hill to our end of the barrio. They rebuilt the latrine with shiny zinc walls and added a new, more comfortable seat. Mami propped up her pigeon pea and annatto bushes, which had been flattened by the storm, and soon they bloomed again, their leaves as new and fresh as babies.

For months after the hurricane all people talked about was money. Money for the cement and cinder blocks that rose out of the ground in solid, grey walls and flat square roofs. Money for another cow, or a car, or zinc for the new outhouse. Money to install water pipes, or to repair the electric wires that had gone down in the storm and hung like limp, useless, dried-up worms.

Even children talked about money. We scoured the side of the road for discarded bottles to exchange for pennies when the glass man came around. Boys no older than I nailed together boxes out of wood scraps, painted them in bright colors, and set off for San Juan or Rio Piedras, where men paid ten cents for a shoeshine. Papi made *maví*, bark beer, and took two gallons with him to the construction sites where he worked, to sell by the cup to his friends and passersby. Even Doña Lola, who seemed as self-sufficient as anyone could be in Macún, cooked huge vats of rice and beans to sell in the refillable aluminum canisters called *fiambreras* that men took to work when their jobs were not near places to eat. Mami talked about sewing school uniforms and actually made a few. But she soon realized that the amount of work she put into them was more than she was paid for and abandoned the idea while she thought of something else.

"Negi, help me over here."

Mami stood in the middle of the room, her dress bunched on her hips, hands holding fast a long-line brassiere that didn't want to contain her. "See if you can catch the hooks into the eyes, all the way up."

The cotton brassiere stretched down to her hipbones, where it met the girdle into which she had already squeezed. There were three columns of eyes for the hooks spaced evenly from top to bottom. Even when I tugged on both ends of the fabric, I had trouble getting one hook into an outermost eye.

"It's too small. I can't get them to meet."

"I'll hold my breath." She took in air, blew it out, and stretched her spine up. I worked fast, hooking her up all the way before she had to breathe again in big, hungry gulps.

"Wow! It's been a while since I wore this thing," she said, pulling her dress up. "Zip me up?"

"Where are you going?"

"There's a new factory opening in Toa Baja. Maybe they need people who can sew."

"Who's going to take care of us?"

"Gloria will be here in a little while. You can help her with the kids. I've already made dinner."

"Will you work every day?"

"If they hire me."

"So you won't be around all the time."

"We need the money, Negi."

Mami twisted and sprayed her hair, powdered her face, patted rouge on already pink cheeks, and spread lipstick over already red lips. Her feet, which were usually bare, looked unnatural in high heels. Her waist was so pinched in, it seemed as if part of her body were missing. Her powdered and painted features were not readable; the lines she'd drawn on her eyebrows and around her eyes and the colors that enhanced what always seemed perfect were a violation of the face that sometimes laughed and sometimes cried and often contorted with rage. I wanted to find a rag and wipe that stuff off her face, the way she wiped off the dirt and grime that collected on mine. She turned to me with a large red smile.

"What do you think?"

I was ashamed to look, afraid to speak what I saw.

"Well?" She put her hands on her hips, that familiar gesture of exasperation that always made her seem larger, and I saw the unnatural diamond shape formed by her elbows and narrowed waist. I couldn't help the tears that broke my face into a million bits, which made her kneel and hold me. I wrapped my arms around her, but what I felt was not Mami but the harsh bones of her undergarments. I buried my face in the soft space between her neck and shoulder and sought there the fragrance of oregano and rosemary, but all I could come up with was Cashmere Bouquet and the faint flowery dust of Maybelline.

She woke early, sometimes even before Papi, cooked the beans and rice for our supper, ironed our school uniforms and her work clothes, and bathed, powdered, and stuffed herself into her tortuous undergarments. In whispers, she gave me instructions for the day, told me when she'd be back, warned me to help Gloria with the children, promised to sew the buttons on Hector's shirt when she came home that night.

Papi was not around as much once Mami began work, and our mornings took on a rhythm that left him out the days he was home, each one of us engaged in our own morning rituals of waking, dressing, eating breakfast, and walking the two miles to school. My classes began the earliest, at 7:30, and I left home while the air was still sweet and the ground moist, our neighbors' houses looming like ghosts in light fog or receding behind greyness when it rained.

My Uncle Candido's house was halfway to school. He complained to Mami that I never looked up when I went by, never greeted anyone, never looked anywhere but down at the ground.

"If you keep walking like that," he said, "you'll develop a hunchback."

But that threat wasn't enough to keep me from wrapping my arms around myself. Books pressed against my chest, I strode head down, looking closely at the way the ground swelled and dipped, listening to the crunch of my hard school shoes on the pebbled stretches and their swish on the sandy patches. And when I didn't look at the ground, I was blind and would sometimes get to school and not know how. On those mornings my eyes closed in on me and showed me pictures inside my head, while my legs moved on their own up the hills, down the ruts, through the weeds, across gullies, between the aisles of my schoolmates' desks and to my own, alphabetically in the rear of the classroom. I'd sit down, open my notebook, write the date at the top of the page, and look up to Miss Jiménez and her cheery *"Buenos días, clase."* I would then realize I'd come all the way to school with no memory of the journey, my mind a blank slate on which I would write that day's lessons.

With Mami at work, I took advantage of Gloria's vigilance with the younger kids to make my own getaway into the *montes,* up trees, behind sheds and outhouses, and once, on a dare, into Lalao's *finca,* where I filled the skirt of my dress with the coveted grapefruits.

"Where did these come from?" Mami asked when she came home from work.

"I found them," I said.

"No, she didn't. She sneaked into Lalao's *finca* with Tato and Pepito." Delsa smirked, and Mami's eyes disappeared behind a frown.

"Haven't I told you not to go in there?"

"They were on the ground, just on the other side of the fence. . . ."

She looked at the grapefruits, green speckled with yellow and tiny black dots. Their citrus fragrance filled the room like smoke.

"Don't go in there again," she said, picking one up, "or I'll really let you have it."

She peeled one in long strips and sucked on the sweet juice hungrily. I sought Delsa's eyes and saw fear, not of Mami but of me, because Delsa knew that while Mami was at work the next day, I'd get her for tattling.

One morning Mami cooked our dinner, left everything ready for Gloria, dressed, and got us off to school one at a time. When I came home, she was still there, her work clothes stretched on the bed, rumpled and forgotten.

"Where's Gloria?" I asked.

"She escaped," Mami said, which meant that Gloria had eloped. No girl ever ran away by herself, although boys disappeared for weeks the minute they thought of themselves as men.

"Is she coming back?"

"I don't know. No one knows the man she ran off with."

Mami couldn't go to work for a couple of weeks, and we had to live with her bad temper and complaints. "I'm not the kind of person to sit around doing nothing," she said to Doña Ana, and I wondered how she could think of her housework as nothing when she spent hours doing it.

"So how do you like the factory?" Doña Lola asked Mami as we shucked pigeon peas in her new kitchen.

"It's good work," Mami answered, pride in her voice. "I started as a thread cutter, and now I'm a sewing machine operator."

"*Qué bueno!*"

Doña Lola's son Tato ran into the kitchen. "Is there anything to eat?"

"Rice and beans in the pot."

Tato rattled lids and dropped a spoon on the new cement floor. Doña Lola stood up with a jerk. "Let me serve you," and under her breath, "Men are so useless."

Tato looked at me from beneath his long lashes. Doña Lola handed him a tin plate mountained with white rice and red beans. He sat in the corner, spooning it in as if he hadn't eaten in a week.

He was a year older than I, skinny, brown as a chocolate bar, his hair orange, his hazel eyes full of mischief and laughter. He was the dirtiest boy I'd ever seen, not because he didn't wash, but because he couldn't stay clean no matter how many times Doña Lola dunked him in the tin tub in back of the house.

Tato was not afraid of anything. He caught bright green lizards, pinched their jaws at the side, and forced them to bite his earlobes, to which they clung like festive, squirming decorations. He trapped snakes and draped them around his neck, where they writhed in sumptuous silvery waves that seemed to tickle. He speared iguanas and roasted them on open fires, claiming that their meat was tastier than chicken. He was an expert slingshot maker, and it was he who taught me to choose the forked branches that we stripped of bark, dried in the sun, and carved until we could tie split inner tube strips and a rubber square that held the lethal stones we shot with uncanny accuracy.

I was as good as he with both slingshots and painstakingly constructed bows and arrows, with which I could drop birds in flight. We had an uneasy, competitive friendship, made more special by the fact that Mami didn't approve.

"You're almost *señorita*. You shouldn't be running wild with boys," she'd tell me. But I didn't have anything in common with the girls my age. Juanita Marín had found more kindred friendships at her end of the *barrio*, and Doña Zena's daughters, who were about my age, were kept on a tight leash because of their parents' religiosity, which didn't allow for outside influences. My sisters close to my age were not as interesting as the neighborhood boys who ran and climbed and didn't mind getting dirty.

Tato put his dish and spoon in the dishwater. "Let's go play outside." His small, dirty face betrayed no hint of what we were really going to do.

"Can I Mami?"

She cracked the tip off a pod, pulled the string, snapped the casing open, slid her thumb inside the slithery shell, and added the peas to the mound in the bowl between her knees. She looked at me with a warning. "Don't go too far. We're going home soon."

I thought maybe she had read our minds, and for a minute I was afraid to go with him.

"Come on!" Tato called from the yard.

I backed out of the kitchen, but Mami and Doña Lola had gone back to their shucking. We ran around the yard a couple of times to throw them off then sneaked into the oregano bushes that grew thick and fragrant behind the outhouse.

"You first," he said.

"No way! You first."

He pulled down his shorts and just as quickly pulled them up. "Your turn," he said.

"I didn't see anything!"

"Yes you did!"

"I didn't. And I'm not going to show you mine until I do!"

Although I'd seen both Hector's and Raymond's penises when I changed their diapers, I'd never seen one outside the family. Tato had no sisters, so I was pretty sure he'd never seen a girl's private parts. I, of course, had seen several of those, too.

"Well, I'm not pulling my pants down again!" Tato said walking away.

"Fine. I don't have to see your silly old little chicken, I've seen my brothers', and I bet they're nicer than yours."

"Those are baby *pollitos*. I'm already big. Mine has hair on it!"

"Oh, sure!"

"It does. And it gets so big, it can already go into a woman."

"You're disgusting!"

"I can get it into a woman and wiggle it around and around, like this." He wriggled his finger in arches that circumscribed a space much larger than his hand, at the same time wiggling his hips in figure eights.

"You're sick!" I ran into Doña Lola's yard just as Mami came out.

"I was coming to find you," she said, looking behind me. Tato watched us from the path into the bushes. "Grab that bag. We're going home."

Doña Lola handed me a sackful of pigeon peas.

"Tato, go and feed those pigs! They've been squealing all afternoon." He ran off, and Mami led the way up the road to our house.

"What were you two doing in back of the outhouse?" she asked casually.

"Just playing." I hoped she hadn't heard us talking. She didn't say any more, and I took the shortcut home, through the yucca plants, past the barren mango tree at the edge of Lalao's *finca*.

Another day Tato and I were behind the latrine.

"I can see it better if you squat," Tato said, crouching in front of me to get a better look at the smooth slit between my legs.

"Forget it!" I pulled up my panties.

"But it's not fair. You saw mine real good!"

"Sí. And you lied. There's no hair on it at all."

"You didn't look close enough."

"There was nothing to see. It's just as shrivelled and small as my baby brother's."

"You have to rub it to make it big."

"No way am I touching your dirty little *pollito!*"

"It'll grow big and long, you'll see!"

"No way!"

"I'll touch you if you touch me."

"I don't want you to touch me!"

"It feels good." He rubbed his crotch as if he had an itch. He thrust his hips out toward me. "Oooh, it's so good. . . . Mmmm!" He closed his eyes and smacked his lips like he was eating the sweetest candy.

I stared at him writhing, his tongue flicking in and out of his mouth, foamy spit at the corners, his eyes rolling in his head, his hands moving faster and faster. "Men are such pigs!" The words flashed into my head like the headline on a newspaper, only I heard it too, in the voices of Mami and Doña Lola, Gloria and Doña Ana, Abuela, *bolero* singers, radio soap opera actresses, and my own shrill scream into Tato's face.

"*Cochino!*" Pig! His eyes popped open, and his mouth dropped into a grimace that became a lewd, ugly, humiliating smile. He tried to grab between my legs, and, enraged, I drew back my foot and kicked as hard as I could so that it seemed that I lifted him on my shin before he crumpled to the ground, hands between his legs, no longer rubbing but holding fast to what I was afraid had come loose.

Mami and Doña Lola came running. Between sobs, Tato told them I had kicked him for no reason at all, and Mami dragged me home, her fingers pinching my bony arm.

I screamed, trying to explain what Tato had tried to do. But Mami wouldn't listen. I pulled loose and ran, and she chased me into our yard and through the house. On the way out the kitchen door, she grabbed a frying pan and thwacked my head. She tied my wrists together in one of her strong hands, and beat me, again and again, raising welts on my arms, my back, the back of my head, my forehead, behind my ear. My sisters and brothers came out from wherever they'd been playing, even Raymond who had just learned to walk, and they watched as Mami lifted the pan over her head and let it fall on the ball I had become, hanging from her hand like an unripe fruit on an unbending tree.

"Don't you ever, ever do that again," she growled, and I wasn't sure if she meant kicking a boy between his legs or letting him see my private parts. Because it seemed to me she knew what Tato and I did behind the latrine while she and Doña Lola talked about their lives. She knew, and she was waiting for me to do something worse than what I could imagine so that she could do something far worse than what I would expect. I let my body go limp to take her abuse, and part of me left my body and stood beside my sisters and brothers, their eyes round, tear filled, frightened, their fingers interlaced into each other's, their skinny bodies jerking with every hit I took.

Gloria came back to live in a neat wood house in the middle of a coconut grove behind her mother's property. Her *marido* was from a nearby *barrio* and worked for the electric company.

"Maybe now," Mami joked, "we'll get light back in Macún."

As soon as Gloria returned, Mami unfolded her work clothes, washed her hair, and polished her shoes. But instead of Gloria coming to our house every morning, we now went to her shady house under the palms.

One day she handed me a small paper bag, tightly packed with something soft. "Throw this into the latrine, would you please?"

"What is it?"

"Nothing that concerns you."

"Then why should I throw it out?"

"Are you this mouthy all the time or just with me?"

"All the time."

"I figured. Take the thing out and I'll tell you about it when you come back."

I was tempted to open the bag and look inside, but she kept her eye on me as she changed Raymond's diaper. When I looked down the hole of the latrine I noticed a couple of little bags like the one I held floating on the dark smelly waste at the bottom.

"Okay, I threw it out." She put Raymond and Edna down for their afternoon siesta. The air was light, breezy, aromatic of guavas, which grew in tall bushes along the side of her house. "What was inside the bag?"

"A Kotex."

"What's that?"

She poured water into a bowl and salted it generously. "How old are you?"

"Ten."

She grabbed two green plantains from a high shelf and brought them to the table. "And Doña Monín hasn't told you about being a *señorita?*"

"She told me I should stop playing with boys because I'm almost *señorita,* and that I should keep my legs closed when I sit."

Gloria laughed so hard she almost dropped the knife she found near the *fogón.*

"What's so funny?" I was embarrassed and pleased. Clearly there was a lot more to this *señorita* business, and Gloria knew what it was. I laughed with her, sensing she was about to tell me something my mother was supposed to but hadn't.

"Do you know where babies come from?"

"Everybody knows that!"

"Do you know how they're made?"

I'd seen roosters chase hens, catch up, climb on top of them, and dig sharp beaks into the hen's head as she cackled and screeched and he flapped his wings. I'd seen male dogs chase females, the male climb on top of the female, ride her while she tried to shake him off, and dig his narrow pink penis into her backside. I'd seen bulls ride cows, horses hump mares, pigs rolling in mud, their bodies connected under the female's tail. And I'd seen eggs laid, bloody puppies wet and shimmery, calves encased in a blue bubble, slippery wet ponies thin and vulnerable, and hundreds of pink piglets suckling engorged teats. But until Gloria asked, I'd never put it together that in order for me and my four sisters and two brothers to be born, Papi had to do to Mami what roosters did to hens, bulls did to cows, horses did to mares. I shuddered.

"Yes, I know how babies are made."

Gloria slit a plantain from tip to tip, peeled the casing back, and cut diagonal slices which she dipped in the salted water.

"Before you can make babies, you have to be a *señorita,* which means you bleed once a month." Gloria then explained what a period was, how long it lasted, what a woman had to do so her clothes wouldn't get soiled. "Very soon you will be a *señorita,*" she said, "and then you have to keep your legs crossed, just like your Mami says, all the time." She laughed at her own joke, which didn't seem so funny to me. "Ay, you're so solemn! I must have scared you. Don't worry, it's nothing. Just a nuisance you learn to live with. Every woman does."

But I wasn't worried about my period, which couldn't possibly be worse than the worms I'd found in my panties. I imagined Mami and Papi, in bed, stuck together in the middle. I remembered Tato's words that he could stick his penis in a woman, and I realized that's what Papi did to Mami after we'd all gone to sleep and the springs on their bed creaked in rhythms that always ended in a long, low moan, like a moo, or a hoarse whimper.

Mami was one of the first mothers in Macún to have a job outside the house. For extra money women in the *barrio* took in laundry or ironing or cooked for men with no wives. But Mami left our house every morning, primped and perfumed, for a job in a factory in Toa Baja.

The *barrio* looked at us with new eyes. Gone was the bland acceptance of people minding their own business, replaced by a visible, angry resentment that became gossip, and taunts and name-calling in the school yard.

I got the message that my mother was breaking a taboo I'd never heard about. The women in the neighborhood turned their backs on her when they saw her coming, or, when they talked to her, they scanned the horizon, as if looking at her would infect them with whatever had made her go out and get a job. Only a few of the neighbors stood by Mami—Doña Ana, whose daughter watched us, Doña Zena, whose Christian beliefs didn't allow for envy, and Doña Lola, who valued everyone equally. Even Tío Candido's wife, Meri, made us feel as if Mami was a bad woman for leaving us alone.

I was confused by the effect my mother's absence caused in other people.

"Why, Mami? Why is everyone so mean just because you have a job?" I pleaded one day after a schoolmate said Mami was not getting her money from a factory but from men in the city.

"They're jealous," she said. "They can't imagine a better life for themselves, and they're not willing to let anyone else have it either. Just ignore them."

But I couldn't close my ears to their insults, couldn't avert my eyes quickly enough to miss their hate-filled looks. I was abandoned by children who until then had been friends. The neighbors on the long walk to and from home were no longer friendly; they no longer offered me a drink of water on a hot afternoon or a dry porch when it rained.

Papi seemed to have the same opinion about Mami's job as the neighbors. He looked at her with a puzzled expression, and several times I heard her defend herself: "If it weren't for the money I bring in, we'd still be living like savages." He'd withdraw to his hammers and nails, to the mysterious books in his dresser, to the newspapers and magazines he brought home rolled up in his wooden toolbox.

I had worried that not having Mami around would make our lives harder, but at first it made things easier. Mami was happy with her work, proud of what she did, eager to share with us the adventures of her day in the factory, where she stitched cotton brassieres she said had to be for American women because they were too small to fit anyone we knew.

But her days were long, filled in the morning with the chores of making both breakfast and dinner, getting seven children ready for school or a day with Gloria, preparing for work, going there and back, returning to a basketful of mending, a house that needed sweeping, a floor that needed mopping, sheets that had to be washed and dried in one day because we didn't have two sets for each bed. As she settled into her routine, Mami decided she needed help, and she turned to me.

"You are the oldest, and I expect you to be responsible for your sisters and brothers, and to do more around the house."

"But isn't Gloria going to take care of us?"

"I can't count on anyone from outside the family. Besides, you're old enough to be more responsible."

And with those words Mami sealed a pact she had designed, written, and signed for me.

"Delsa, you'd better get in here and do the dishes before Mami gets home."

Delsa looked up from the numbers she wrote in her composition book. Rows and rows of numbers, over and over again, in neat columns, in her small, tight script. "It's not my turn." She went back to her homework.

"Whose turn is it then?"

"Yours. I did it yesterday."

The sink was full. Plates, cups, spoons, pot lids, the heavy aluminum rice pot, the frying pan, all half submerged in gray water with a greasy scum floating on the top. "Norma!"

"What!"

"Come here. I'm going to teach you to wash dishes."

"I'm watching Raymond."

"Well, let Hector watch him."

"I don't want to."

"If these dishes aren't washed by the time Mami comes home . . ."

"You do them, then."

I didn't want to either. I didn't want to do any of the things Mami asked of me: feed the kids an after-school snack; make sure they did their homework; get Raymond and Edna from Gloria's; change the water on the beans and put them on the stove to cook over low heat; sweep the floor; make the beds; mound the dirty clothes in the basket; feed the chickens and the pigs. Delsa and Norma were supposed to help, but most of the time they refused, especially when I tried to get them to do the unpleasant tasks like changing Raymond's diaper or scrubbing the rice pot. Almost every day just before Mami came home I scrambled around to do all the things she'd asked me to take care of that morning. And almost every day I received either a lecture or *cocotazos* for not doing everything.

"You're almost *señorita*. You should know to do this without being told."

"I just can't . . ."

"You're lazy, that's your problem. You think everything will be handed to you."

"No I don't," I whimpered, my hands protecting my head from the inevitable blows.

"Don't you talk back!" And she pushed me away as if I were contagious. "The least you can do is set an example for your sisters and brothers."

I looked at Delsa, who at nine could already make perfect rice, and at Norma, who swept and mopped with precision, and at Hector, who dutifully changed out of his uniform into play clothes every day without being told. "What makes them so good and me so bad?" I asked myself. But there were no answers in Delsa's solemn eyes, or in Norma's haughty beauty, or in Hector's eagerness to please. Every night Mami told me how I had failed in my duty as a female, as a sister, as the eldest. And every day I proved her right by neglecting my chores, by letting one of the kids get hurt, by burning the beans, by not commanding the respect from my sisters and brothers that I was owed as the eldest.

Madeline Coopsammy

THE TICK-TICK BICYCLE

EVERY NIGHT AFTER SUPPER, Sharon heard it. Tick, tick, and the lights would flash, like those of a circus horse. She would see him, learning backwards on his bicycle, grinning sardonically, and looking into their front porch. In spite of the semi-darkness of the porch, the street light would reveal, to her frightened eyes, his form elevated to a mysterious strength and power by the shining glory of the bicycle. She had seen him when he was not astride his flashy machine in its souped-up beauty, how ordinary and insignificant he was. But when he rode through the streets of San Juan de la Pina on his tick-tick bicycle, he owned the world.

She began to dread going out on the porch after supper. Yet to remain inside the house, where the tropical heat saturated her body and seemed to addle her mind would be to admit her guilt. She would wait until she thought it was safe to come out. But often she miscalculated his hour, or he had returned, not having seen her the first time. After he had gone, she found it difficult to concentrate on her studies, and too often she could not fall asleep. Sometimes, long after everyone was sleeping, she was sure that she heard it again. Tick, tick, and through the fine weave of the lace curtain, she thought she saw the flash of lights as his bike went by. She would get up and make sure that the window was shut tight, though the heat would almost suffocate her.

They called him Wild Bill Hickok, most often, Wild Bill. The Caribbean island of Santa Maria in the 1950s was by no means the plains and mountains of the American Wild West. But Santa Marian youths, for a few cents, could relieve the tedium of their lives by absorbing the celluloid fantasies of Hollywood. And so it became easy for them to adopt the names of its heroes and vagabonds, no matter how incongruous. Wild Bill was known to all the residents of San

---

Juan de la Pina, an amorphous part of the town that could not be classified as a suburb but was not completely part of the business world.

The district of San Juan de la Pina was bound by two parallel arteries, each the opposite of the other. On one side was the Northern Main Road, bustling with commerce, traffic, and bacchanalian revelry every night of the week. On the other was the softly residential avenue known as Cumana. Several nondescript but divergent streets linked these two passageways. But Wild Bill made himself equally at home on his tick-tick bicycle as he veered casually between the two territories. Everyone knew him, accepted him as part of the landscape, as just another idler, another young man who lounged about the clubs and cafes, or "parlours" as they were called, of the Main Road. How he lived, no one knew or cared. Wasn't it enough that he owned a tick-tick bicycle, the most flamboyant of its kind? But to Sharon, consumed with fear of him, hating him for the chaos he was wreaking on her hitherto peaceful life, he was more than an idler. She had heard it whispered that he was dangerous. But why exactly, no one dared to say.

And so, she had always kept her head high when she passed him on the Main Road, as he slouched against a post or learned against his bicycle; and even though he always muttered sly remarks under his breath, or whistled at her, she never looked at him as she had been warned. She treated him as any other wastrel. But that was before. Now it was different. In the past, he had appeared and disappeared at irregular intervals. Now he was always around. She began to fear walking on the Main Road alone. But most of all, she dreaded the hour after supper when he would be sure to ride by, the tick-tick of his bicycle echoing every fearful beat of her own heart.

Perhaps, if he were not the proud owner of such a status symbol as a tick-tick bicycle, she could dismiss him as of no consequence. But because of the bicycle, he considered himself King of the Main Road, where all the unemployed and unschooled young men congregated, doing odd jobs, or shooting pool in the beer parlors. When he was not standing on the corner of the Main Road, sniggering at the girls, he was seen crouched over the low handlebars of the ten-speed bicycle, which was shinier, newer, boasted more lights and more gadgets than that of any other youth. Above all, it seemed to have the loudest, most persistent tick-tick in the area. What he had added to the bike to create that sound, Sharon never knew.

When Sharon and her mother were returning from visiting relatives, many blocks away, they saw him, hanging backwards on his bicycle, grinning at them. Her mother had cautioned her not to show any fear, saying sternly, "He's only one of those no-good idlers. Besides, he's a big coward, everyone knows that. He'll never molest us."

If you had said that a few months ago, Mother, you might have been right, Sharon thought. But now, it's different. And she trembled when he passed by. Still, she dared not say anything to her mother. For her mother would only worry, as she always did. Sharon was old enough to know that life was not easy for her mother, having to bring up five daughters by herself, while her husband worked in Venezuela, "in the oil fields" as people in Santa Maria always described it. Sharon had heard that expression so often in her childhood that she had imagined the neighbouring country as one huge field of oil, and its landscape broken only by enormous derricks. As she grew older, she became more accustomed to the reality of a father absent most on the time; on his trips home, she learnt to make fine distinctions about the country in which her father spent most of the year. She began to understand that Maracaibo was different from Caracas and that Venezuela, though only eleven miles away, had little affinity with British Santa Maria. But her father's twice a year visits were never enough. When she complained, her mother explained that this was the only way in which they could be brought up in the style to which they were accustomed. "Times are hard now" her mother said, "and people like us are not common people." But because she had no brothers, and because her father was never there, Sharon felt that they had no one, no strong man to protect them from Wild Bill.

She never told her mother: how could she bring herself to explain that Wild Bill had taken to riding past their house more regularly now than before, and that she—and no common girl of the street—was responsible for this? That he was pedalling his tick-tick bicycle up and down their quiet, respectable street because of her and not because he was waiting for some servant girl from one of the neighbouring houses? That if it hadn't been for her, he would now be hanging around the Main Road rather than disturbing her serenity by the nagging tick-tick of his bicycle down their street every night? If only she had not been so self-willed. She shivered whenever she heard the sinister sound of the bicycle. In the daytime, when she took the bus to go to school in the town, she felt safe from him. It was too early for him to be about, idler as he was.

But in the afternoons, after school, she could never bring herself to go to any of the stores on the Main Road, even though it was necessary to do so. Perhaps she had to buy some lace or ribbon for her sewing class the next day, or else incur the wrath of Sister Veronique, the sewing teacher. Now, however, she would have to wait until one of her sisters could go with her, for he would be sure to be there, not sitting or standing, but half-leaning against a pillar or his bicycle. Often,

Sharon wondered why it was that Wild Bill managed to convey the impression of evil, even though he was, in reality, quite nice-looking. He was never drunk, nor did he ever smell of rum. He was always well-dressed, in the jeans and wide belts that were becoming fashionable in Santa Maria at that time. But whenever Sharon looked directly into his eyes, their smallness never ceased to amaze her. There was something strange about them, she would think. And why did he have to straighten his hair, instead of letting it curl in its natural way? Surely that was the mark of an idle young man's vanity. Everyone had come to expect Negro women to straighten their hair with a hot comb and lots of brilliantine. All modern Negroes did it, instead of plaiting their hair in the corn-row style of their African cousins. But sensible people could not abide seeing such straightening in a man's hair. Respectable old men never indulged in such vanity. But the "Hot Boys" of the town, as they were called, those frequenters of the "Pit" section of the cinema, were the ones who sported such a fashion. But Sharon had to admit that the eyes, the straightened hair—they were of no consequence. It was the mouth, the cynical, sneering mouth, the lecherous grin that never ceased to dismay her.

Although she was sure everyone in her family knew of her fear, and that they hated her for the disgrace she was going to bring upon them, she could never bring herself to talk about Wild Bill. She was too ashamed of her weakness and bad judgement and of how she had pestered her mother to go to the Allens' party that night three months ago. Her arguments with her mother had been long and bitter.

"But everyone—all my friends in class—are going, Mother. Why I alone must stay home every Friday night? I never get to go to *fetes* like everyone else."

"You can go to *fetes*, yes," her mother would counter, "but *fetes* in decent places, to nice people's homes, not with people like that."

"But the Allens are decent people, Mother. They come to Church every Sunday."

"You are too young to understand, girl. You will be sorry later on in life. I don't want you going out with any and everybody. Remember who your grandfather and uncles are."

"So my grandfather is a white man, and my uncles are doctors. But my father is a brown man, and we live in this rat-hole and pretend that we're better than everybody else. Well, I don't want to pretend any more. I want a normal life."

Her mother's face had taken on that veil of fear and hurt over it that always frightened Sharon. This always had the effect of making her back off from any further confrontation with her mother. Mrs. Damien was a thin, nervous woman who sometimes retreated into her own fantasy world when life's realities became too much for her. Always fearful of her mother's precarious hold on the world, Sharon had resigned herself to not going. But then Mrs. Danien had suddenly announced, "I asked Aunt Margie if I should let you go to the Allens' *fete,* and she said it should be okay."

Surprised, Sharon had nothing to say, but one thought was uppermost in her mind. You asked Aunt Margie, a worse snob than yourself? And she said yes? Aunt Margie? That is really strange. It suddenly came to her that the Allens were relatively well-off. Aunt Margie usually rated people according to how "high-coloured" they were; that is, according to how much white blood they showed. Could it be that the old biddy felt that the Allens' money made up for their lack of "high colour"? Sharon decided that it was too complex to worry about. She could already hear the steel band music pounding in her ears and feel the calypso rhythms in her body. She could see her classmates' laughing faces. And she knew which boys would be there too, but it didn't matter, for the Allens' second boy would be there for sure. And she couldn't wait to talk to him again. He was so intelligent; his eyes behind his horn-rimmed glasses were so deep and kind.

And then Wild Bill had to spoil it all—by crashing the party. And no one, none of the adults or young men there had cared enough to throw him out. And though everyone was having a good time, she felt that many of them looked as if they had had too much to drink. She found it strange that there were so many adults. She could not imagine her mother or any of her aunts at this kind of party, so relaxed and comfortable, and laughing and teasing the teenagers. Now at last she had a glimpse of another Santa Maria, the Santa Maria of the "common people" from which her mother and her aunts shielded her so well.

And when Wild Bill had come in, he had walked straight up to her. It was as if he had sensed that she was easy prey. And her fear of offending, her desire to be liked by these people, even though they were people that her mother might call common, was uppermost in her mind. Wild Bill had stood in front of her and asked her for a dance! For a few seconds, which seemed like hours, Sharon just sat there, unable to either refuse or accept. But her inexperience, her self-consciousness and sensitivity made her feel as if everyone waited with bated breath to see what she would do—for Sharon was aware, from the moment she walked into the room, that she was the only one of her kind there. Her skin was white, that pasty white of the Trinidad white, and her hair showed traces of negro blood visible only to the sharp-eyed who looked for such things. Perhaps everyone there would think that she was snubbing Wild Bill because she felt superior to them all.

And so she got up. Got up to dance with Wild Bill! If her mother or any of her sisters were to see her, she knew that she would die of shame. But they weren't there, and she tried to hold herself stiffly and prayed that the dance would soon be over. But he wouldn't let her. He clutched her suffocatingly close to himself. She cringed, inside herself. But outside, she was dancing around the floor with him, and she felt every eye in the room riveted on them, every voice censoring her. But what could she have done? She was not experienced enough to know that Wild Bill would never have been an invited guest, that in spite of the happily-intoxicated older people, it was still a "decent" party. The youngsters there were all high school students, a privileged class. They were far removed from someone like Wild Bill, idler, lounger-at-large, and unemployed in spite of his tick-tick bicycle and its flashing lights.

In her reflective moments, when she tried to convince herself that Wild Bill would not dare to harm her, she replayed in her mind's eye the scene of that night, what she had done, how she had acted, and how she had looked. Then she was convinced that it had been her fault. For again Wild Bill had come back and asked her to dance. And having danced once, how could she refuse? And the third time. But then, the Allens' second boy who had been sitting next to her and talking about *The Aeneid* and Vergil, had suddenly got up and said to Wild Bill, "Sorry, boy, she's dancing this one with me." And she had been saved. Wild Bill had never come back and asked her to dance again, contenting himself with ogling her in a slimy way from across the room. But Sharon felt dirtied, almost as if she should go to confession. Or as if she had broken one of the most sacred rules of the convent, and that the nuns would soon be asking her to leave, the ultimate disgrace that could befall a convent girl. For she was no good, she associated with Wild Bill Hickok, anathema to all they hold dear.

Sometimes when she couldn't sleep at night, she thought about how the characters in books and movies would get away from people like Wild Bill, and she often thought that the easiest would be to fall under a car. At other times she was sure that he would come to her house that night, perhaps when she was asleep, and he would break open the window. What would be even worse, he would park his tick-tick bicycle in front of her house and walk up their front steps during the hour after supper when her whole family was sitting on the porch. And he would walk up the steps and stand on their porch just as if he were any of the "decent" boys that came to visit. Then her mother and sisters would find out, and they would be hurt and embarrassed. They would blame her for bringing this shame upon them, this association with the lowest of the low, with this toad that idled his life away on street corners calling out names to the girls as they passed by.

A day passed by and she saw no sign of him. Then another day. After a week had gone by and he still had not appeared, she hoped and prayed that he had moved away and that she would never see him again. Or that by the time he returned, she would be grown-up, with a boy-friend or husband so big and strong that Wild Bill would not dare to trouble her any more. Or that she might have left the island, "gone away" as most young people did when they finished high school. Then one day a headline in the newspaper caught her eye:

Wild Bill Sentenced to Five Years

William A. Carter, also known as Wild Bill Hickok, of no fixed place of address, was yesterday sentenced to five years in the Royal Gaol for breaking and entering. Carter, who had a record of previous offences, had been convicted before on charges of "peeping Tom" behaviour and of molestation of females.

An earlier charge against Carter, that of statutory rape, had been dropped. In sentencing Carter, the Judge made it clear that he would have been more lenient with him, if only he could have ascertained that Carter, at any time in his life, had held down a steady job. "Instead," the judge continued, "the evidence of the Court proved that you spend your hours on street corners, badgering females, and scrounging a meal from anyone you can find. And so," added the Judge, "I feel compelled to put you away for five years."

Merle Hodge

INEZ

MRS. HENRY WAS READY to call the police. The children and the dogs had to get breakfast, she and Henry had to have their coffee, and the confounded girl was ten minutes late. And she had warned her, two years ago when she started, that if she ever came late, every minute would be deducted from her wages. This was the first time, but it would also be the last.

And to think that the facety girl had just the day before put God out of her thoughts and asked for an advance on her week's pay. In the middle of the week!

"Only five dollars, Ma'am."

"Five dollars! But that is half your pay—you can't get half your pay in the middle of the week!"

When the clock struck eight, Mrs. Henry was seized with panic. Suppose she had been fool enough to give her the five dollars! She had no idea where the girl lived; she knew nothing about her; she would have just disappeared like that with her five dollars.

Mrs. Henry now wanted to phone Matilda's Corner Police Station and report an attempted robbery.

The roll call revealed twelve absences. Praise be, sighed the teacher, God forgive my thoughts. But see my trial if all fifty-five of them turn up here one morning. And thank you Jesus, Carlton didn't find his way to school today again. (Forgive me Lord.) He must be in the Plaza begging five cents, or his mother must be catch him up there yesterday and break his foot. (I not wishing it on him, Lord.)

But where is Maxine?

Reprinted by permission of the author.

Maxine was very rarely absent, or late. She always arrived shining clean, her hair neat, her uniform well ironed, although it had long lost its color. Maxine with a wisdom beyond her years. She was bright, bright, and would learn rapidly, if there was more time to teach her.

Yesterday Maxine had inquired of the teacher whether there was any way she could turn into a boy.

It was because the Baby-Father had said to her mother that the Last One still didn't look much like him, so he wasn't bringing one cent more. She could get his father to support him, and furthermore he wasn't bringing a cent more for Audrey either, though he wouldn't say it wasn't his pickney, for gal-pickney grow into woman, and woman is a curse, don't the Bible say so? All women bad like Satan.

So Maxine wanted to turn into a boy as soon as possible.

Afterwards, Miss Williams had gone into the Principal's office and looked into the records, just to make sure. But she was not mistaken: Maxine's date of birth made her seven years old at her last birthday.

Where was Maxine today? The teacher felt a vague uneasiness. Then her heart sank. Oh God! Suppose. . . .

Maxine had related to her how the Baby-Father had tried to box her mother (Maxine wasn't sure why), and how when she picked up the kitchen knife he left, swearing he would bring the police for her.

ℰ

The father of Maxine, Donovan, and Junie had posted his guard at the gate, as usual, for it was the last day of the month. But the boy had not yet raised the alarm. Almost two hours and his spar Nelson was still on standby, ready to take over his domino hand for him when he would have to make a hasty exit.

There had been one false alarm. Out of the corner of his eye he had seen the little boy coming into the yard and he had sprung from the bench—dominoes flying left and right—reached round the side of the house and dived into Wally's room. But David had only come in to use the toilet.

Malcolm was beginning to relax—maybe the miserable woman wasn't coming this month to hold out her hand. How was a man supposed to feed himself and *three* pickney out of what he got at the end of the month? He had told her to give the children to the Government, and that was final. Let the Government feed them, they had money to buy thousand-dollar suit from England for the Governor-General, so they must can feed the pickney them.

Presently, David came back into the yard, reported that the Baby-Mother was still nowhere in sight, and collected his ten cents.

It was dark now, she never came this late. Nice, thought Malcolm. She must be decide to rest me. She must be decide to carry the pickney them go give the Government.

Cho, she no just haffe box-down one of them, break them hand, for police to come charge her for ill treatment and carry-way the whole of them?

❧

The landlord arrived, punctual as doom. The tenants paid, or tendered their excuses, and Mr. James was waiting for Inez. It was seven o'clock and none of the tenants had any idea where she was. The room was empty, and not a single one of her children was to be seen either. The yard neighbor who kept an eye on them in the daytime had not seen them all day.

Inez owed three month's rent. The door of the room was not locked. Mr. James opened it and stood, dejected, looking in. He shook his head wryly. It was a detestable business, what he was going to have to do. For if he didn't, his wife would come down and personally carry out the operation, and then it would be even more unpleasant.

Mrs. James had no use for sluttish women who spent their lives breeding bastard children and then expected you to feel sorry for them when they couldn't pay their debts. She was always willing to teach them a lesson.

He was all for selling the damn properties so he would never have to walk into a tenement yard again, stepping over dusty, snotty children to confront the stone-faced hostility of their parents. He would gladly sell all the properties. But over her dead body.

Now once again they were going to have to evict, seize . . . seize what? The Klim tin sitting smoky and awry in the dead coals? The low, lumpy bed with the deep well in the middle?

He wished with all his might that Inez could come through the gate this very minute, bringing even part of the rent; then he could give her some more time—Mrs. James might not object to that. Otherwise . . . it was a scene that he never got used to; each time made him years older. A shouting, swearing woman, her children screaming, crashing of kitchen utensils, crowd gathering, police. . . .

❧

The nurse on her way out noticed the same silent knot of children still sitting on the bench. The waiting room was nearly empty now: most of the day's crowd had been seen to; there were not many numbers left.

She stepped back and went over to them. The younger ones drew closer round the girl who sat clutching a paper bag and an empty rum bottle.

"Where is your mother?"

"She soon come, Ma'am," said the girl, without conviction.

"You have a number? One of you sick?"

"No Ma'am."

"Then what are you doing here?"

The children stared, mute. Maxine lowered her eyes. "Don't know, Ma'am," she whispered.

The nurses fed them, bought them ice cream, put the youngest ones to sleep on an examining table.

When the police came, Nurse Johnson asked one of the officers what they were going to do. He threw her a glance of part weariness and part scorn as though she had asked a naive and unnecessary question.

"Look for the mother, Ma'am," he explained in a long-suffering voice, "and charge her with abandonment."

ᔆᔆ

The dogs had been barking at the edge of the gully for a full hour, an ominous, nerve-racking sound, for it echoed down the gully and from the caves on the other side.

But now there seemed to be another noise that chilled your spine—a long scream of a baby crying; and now it was all the dogs in the neighborhood barking, shrieking at the edge of the gully.

Mrs. Campbell pulled in her children, locked the doors and the windows, and sent the maid down to the gully to look.

The maid flew back, holding her head and screaming. Before she reached the house, Mrs. Campbell was on the phone to the police.

She lay on the bottom of the gully, face downwards. The Last One lay cozy in the crook of her dead arm, but he was crying now because his bottle had rolled away from him, his bottle of corn meal and water.

Elizabeth Nunez

excerpt from
BRUISED HIBISCUS

ON THE OUTSKIRTS OF Port-of-Spain going south and then further inland to the east, the cool salt wind that blew off the Gulf of Paria across the filth of Nelson Street turned fresh and began to smell of the long green leaves and candy-sweet stalks of sugar cane near harvest time. It blew past the Croisee with its stench of rotting fish, past where the sailors took prostitutes in the narrow crevice of dilapidated buildings and warehouses bursting with bags of sugar and cocoa stacked to the roofs squeezed against banks with names like Barclays of London and Chase Manhattan. It swirled dirty paper and dried animal droppings off the pavements in Nelson Street and then raced through the La Basse chasing after children fighting corbeaux for scraps of food in the piles of garbage on the sea side of the Churchill-Roosevelt Highway, opposite Shanty Town that spilled out of the foothills like an infectious disease spreading sores of cardboard shacks. Eyesores, the ladies in St. Clair Park called them, yesterday's newspaper and the bright colors of last Sunday's comics plastered on their outsides like paint, a few lengths of rusty galvanize laid on top to ward off the rain.

Now buffeting down the Churchill-Roosevelt through the canefields fields towards the Caroni River, the wind was beginning to lose its salt-sea smell and the mango-sweet stench of the garbage from the La Basse. It crossed the zigzag of ditches dug patiently, then frantically, by East Indians who kept believing they could lick the power of the thunderstorms—at least their gods could—the inevitable thunderstorms that each year ruptured the banks of the Caroni, flooding the rice paddies, even the meticulous rows of tomatoes, cabbage and eggplant they planted safely (so they thought) near the edge of the highway.

Reprinted by permission of the author.

Now in the rapid descent of nightfall, the sun slipping into the horizon as if it had no energy left to linger, the wind curled softly around palm-roofed mud huts, picking up the stink of manure to be sure, the pungent odor of curry and dahl from black cast iron pots, but earthy now, smelling of the land. Never mind the sudden flurry of San Juan with its nest of cars swirling around the roundabout, to the right, then straight or to the left, then straight, or round and round in circles. A tiny town, no competition for Port-of-Spain, though it had its markets and its shops too, and its share of crime (Boysie Singh had two women there and scores of boys in training to follow his footsteps). The wind breezed past it in minutes, rolled lazily over the wide open plains towards Tacarigua on the edge of the Orange Grove sugar cane estate. Blew out the thin, white curtains in the dining room of Rosa DesVignes' pretty house and fanned the fire on the stove in the kitchen so she had to shut the window tight. But not before Cedric heard it bang.

"You didn't latch the window, Rosa?"

A night like any other night when Rosa anxiously tasted the food still on the stove in pots, hoping the pinch of salt she added or the pepper was just right. That what she cooked would please her husband, Cedric. Except that night, anxiety turning to fear as she felt the germ loosen in her breast where it was buried. A germ like Zuela's. Because before the window banged and the fire on the stove flared and Cedric shouted, he had walked unexpectedly into the kitchen, caught her with the salt in one hand and the spoon to her lips. Said not a word about her cooking, which she was braced to hear, but cool as ice water, not facing her directly, gave her the news that had spread up north that night. Of a white woman stuffed in a coconut burlap bag in Otahiti, her eyes and lips and tongue eaten by fish, her body dumped between the bamboo in Freeman's Bay, corbeaux circling to finish her off.

"Bet they all think is Boysie. But that has no signs of Boysie. Crime passionnel," he said, pleased with the sounds of his words. He was studying French, Greek and Latin. "A man caught his woman *in flagrante delicto*. And then CRACK . . ."

The word cut across the room. Ugly. Like the brittle sound of a centipede's back snapping.

Rosa jumped. The next moment she was grateful for the wind that had left Nelson Street and blown through the canefields banging the kitchen windows shut, so hard that they sprang open and struck the walls again, like their own echo. For Cedric didn't see the blood rush from her face, and later at dinner, when she brought his food to him in the dining room and he repeated *in flagrante delicto* knowing well enough she knew no Latin, she had time to control the color in her face again. But not her head that throbbed now, stabbing pins in her eyes.

Flagrante delicto. Even if she were not certain of the words, she understood the meaning. *Caught his woman . . .* And she had seen that smile on Cedric's face. She knew that smile, the wet smile he wore only on his lips, the smile that never touched his eyes. A camouflage she had long learned to spot. He used it because he wanted to be considered cultured and educated and thought it would hide the pictures he had in his heart. But she saw them and pain broke through her temples for they reflected the very images that had come suddenly to her in the kitchen the moment he told her of the white woman in Otahiti, a cord around her throat, her eyes, lips and tongue gouged out by fish. His images reflected in her mind as in a mirror but in reverse, so that where he saw woman, she man, and she put her hand to her forehead to push them away feeling too late Cedric's eyes on her.

"What's the matter Rosa? Sick again?"

"No." She answered quickly. "No."

"Headache again?" He didn't look up from his plate.

"No."

"Then what?"

"What you said."

"About the woman in Otahiti?"

He glanced at her. *"That* bothers you?"

"It's so sad."

"Sad?"

"That she was murdered."

"Didn't you hear me, Rosa? In the kitchen? I said, *in flagrante delicto.* At the very moment in the act. You understand *that,* Rosa? In the very act. *In Flagrante delicto."*

"I mean, to murder her like that?"

"Like what?"

"To put her in a bag and dump her in the sea."

Cedric put down his knife and fork, dug his elbows on the table, arched his hands above them, and looked steadily at her. It was a look she had seen many times, in the last year more than she could bear. The first time he stared at her like that, he told her why: He had married a white woman. Like a fool, he had married a white woman. At another time he spoke of her eyes. Like cubes of frozen iced-tea, he said. "But your skin, not your skin. It gives you away." He told her that the sun had burnt it so brown it betrayed her. Let English people know that she lived here not there; that she belonged here, not there, though there had been ancestors there once in the blinding white.

Now he spoke slowly looking obsessively at the white spot that had begun to form on her lower lip where she bit it, watching the blood drain slowly into the corners of her mouth. "When a woman forgets. . . . Thinks she can go out and take it somewhere else . . . When a woman betrays. . . . You understand me, Rosa? A man has no choice. And if he catches her *in flagrante delicto . . .*" He paused, still studying her lips. "Such a man cannot be held responsible. It's a crime du passion that even the courts understand." He shifted his eyes to hers.

Rosa felt her lips tremble. "But it could have been Boysie," she said.

He held his eyes on her.

"He did it before. Don't you remember?" She looked away. "Don't you remember the body that floated out of the sea near the Yacht Club?"

"No one could prove it was Boysie."

"Well, it is possible. Justice Vincent-Brown said . . ."

"He didn't say that, Rosa."

"He said . . ."

"Not that, Rosa."

"He convicted him."

"Yes."

"And people said Boysie took out the man's heart."

"Not true."

"They say Boysie does that all the time. Cuts out people's hearts and rubs them on the hooves of his horses. This woman could be another one, Cedric. Like that man in the water at the Yacht Club."

"I warn you, Rosa, that man's heart was not missing."

"The judge said . . ."

"His heart was still in his body."

"He said . . . People say . . ."

"Shut up!" Cedric brought his fist hard down on the table. Rosa felt the tears gathering in her eyes, but still she persisted, her voice shaking. "Maybe he didn't get a chance . . . Maybe someone caught Boysie before he could take out the heart . . ."

Frowns rolled like wavelets on Cedric's forehead. They gained speed and then almost on the verge of crashing they suddenly retreated, grew calm, disappeared. He threw back his head and laughed: "That's what I like about you Trinidad white people. You believe in more foolishness and superstition than colored people themselves. You believe in soucouyant and diablesse and duene. Long after black people stop believing in foolishness like that you Trinidadian white people still holding on. So Boysie using human hearts on racehorses? It would take people like you to believe that. Boysie must think you're some fools."

The pain behind her eyes ached, and Rosa pressed her thumbs against the sides of her head.

Cedric leaned forward towards her. "You can't again tonight?" he asked. "Headache?"

She shook her head. "No, no. I'll clear the kitchen."

"Because last night . . ."

"I'm fine."

"Look, just get that Boysie nonsense from your head."

"It's okay, Cedric."

"Then I'll be in the study."

Cedric brought his knife and fork together in the middle of his plate and stood up. Almost gently he added, "The dinner was good tonight, Rosa," and surprised her.

When he left she surrendered to the tears that pricked the backs of her eyes. She knew what he wanted, what he meant by his *in flagrante delicto,* looking steadily in her eyes. By his question. You *can't again, tonight?* His tone caustic. Mordant. It seemed like a lifetime but it was only three years ago when he didn't have to ask, when she couldn't wait until he came from the study. There, with the dishes still spread on the table she'd look across at him and he'd know. He would take her then. Sometimes on his chair pulling her legs astride on his lap. He would wait only for her to unbuckle his pants and slip them down his thighs. Sometimes on the hard floor and later she would have to take slivers of wood out of her backside. She knew always to close the windows and draw the curtains before dinner, and months after she had stopped, had removed the drapes and left only the sheers, he seemed not to notice, except on nights like that one when the wind banged the window against the wall and then blew it shut again and the noise brought him early to the kitchen.

How had she reached that moment when the thought of waiting for him in their bed until he was finished with his books brought tears to her eyes. When now she took as long as she could in the kitchen, and bathing before she went to bed was painful, washing the places he would touch.

She had wanted him from the beginning. Not him as a person, but sex. That was what she had wanted and he found her out. Twenty-eight, the last of three sisters and still unmarried, living in a residential camp on the Orange Grove sugar cane estate in the full languor of its decadence. Yellow pawpaws like the swollen udders of cows hanging heavy, plump, overripe in bunches from the tops of long slim trees in backyards. Avocados left to rot in the sun, their pale yellow flesh slimy and slithery, turning black and hard in the burning heat. Mangoes squashed about the lawn, seeds and fleshy pulp mashed into wet grass. An experiment with flowers abandoned out of

248 ⟶ Elizabeth Nunez

boredom and excess, so hibiscus forced to be roses ran rampant, the elegant simplicity of their single-layered petals curled into ruffles like a French petticoat. Poinsettia once wild, tall and wiry, now tamed, short and stumpy, threatened into extinction by the thorny grip of bourganvillea that had defied a determination to train them into fences. Now bourganvilleas scaled walls like ivy, and poinsettia bloomed way before Christmas.

They had cut down the big trees on the Orange Grove Estate, the wide-trunked samaan, the spreading immortelle. They needed the space, they explained, for a clubhouse for the women to play bidwhist and bingo and for the men to gather at night over scotch, cue sticks in hand, stabbing balls across a grass-carpeted table.

So it was in Orange Grove after the war when Rosa was a young girl. When chocolate was the rage again and English chefs and bakers could indulge in dreams about sugar for cakes. No one remembered the depression of the 30's or that Europe had been sweetening its tea with beets instead of cane and could do so again. Orange Grove bloomed. New machinery, new factories. Its future was its present, so it thought, and it splurged, believing that children loved to chase vultures and cane cutters were happy with ten cents a day. For sure no one would tell the people in the La Basse that they were due more than cardboard plastered with yesterday's newspapers. Orange Grove sent its children to England for mates so the Trinidad's white blood would stay white. Rosa's parents did too. Sent her two sisters, but not her. Not Rosa. Her mother protected her. And even when some of the women returned from ruined marriages, there were Trinidadian white men to be found because they too could not explain to their English mates why they threw salt behind their backs and crossed themselves, or why they too cut loose strands of their hair from combs and brushes and threw them in the fire. Or why they couldn't stop doing things like that.

Both of Rosa's sisters who left husbands in England found white men again in Trinidad. Not her. Not Rosa. Her mother still held her shut behind closed doors.

"She love you too much," the black woman who cleaned their house used to say to her. "She think you too good to give away."

Another woman had said the same thing. A woman with a butterfly on her face and a name that was both a first name and a surname. Mary Christophe. She said to Rosa when Rosa asked, fearing her turn was next the fifth time her mother had gone to England with her sisters: "Will she take me away there too?"

"No," Mary Christophe answered. "You belong here. You one of us. She know that. She won't take you away. You *too good to give away.*"

Yet when Cedric came, his hat in one hand, his books in the other, her mother said yes: "Yes, you can marry her."

Maybe it was because by then she had become an embarrassment to her mother. For in an age when women were wives way before twenty-one, she was already an old maid, one whose habit of withdrawal was causing a gossip about an unnatural woman who didn't like men. Yet it was not reason enough to explain why after so many years of claiming no one suitable for her daughter, Clara Appleton would surrender, throw out her scruples. And for a black man.

There was speculation: At long last Mr. Appleton was dead and buried. But people observed too that Cedric was not pure black. Not offensively black. Some other blood had loosened the curls in his hair and tempered the dark color of his skin. He was brown, café au lait. And an educated man. A school teacher. A headmaster. A fact they knew was not lost on Clara Appleton whose education, like that of white women of her time in the Caribbean island colonies, was below the secondary school level. For schooling was unnecessary for the daughters of the marooned when there was an overseer to find, a landlord, in islands where England had abandoned their great grandfathers for her profit. When there was bait they could use in England if fishing became necessary: A promise that in the colonies a white man was worth his weight in gold.

Clara Appleton must have been impressed with the high sounding letters of the books Cedric carried: *Ars Poetica,* the *Decameran,* the *Iliad,* the *Odyssey.* She must have swooned with ecstasy when he quoted to her from the *Aeneid* in Latin. Still, she must have been surprised that Rosa did not oppose her. That Rosa seemed anxious, eager even to be with Cedric, that she said yes without hesitation. Yes quietly, though not once in the sixteen years since she had become a woman, had she shown the slightest interest in men. But Clara Appleton did not know of the passion that burned in her daughter's heart. A desire that consumed her and terrified her too for the power it gave her since she was twelve, lying on her belly at nights rubbing her bare skin against her mattress. Since the day she and a little girl had witnessed behind a hibiscus bush a scene so devastating she had willed herself to forget. Willed herself to forget too that she and the little girl had ever played together like sisters. Had ever been children.

Until she saw Cedric, Rosa had managed to control the lust and the feelings of power too. Perhaps it was simply timing, she thought, as so often no matter how much a person plans, arranges and organizes, timing is the only explanation that makes sense out of why things, events and people that under ordinary circumstances would never come together, suddenly do. Perhaps it was simply that Cedric had accepted the job to tutor children on the Orange Grove Estate at the very time that she had reached the limit of her ability to bottle the passion she had suppressed for so many years. When she saw Cedric striding past her house she had already lost control. His long legs, the ripple of muscles along his thighs against his thin pants, his full lips beneath his dark mustache, the sensuous flaring of his nostrils tortured her. She thought only of having him.

On the nights of the days when she saw him, she tossed restlessly on her bed, finding no satisfaction in the rubbing of soft flesh against hard mattress, consumed by the thought of Cedric's legs wrapped around hers, feeling the throbbing of his heart above her, his breath in her mouth. She woke up in a sweat and with a longing that left her panting until she stopped him one day and asked, would he consider tutoring a new student, a woman of her age. In fact a woman her age. Her. She, Rosa, since she had never finished secondary school. She didn't say this last directly, but saw in his eyes when he said yes he would tutor her, that he understood why she wanted to be tutored.

He came the next day, and she led him to the room she had chosen for her tutoring in the back of the house where the grass grew tall and wild and shaded the windows. She closed the door and put his fingers in the slit between the buttons on the front of her blouse, and knew he would reach for her breasts and when he found them naked and trembling, her nipples hard and erect, that he would tear her dress apart and discover that not only had she not worn a bra or a slip but nothing else either.

They were married within three months and for six months after that it was never enough for her when he took her without relenting twice a day, sometimes more. Then one day, suddenly, her passion died. Her passion premeditated, that is. Suddenly, one night on the dining room floor when without warning she caught the pictures behind Cedric's smile.

She could not explain it. Not sensibly. If anyone were to ask she would have to say she didn't know what he thought, how he felt. *Exactly.* How could she have known what pictures were in his mind? She hardly knew him. Had not bothered to know him. Sex was what she married him for, what she was willing to give up everything for. The things that mattered, like the Church that consoled her when there was no one else. Every Sunday at mass, the Body of Christ taken on her tongue. Then, with Cedric, she no longer felt she could receive communion. Not with lust in her soul.

Sometimes she waited until late on Saturday to make her confession, but even then she knew that by nightfall she would have broken her promises. And wasn't she married? Hadn't she received the sacrament that made it now holy? That was what her Confessor told her each time she went and he was puzzled by her breathlessness, her urgency for penance.

"Six Hail Mary's? Is that enough, Father?"

"But you've done nothing, child."

"I said three times, Father. And on Friday, four. I couldn't stop . . ."

"It's God's will."

"I don't do it for children."

"In Holy Matrimony . . ."

"I don't think about children."

"You are married, child."

"You don't understand."

"Unless you do things that do not lead to procreation." "I do, I do."

Still it was not enough for the priest. Still she could not convince him that there was nothing she felt for Cedric but desire, the actualization of dreams that tormented her when she lay on her belly rubbing herself against the hard mattress on her bed. Since she was twelve and frightened by the passion that consumed her. And she told no one, not even the girl whom she could no longer remember, perhaps because she chose not to, or because she couldn't. For the thing they saw together had made them both lose memory.

Why did the passion for Cedric die so suddenly? How did the pictures she saw behind his smile that day blind her to all else? (How could she see them?) Blind her until she saw shadows of what she and that little girl had seen. (Her name? It had sunk so far in her memory she wondered now if the girl had existed at all.) What was it they saw through the tangle of vines that wove the wild hibiscus bushes together like a curtain: green splashed with the bright reds and pinks of petals; long, thin stamens protruding provocatively from their centers. What was it the little girl (Was she real?) had told her afterwards that revolted her?

Perhaps it was because she had not clearly seen them. Had not acknowledged she had seen them. Then there they were on Cedric's smile that night threatening to surface through his words: *Beg. Beg. You like it so, Beg.* They flashed in a blur above her, her back pressed into the wood boards of the dining room floor, and were gone before she could be sure she had seen them. But the half memory had clogged her throat and she gagged. Then vomit spewed from her mouth, thick, sticky, stinking across Cedric's chest at the very moment he reached orgasm, so that from top to bottom they were covered in warm liquid, his, white and shiny, sliding down her legs. She didn't want to do it after that and grew to despise herself for the passion that had ruled her, and still did.

Not so Cedric. When the next day she turned away, he pulled open her legs. He didn't take her in the kitchen or the dining room, or the many places in their house when a touch from him used to send her fiddling with his belt buckle, but in his bed. There he took her. Every night.

Now Rosa pulled her nightgown over her head and waited for him. She had heard his footsteps on the stairs. *In flagrante delicto.* She knew he thought she had taken a lover. More than once she had caught him searching through her dirty underwear. More than once he had left her stained panties on the bed carefully placed there so that the crotch was laid open. A scratch on her back he had made, black and blue marks on her legs where he had squeezed her and seemed to forget then later would ask, with his smile and dirty pictures: "How'd you get that, Rosa? Who put that there, Rosa." Smiling.

He would warn her not to answer. "Shh. You better not tell me. Shh. You could incriminate yourself." Smiling.

Sometimes she would try. "Last night . . . You remember . . ."

"Don't tell me. I don't want to know." He would put his hand across her mouth.

So it continued, the marks on her skin and his questions. Her dirty panties spread out on her bed. His refusal to hear her answer. Until she became her own accuser, incriminator, delator, informer. Confessing her guilt with her silence.

"No," he would whisper, his hands over his ears as if she had spoken. "No names. I want no names." Then the smile again with the pictures, wet and ugly. "White skin you say bruises easily? White skin you say shows it up? If that is what you say, but no names. I want no names."

She offered him no resistance. She let him think what he wanted. Now it was that white woman in Otahiti. He would want to catch her too *in flagrante delicto.* But a germ had shifted in Rosa's breast. Broken through its encasement and sprouted roots. She would content herself no more with praying for his death, that God would take him quietly in his sleep, that he would get some painless illness and die quickly. That other woman, her eyes and lips and tongue gouged out by the fish, her flesh rotting, beckoning vultures, had slid into the darkest part of her soul. "Murder," she whispered and then was terrified by the sound of the word lapping against her ears.

The next morning *The Trinidad Guardian* carried a small article on the front page, reporting what a fisherman had discovered floating between stumps of bamboo on a sea splashed with slivers of green sea reed and the rusty brown olive leaves of ancient almond trees. A tiny column not given much significance, for the reporter who had brought in the story had himself doubted the gossip when he had heard it. A white woman murdered in Otahiti! He knew that Trinidad would have done its best to protect her. Still he was curious, and since he was in San Fernando not far from Otahiti, he decided to take a look. Saw the body bloated and dark, saw the straight black hair falling past her shoulders, and mumbled under his breath, *the masses are asses.* An East Indian woman, so he thought, and penned his report on the way to Port-of-Spain between stops to let loaded bison cross the road or trains with carriages crammed with stalks of sugar cane bound for Usine Ste. Madeline, and then again when he reached Arima where lines of cars swirling around the roundabout had literally snarled themselves to a halt. There he finished his piece, waiting for tempers to subside and a policeman to disentangle them all, satisfied, in addition, with the moral indignation he had gratuitously expressed: *Once again a poor, unfortunate East Indian woman had been a victim of the wave of senseless violence that is growing wild all over Trinidad. Can a woman, even a poor peasant, be safe anywhere? Isn't it time that the little men learn that they can't take out their frustrations on their women? Violence is not the answer.*

Cedric was devastated when he read the newspaper the next morning. All his theories fine-tuned to fit Rosa confounded by an insignificant, self-righteous newspaper. An East Indian woman! But by dinner he had regained his confidence. When he spoke to Rosa again that night, he strung *inflagrante delicto* and *crime de passion* around her neck like a noose, certain then that the reporter was not only wrong but stupid, and that what he had told Rosa the night before was indeed correct. That the woman found floating in the sea in Otahiti was in fact a white woman. Now he knew too who she was and who had murdered her, and why.

He had first found reason to believe she was white when he had finally put in place the last piece of a jigsaw puzzle that had tormented him all that day. Ironically, the part he needed came from the mouths of the very people he scorned: the uneducated masses. Scavengers, he called them, raking the streets for gossip they substituted for true knowledge they could get from books. Yet it was that very gossip, traveling the same route north it had taken out of Otahiti to a Chinaman's shop in Nelson Street, that gave Cedric the information he needed to make sense of the riddle that had spun his head in circles all day.

Ordinarily he would not take notice of anything they said, but when he collided with an unruly crowd spilling out of rum shop along the road from the school where he was headmaster, he caught between their curses and shouts the pieces he needed for Rosa that night. Not about the who and why of the mass the fisherman had found floating in the sea in Otahiti, for he already knew the answers to those questions. Such killings were common enough. And understandable. A lecherous woman, a man with no other defense but to stop her and so redeem his name. But the what arrested him. The what that drove the people in the rum shop deeper into drink with the impossibility of it. A white woman? A real, real white woman? And fish gouge out she eyes and lips and tongue? A true, true white woman?

It was all Cedric needed. He locked it in with the other piece he had. The call he received at lunchtime that had started the spinning in his head, from Headley Padmore, his cousin, who, like him, had taken flight from Cedros terrified by nightmares of a lifetime of ripping his hand to shreds pulling out salt-crusted seines from the sea and gutting fish with a beach full of men with rum-red eyes and skin coarse as raw leather. They had an old resentment between them, these cousins, over the careers they had chosen: one the police force, eschewing the merits of secondary school; the other Teachers Training College, choosing the mind over brute force, he told his cousin.

"You wouldn't believe who came in the Police Station this morning, Cedric. One of your bookman. Wanted to report his wife was missing. A doctor. He walked in my office just a few hours ago. In shirt and tie and jacket. A doctor. Said he can't find his wife since Tuesday. You know which doctor I talking about? Well maybe you don't know, seeing as how you living in that one-horse town. The Indian man that marry that white woman. I hear she was horning him. And he come pretending in my office like he don't know where she is. I almost told him to a man where he could look for her. She sleeping with everybody. Tom, Dick *and* Harry. Dick that's where she is. With Dick. With Dick in her." He roared with laughter. "Probably Dick got stuck on her, or stuck in her."

Cedric slammed down the phone in disgust but his mind raced. All that day he paced up and down, struggling to fit together the curved loops of the puzzle that was scattered in his head. His blood beat against his temples and his temper rose with the stifling heat of the early afternoon in the close quarters of his classroom. He shouted at the children and brought his cane viciously down on the open palms of boys unlucky to have the wrong answers to questions he barely formed. Over and over he shifted the pieces: An Indian doctor married to a white woman. One piece. He, a colored headmaster married to a Trinidadian white woman. Another piece. The doctor with horns jutting from his forehead. Another. A white woman, legs sprawled wide open on a bed for every Tom, Dick and Harry. Another piece. Rosa, his Rosa. Once, now no more. She could

never have stopped so suddenly on her own. There had to be someone, somebody else taking his place. He would catch her *in flagrante
delicto*. He barely saw the road in front of him riding his bicycle home
that evening by force of habit. When he ran into people from the
rum shop, he couldn't tell where he was, *in flagrante delicto* humming
through his brain like a buzz saw. All he needed were the parts they
gave him, shouting to each other and to him. The picture became
clear. A white woman murdered in Otahiti, dumped in Freeman's
Bay. A missing white woman. A woman who had made a cuckold of
her husband. Now this. A body floating in the sea in Otahiti. He
threw out his net of *in flagrante delicto* and *crime du passion* like a seine
over Rosa. (Later he would make it a noose.)

When he made love to her that night believing he had caught
her and there would be time enough to pull her in on the beach like
a fish, flapping, he studied her. Her honey brown hair splayed on the
pillow like a fan above her head, the nervous jumping of her eyeballs
beneath the pale thin covering of her eyelids, the shapely curve of
her eyebrows. He stopped and bent closer over her, still pumping.
Two tiny dry dots of blood on the corner of her eyebrow. Another
piece snapping in place in his jigsaw puzzle. She had plucked out the
hairs beneath the curve above the corners of her eyes—for whom?
For whom had she set her trap with her longing now that she no
longer wanted him?

No expression on her face. No movement except the jumping of
her eyeballs. The lips draw to a line. Soft, soft. The brows smooth, the
cheeks unflushed and yet he saw the disgust he knew she felt for him
the day she stopped. Still he pumped. He would catch her. He
pumped. *In flagrante delicto*. He pumped, then waited for the low
moan that would filter through her lips. Waited for it, for though she
hated him, he knew it would come. And when it came, he plunged
deep within her.

The news in *The Guardian* the next morning threw him into confusion, unhinged the pieces in the picture that had formed so clearly
in his mind. He had planned to show the finished puzzle to Rosa at
breakfast, to let her know he was no fool, no stupid horned cuckold.
Then he read about an East Indian woman and the parts began to
slip apart again. An East Indian woman! Not the doctor's wife? Not
the white woman who opened her legs to every Tom, Harry and
Dick? He left early that morning in a state of intense agitation. But by
dinner-time he was calm again, his facts confirmed by his police
cousin gloating: "Told you the doctor was lying. He knew where she
was. Every Tom, Dick and Harry. Told you."

"Paula Inge." He gave her name to Rosa at dinner. Quietly. Not
looking up from his plate. "A German Jew."

"Who? What are you talking about?"

"The woman in Otahiti."

"Which woman?"

"The woman they found in the sea yesterday morning." "The one the fisherman found?"

"Yes. Paula Inge. The doctor's wife." "The doctor?"

"Dr. Dalip Singh's wife." "I'm sorry," she said.

He looked up at her. "What for?" "For the doctor," she murmured. He frowned. "The doctor?"

She shook her head. "No. No. For the poor woman." He smiled.

"To die like that." Her eyes misted. "She deserved it," he said.

She squeezed her eyes shut and bit her lip.

"She deserved it," he repeated and sawed his meat. "No. Not like that."

"I told you. *In flagrante delicto.*"

She looked away from him. "Boysie," she said. "Boysie, that's what people are saying. He cut her throat and slit open her chest."

He held the knife in his hand still and told her to be quiet. "Boysie," she repeated. "He took out her heart."

He warned her to stop.

"For his racehorses. He slit her open right down her belly. For his racehorses." The words rolled off her tongue as if by a will of their own.

He warned her again.

"He took out her heart . . ."

He slammed his fist down on the table. "Enough!"

She got up. "Boysie," she whispered.

He ordered her to sit down. "Now. Now. Down!"

She backed into the chair.

"*In flagrante delicto.* Understand? *In flagrante delicto.*"

"No, Cedric."

She wrapped her arms around her waist. He leaned over to her. "She left her husband's bed."

"No, Cedric."

"Her husband's bed!"

She did not answer him this time so he taunted her. "Talk. Tell me again. Tell me what you have to say."

"Boysie . . ." she began again quietly.

"Watch out, Rosa."

"She was faithful . . ."

"Careful, Rosa."

"To him."

"I don't like to wear horns, Rosa."

"And I feel sorry . . ."

He stared at her. "For him." The tangle of nerves at the base of his neck tightened. Pain flared up the side of his face. *For him? For him?* He released it. "It's the woman who's stinking goddamn you! Goddamn you!"

She put her hand to her lips. "I pity him," she said.

He lunged across the table towards her "He's alive. Alive and getting drunk in the Pelican. Having a good time. Alive!"

She pressed her fingers deeper into her lips but she did not back away.

"You better watch out, Rosa." He leaned back in his chair.

Still, she repeated: "I feel sorry for him."

"You better watch out when you're with every Tom, Dick and Harry, Rosa. You better watch out."

"I feel . . ."

He lunged again. "Stinking!"

Still, she continued, " . . . sorry for him."

"Stinking, goddamn it!"

"No, Cedric."

"Drunk as a fish in the Pelican."

"You're wrong, Cedric."

"Liar!"

She looked down on her hands. "She was a good wife. A decent woman."

He jumped up. "Liar! You think because I'm black, I'm stupid. You think because I'm black I can't read behind that white skin of yours."

"He was wrong. You're wrong." Then she looked directly up at him. "I pity you both."

At first Cedric simply stood still as if he were waiting for her to say more, but when she did not it was as if he had finally heard her. He brought his face close to hers. His lips almost grazing hers, he breathed on her: "Who the hell do you think you are, white lady? You think I'm going to beg for that space between your legs?"

Tears gathered in Rosa's eyes.

"Pity yourself, white lady." His voice simmered to a hoarse whisper. "Careful. It's mine." He waited until a tear trickled down her cheek and gently he brushed it away. A caress. "Shh. Quiet. Careful." A lover's solicitude. Lethal. "Don't give it away. For then it won't be me you'll feel pity for, white lady. It won't be me."

That Saturday, on The Feast of Our Lady of Fatima, Rosa caught a taxi to take her to the foot of the hills in Laventille. Anyone who had seen her fingering the beads of her rosary, her black lace mantilla fastened with a clip on the top of her head, its sides casting dark shadows across her face would have thought: This is a woman in mourning, a woman praying for a soul that had recently departed. And that person would have been partially right, for Rosa was praying for a soul, but not for a soul that had left this earth or one that was about to leave this earth, in spite of her husband's threats, but for a soul that could cause the departure of another soul. Her soul. She was praying for *her* soul, rolling the balls of her fingers across the black beads of her rosary, fixing her mind on the purity of the Lady. Begging the Lady to help her to be pure too; to push back the evil seed that flared out of the hollow of her breast where she had hidden it; to cast out of her mind the thought that had set her brain on fire. *Our Lady of the Immaculate Conception, Our Lady of Fatima who had appeared to three innocent country girls.* She implored the Lady to work a miracle on her, to cure her too, to wash away the sin she had not yet committed, but in her thoughts: Murder. To erase the reflection of the mirror she saw in reverse in Cedric's eyes: Where Paula Inge, she saw him; where Dr. Dalip Singh, she saw herself.

Jan Williams

ARISE, MY LOVE

EVER SINCE FRANK COULD remember, he had lived on the island. There was the high blue smudge of St. Vincent to the north on clear days and nearer and clearly marked, if you turned your head, the sharp, saw-toothed hills of Union Island, with Carriacou as a blue backdrop beyond. He knew all the islands by name—all rocky, dry and reluctantly giving up during the short rainy season a pathetic little crop of cotton, corn and peas.

"Ain' nothin' ever happen," Frank had been saying since he was small, although big enough to lend a hand in the boat and pull on an oar as he went out with Grandmere into the clear green waters within the reef to tend the fishpots and dive for lobsters and conches.

"Ain' nothin' ever happen nowheres 'cept birth an' death an' livin' in between," Grandmere would say, pursing her thick lips and resting on her oar as she wiped the sweat off her face. And then she would go on rowing in short, swift jerks from the wrist, stopping every so often to peer into the clear green depths or to slip over the side to dive towards some rocky cavern in which her sharp eyes could see a lurking lobster or a bed of rock where the conches clung thickly.

Sometimes at low tide they would row within the waters of the reef out to Shell Island, a sandy shell-strewn spit on which in the old days a few coconut-palms had fought their losing battles against the sea. Nothing was left of them now but a few stumps, soggy and shell-covered, in a desert of whitened shells and coral, brightened at times by a yellow sea fan, a pink conch, a large, dappled brown cowrie hurled up by the rising tide and left to fade under the merciless sun and to whiten like old bones.

Frank loved Shell Island. So did Fibi, his little cousin. Fibi's mother, Frank's Tante Mallie, had died when she was born; of a broken heart, some folk said, when the young Bajan from St. Vincent had stopped coming to the island in his sloop, leaving Mallie to fend for herself, as men so often did. Frank remembered when she had died; remembered the muffled crying of Grandmere as she followed the coffin down through the valley and along the narrow hillside path to the little cemetery. He remembered, too, the shock of realisation that Mallie's voice was forever muted, leaving in its turn the weak wailing of Fibi, that was so easily silenced by a rag dipped in sweet water or by gentle rocking.

When she was a baby he used to sit for hours on the step of their thatched hut, holding her in his arms, marvelling at her pale-gold skin, the soft fine hair like the down of a baby chick, and her blue eyes flecked with brown like little freckles. His small black hands looked so dark and out of place as they held her and in his mind he early set her apart.

When she was big enough to go out in the boat with Grandmere and himself, he plaited her a hat from wild cane to protect her hair and face from the sun. But in time the sun had its way and Fibi at fifteen was a warm golden brown, her hair bleached yellow by salt water and sun.

Frank's heart would twist within him at the sight of her thin body in the sea-stained and tattered dress which was practically the only garment she possessed, her golden legs powdered grey by the dry dust or glistening a deeper gold when she scrambled back into the boat with a lobster or a conch.

"Fibi hadn't oughta look like dat," he told himself, seeing in his mind's eye a picture of Fibi dressed like the girls in the magazines the padre sometimes gave him. He saw her in a clean white dress, her hair combed smooth, with perhaps a ribbon in it, instead of tangled and flying in the wind, or plaited pickny fashion by Grandmere on a Sunday, until the smooth strands escaped and grew tousled again in the wind. She would look good, too, he told himself, with lipstick and a dab of powder on her straight little nose with the gold freckles sprinkled across its bridge.

"One a dese days," he told himself, "I gettin' 'way from dis island. I going to Aruba or Trinidad or some place an' earnin' plenty plenty money for Fibi." But he knew that as long as Grandmere lived he would have to stay, since there was no one to work their little plot of land or to catch fish to eke out their crop of dried peas and cornmeal.

His dark eyes would grow broody as he remembered the time when going out in the boat with Grandmere had been an adventure.

But that had quickly dulled with the passing years and had become, as Fibi and he had grown older, a grim, everyday search for food, as it was for Grandmere and most of the other people on the island. But the dream of earning money persisted, tinged though it was with hopelessness when he thought of Fibi and all he wanted to do for her. Her casual acceptance of things as they were crushed him into despair. His love she accepted too, without being aware of his growing fear of the day when the quiet backwater of her childhood would burst the dam and fling her into the stormy waters for which her comeliness had destined her. To Frank, Fibi was the one lovely thing in a life which held out no hope for the future; but behind the loveliness was fear.

Then one night it came upon him with full force like a blow between the eyes: he had to do something positive to prove his love for Fibi. He was returning to the village after hours spent on the rocks, catching crabs for bait by the light of a flambeau. He was going to catch fish from the rocks the next day, for they needed more mullet and chub than they could catch to make a meal, now their corn was all gone, and there was no money to buy any from the shop. He was going to try for something bigger—a red snapper or two, perhaps, or a cavalli. Then he might manage to sell one or two, to the agricultural officer who had just arrived at the government rest house. There were so few visitors to the island, this was an opportunity he dare not miss.

Picking his way carefully along the stony track that wound round the hill towards the village, he saw the slender mast of a sloop at anchor in the bay, silhouetted against a sky studded with stars and in which hung the silver thread of the new moon. Then he heard voices—the deep rumbling of a man's and the shrill laughter of a girl. It was Fibi. On an island where everybody knows everybody else, Frank knew that the man was a stranger. He stood still and listened. All he could hear was a faint rustling among the sea grape bushes bordering the beach.

"Dat yo, Fibi?" he called.

He waited and thought he caught a faint "Ah" followed by a suppressed giggle.

"It latem, Fibi," he persisted. "It time yo' in bed long long time." The only answer was the sound of the sea lapping the white sand with deep sighs. He walked to the village slowly.

He lay in his corner in an agony of misery. Grandmere was snoring. A rooster crowed and another answered it. And somewhere a dog howled. The sound was mournful and eerie in the night. Until now he had seen Fibi as a child—a gay, uncomplaining companion of days in the boat or out hoeing in the hot sun—a golden creature whom he, dark and uncouth though he was, would one day rescue from a way of life into which an unkind fate had flung her. His mind stumbled numbly over the fact that Fibi, for all her golden skin and blue eyes, was as coarse as her environment had moulded her; that she was no different from the other girls on the island. Fibi in a temper could curse like the rest, pull out hair and throw stones. Fibi noisily sucking up fish tea from a tin pot, sucking and gnawing a fish head and spitting out the bones, belching loudly and wiping her mouth clean with the back of her hand, might look different from the darker girls, but she was no different really.

The realisation of this was like the stubbing of a toe against a sharp stone. It hurt.

Frank carried the hurt around for weeks, helplessly casting about for the right to speak to her, to make her understand; but finding he had no right. Who was he, he asked, to tell Fibi that he loved her?

After a few days, the sloop sailed, and Fibi's nocturnal disappearances ended, though Frank, watchful, saw a subtle change in her as the weeks merged into months. Always thin, she grew thinner, and the fine modelling of her face grew even finer, giving her a look of transparency which the blue veins at her temples accentuated.

She no longer sang as they rowed the boat. And once or twice he heard her crying in the night. He longed to take her in his arms, as he had done so often when she had been small; but he knew that his desire for the feel of her thin body against his own was for his own comfort as much as for hers. But she would only say, as she had been accustomed to saying, recently, whenever he touched her tousled head, "Tak yo' han's offen me," in a sharp, bitter voice so unlike her own. He retreated with his misery, just as Fibi did with her own.

One morning Grandmere did not get up. She lay on the torn canvas cot against the wall of the hut, her legs drawn up to her lean belly, shivering and mumbling to herself. Without the white cloth she usually wore twisted around her head, she looked very old, Frank thought, binding the leads along the edge of his cast-net while Fibi bent over the coal-pot by the door. His belly growled as he watched Fibi stirring sugar in the milk-can of hot water and then pouring it into the three tin pots.

"Ain' got no bakes this morning. Ain' got no more flour," Fibi told him as she handed him the pot of sweet water.

"Dat a'right, Fibi. I ain't pertickler hungry dis mornin'," he replied.

He wanted to make an early start because the agricultural officer had said he would like some lobster and a big string of mullet to take back to St. Vincent with him on the launch that afternoon. With luck they might catch enough to buy a little cornmeal and flour. Fibi could go into the shop. The sight of the tins of sardines, corned beef and salmon, the barrel of biscuits, the rum on the shelves, was torment to Frank. And the shopkeeper liked Fibi. Sometimes she managed to wheedle a penny loaf or a handful of broken biscuits from him.

Grandmere turned her head to the wall when Fibi took her the "tea." She left it on the floor beside her as they went out, Fibi carrying the net and gaff and Frank the oars and row-locks.

Rowing in silence, Frank kept his eyes on the church and the huddle of thatched huts that had once been a prosperous village in Grandmere's youth, when most of the island had been one estate. Frank wanted to look at the little gold tendrils of Fibi's hair and to imagine the lay of muscles under the bedraggled loose dress with the patch across the back—a patch that in its turn was soon going to need yet another patch. He wanted, too, to grip her arms until he hurt her, to shake her and say: "Listen, Fibi, you gotta listen. Yo' gotta be different to de other girls, see, yo' just gotta."

Then as they left the bay and were out round the point in the shallow green water within the reef, he became grimly intent on the day's work; years of habit, years of grappling with the sea to give up its life for food, translating from thought to instinct. And, as if by unspoken agreement, they both began to pull more slowly, their eyes searching the green depths for what they sought.

Twice he shipped his oar, slipped silently over the side, dived, came up for air, dived again, his grimy sea-and-work-stained shorts and shirt which were a miracle of patching, clinging to his lean body. Then he pulled himself into the boat, throwing Fibi a smile as he threw a lobster, tail thrashing, into the bilge. Time and again he and Fibi slipped over the side into the clear depths, until they reached Shell Island, for it was on the ledge of rock that ran like a spear out into the deeper water towards the reef that he would stand waiting to cast his net, while Fibi cruised around in the shallower water on the look out for lobsters and conches.

Just before they reached the ledge, Fibi suddenly shipped her oar and leaned over the gunwhale, retching miserably. Frank, appalled that what he had feared was now a fact, was filled with a blinding rage, not only against Fibi and himself, but against the island itself that had bred her. It crashed over him like a gigantic wave and the blood pounded in his head.

The instinct to destroy blotted out all else. Fibi was suddenly no longer to be rescued but to be destroyed, to banish his own anger and shame. Hardly knowing what he did, he suddenly brought his fist down on her golden head, bent miserably over the boat's side, with a violence that jarred his whole body.

Then, because the crumpled figure, with head lolling in the bilge where she had fallen, urged in him the stirring of fear and pity he could no longer bear to feel, and with a wild, searching glance at the shimmering white sand of the beach and the impertinent blue of the sea beyond, he lifted her and dropped her over the side of the boat. He leaned over and watched her, a wavy-edged, distorted figure in the clear water, as he had watched her many times before.

Then before he knew it, he dived towards her and she was no longer distorted like a figure in a fantasy but close and near to him. He tried to take hold of her but time after time she eluded him, carried this way and that by shining currents. Again and again he rose to the surface, filled his lungs with great gulps of air and dived. When at last he managed to hold her and felt her body limp in his arms as he brought her to the surface, he suddenly became panic-stricken at what he had done. Thought, and with it terror, seeped into him again slowly.

Taking a deep breath, he dived again, down into the familiar depths they both had known so intimately in the past. Fighting the pressure of the water until little explosions went off inside his head, he pushed her body with all his remaining strength into a cleft in the rocks; went up for air and dived again to seize a huge chunk of coral to wedge her body more securely in the cleft.

Exhausted he dragged himself to the hot white sand and coral of the island, staring dully at the sky and the white scudding clouds racing across it, not sure if the thunder he heard was his own blood pounding in his head or the thunder of the surf on the reef. Love for Fibi burst like a great white light over him, wave after wave of timeless white light until, blinded by it, he slid into the water to escape its searing brightness. He had to see her once more. He could never go back now, back to Grandmere and life, any more than Fibi could. He saw one golden-brown arm waving in the water like a reed, and touched it, dislodging the rock that had held her down. Opening his mouth, he tried to speak, and that was the last he saw of her as her slim brown body rose gracefully to the surface.

About the Authors

PHYLLIS ALLFREY   Phyllis Byam Shand was born in Dominica, B.W.I., in 1915. Her long West Indian lineage dates from the mid-seventeenth century. As a young woman she went to England and married Robert Allfrey. After several years in England and the United States, she, her husband, and their two children returned to Dominica. Allfrey left her native island temporarily to serve as the minister of labour and social affairs in the federal government of the West Indies. When the Federation collapsed in 1961, Allfrey returned to Dominica from Federation headquarters in Trinidad and never again left her home island. She is best known for her novel *The Orchid House*, which was published in England, France, and the United States in 1953 and 1954. Allfrey also privately published several collections of poetry—*Palm and Oak, Palm and Oak II*, and *Contrasts*—in London, Dominica, and Barbados. She is the author of at least two dozen short stories, some of which were published in various magazines in England. More recently, her poetry and short stories have appeared in anthologies published in the United States, Britain, and the West Indies. Her biography by Lisa Paravisini was published in 1996 by Rutgers University Press.

LOUISE BENNETT   Louise Bennett, one of the foremothers of West Indian literature, was born in Jamaica in 1919. She began writing poetry in Jamaican vernacular and presenting it in traditional Jamaican dress in 1938. In the late 1940s, she won a British Council Scholarship and went to study at the Royal Academy of Dramatic Art in London. When she returned to Jamaica, she taught drama to youth groups and at the University of the West Indies Extra Mural Department. In 1966, she published *Jamaica Labrish*, which contains over two hundred pages of her poems. She has also produced a number of recordings, one of which is "Children's Jamaica Songs and Games." *Selected Poems* by Louise Bennett collected by Mervyn Morris (Sangster's 1982) is an excellent source of many of her later poems. Bennett was awarded the M.B.E. for her contribution to Jamaican cultural life and also the Musgrave Silver Medal, a Jamaican award in recognition of her achievements. She received an honorary doctorate from the University of the West Indies in January 1983. In private life she is Mrs. Eric Coverley.

ERNA BRODBER   Born in rural Jamaica in 1937, Erna Brodber spent her childhood in Woodside, St. Mary. After graduating from high school, she worked in the civil service, then taught in Montego Bay. She received her B.A. honors degree from the University of the West Indies and later received an M.S. in sociology. She served as head of the history department at St. Augustine High School for Girls, then became children's officer with the ministry of youth and community development in Jamaica. She was awarded a doctoral fellowship to the University of Washington, where she studied psychiatric anthropology. In 1984 she founded BLACSPACE, a company promoting research on the African diaspora. Brodber published her novels *Jane and Louise Will Soon Come Home* in 1981, *Myal* in 1988, and *Louisiana* in 1994. She has also published poetry in *Festival Commission* and in *Pathway.*

MICHELLE CLIFF   Michelle Cliff was born in Kingston in 1946 and grew up in Jamaica and the United States. She was educated in New York and London. She holds a B.A. in European history and an M.A. in philosophy. In the 1970s she became active in the feminist movement, producing essays, lectures, and workshops on racism and feminism. With Adrienne Rich, she co-edited the journal *Sinister Wisdom* (1981–1983). She wrote *Claiming an Identity They Taught Me to Despise* in 1980, *Abeng* in 1984, and *No Telephone to Heaven* in 1987. She is the author of a book of short stories, *Bodies of Water,* and of *The Land of Look Behind: Prose and Poetry.* Her poems also appear in magazines and scholarly journals.

MERLE COLLINS   Merle Collins was born in Aruba and grew up in Grenada. She was a public worker in the Ministry of Foreign Affairs during the Grenada Revolution and a member of Grenada's National Women's Organization until 1983. Before coming to the United States, she lived in London, where she was a member of African Dawn, a group that performed dramatized poetry accompanied by African music. She is presently a professor of English and comparative literature at the University of Maryland. She published her first novel, *Angel,* in 1987, and a second novel, *The Colour of Forgetting,* in 1995. She has published a collection of short stories, *Rain Darling,* as well as two volumes of poetry: *Because the Dawn Breaks* and *Rotten Pomerack.* In addition, she co-edited *Watchers and Seekers: Creative Writing by Black Women in Britain* in 1987.

MARYSE CONDÉ   Maryse Condé was born in Pointe-à-Pitre, Guadeloupe. She is the author of nine novels, seven short stories, more than ten essays, and four plays. She has written children's literature, edited three anthologies, and granted numerous interviews. Her recordings are available from Radio France International. Condé earned a doctorate in comparative literature from the Sorbonne. She has lived in Guadeloupe, Africa, Europe, and the United States. She currently teaches at Columbia University and resides with her husband and translator, Richard Philcox, in New York. Her novels include *Hérémakhonon* (1976), *En attendant le bonheur* [*Hérémakhonon*] (1988), *Ségou I: les murailles de terre* (1981, 1984), *Un saison à Rihata* (1981), *Ségou II: la terre en miettes* (1985), *Moi, Tituba, Sorcière noire de Salem* (1986), *La vie scélérate* (1987), *Traversée de la Mangrove* (1989), *Les derniers rois mages* (1992), *La migration des coeurs* (1995), and *Desirada* (1997).

MADELINE COOPSAMMY   Madeline Coopsammy was born and educated in Trinidad, where she remained until she was twenty-one. She won a scholarship from the government of India to study at Delhi University, from which she earned a B.A. degree. She afterward migrated to Manitoba, Canada, and attended the University of Manitoba, earning bachelor's and master's degrees in education. She and her husband live and teach in Winnipeg. In addition to essays and reviews, Coopsammy has published poems in *HERizon Magazine*, *Caribe*, *Other Voices*, *Writings by Blacks in Canada*, *Breaking Through*, *Creation Fire*, and *New Worlds of Literature: Writings from America's Many Cultures*. She is also the author of short stories published in *Other Voices*, *Caribe*, and *Shapely Fire* (Mosaic Press).

CHRISTINE CRAIG   Christine Craig was born in Kingston, Jamaica, in 1943. She was an honors graduate of the University of the West Indies, where she specialized in English and mass communications. She was a founding member of the Caribbean Artist Movement of London, and after returning from London to Jamaica, she worked with the Women's Bureau. She published several books for children, including *Emmanuel and His Parrot* (1970). Her nonfiction manuals of that period reflect her involvement with feminist issues and health topics. She is also the author of short stories and poems that appear in Jamaican, British, and North American anthologies and journals. She published *Quadrille*, a collection of short stories, in 1984. In 1993, Heinemann published *Mint Tea*, a collection of short stories.

EDWIDGE DANTICAT   Edwidge Danticat was born in Haiti in 1969. She came to the United States when she was twelve years old, and within two years she began writing in English. Danticat graduated from Barnard College with a bachelor's degree in French literature and subsequently earned a master of fine arts degree from Brown University. Her first novel, *Breath, Eyes, Memory*, was published in 1994 by Soho Press and subsequently by Vintage Books. Her collection of short stories, *Krik? Krak!*, was published by Soho Press in 1995. Many of the short stories appeared earlier in various periodicals, primarily *The Caribbean Writer.*

SUZANNE DRACIUS   Born in Fort-de-France, Martinique, Suzanne Dracius grew up between Terres-Sainville and the heights of Balata in Martinique. She moved to Sceaux, France, but returned to Martinique where she serves as professor of classics at the University of Antilles-Guyane in Fort-de-France. During the fall quarter 1995, she was guest lecturer in Caribbean literature at the University of Georgia. *L'autre qui danse* (1989) is her first novel. She is presently working on a second novel. She wrote two stories, "Virago" and "Sweat, Sugar, and Blood," translated by Doris Kadish from "De sueur, de sucre et de sang," published in *Le serpent à plumes* (1995).

NYDIA ECURY   Nydia Ecury was born in Aruba in 1926 and for many years has been a well-known poet and actress in Curaçao. In 1972, she published her first collection of poetry in Papiamentu with Mila Palm and Sonia Garmers. In 1978, she published a second poetry collection in Papiamentu, *Na mi jurason mará* (*To My Heart Attached*). Her theatrical activities include roles in Dutch films and a one-woman show, *Luna di Papel* (*Paper Moon*), which she created and presented numerous times in Curaçao and in Holland. In 1984, Ecury published her first poetry collection written in both English and Papiamentu, *Kantika pa Mama Tera* (*Song for Mother Earth*). She is preparing a new English/Papiamentu poetry collection, *Mi amor, un sinta den bientu* (*My love, a ribbon in the wind*).

ZEE EDGELL   Zee Edgell was born in Belize, where she also grew up. She worked as a reporter for the *Daily Gleaner* of Kingston, Jamaica, and was also editor of a small Belizean newspaper. From 1966 to 1968, she taught at St. Catherine Academy in Belize City. She subsequently traveled extensively, living in Jamaica, Great Britain, Afghanistan, Nigeria, Bangladesh, and the United States. She returned to Belize to teach and was appointed director of the Women's Bureau in the government of Belize for the period 1981 to 1982. From 1986 to 1987, she was director of the Department of Women's

Affairs. She lectured at the University College of Belize from 1988 to 1989 and was visiting professor at Old Dominion University in Virginia in 1993. Edgell now teaches creative writing at Kent State University. She is the author of *Beka Lamb* (1982), *In Times Like These* (1991) and *The Festival of San Joaquin* (1997). She is presently working on her third novel. "Longtime Story" is Edgell's first short story.

BERYL GILROY   Beryl Gilroy was born in Guyana, where she became well-known as a school teacher. In 1951, she went to England, where she worked as a factory clerk and a maid before being able to serve again as a school teacher. While raising her children, she worked as a freelance journalist, as a book reviewer on the BBC Caribbean service, and as a publisher's reader. She eventually became headmistress of a North London primary school and is now attached to the Institute of Education at the University of London. She has written a series of children's books, published by Macmillan, and in 1976 she published an account of her experiences as the only black headmistress in her London borough: *Black Teacher.* In 1982, she won the GLC Creative Writing Ethnic Minorities Prize for *In For A Penny* (Holt Saunders). In 1985, her novel *Frangipani House* (Heinemann) was a prizewinner in the GLC Black Literature Competition. In 1989, she published the novel *Boy-Sandwich.*

LORNA GOODISON   Lorna Goodison was born in Kingston, Jamaica, in 1940. She attended the School of Art in Jamaica and later the Art Student League of New York. Goodison has been an art teacher, an advertising copywriter, a scriptwriter, and a teacher. She has illustrated her own books and exhibited her paintings in Jamaica and in Guyana. Her poems appear in anthologies throughout the world. Her publications include *Tamarind Season, I Am Becoming My Mother, Heart Ease, Selected Poems,* and *To Us All Flowers Are Roses.* Her collection of short stories, *Baby Mother and the Kink of Swords,* was published by Longman in 1990.

MERLE HODGE   Born in Curepe, Trinidad, in 1944, Merle Hodge lives and writes in her native island. She studied French at the University College in London, where she received an honors bachelor of arts and a master's degree in philosophy. She subsequently traveled throughout Europe and lived in Africa. She returned to Trinidad in the early 1970s, where she teaches French, English, and West Indian literature at the University of the West Indies in St. Augustine. She has also lectured in French Caribbean and French African literature at the University of the West Indies in Jamaica. Her publications include *Crick-Crack Monkey* (1981), the short story "Inez" (in *Callaloo,* fall 1989), and *For the Life of Laetitia* (1993). She has published essays on Caribbean literature and children's literature as well as the short story "Millicent" in *The Shell Book of Trinidad* (1973). She has also translated *Pigment,* a collection of poems by Léon Damas.

JAMAICA KINCAID   Jamaica Kincaid was born in St. John's, Antigua, and although married and living in the United States she remains a citizen of Antigua. She came to the United States in 1966 and began writing in 1973 or 1974. She worked as an au pair and went to college in New Hampshire, although she didn't graduate. After meeting a writer for *The New Yorker,* she became a staff writer for that magazine. Her stories written at that time also appeared in *The Paris Review* and in *Rolling Stone.* In 1978, she published her first book, *At the Bottom of the River* (Farrar, Straus & Giroux), for which she received the Morton Dauwen Zabel Award of the American Academy and Institute of Arts and Letters. Her second book, *Annie John,* was published in 1983, also by Farrar, Straus & Giroux. In 1988, she published *A Small Place,* which has been called "an expansive essay" rather than a novel. In 1990, Kincaid published the short novel *Lucy.* In 1996, she published *The Autobiography of My Mother,* and most recently, *My Brother.* She lives in Vermont with her husband and two young children.

CHRISTABEL LARONDE   Christabel LaRonde was born in Dominica and lives in Pottersville near Roseau. She was Phyllis Allfrey's young protégée and was inspired by Allfrey to write poetry. Some of her best poems reflect the mystical beauty of Dominica. She also writes in tribute to Jean Rhys, a Dominican writer whom she very much admired.

UNA MARSON   Una Marson was born in Jamaica in 1905. She was a poet, playwright, and broadcaster. In addition, she was an editor (*Poetry for Children by Poets of Jamaica*), an activist (secretary to the League of Coloured Poets), a social worker (Jamaica's Save the Children Fund), and a publisher (*The Cosmopolitan*). She also served as secretary to the Emperor Haile Selassie during his exile in England during the mid-1930s, and she received the Institute of Jamaica's Musgrave Medal for poetry in 1930. She is credited with having started the BBC's "Caribbean Voices" program in 1942. Her four substantial volumes of poetry include *Tropic Reveries* (1930), *Heights and Depths* (1931), *The Moth and the Star* (1937), and *Towards the Stars* (1945). She wrote three plays: *At What a Price,* which was produced in London in 1932, and two unpublished plays, *London Calling,* which was to serve as a vehicle for black West Indian actors in England, and *Pocomania,* which is set in Jamaica. She died in 1965.

GILDA NASSIEF   Gilda Thébaud was born in Port-au-Prince, Haiti, the daughter of Dr. Jules Thébaud and Ella de La Fuente, and was educated in Montreal, Canada. She is the mother of three children, Ivor, Maroussia, and Gregor, and has lived in Dominica all her adult life. She is a poet and an artist; her first volume of poetry, *Glimpse*, was published in 1976. It contains 21 poems that she also exquisitely illustrated. Nassief, now Gilda Thébaud Mansour, is currently serving her country as high commissioner for the Commonwealth of Dominica, stationed in India. She has completed a series of love poems collected under the title *Miel (Honey)*, which she is currently illustrating. Her poetry-illustration work in progress is entitled *Pearl Drops*.

GRACE NICHOLS   Grace Nichols was born in Guyana in 1950 and moved to Britain in the mid-1970s. Her work is better known in Britain than it is in the United States. She has had poems published in *Frontline, Ambit, Kunapipi,* and *Poetry Review,* among other journals. She has read her poems for the BBC and for Australian radio, and she participates in the Black Arts Festivals in London. Nichols is the author of two children's books: *Trust You Wriggley* and *Baby Fish & Other Stories.* She published her first collection of adult poems, *i is a long memoried woman,* with Karnak House in 1983. More recently, she has published *Fat Black Woman's Poems, Lazy Thoughts of a Lazy Woman,* and a novel, *Whole of a Morning Sky,* all with Virago Press. She has also edited *Can I Buy a Slice of Sky?,* which is a collection of Black, Asian, and American Indian poetry, and *Poetry Jump-up: An Anthology of Black Poetry.*

ELIZABETH NUNEZ   Elizabeth Nunez was born and grew up in Trinidad. After coming to New York, she married, had two sons, and in 1986 published her first novel, *When Rocks Dance,* under her married name, Elizabeth Nunez-Harrell. She became a member of the faculty of the humanities department of Medgar Evers College, the City University of New York, where she serves as chair of the department. She is author of the forthcoming novel *Bruised Hibiscus* and the unpublished novel *Beyond the Limbo Silence.* She is also author of the *Modern Fiction Studies* article, "The Paradoxes of Belonging: The White West Indian Woman in Fiction" (summer 1985).

ESTHER PHILLIPS   Esther Phillips is a Barbadian who was born in 1950. Her poetry was first published in *BIM* magazine in 1969, and her first collection of poems, *la Montee,* was published in 1983 by the university press U.W.I. She is a tutor in English literature at the Barbados Community College and is now working on another collection of poems, which she hopes to publish soon. She has had short stories published and has recently ventured into play writing. Poetry, however, is her first love. She has a daughter, Simone.

VELMA POLLARD   Velma Pollard was born in Jamaica and grew up in Woodside, St. Mary. Her sister is the writer Erna Brodber. Pollard received her Ph.D. in language education and has taught in Canada, the United States, Guyana, and Trinidad. She is presently the dean of the faculty of education at the University of the West Indies in Jamaica. She specializes in teaching English in a creole-speaking environment, language in Caribbean literature, and the language of the Rastafari. Her critical articles, poetry, and short stories have appeared in *BIM, Caribbean Quarterly, Over Our Way* (D'Costa/Pollard), *Jamaica Woman* (Mordecai/Morris), *Focus, Pathways, Voicepoint, Kyk-Over-Al, Her True-True Name,* and *Caribbean New Wave.* Her publications include *Crown Point and Other Poems, Shame Trees Don't Grow Here,* and a collection of fiction, *Considering Women.*

JEAN RHYS   Jean Rhys was born in Dominica in 1890 and left for England at the age of 16. She returned to visit Dominica only once. In London she briefly attended the Perse School and the Academy of Dramatic Art. She published five books before World War II, the first a collection of short stories and the other four novels. Her first book, *The Left Bank: sketches and studies of present-day Bohemian Paris,* appeared in 1927, followed by the novel *Postures* in 1928. *Postures* was republished as *Quartet* by André Deutsch in 1969. *After Leaving Mr. Mackenzie* came out in 1930, *Voyage in the Dark* (based on Rhys's first piece of sustained writing) was published by Constable in 1934, and *Good Morning, Midnight* was published in 1939. Rhys subsequently disappeared from the literary scene. Her best-known novel, *Wide Sargasso Sea,* was written during the late 1950s and early 1960s and was published in 1966 when she was in her mid-seventies. A collection of her short stories, *Tigers are Better Looking,* was published in 1968, and another collection, *Sleep it off, Lady,* in 1976, both by André Deutsch. In 1978, Jean Rhys was awarded the C.B.E. for her services to literature. She died in May 1979. Her unfinished biography, *Smile Please,* was published by the estate of Jean Rhys in both British and American editions in 1979.

ESMERALDA SANTIAGO   Esmeralda Santiago was born in rural Puerto Rico, one of seven children. As a young girl she was taken to New York City, where she won a scholarship to New York City's High School of Performing Arts. She then went on to Harvard from which she graduated with high honors. She subsequently earned an M.F.A. from Sarah Lawrence College. She is married to the director of a film production company based in Boston and has two children. Her publications include *When I Was Puerto Rican* (1993) and *América's Dream* (1997).

SIMONE SCHWARZ-BART Born in 1938 in Guadeloupe, Simone Schwarz-Bart attended school in Pointe-à-Pitre before completing her education in Paris and in Dakar. She lived in Switzerland with her husband, the writer André Schwarz-Bart, with whom she wrote the novel *Un plat de porc aux bananes vertes* (1967). Her works include *Ti-Jean L'horizon,* translated as *Between Two Worlds;* her prize-winning novel, *Pluie et vent sur Télumée-Miracle* (1981), translated as *The Bridge of Beyond;* and a play, *Ton beau capitaine* (1987).

OLIVE SENIOR Olive Senior was born in a Jamaican village in 1943 and was raised by urban relatives. She was educated in Jamaica and in Canada and worked in journalism, public relations, and publishing. She served as the publications officer at the University of the West Indies Institute of Social and Economic Studies, as managing director of the Institute of Jamaica Publishing Company, and as editor of *Jamaica Journal.* Her publications include *Down the Road Again, The Message Is Change, Stranger in Our House,* and *A-Z of Jamaican Heritage. Talking of Trees* and *Gardening in the Tropics* are her two collections of poetry. She won the Jamaica Centenary Medal in 1980, the Commonwealth Literature Prize in 1987, and the Silver Musgrave Medal for Literature in 1988. She won the first Commonwealth Writers Award in 1986 for *Summer Lightning and Other Stories,* which was followed by *Arrival of the Snake Woman and Other Stories* in 1989 and *Discerner of Hearts* in 1995.

CARMEN TIPLING Carmen Lyons Tipling was born in Port Antonio, Jamaica, and attended school in Kingston. She went away for college to the Culver-Stockton College in Missouri, where she majored in journalism and drama. While in college, she began writing plays, including "The delicately wounded." She subsequently wrote other one-act and full-length plays, one of which is *Lunchtime Revolution.* She has won numerous prizes in the annual Jamaica Festival of Arts for her plays, which include *Straightman* and *The Skeleton Inside.* She co-wrote the musicals *Port Royal Ho* and *Arawak Gold.* The latter was produced in 1992 and played at the Ward theatre for 40 performances. Tipling worked as a personal assistant to the Jamaican minister of foreign affairs and more recently served in New York City as the overseas public relations consultant for Jamaica. She now works in Kingston, Jamaica, as a communications consultant.

ANA LYDIA VEGA   Ana Lydia Vega was born in Santurce, Puerto Rico, in 1946. She earned a Ph.D. in comparative literature from the University of Provence, France, and in 1982 she received the Casa de Las Américas prize for her short story collection *Encancaranublado y otros cuentos de naufragio*. She is a three-time winner of the P.E.N. Club of Puerto Rico award for best short story collection. In 1984, she was awarded the Juan Rulfo International Award for short story ("Pasión de historia") in Paris. In 1989, she received a Guggenheim fellowship for literary creation. Among her many publications are *Vírgenes y Mártires, Encancaranublado y otros cuentos de naufragio, Pasión de historias y otras historias de pasión, El tramo ancla, Falsas Crónica del sur* (translated by Andrew Hurley as *True and False Romances*), *Cuentos calientes,* and *Esperando a Loló y otros delirios generacionales*. Among Vega's pedagogical books are *Le Français vécu* (with Villanua, Lugo, and Hernandez) and *La plume à l'oeuvre* with Ada Vilar. With González, Baralt, and Collazo, she published *El machete de Ogún, the Slave Revolt in Puerto Rico*.

JAN WILLIAMS   Information about this author is limited. We only know that Jan Williams was born in Trinidad and lived in England and in Guyana. Two of her short stories have appeared in *BIM*: "Fugitive" and "Pinch of Snuff."

About the Editors

ELAINE CAMPBELL is lecturer in writing at the Massachusetts Institute of Technology (MIT). She holds a Ph.D. in English and an M.S. in education with a specialization in TESOL (teaching of English to speakers of other languages). Dr. Campbell is the author of chapters, articles, and reviews of Caribbean literature and culture that have been published in scholarly journals throughout the world. Recently she published *English As a Second Language Resource Book*. She is currently completing a novel, *The Brass Ring*.

PIERRETTE FRICKEY is associate professor of French and Spanish at the University of West Georgia. She holds a Ph.D. in comparative literature, an M.A. in French, and an M.S. in psychology. She is the author of essays and chapters on Caribbean literature and the editor of *Critical Perspectives on Jean Rhys*. Her publications also include articles on twentieth-century French literature, and her most recent essay on the French poet Aragon appears in *Modes of the Fantastic*, published by Greenwood Press. She is now working on a new book, *The Dialectic of Exile*.